APPRENTICE TO THE GODS

BOOK FOUR OF
THE SEVENTH SHAMAN

D.T. Read

Theogony Books
Coinjock, NC

Chris Kennedy/ Theogony Books
1097 Waterlily Rd.
Coinjock, NC 27923
https://chriskennedypublishing.com/

Publisher's Note: This is a work of fiction. Names, characters, places, and incidents are a product of the author's imagination. Locales and public names are sometimes used for atmospheric purposes. Any resemblance to actual people, living or dead, or to businesses, companies, events, institutions, or locales is completely coincidental.

Cover Design by Shezaad Sudar.

Ordering Information:
Quantity sales. Special discounts are available on quantity purchases by corporations, associations, and others. For details, contact the "Special Sales Department" at the address above.

Apprentice to the Gods/D.T. Read -- 1st ed.
ISBN: 978-1648556494

For Joshua Essoe and James Artimus Owen,
who accepted me as their apprentice
in all the arts of storytelling.

For Kim,

"Answers only come when
you ask the questions."

Best

J. T. Read

Chapter One

Derry gasped at the sight of my bruised face in her link's display. "Oh, my hear', Kew, wha' happened?"

"We held the second night of Coming of Wanikiya," I told her, "here in Old Trade Center, using the traditional chants." I spoke in short phrases, between shallow breaths, because of my cracked ribs. "Somebody called the security forces. They roughed up a few people." *Mostly me. Could've been a lot worse, with all the elders and children there.*

My wife's eyes widened in obvious shock. "Law enforcemen' did tha'? Wha's traditional chan's go' to do with i'?"

"It wasn't the civilian InterClan Law Enforcement officers, little bird." My tone dropped to grimness. "It was Great Council Security Forces."

Her jaw hardened, visible even in my link's small display. "The Hevos."

When I nodded—only slightly, to prevent a twinge in my neck—she asked again, "Why, Kew?"

I'd considered several possible reasons while I'd lain awake nursing my various aches during the previous night. Two thoughts had persisted.

"Chief Hevovitas and her supporters in the Great Council," I said, "consider themselves nobility because their maternal lines go back to Shaman Huyana. They believe they're the wise ones, who know better

5

than 'ignorant' people from desert clans. They're determined to do away with what they call 'the foolish traditions of our grandfathers' and replace them with their own 'truth.' They're starting with the children."

I paused, my jaw tensing, too, at recalling my stepbrother Bimisi's dismissive statement about letting the elders die off and take their traditions with them.

"Wha' d'yew mean?" Derry asked. She scrunched her forehead, puckering the long scar that ran across it.

"They changed the ceremony," I said. "If it'd just been using antigrav and wrist rockets in a ceremonial center that looks like a torgus tank, instead of the traditional dance pageantry on a plaza, it would've been fine. That was really good, really effective. But they altered the chants themselves.

"Now they call it *Remembering* Wanikiya instead of *Coming* of Wanikiya," I explained, "and they present it as if he, uh, *I* already came a couple centuries ago."

Derry appeared puzzled. "Do they know yew're Wanikiya? How would they know i', and why does i' matter to them?"

"Ya, they know," I said. "You met my stepbrother Bimisi, didn't you, when we went to Red Wash for... the funeral?"

Bimisi's sneer burned in my memory, making it clear he knew very well what I'd been instructed not to reveal yet.

"Aye." Derry wrinkled her nose with its sprinkling of russet freckles. "The arrogant one who could call snakes ou' of the deser'. He seemed slippery as a snake himself."

"His mother probably told him what was in my Birth Chant as soon as the man in our family died," I said. "Maybe even before. She was one of the four people who heard him pronounce it."

I'd talked with Bimisi after the first night's ceremony.

"Surely you don't truly believe we're still *waiting* for Wanikiya, do you?" he'd asked, watching me closely. "I'd be careful not to let that become public knowledge if I were you, little brother. Our great chief considers such views to be seditious."

I lowered my voice, though I sat alone in Gram's dwelling, upstairs from her herbal apothecary. "Bimisi is the Hevovitas clan's chief chanter now. Has been for a while.

"Having the long-awaited seventh shaman suddenly appear matters to the Hevos because it'll divide our people between them and... me." I had to force the final word. *Why me? I'm not wise enough. I'm definitely not holy enough.* I pressed on. "It'll draw attention to the Hevos' increasing tyranny and encourage people to resist them."

I shrugged and instantly regretted it when pain like a wildfire swept across my beaten shoulders. Trying to minimize a flinch, I concluded, "The Hevos can't have that—not when they're trying to consolidate their own power—so anyone who tries to preserve the old ways is now considered a subversive."

Horror widened Derry's storm-gray eyes again. "Yew've no' even declared yerself. Wha're yew going to do?"

"What Shaman Shiye called me to do," I said.

* * *

By early afternoon, injuries or not, I couldn't stay still any longer. I'd spent a lot of time pacing the corridors of Belsken Field's medical facility during rehab for my wounded right arm. Exercising, even if I couldn't do a complete workout, was part of my daily routine.

Dressed in nondescript farmer's clothing, I examined my face in Gram's washroom reflector. Since last evening, a few applications of her homemade healing salve had reduced the swelling and discolorations enough that one would have to study my face to see them.

I debated about carrying my boot knife. Habit urged me to do it, but Shaman Shiye's quiet voice in my mind said, *Leave it.* I knew why. The Great Council would likely have its enforcers patrolling the city. If they concocted some excuse to search me, I knew it wouldn't end well if they found my knife. Besides, most of my childhood training had been in weaponless combat.

Best to just keep my head down. Anything I have to do with cracked ribs is going to be painful.

That included descending the adobe-brick stairs from Gram's dwelling into her shop. I eased myself down one step, one foot at a time, teeth gritted so my breaths hissed between them.

There weren't any stairs at Belsken's med center, and only my arm was wounded then.

In the shop, another thought occurred to me. *Better leave my link here, too. It's got contact codes for my family, my TDY orders, everything important in it. My military ID ring, too, with its chip containing my military record and pay account. And especially Gram's little bag, with the ancient link containing my Birth Chant. Anything I'd leave in the intel shop while flying a mission should stay here. The city is now enemy territory.*

Because I planned to buy some earrings for Derry from a local jeweler, I used my link to transfer credit from my account to Gram's and took the amount from her cash drawer in rel coins. I had no bag or wallet, but the coins' small size allowed me to conceal them in the deep thigh pockets of my farm trousers.

They couldn't track purchases with coins the way they could electronic payments.

Last, I removed my dog tag's neck chain, put the chain with my other belongings in a drawer behind Gram's counter, and pushed the tag itself to the bottom of one pocket, under the coins. *That'll be enough ID if I need it.*

With Gram out of town, serving as midwife to my stepsister, I let myself out the rear door from the storage room into the side alley, the same way I'd entered. I ensured its locks were secure before I set out.

I scrutinized the plaza while I limped across it. No signs of last night's skirmish remained, except the out-of-town merchants hadn't set up their tents and stalls.

Ya, I thought it seemed too quiet this morning. The plaza's usually a festival during ceremony days, so loud we can hear it indoors. Did the council's enforcers intimidate them?

I didn't see old Demothi anywhere, either. For years, I'd skirted the one-eyed crazy man from his blind side to avoid becoming the object of his wailing rants. During the confrontation on the plaza, however, he'd interceded and drawn the blame for the unauthorized ceremony to himself.

Sure hope they didn't haul him off somewhere. He probably wouldn't survive a beating.

As it had through the past few days, lightning continued to crackle outside the plaza's nironnium dome. Gray smoke rose from the surrounding dwellings and drifted toward fanned vents in the enclosure, and the sand whipping across its panels dimmed the multi-forked strikes. Still, distant thunder rumbled like muffled drums.

Storm fronts have probably shut down the vortex terminal. As usual. I really don't want to be stuck here past the date on my TDY orders.

Knowing the public transports would jar my ribs more than traveling on foot, I chose to walk around the city. Eventually I'd return to Gram's home and watch the ceremony's third night on my link.

I sighed. Carefully. *Really would like to talk with her about all of this.*

On my first day back in Awénasa City, the lanes I'd strolled had been decorated with four-span-long white and golden fringes. They'd draped shop fronts and fluttered across narrow lanes. Intricately cut paper birds, brown and golden and white, had twirled on mobiles hung from shops' doorway lamps.

This time, I found the decorations torn down. A few paper birds and shreds of fringe bearing gritty boot prints lay crushed on the cobbles.

Two days ago, I'd jostled about with crowds in a celebratory mood. I'd heard numerous regional accents and seen enclave totems from across the continent—maybe from around the planet—on people's braids and horsetails. Everyone had exchanged greetings and genuine smiles as we'd passed one another. Out-of-towners had thronged the merchant stalls, bartering for goods they couldn't get at home.

Few people occupied the pedestrian lanes to Awénasa City's center this afternoon. Those who were out rushed along on their way, seeming intent on reaching specific destinations without stopping to browse. Most kept their gazes lowered except to furtively peer around, as if they shared my sensation of being watched.

They had good reason. Enforcers stood in the open, batons hanging at their hips and duty links gripped in their hands, at the intersections of the busiest lanes. I kept the troopers in my peripheral vision while I pressed on.

Once I overheard a snatch of conversation between an older couple with anxious expressions. "... hear what happened in Old Trade Center last night? They almost killed a young man!"

I resisted the impulse to glance at them. Instead, I studied the adobe-and-brick canyon of the lane ahead. Twenty or so arm-lengths away, a jeweler's shop caught my eye. *That's the place with the earrings I really want for Derry.*

On entering, I searched the artisan's showcases. One displayed earrings shaped into intricate flowers, suns, and geometric designs. Some pieces had been carved from coral and turquoise; others were hammered silver inlaid with semi-precious stones.

In the past, I'd seen pairs of tiny birds with outstretched wings shaped from opalescent milkstone. They'd gleamed like stars on the midnight-blue velvet. *Perfect for my white bird, my Anataqa.*

When I didn't find them, I inquired. "Do you have any white bird earrings left? I know I've seen them here before."

The shopkeeper, a heavyset man with pouchy eyes, studied me with undisguised suspicion. "No," he said, a little too sharply, "I don't. You must be thinking of another shop."

"Fine. Thanks." I quirked an eyebrow as I exited. *That was strange.*

I tried three more jewelers, two of them on narrower side lanes. Every merchant eyed me warily and staunchly denied he or she had *ever* sold white, bird-shaped earrings.

Do they think I'm an undercover inspector for the Great Council or something?

Word clearly gotten out about the altercation in Old Trade Center, most likely spread by the Great Council itself as a warning.

Ironic that people fear me as a council spy when I was the one the Hevos beat up to be the example.

* * * * *

Chapter Two

In late afternoon, people began to emerge from the city's scattered public lodges, usually in family groups, to migrate toward the ceremonial center. Their scuffing shoes stirred up small, dusty puffs about their ankles.

I stayed in the milling press as much as I could. However, when my stomach reminded me with a rumble it'd been a few hours since I'd eaten, I followed the scents of seared meats and frying maize bread to a streetside stall.

My mouth remained raw and tender enough that I tasted blood if I spoke too quickly, so I chose pulled shegrul with mild seasonings—not my usual preference—steamed in rolled rounds of maize bread. I also ordered a container of thick chicken-and-maize soup, a bottle of chilled water, and several awanatas. Sore mouth or not, I couldn't resist my favorite feast-day pastries.

The middle-aged woman behind the table, with sweat produced by her flaming braziers gleaming on her face, packed my selections into an insulated box while I counted rel coins out for her. She offered a hesitant, "Remembering Wanikiya," as she handed the box to me.

Somewhere in the past two days, I'd learned the expected response was, "May his memory be long with us." I couldn't bring myself to say it. I only said, "Thank you," gave a slight nod, and wheeled away.

Easing my way through swelling crowds heading the opposite direction proved more difficult than I'd expected. I tucked my arms to my sides to protect my ribs, but I couldn't avoid every inadvertent push or bump. I set my teeth against jabs and pangs, and weaved through each momentary gap I spotted.

Halfway back to the arch into Old Trade Center, a heavy hand clamped onto my left shoulder. The one with the worst bruising and most baton-inflicted welts, of course. I couldn't prevent the cringe. I shifted my head cautiously and saw my face reflected in the dark helmet plates of two Council enforcers.

"Going the wrong way, aren't you?" asked the one whose steel-sheathed fingers gripped my shoulder. He tightened them, an eagle's talons piercing its prey. Even with its electronic modulation, I detected an unfamiliar accent. *Not Chalca.*

Is he studying my face, or am I being paranoid? Regardless, I held his stare and said, as clearly as I could around my cut tongue, "My wife gave birth to our first baby. She can't come to the ceremony tonight. Thought I'd pick up some supper…"

All technically true, though our baby would be a month old by the time I saw him. He and Derry awaited me on Solienne, 75 lightyears from Tempest, and the food was for me, not her.

"Open the box," the second troop ordered. His hand hovered at his belt, where his baton hung.

I popped the cover, held the box out to them. Both assessed its contents. The second man poked through the shegrul rolls and awanatas with his gloved hand for what seemed an interminable space. I got the impression they would've helped themselves to my meal without a qualm, maybe eaten the whole thing, if they hadn't been wearing helmets.

Finally, the first trooper released my shoulder and said, "Close it, set it on the ground between your feet, and put your hands on your head."

I complied, suppressing a wince and caging my eyes on some spot well up the lane to keep my expression neutral. Hard hands patted me down. Somehow, I managed not to flinch at their less-than-gentle contact with my ribs. When steel-clad fingers searched inside my boots, I closed my eyes. *Thank you, Shaman Shiye.*

At last they backed off. "Take the food to your wife and don't waste time going back to your ceremony," the first trooper said.

"Yessir."

They stood there and watched me stoop gingerly to collect the food box.

I didn't continue toward Old Trade Center. Instead, I entered a side lane where I knew several public lodges stood, then ducked into an alley between two lodges near the lane's far end. Even then, I froze to check my surroundings at every rattle of a pebble, scrabble of a kosa, or echo of a distant voice in the tight passage. *Like being hunted by Shiraganji again.*

Several side alleys later, including a couple I knew were too narrow for large men in security forces gear to squeeze through, I stood at the lip of Old Trade Center's arch. Sweat dampened my loose shirt's armpits, and I clutched the food box with both hands to still their quivering.

The flow of ceremony goers had ceased, except for a few stragglers. I searched the area for enforcers. They seemed to have followed the crowd, but I stayed to the plaza's periphery rather than openly striding across it to Gram's shop.

Having gathered my personal belongings from the drawer behind the counter, I labored my way up the stairs to her dwelling and sank onto the familiar red-and-black sitting rug in her gathering room. My injuries throbbed from the exertion, but I felt most surprised by my exhaustion.

Been away from Tempest's higher grav for too long.

With my hands' trembling subsiding, I checked my link's chrono. *Not too late to call Gram.* I touched in her code.

The distant ringtone sounded several times before her face appeared in my display. She seemed harried, but she beamed. "Ai, Akuleh. Are you on Solienne now?"

"Still on Tempest," I said. "Do you have time to talk?"

Her smile faded, and regret shaded her tone. "Not right now. Kotori had a hard labor and delivery, and she needs a lot of care." Gram smiled once more. "I'll *make* time for you tomorrow, Akuleh. Please stay in my home as long as you need to." She glanced around her shoulder. "Now I need to go back to Kotori."

"Right. Thanks, Gram," I said and ended the call.

I laid out the container with my meal, resisting the urge to inhale its aromas of meat and maize too deeply on account of my ribs, before I initiated a search on my link for recordings of the ceremony's third night.

That's the part I remember the least, the part I need most to relearn. Must be hundreds of old ceremony vids out there. Shouldn't be too hard to find one.

My search for Coming of Wanikiya Ceremony, third night did yield, as I'd expected, several hundred listings. I scrolled through them in mild amazement. *Has every enclave on the planet recorded every one of its ceremonies?*

I paused when one entry caught my eye.

YELLOW ROCK WAS THE FIRST ENCLAVE ESTABLISHED OUT-SIDE AWÉNASA CITY, AND THE LAST KNOWN HOME OF CHANTER YUMA BEFORE HE DISAPPEARED IN THE DESERT.

Yellow Rock Enclave. I've heard of that. Think Chanter Wahkan mentioned it to me once.

I checked Yellow Rock Enclave's ceremony list and selected a video made a few years before my birth. *Won't be any unauthorized updates there.*

Sitting with my back to the warm brick wall with my link propped on my travel pack where I could see it clearly, I dug into my meal.

Traditional enclaves were circular, about a quarter of a range across, and originally sheltered from Tempest's extreme elements by vented roofs built of heavy logs and mounds of soil. Nironnium domes, imported from Solienne, had come much later, during my childhood. Inside the fortress, adobe or stone dwellings were constructed against the outer wall like odd boxes in tiers, usually three layers high.

The video I'd chosen opened on a dirt-floored plaza beneath an arched, timber-and-soil roof. Smokey torches supplemented ten or twelve bonfires outlining the plaza's perimeter. A few people still milled about, but most already perched on lower-level roofs to watch.

The videographer must have been positioned near the drum circle, because I heard only its deep beats and the clear tones of flutes while the dancers emerged on ladders from one of the four underground ceremonial lodges.

The pageant opened with the Wanikiya and Anataqa dancers; he in regalia of golden plumage, and she in equally elaborate white. They moved gracefully among small clusters of people seated on the ground. Their dance depicted healing and teaching, and choosing others to labor with them.

A pack of wolf dancers, wearing shaggy pelts complete with the heads, appeared from the other three subterranean chambers. Dancing back and forth with aggressive, stomping steps, they threatened Wanikiya's people with clawed gloves. The Wanikiya dancer, leading a band of figures in brown eagle regalia, drove the wolves off several times.

Then the drumming rhythm changed again. The beats grew quicker and sharper, and the Machitew dancer skulked in from the darkness outside the encircling bonfires. He shook his black-rag mane, snapped his wooden mask's hinged jaws, and flexed naked limbs smeared with black ashes. With displays of strength and baskets of gifts, he lured people away by ones and twos, into the shadows from which he'd come.

Finally, Machitew led a massive attack against the remaining people of Wanikiya. His hordes, a massive pack of wolf dancers, charged across the plaza. With only a handful of sword-bearing eagle warriors still at his side, Wanikiya held them off, while Anataqa led their people to safety in the underground lodge where she'd waited earlier.

More drums joined the first one. They crashed and thundered while the battle played out. Eagles and wolves fought and fell. When Wanikiya finally came face-to-face with Machitew, one wolf dancer threw off his pelt, revealing eagle regalia beneath, and joined the surviving eagles. Undaunted, the wolves surged forward, and Wanikiya went down in the mêlée.

At a victory shout from the Machitew dancer, chanter apprentices posted around the plaza simultaneously doused every bonfire with buckets of water. Total darkness swallowed the enclave, as complete as an askuk's gullet. The drums instantly ceased. But for a few babies' frightened cries, the audience lapsed into breathless silence.

My hand closed, white-knuckled, on my barely touched water bottle.

* * * * *

Chapter Three

After several seconds, the single drumbeat resumed, slow and quiet, but it still echoed from the surrounding enclave walls. I glimpsed hurried activity in the gloom, dark-clad shapes bearing shielded lamps, who dashed up the stone stairs flanking the enclave's east-facing gate.

I waited with my heart pummeling my ribs. I actually started when twin fires leaped to life above the gate, at opposite ends of a lintel stone broad enough to be a stage. Towering flames like beacons cast a vibrant, golden light across the whole plaza.

Between the pillars of fire stood a regal figure wearing a crimson robe that reached his heels, and a wooden headdress carved and painted to resemble the sun. He stretched out his muscular arms in a gesture of welcome.

Shaman Shiye. I swallowed my emotions at the rush of memories. *He reached out to me the same way in my shaman vision.*

A melancholy flute melody began, and three torches flared to life on the plaza below, borne by eagle dancers who searched among the fallen.

One found the Wanikiya dancer and extended a hand to raise him to his feet. The other eagle dancers did the same for his two companions, a warrior who'd stayed at his side through the entire pageant, and the one who'd shed his wolf pelt to join Wanikiya at the end.

The first one's Kota. I know that. But who's the other?

I pushed away thoughts of what the trio's fall in the battle must mean.

Like a chief's guards, the three torchbearers accompanied Wanikiya and the two warriors across the plaza with great dignity. When they started their march up the eastern stairs, the enclave's gathered chanters burst into a new song, this one triumphant.

> In the season when darkness falls,
> Wanikiya will defend us.
> Like a warrior with a sword
> will Wanikiya guide us,
> up the Ancients' Path
> into the land of sunrise.

On the lintel platform, aglow with the two fires' dancing light, the Shaman Shiye figure embraced Wanikiya and the two warriors, then stepped forward and beckoned.

New torches flared on the plaza. Their bearers, made visible by the swaying, orange light, waited near the entry of the chamber in which Anataqa and her people had taken shelter. The bearers assisted each person off the ladder. They escorted the group across the plaza and up the stone steps while the chant reverberated through the enclave's hollow.

> Like a guide with a torch
> will Anataqa lead us,
> up the Ancients' Path
> to join them
> on the Sacred Mountain.

I sat motionless for some time after the vid ended, sagging under the burden of it. My maize-and-chicken soup had gone cold, the maize bread enveloping the pulled shegrul had crumbled, and my anticipated awanatas lay untouched.

I replayed the battle's conclusion several times, zooming in to study Wanikiya, sword in hand, facing Machitew. *I'll have to fight him in the end.* I felt no surprise, only a soul-deep confirmation. *Will it be a physical battle, or one of chants?*

A memory seized me, of a cold night in my dorm room during pilot training, of Machitew contorting my limbs until I thought they'd break and using my mouth to voice a demon chant.

Gritting my teeth, I struggled to my feet and recited the Warding Chant.

> Shield me from the spirits of the Dark,
> O Sower of the Stars.
> Shield my mind against them
> that I may know your wisdom.
> Shield my heart against them
> that I may have your peace.
> Shield my hands against them
> that I may work with skill and patience.
> Shield my feet against them
> that I may walk your Path in safety.
> Shield me from the spirits of the Dark,
> O Sower of the Stars.

I repeated it, half shouting, until the memory dissipated.

Physical trembling remained when I returned to my place on the rug, but I'd calmed. *Barely escaped him that night, but I'm stronger now. Stronger than him.*

Once more I watched the final blow in the vid, as Wanikiya shielded Anataqa and their people from Machitew. *Will I have to die to save them?*

A new memory flooded my mind, from about a year and a half ago. On that night, sitting in this room on the same red-and-black rug, Gram had given me the little leather bag I now wore on a long, yellowed cord about my neck.

"Sometimes," she'd said, "the Ancients require sacrifice, Akuleh. Sometimes, when the outcome is very important, sacrifice is the only way. The woman who bore you knew that. Her husband knew it, too. In time, you'll come to understand it yourself."

"Did *he* have to sacrifice himself to save our enclave from the storm?" I'd asked her. "Did *she* have to sacrifice herself to give me life?"

"Ya," Gram had said, and nodded, "and ya. Her last words were about you." She'd squeezed my hand in an attempt to offer comfort.

My throat tightened at remembering. I dropped my gaze to my lap and pondered my parents. The father I'd idolized. The mother I'd only seen in holoimages and learned about through family tales.

"They sacrificed their lives," I'd murmured at last, and asked Gram, "What will I have to sacrifice? My soul?"

"Not your soul, I think," she'd said.

I released a resolved breath. *Better my life than my soul.*

* * *

I woke from a dream of swords and smoke and shouting when my link chimed with an incoming message. Rolling to my belly to reach for the link, I grimaced at a jab through my ribs, and squinted in the dimness to read the text in its display.

CONTACT LOCAL VORTEX TERMINAL TO CONFIRM SCHEDULED
PASSAGE TO BELSKEN FIELD, OSFELGA, SOLIENNE.

Good. Maybe I'll get out of here today after all. Still propped on my elbows, I tapped the terminal's site to check in.

A muted flash outside the gathering room's window and a thunder
crack like a rocket strike on the nironnium dome pressed me facedown
to the stone floor with my arms over my head. My heart seemed to
stop for an instant. *Not a positive indicator for being able to leave.*

I couldn't access the military terminal's check-in site. Instead, a
screen full of text appeared.

AWÉNASA CITY MILITARY VORTEX TERMINAL IS CURRENTLY ON
STANDDOWN DUE TO CATEGORY-4 THUNDERSTORMS IN THE VICIN-
ITY. DO NOT COME TO THE VORTEX TERMINAL UNTIL NOTIFIED TO
DO SO. TO RECEIVE A NOTIFICATION WHEN OPERATIONS RESUME,
ENTER YOUR NAME, SERVICE NUMBER, TRAVEL ORDER NUMBER, AND
VIDMAIL IN THE FORM BELOW.

I did, with frustration furrowing my brow.

Then I called Derry. "Doing all right, little bird?" I asked when she
appeared in my link's display.

"Kew!" Her eyes widened. "Yer face looks much better. Are yew
coming in today?"

"If the storm passes," I said.

"The vortex terminal's shu' down again?" Her voice carried disappointment. "A new storm?"

"Same storm, new front, but I'll be in the first portal to Belsken as
soon as it reopens."

The loneliness in her eyes at that news matched the emptiness in
my own heart.

The third night of the Wanikiya Ceremony flooded my mind, and I gazed wordlessly into her eyes for some time. *My white bird. My Anataqa. You have no idea how much I'm going to need you—how much I need you right now.*

"Are yew a' righ', Kew?" she asked. "Do yew still have pain? Yew seem sa sad."

"Missing you," I said. *This isn't the right time or way to tell her all of it.* "I'll get there as soon as I can. *Ti qala bé messa tai messa,* Derry."

Thunder continued to crash, and tornado-velocity winds shrieked and roared outside Old Trade Center's dome throughout the morning. I bathed, though the storm had blocked the sunlight from the rooftop cistern long enough that the water I pumped into Gram's trough-like tub triggered chilly shivers when it rolled down my spine. The bruises and welts on my upper back and shoulders had begun to heal, but they remained tender.

Breakfast consisted of my unfinished supper, rewarmed over a small fire I built in Gram's oven. *Not as good as eating it fresh, but better than more canned goods.*

After cleaning up, I settled on the familiar rug, set my back gingerly to the wall as before, and touched Gram's call code on my link.

She answered at once, as if she'd been waiting for me. When I recognized Red Wash Enclave's well house behind her, I knew at once where she sat. A small circle of benches had been built near the well house, a place for the elders to gather. Leaving the crowded family dwelling would allow her to have a private conversation.

Gram smiled. "Good morning, Akuleh. How are you doing?"

"Much better," I said. "Can you talk now?"

"As long as you need," she replied. "Kotori's sleeping. Her husband sat with her all night, and her mother's tending to the baby now. It's a girl."

"Good," I said, and sighed. *So much to discuss with her. Where do I start?*

I began with the first night's ceremony, and the changes to portray Wanikiya as a figure from history. I recounted my conversation with Bimisi afterward, including his position with the Hevovitas clan and their campaign to destroy the traditions given by the Ancient Ones.

Gram shook her head heavily. "I'm sorry he's with the great chief's clan. They're only interested in being important in their own eyes and exercising authority, not serving the people. Losing our traditions will endanger our people. It did before."

I nodded in agreement and went on, "I stayed at Sunning Lizard House the first night, before Kimmie called to give me the new lock codes to yours. The next morning, the other people staying at Sunning Lizard discussed it. Most of them thought the changes were wrong, too, so they decided to hold their own second-night ceremony here in Old Trade Center.

"All the shopkeepers and everybody got involved," I said. "They contributed old clothes to make the regalia and brought out their hand drums and flutes.

"Even Demothi showed up. I don't think I've ever seen him actually happy before in my life." I grinned at remembering his childlike excitement. "He kept saying, 'This is good, this is good!' and waving his arms, but then—" I narrowed my vision on Gram's "—his voice changed. It got stronger, almost commanding, and he said… I hope I can remember his exact words…"

I rubbed my forehead for a few seconds and concentrated. "He said 'Hear the words of Shiye, your first shaman. Wanikiya, your seventh shaman, already walks among you. You will not know him if you see him, but two years from this night he will declare himself. You will know him because he will bring an end to the war, his first act as your seventh shaman.'

"He assigned everyone their roles for the ceremony, and—" I paused and swallowed "—he chose *me* for Wanikiya." I cocked my head and peered at Gram. "Did he make a real prophecy? Does he really know things, or is he just crazy? How in Yuma's name am *I* supposed to end the war in two years?"

Gram chuckled, deepening the crinkles around her eyes. They held a knowing glitter. "I don't believe he's completely crazy, Akuleh. How did the ceremony go?"

"It was good," I said, "until Great Council Security Forces showed up. They herded everybody into the middle of the plaza and threatened us with charges of sedition. Thankfully, there were only a few injuries, nothing serious." *She doesn't need to know I was the one who got injured.*

Gram's expression sank into solemnity, and her voice matched it. "It's becoming dangerous to walk the Path, Akuleh. One local chanter has been imprisoned already because he called out the Great Council for corruption." *You're going to face this yourself,* her eyes warned.

I nodded. "Bim was the one leading the enforcers, Gram. He knows about my Birth Chant."

Gram sighed. "He's jealous. He's been taught that your Birth Chant should've been given to him, but the man who pronounced it gave it to you because of his relationship to you." Her features grew serious. "That man did not speak wrongly, Akuleh. Nor did the Sower of the Stars, who spoke the words into his mind. Always remember that.

"And ya—" she brightened a bit "—I do believe what Demothi said was a prophecy. Record it, just as you told it to me, in the link you wear around your neck." She indicated my chest. "The link holds many other sacred things. Listen to them to learn your calling, and in times when you need strength."

When I nodded solemnly once more, she added, "Coming of Wanikiya Ceremony is prophecy, too. The Great Council wants to change it because its fulfillment will mean the end of man-chosen chiefs and their authority to rule."

I straightened in surprise. "Completely? I didn't know that. No wonder she feels threatened. She's trying to become chief for life."

Gram said, "Remember what Demothi has been shouting in the market all these years? 'Wanikiya will battle Machitew for the *souls* of the people.' In times when the Chalca kept to the Path, their only chief was Star Father, speaking to them through his Ancient Ones." She gave me a motherly smile. "In time, he will speak to them through you, Akuleh."

I shifted against the adobe wall, and the rough bricks prodded my raw shoulder blades. "I'm not ready for this, Gram." I let my head droop and shook it slowly. "How will I *ever* be ready?" I met her gaze again. "I watched the ceremony's third night on my link. I have to die to save our people."

* * * * *

Chapter Four

Gram's face softened. "Maybe. There's a lot you must do before that might happen. What else did you see?"

"I saw Wanikiya and Anataqa," I said, "teaching and healing people together, and choosing others to help them, and Wanikiya protecting the people from enemies in wolf costumes." I puckered my forehead. "What do gray wolves mean? I know I learned it once, but I don't remember."

"They represent hunger and violence," Gram said. "You must prepare our people to face them. Teach them about the protection that comes from keeping to the Path and make sure to prepare others to lead."

I gave a wry smile. "So they can take over when I'm gone."

"If it becomes necessary," Gram agreed, "but giving others some of the responsibility will lighten your own load."

Need to remember that as a flight commander, too. "My load." I sighed. "It feels heavy already."

Gram seemed about to say something else, but a sharp call rose behind her. She twisted to respond, then returned to me. "I'm very sorry, Akuleh. That was Taima; they need my help. *Please*, vidmail me whenever you can. I love you."

I swallowed disappointment. "I will, Gram. Love you, too."

Ending the call left me feeling abandoned. I sat holding my blank link for a minute, like a lifeline, before I set it down to work the ancient one out of the leather bag at my neck. While it took its time to power up, I wondered, *Is there a correct way to record a prophecy? Maybe I should listen to some of Grandfather's recordings first.*

The old link contained more than two centuries of entries. My great-grandfather hadn't been its first owner. I found chants about Chatima, the sixth shaman, and his death at the hands of Winéma's followers shortly before they became Pahana.

I know Shaman Shiye was killed, too. Wonder how many of my predecessors were martyred?

Half the contents covered the War of Extermination, Chanter Yuma, and the Crossing to Tempest. I listened to one of my great-grandfather's chants.

> We call to the one
> who has eyes to see,
> the one left to lead us.
> Go to the desert, we say.
> Seek wisdom from the Stars.
> It is not I, he sings,
> It is not I.

I scrunched my forehead. *Do I have to chant the story of Demothi's prophecy and how he made it?*

Even after listening to several entries, it took me what remained of the morning to make a recording I felt comfortable with. I began by keying a heading into the contents list.

TWENTY-FIFTH DAY OF ELEVENTH MONTH OF INTERSTELLAR STANDARD YEAR 241. PROPHECY OF SHAMAN WANIKIYA'S COMING

GIVEN BY DEMOTHI, CLAN UNKNOWN, RECORDED BY AKULEH OF
CLAN MASOU.

Tipping my head against the knobby bricks, face upturned, I closed
my eyes to consider the words for my chant. I fumbled for appropriate
phrases at first.

"Doubts shadow gathered faces," I began. "Questions come,
questions about sacred things. Some mock. Some taunt the elder. They
whisper like sand driven by wind against the walls."

As I went on, my confidence grew. The words rose within me.

"Above the whispers, truth roars. Like lightning through dark
clouds, words of truth pierce the storm. Words of truth bring certainty.

"'Hear the words of Shiye, your first shaman,' Elder Demothi says.
'Wanikiya, your seventh shaman, already walks among you. You will
not know him if you see him, but two years from this night, he will
declare himself. You will know him because he will bring an end to
the war, his first act as your seventh shaman.'

"These words Shaman Shiye spoke to the doubters through Elder
Demothi."

The effort left me exhausted to a degree I hadn't known since my
vision in Caerden's mountains and starving as if I hadn't eaten for a
phase. I needed several minutes to regain my energy to venture downstairs.

Lightning and wind still battered the dome above Old Trade Center. Through the shop's front window, I watched the swish and swirl
of sand upon its surface for a few minutes, mesmerized by the power
of it, before I headed down the aisles where imported canned goods
filled the shelves.

Having paid with another transfer to Gram's account, I labored up the steep flight once more. I spent the afternoon watching the first two nights of Yellow Rock Enclave's Wanikiya ceremony.

No anti-grav tank and wrist-rockets. No lighting except the torches and bonfires, but the dancers' eyes and smiles radiate an inner light. I like this one best.

I cleaned up the evidence that I'd stayed in Gram's tidy dwelling, loaded my travel pack, and settled in early to sleep.

I felt thankful I had when my link's chime woke me just after 0200. Guided by its display's glow, my hand closed on it at once, and I read the brief message.

AWÉNASA CITY MILITARY VORTEX TERMINAL HAS RESUMED OPERATIONS. CONTACT AT ONCE TO CONFIRM SCHEDULED PASSAGE TO BELSKEN FIELD, OSFELGA, SOLIENNE.

"Finally!" I opened the terminal's site to check in. The confirmation message brought the first genuine smile to my face in close to a phase.

REPORT TO ACMVT NLT 0800 FOR YOUR 1100 PASSAGE TO BELSKEN FIELD.

I called Derry first. *It'll be a little past 0900 there.*

"Wha's the word, love?" she asked when she answered.

"Got an 1100 vortex, if all stays clear," I said. "Should get me to Belsken Field about 1800 your time. I'll call you from the terminal's crawler stop."

"Brillian'!" Radiance replaced her evident anxiousness. "I canna wai' to see yew."

I set my link's wake-up tone for 0500 and returned to sleep in minutes. On rising three hours later, I donned my flight suit and placed my flight jacket on top inside my pack, covering the service blues I'd worn for my arrival as an honor guard. *I'll need the jacket when I get to Osfelga. It's winter there.*

Reaching the transport stop, I felt unexpected relief to see Demothi at his accustomed spot, appearing none the worse for facing down the enforcers. *Maybe they figure he's insane, so not worth beating up.*

The wild man ceased his ranting to follow me with his lone eye. "You must bring your son home soon," he croaked at me.

"I will, Elder," I replied.

He sees far through his lost eye, Shaman Shiye's quiet voice said in my mind. *My servant, who is called Demothi by many, speaks the truth.*

I froze in mid-stride for a split second. Then my thoughts kicked in to match my pace. *How am I supposed to bring them home, Shaman Shiye?*

It is in my hands, my son Wanikiya.

Alone at the transport stop in the early hour, though the sun never set during Tempest's six-month, northern-hemisphere summers, I lifted my arms skyward and sang the Chant to Welcome Dawn.

Minutes later, when the transport exited the city's domes, I narrowed my eyes against the perpetual daylight. Thunderheads pierced with electric-pink flickers mounded on the horizon, but no wind whipped the desert dust at the moment.

The calm between fronts. Please, Shaman Shiye, help me get off Tempest before the next one hits.

* * *

I didn't breathe freely until I burst from the vortex into Belsken Field's Military Terminal. I retrieved my flight jacket from my pack and shrugged it on before I strode outside.

As I had the first time I'd arrived on Solienne, I bounced my first few steps in the post-Tempest lower gravity. This time, at least, I knew to expect it.

Winter's early darkness—the first I'd seen in days—had fallen hours ago. Fresh snow gleamed stark white in contrast. Fine snowflakes filtered from clouds lying low enough to conceal the towering Hamskjold Mountains, the teeth-like peaks marking Osfelga's western border.

I checked my link's chrono. *Past 1800 hours. It'll be close to 1900 by the time I get home.*

Home. Warmth filled my soul. I smiled at everyone I passed.

Entering the crawler stop, I exchanged salutes with other personnel and unpocketed my link. "Waiting for the crawler," I said when Derry answered. Anticipation left me unable to stand still, so I stepped outside. "ETA about forty minutes."

"We're waiting supper for yew." Derry's eyes sparkled. "I made awanatas for the occasion."

I chuckled. "That's perfect, little bird, but all I really want is you."

I smiled throughout the ride to the housing annex. It was too dark to watch the rugged coastline slide by, but I wouldn't have seen it anyway. Two faces filled my mind's eye.

Donnol, bundled to the ears and wielding crutches, burst from our front door as the crawler lurched away. Puffing a vapor cloud with every swinging step, he intercepted me halfway to the townhouse. *He's grown since I left.*

"Thought you dumped those," I said with a grin and pointed with my chin at his crutches.

"This's easier on the snow," he replied.

The walkway around the circle had been cleared, but I knew slippery spots remained. I slowed my pace enough for him to keep up, not to mention favoring the lingering soreness of my ribs.

He chattered the whole way. "Can yew stay here forever now, Kew? Can yew say where yew were? Wha's it like there? Did yew miss me?"

I grinned. "Yes, I missed you, Donnol. Did you remember your promise to help Derry?"

"Aye." He nodded solemnly. "'Specially now with Garny."

"Good. We were right to choose you for our Guardian."

Supper smells swept through the door when Madam Graebel opened it, and my stomach growled. She greeted me with a tight hug before I'd even shed my pack. "Upstairs," she said with a knowing wink as she released me.

I worked my way up the steps, mouth pressed closed on a grimace, and paused at the top when I noticed a single dim light glowing in our bedroom. I called quietly, "Derry?"

"Oh, Kew! Do come in." Her face bore the same radiance I'd seen on our wedding day. "He only jus' wen' to sleep. Come see."

She sat curled in a large armchair near the foot of our bed, cradling a blanket-wrapped bundle to her heart. She seemed small in the chair, and somehow fragile, but I smirked.

Any woman who can get her troops out of a bombed building through a crumbling tunnel with her wrist broken, her face cut up and bleeding, and one eye blinded isn't fragile. Not to mention giving birth.

"You first, Derry." Abrupt tightness in my throat reduced my words to a rasp. Crouching beside her chair, I slipped my hands into her hair, longer than it'd ever appeared in her vids, to cradle her face and lean in. Our mouths met, and for the next few minutes we strove to make up for every lonely moment of the past nine months.

Until a cry startled us apart.

"Oh dear, we've woken him," Derry whispered.

I could see him fully then, his miniature face with eyes squeezed shut, toothless mouth wide open as a baby bird's with his squalling, and lots of black hair.

In the next heartbeat, Derry eased him into my hands.

The whole universe could've disappeared right then, and I wouldn't have noticed. *My child.* The pinching sensation closed my throat again, leaving me completely unable to speak, so I buried my nose in his fuzzy hair and nuzzled his head. *This miniature, wailing person squirming in my hands is* my *child.*

"Bounce him a bi', jus' gen'ly like this," Derry said and demonstrated. "Tha' usually stops him crying."

When he finally did stop and opened his eyes, we searched each other's faces. Each other's souls. He gurgled and waved his tiny fists, and my heart went into orbit. I couldn't stop grinning.

Words from my Birth Chant whispered across my mind.

Maize kernels rest in fertile earth.
In desert earth they grow strong roots.
From desert earth they grow tall stalks.
Firm against storm winds they stand,
Good stalks full of ears, of kernels,
Good kernels to nourish our people.

Maize kernels growing into strong stalks meant children becoming strong adults. Kernels to nourish our people meant my children would serve our people.

Another fulfillment of my Birth Chant. Now I need to perform his. Overwhelmed with the magnitude of it, I kissed his warm head. *'Joy' isn't a powerful enough word. I finally know how my father felt about me.*

"Kew?" Derry asked.

Her query returned me to the present, and my voice restored with it. "I need to take you and Garnan home to Tempest. Soon." I told her about Demothi's admonition and the confirmation I'd received from Shaman Shiye. "It's important."

I knew that for sure, even if I had no idea why.

* * * * *

Chapter Five

I carried Garnan when Derry and I went downstairs a few minutes later. Her mother placed a pot of Caerdish cabbage soup, seasoned with onions and herbs, and a loaf of seed-laden black bread on the table, and Donnol and Derry set out bowls and utensils.

"Yew canna hold him and ea' a' the same time, Kew lad," Madam Graebel teased.

"Probably can," I returned with a grin, but I allowed her to take him from my arms.

Donnol filled me in on recent events while we ate. I came close to choking on my soup once, trying not to laugh at his earnest report of hunting for a noisy squirrel in the attic.

After supper, I let him beat me two out of three at one of his vid games. Then I contacted Chanter Wahkan.

"Akuleh!" He beamed when he recognized me in his link. "Have you returned to Tempest to accomplish your preparations?"

"Not yet, Chanter, but I will soon." I told him about the three-day pass my wing commander had granted me during the return trip from honor guard duty. "I need to do a purification so I can perform my son's Birth Chant before I go back."

"I'll meet you at the chaplains' office at 0500 tomorrow," Wahkan said.

* * *

41

I waited until after Derry and I had made love that night, while we still lay in each other's arms, to tell her about my appointment to flight commander and the reason for it. She'd never met my trainee, Nawat, but she'd known my late flight commander and my Fuago Monoan friend Yobo, as well as his wife Ga'olani. She understood without me using their names, according to the Chalca taboo.

"I'm sa sorry, Kew," Derry said. "Please give Go my love and condolences."

"Things are changing on Tempest," I said. "I told you most of it the other day. It seems limited to Awénasa City right now, but it'll be influencing the remote enclaves before long."

"Wha' will the people do?" Derry asked. "How will they reac' to the Hevos' dicta'es?"

"I don't know." I sighed. "I only know we need to return there soon." When she questioned me with her eyes, I said, "It's in Shaman Shiye's hands."

I didn't tell her about Demothi's prophecy. *Not yet. I'll wait until we we're together with Chanter Wahkan.*

* * *

When Garnan woke us with hungry cries for the third time, this time shortly after 0300, I knew I wouldn't return to sleep before my link's wake-up tone sounded. I dressed in civilian clothes and told Derry, "I'll be gone all day."

"There's juice and toas' in the kitchen," she offered with a yawn.

"I need to do this fasting, White Bird." I kissed her, stroked Garnan's cheek with a fingertip, and burrowed into my parka.

The crawler didn't make frequent runs to our base annex at such an early hour, so I had to wait a while in the crystalline cold. By the time I disembarked near the chaplains' section, my link read 0509. I strode briskly up the street to the building, crunching over frozen snow and leaving contrails of my breath on the motionless air.

In the grounds behind the base chapel, half buried under snow, lay the shallow-mounded roof of a ceremonial lodge. Chanter Wahkan straightened from tugging the cover off its square entry hole when I drew up. He caught his loose, gray-streaked hair away from his face and studied me for several long seconds. His smile deepened his face's wrinkles, so reminiscent of Gram's. "Akuleh. This is a happy occasion."

"Ya, it is, Chanter." The swell of joy I'd felt at holding my child the previous evening resurfaced.

I found the ladder lying in the snow a few spans away and lowered it into the opening. When I'd descended, he followed me down. We assessed the lodge's interior by his oil-burning lantern's flickering light.

Large enough to seat ten men, I estimated, and just high enough for the ceiling's woven logs to clear a typical Chalca's head. Taller other-worlders would have to duck or stoop.

A veneer of beaded ice—vapor that had frozen after earlier rituals—coated the circular walls, ceiling, encircling bench, and the raised hearth built in a niche on the east side.

Two buckets stood on the bench. Beneath it I found a stack of split hardwood for fuel, and boxes of tinder and kindling. Covered clay pots filled with purifying herbs, and a bowl of coarse sand for cleansing oneself, stood ready as well.

"Do you want assistance?" Wahkan asked.

"I'll need water," I requested.

I handed the buckets up when Wahkan had climbed out and reached back for them.

Alone, I began the Chant to Ignite Sacred Fires. The formal ceremonial chant, not the simple one for teaching apprentices.

"O, Ancient Ones, who light the skies with stars and warm the Mother Worlds with sun," I sang quietly while I worked, "send to me fire spirits from the stars to light sacred this lodge. Send to me fire spirits from the sun to warm this lodge and teach me how to live in beauty."

By the faint moonlight sifting through the roof entrance, I arranged tinder and kindling in the firebox beneath the stone hearth. I continued the chant as I touched balls of dried grass with my cold-wizened finger. A tiny flame rose from each one. I crouched, ignored the jab in my ribcage, and blew gently until the tinder ignited.

Wahkan returned with full buckets, and I climbed up to take them one at a time. "Thank you, Chanter."

He acknowledged with a nod. Then his footfalls withdrew.

Resuming the chant, I lay hardwood lengths on the kindling. Flames obediently enveloped the wood. I inhaled the smoke's sweet aroma when I stood. My hands, already stiff with cold, ached at unfastening my parka.

I dipped water from one bucket into a drinking pot, added herbs, and set the pot on the stone hearth to heat before I shucked the rest of my clothes. By then, the ice glazing the ceiling beams above the firebox had begun to melt and drip. Clad only in a traditional loincloth, I shivered and my teeth chattered.

The complete purification ceremony required performing the cleansing ritual seven times, once every hour, between prayer chants and meditation on the sought-after blessing. The lodge grew warm, then hot, a heat intensified by rising steam. Chanter Wahkan returned regularly to replenish my water buckets.

"Star Father, Sower of the Stars," I chanted, ignoring the sweat dripping off my nose and earlobes, and streaming down my temples to my mouth, "grant me your words for my son. Show me your Path for his life."

When vapor curled from the pot of cleansing tea for the seventh time, I knew it and the stone hearth had grown hot enough. I sighed. *One last time.*

Sitting cross-legged on the wooden platform before the hearth, I took the clay pot in both hands and lifted my gaze to the ceiling.

"Pour your spirit into me with this bitter cup, O Sower of the Stars." My voice had faded to a whisper by then, but I persisted. "Let it wring from my blood and skin the impurities of the worlds. Let it press from my bowels and bones the infirmities of the worlds, that I may climb the Sacred Mountain and approach you in worthiness, O Sower of the Stars."

I tilted my head back, tipped the pot, and drank quickly. The tea warmed my throat. My eyes and nose watered, and sweat broke out once more on my body.

I set the empty pot aside. One bucket stood at my right, the other at my left. The right one held a weaker version of the tea and a gourd dipper. I scooped the dipper full and sloshed its contents across the hearth.

Vapor rose with a sizzle like the voice of a malevolent spirit, leaving droplets to dance and spit on the hot stone. I closed my eyes and scooped with my hands while I chanted in the aromatic cloud around myself. I inhaled its pungency slowly and deeply, again and again, to cleanse my lungs as well.

Sweat streamed from my pores. It represented evil as a substance, and I visualized it oozing from my face and forehead, dark and oily. It ribboned my temples and throat and soaked my loose hair into lank tendrils across my back. Sweat rolled down my sternum and spine. I sat motionless, eyes still closed, and repeated the chant.

When the hard sweat ended, but before drafts through the covered entry began to cool the foggy heat, I scooped sand from the shallow bowl, near the bucket at my left, and scrubbed myself. The repeated applications left my skin raw. I gritted my teeth against the smarting as I worked.

Kneeling on the platform, I seized the left bucket and poured its icy contents over my head. It took my breath as it had each time before. I gasped and spluttered and began to shiver violently as I swept off the last grains of coarse sand with both hands.

Wahkan had brought dry towels each time he'd refilled the buckets. I snagged one off the bench, flung it across my back, and rubbed myself dry, wincing at the raw spots that left red smudges on the pale cloth.

For long minutes afterward, huddled under a heavy towel, I sat motionless and studied the twined logs supporting the roof. Condensation drizzled and dripped from them, hypnotic in their steady rhythm.

No vision came. *Do the words come in a vision?* I heard nothing from the familiar, quiet voice that so often whispered through my mind. *Where are you, Shaman Shiye? I'm as prepared as I can make myself. I'm waiting to receive your words.*

The entry cover grated and slid aside, startling me from my concentration, and Chanter Wahkan's face appeared in the square hole. "Akuleh, it's time."

I dressed, climbed shakily out of the lodge, and he helped me draw up the ladder.

"I don't know what I'm supposed to say in the Birth Chant," I told Wahkan minutes later while we waited for the crawler.

He glanced across at me and smiled, a crinkly, wise expression. "Most fathers don't know until they're holding their child."

"What if nothing comes then?"

"Something will," Wahkan said with certainty.

We rode the crawler in contemplative silence amid the chatter of people heading home from a day of duty. I kept my gaze on the gritty floormats between my boots. *What if nothing comes?*

Madam Graebel had supper ready. After my day-long fast, my mouth watered at the aromas drifting into the living room as the chanter and I entered the house.

Derry, sitting on the old sofa, rose and crossed to us at once. Garnan gurgled in her arms, gazed about, and reached out for us. Wahkan smiled at him and stroked his hair before he greeted everyone else. Derry queried me with only her eyes.

I pulled my leather bag out from under my shirt and off over my head, and handed it to her before I took our son in my arms. "Record his chant after mine."

The old link needed a full minute to power up, and several more seconds for Derry to scroll through its contents. "Wha's this?" she asked, angling the display toward me.

Demothi's prophecy. "Something you, Wahkan, and I need to talk about later," I said.

Derry only nodded, pressed the Record button, and said, "I's ready."

Donnol and Madam Graebel watched, clearly curious, as Wahkan positioned himself at my right and placed a hand on my shoulder.

With Derry's family there, something else occurred to me. "I'll have to speak this in Chalca," I told them, "but we can translate it from the recording afterward."

"Thank yew," Madam Graebel said a bit stiffly.

Garnan cooed and waved his arms. When he stared up at me, his mouth open as if to speak, my throat promptly constricted once more. *Why does even looking at him do this to me?* I drew a deep breath to steady myself and closed my eyes for a second. *Help me do this, Shaman Shiye. Tell me the words I need to say.*

I knew how to begin, at least. I gave my full attention to my child. "Garnan, son of Derry and Akuleh," I said. "Garnan, spirit child of Star Father, Sower of the Stars. Star Father pours out His power like a river flowing to his chanters. Star Father pours out his blessings like a spring flood upon his people."

My throat relaxed, but I had to lift my vision from my son's face and close my eyes again.

Finally, images appeared in my mind, accompanying chanted words as unmistakable as every silent directive I'd ever received from Shaman Shiye.

"Listen, Garnan, as I sing the Path of your life, as I sing the tasks of your life. Follow the flight of the golden eagle. Follow his Path as far as you can. Soar in his Path as high as you can, and learn wisdom in the shadow of his wings."

I had to pause. *The golden eagle is me. I know that, but how can I teach him wisdom when I need to learn it myself?*

It took a few seconds before I could continue. "Listen to the counsel of the white bird, for her words will keep you safe. Her words will give you strength and peace for your Path."

I knew her symbol well by now. *Derry is the white bird. Mothers are always the greatest influence on their children.*

"Learn from little brother creatures on the world you will know," I sang. "Learn from those that gather and store. Learn from those that build, so you may teach your people. Teach them to feed themselves. Teach them to shelter themselves, so they may be strong and safe."

One detail burned with clarity. *Not Tempest? A different world?*

I didn't have time to ponder it. The chant continued to flow, like the voice of living water from a spring on the Sacred Mountain. "Learn from elder brother eagle, he of far sight, to see the distance of the future, to know and be prepared."

Understanding opened, and my heart swelled inside my ribs. *My son will be a powerful chanter in the world he'll know.*

"White wolves pace before you," I chanted. "White wolves pace beside you. Listen to their voices, their calls on the winds among the stars, for they speak wisdom. They speak truth and strength."

I hadn't forgotten the symbol of white wolves from my chanter apprenticeship. With their luminous coats, they represented the Ancient Ones, the guardians of mortal chanters. *My son will have access to the guidance of the Ancients.*

I swallowed a new tremor of emotion so I could continue. "White wolves call to you, my son. They have called you Hiamovi, the high chief who will lift our people from the dust, who will lead them in the Light. This is the song of your Path, my loved son Hiamovi."

The river of words into my mind ran dry. I opened my eyes, gathered my infant tightly to myself, and kissed his forehead.

The others stared at me, Derry and her mother and Donnol with curiosity, Chanter Wahkan with the same awe as when he'd heard my Birth Chant.

Wahkan held out his hand for the ancient link and addressed Derry and her family. "I will explain the chant to you in detail, but simply put—" he pointed to Garnan with his chin "—it means Akuleh holds the future of the Chalca people in his arms."

Later, when Madam Graebel, cradling Garnan tightly, took him and Donnol upstairs to put them to bed, I stopped Chanter Wahkan when he started toward the door. "There's something else I need to show you and Derry." I scrolled the link's contents back to the one Derry had found earlier. "This happened a few days ago."

I translated Demothi's prophecy for Derry when the recording ended. I felt every bit as overwhelmed, hearing my own voice recounting it, as I had at the time Demothi declared it, but no doubt shaded my wife's features.

"Keep his prophecy sacred," Wahkan said, "until it's accomplished. Shaman Shiye will show you how when it's time."

* * * * *

Chapter Six

Derry returned to sleep quickly after feeding Garnan sometime around 0200, but I couldn't. Lying spooned with her, body-heat warm under our white, yellow, and green wedding blanket, I slipped my arm around her and snugged her closer to myself.

Words and images tumbled through my mind like debris caught in a tornado. Nawat's fireball in space. Yobo's fireball on the runway. Nawat's mother shouting accusations and Machitew's cold presence echoing them in my ear. Demothi's searching eye and warning. His prophecy of my arrival as Wanikiya in two years. The final battle between Wanikiya and Machitew in the third night of the ceremony.

Can't do anything about any of it right now. Need to find a distraction… What I really need to do is get started on the flight commanders' SOP.

I eased myself apart from Derry, sat up, and reached for my link, which lay on the bedside cabinet.

My outstretched hand closed on the remote instead. I gave it a moment's mental debate, then touched Mute and switched on the vidscreen on the facing wall. *Quick check of the news first.*

The screen rippled to life in the middle of what appeared, by the subtitles sliding across the bottom, to be a eulogy.

A TRIBUTE TO KING SAUVAR'S LONG AND BENEVOLENT REIGN.

Did he die? I straightened abruptly where I sat. *Does Mogen know, out on Tobe?*

At my own movements, Derry shifted and blinked at the vid's flickering light. She sat up, too, her features firming into the intelligence-officer-on-duty expression I missed so much at the briefer's podium at Lybjevyk Base.

"Sorry," I said at once. "Didn't mean to wake you."

"It's a' righ', Kew." Her hand brushed my abs, sending a little thrill through me, when she reached across for the remote to switch the sound on.

It came up quietly in the middle of a female news presenter saying, "… unanimous vote by Osfelga's parliament, for the king's abdication in favor of…"

"They did i', then," Derry murmured. "It's been the subjec' of discussion on the news ne's for days now."

Images captured at major events in the king's life appeared one after another in the vid. His elaborate state wedding and coronation, his initiatives in economics, education, and industry that had improved his people's lives, and clips of several speeches given at critical points in Osfelga's recent history.

"… physicians have determined he is no longer mentally capable of governing," the woman continued. "Sauvar the Fourth will ascend the throne…"

When I glimpsed a small man in dark robes standing behind the king's shoulder at one speech, I froze. "Pause."

Derry crimped her brow in a quizzical expression but said nothing while I tapped the remote to reverse through ten or twelve images.

"Him." I pointed out the diminutive, robed figure. "I'd forgotten about him. I saw him in a vid during our pre-mobilization briefing for Ardonar, hovering at the king's shoulder the same way."

"Who is he?" Derry asked.

"Soola ka' Remmet," I said. "Mogen told me he's his father's chief adviser. He also once told me Soola had 'become indispensable' since his father's memory had begun to fail." My gut twisted at the sight of the stringy mustache and hooded eyes. "I don't trust him, no matter what Mog thinks. Mog said he was a coronation gift from some nobleman on Jassem."

Derry's eyes widened. "On *Jassem*?"

"Ya. The lumpies learned the locations of our bases on Ardonar somehow—you probably know more about it than I do—and which space stations had been rigged with explosives and stuff. Soola would've had access to all that, and the means to relay it. Any chance intel has a dossier on him?"

Derry kept her face expressionless. "I don' think sa. He's par' of the royal household, isn' he?"

"He didn't come freely as an immigrant," I said. "I can't help wondering if whoever gave him to King Sauvar had ulterior motives."

"I's a possibili'y, of course," Derry replied, "bu' he's had two decades to compromise House Reskag if he were going to. I rather doub' he'd wai' this long to do i'."

I huffed a breath in frustration. "Will you do something for me? When you've got time, once you're back on duty, do you think you could do a little research on him?"

"Open sources and Resistance Pac'-releasable materials, to which I'm limited as a Join' Services Exchange officer, wouldn' provide wha' yew wan' to know."

"Being a Joint Services Exchange officer is the answer," I said. "Don't you have to communicate with your Caerdish chain of command sometimes? Could somebody there do the research? You're not a subject of the Soliennese Commonwealth, and neither is he, so Commonwealth laws don't apply."

"We have our own laws," she said, "and there's no Caerdish secure facili'y at Belsken Field. I have to go into the city, to Resistance Pac' Headquarters, for vid conferences." In another instant she gave me an impish smile, puckering the scar across her forehead. "I couldn' tell yew anything I learn' anyway, Kew. Yew're no' cleared fer Caerdish classified."

"Intel Rogue," I muttered and lowered my head to nibble the rim of her ear. "I'll seduce it out of you."

She gave me a playful push.

I resumed my seriousness. "I don't need details, Derry. All I need to know is whether he's trustworthy. You can say 'yes' or 'no' without compromising anything, can't you?"

"I' depends on the source." She eyed me. "Wha' would yew do with any answers I turned up?"

The maelstrom churning in my mind minutes earlier swelled to a keen urgency. "I don't know," I admitted, "but I have a feeling Remmet's behind a lot of our Ops stuff getting compromised."

She studied me more intently for several heartbeats. Then she grinned, snatched the remote from me to switch the vidscreen off, and said, "Le's see who's seducing who."

* * * * *

Chapter Seven

Derry strolled to the cul de sac's crawler stop with me on my third afternoon, her slender fingers intertwined with mine. The solemnity shadowing her face mirrored the heaviness I felt in my soul.

I enveloped her in my arms while we waited for the snaky transport. When it appeared in the distance, spouting vapor and gray slush from its undercarriage, I drew her as tightly to myself as I could, in the futile hope some of her warmth would linger with me. I savored every second of our kiss.

How can I leave her again so soon, her and Garn? I thought it was hard when I had to leave her before, newly pregnant. I haven't had enough time to bond with Garn. Who knows when I'll see them again?

Derry's wistful words shattered my melancholy reverie. "Vid me when yew ge' there, love, and don' worry abou' taking us back to Tempes'. We'll sor' i' ou' somehow."

"Shaman Shiye will sort it out, White Bird." I stroked her cheek with a fingertip, we exchanged a last quick kiss, and I tore myself away to board the crawler.

Fresh snow falling through the early darkness swept the crawler's windows. I didn't look out. I forced my vision forward through the long ride to Belsken Field's vortex terminal.

* * *

My return orders, I learned at the check-in counter, would take me to Satha without having to retrace my route via Tempest, but I'd have the usual three-hour wait for my portal at Belsken Field. *Plenty of time to study Standard Operating Procedures for Flight Commanders.* I yawned at the thought.

I hadn't left the counter before the terminal's double doors *whooshed* open. A mix of cheerful voices preceded their owners inside, along with a swirling burst of snow-laden wind.

A gaggle of apprentice officers, wearing flight jackets and guiding remote-controlled repulsor trunks with C-bags strapped securely on top, crossed to the counter with the unmistakable swagger of newly pinned pilots. They snatched off their flight caps, shook out the snow, and a dark-skinned young man with a thick Obollan accent exclaimed, "Please, gods, just let us end up somewhere warm!"

The whole group queued up behind me, and the joking around subsided to quiet chatter.

When I pivoted to move away from the counter, every one of them snapped into a brace. I found myself facing six Solis or Sathis, four Fuago Monoans, three Obollans, and three Chalca, an even mix of men and women. Every pair of eyes focused on the unit patches on my flight jacket or on my face.

"Sir," said the young man at the head of the line. Sathi, I thought by his accent.

I chuckled. "As you were." I indicated the rank pin at my collar. "I'm an apprentice, too."

Not for much longer, I realized in another second. *I'm coming up on my two-year mark. I'll pin on intermediate officer in a couple more phases. Or journeyman—and sooner than a couple phases—if MinDef concurs with Teichert's request.*

That means I need to get moving on my application for the Qaletaqa.

My late cousin, Hanuk, and I had dreamed of joining the Chalca special operations force from the time we could pronounce its name.

A sudden notion, like pieces in a wooden puzzle snapping together, caught me in mid-step. *That's it. Being accepted for Qaletaqa training will mean I'll have to return to Tempest.*

"Next," said the man behind the counter, and the Sathi youth stepped forward. The others bunched loosely about me.

"15th Aerospace Combat Wing." The tall Obollan who'd loudly hoped for a warmer destination indicated the command patch on my chest. "That's where we're going." He didn't quell the eagerness in his eyes and tone.

"The 15th?" A slim Fuago Monoan youth edged closer. "What can you tell us about it?"

I grinned. "Check in first. I'll be over there." I pointed with my chin toward the opposite wall. "We'll have plenty of time to talk."

I stopped at a vending machine, bought some packages of jerky and a bottle of water, and settled into an empty seat against the cavernous waiting area's side wall. From there I had a clear line of sight on all the entries and exits, including the vortex portals.

The first two young men to saunter over took the seats at the end of two forward-facing rows and leaned across the narrow aisle toward me.

"Apprentice Masou?" one of them asked, with a glance at my name patch.

"I'm called Ku." I tore open a bag of jerky and offered it. They picked out a few strips and told me their names, Manoq and Swa'ako from Satha and Fuago Mono.

The whole flight joined us in ones and twos during the next several minutes. They maneuvered several chairs out of the rows to press in around me as well as they could, as if I were some kind of wise elder, and I surveyed them. *They look like youngsters, all excited, no idea what they're about to get into.*

I thought about Nawat, and how he'd felt like my younger brother. *Burn.*

Another thought struck me. *They're the replacements for our combat losses. Bet most are going to 1st Squadron. That means some of them will be in Lance Flight.*

My flight, I abruptly realized. *Some of these new pilots will be* my *responsibility.* My innards tensed, but I asked, "What do you want to know?"

"Tell us about the 15th," said the Fuago Monoan boy.

I nodded. "It's a good organization. Teichert's a good commander. I've been in it since it stood up two years ago, same time I was commissioned."

"So you fought at Nichi and Ardonar?" asked the Sathi who'd called me 'sir.'

"Yes." I dropped my gaze to the jerky bag.

"Is anyone else from the 15th here, too?" the one Obollan young woman asked.

"No, just me right now," I said. "TDY for a few days." *Don't ask what for,* I thought. *You don't need to know I just served as honor guard for my latest lead-in trainee.*

Two or three fixed me with curious expressions, but since no one asked directly, I didn't answer. Instead, I volunteered, "Commander Teichert gave me a three-day pass on the way back, to see my wife and baby. I wasn't expecting it, so that made it even better." Thinking of Derry and Garn prompted a broad smile. "My son's a month old now."

"Ooo!" A Sathi girl leaned in. "Do you have any eemages?"

Madam Graebel had used her link to capture countless images while I was home, with a promise to forward all of them. *They'll be waiting in my vidmail when I get there—if they don't swamp my account,* I thought.

A search of my link produced only two, both of Derry cradling Garnan. The girls passed the link around and exclaimed at how adorable he was, with his bright eyes and abundant black hair. I beamed. I couldn't help it.

At last, one of the Soliennese girls returned my link and asked, "Where's the 15th deployed now?"

"Can't tell you that," I said. "There's a reason it says 'classified' on your orders."

They all fell silent and exchanged glances. Several faces bore mildly uneasy expressions. After a minute or two of wordless gnawing on jerky sticks, they ask questions about flying Rohrspachen-55 Spearheads in real-world conditions.

"24/7 ops," I said. "No more sim-munitions. You know the high-tempo exercise during your last phase?"

Heads nodded. Every pair of eyes focused on me.

"That was pretty close to reality," I said. "Not constant, but when it happens, it can go for more than a month. It did on Ardonar."

"How can we communicate with our families if it's a classified location?" asked a Fuago Monoan girl.

"We have a secure comms center," I said. "You can sign up to check your vidmail every three days."

On noticing a few cocked eyebrows, I explained, "To keep it from being detected and intercepted, they send encrypted vidmails in blocks at random intervals, using split-second laser bursts via deep-space relays. At our comms center, technicians decrypt the block and disseminate the vidmails to everybody's accounts. Outbound vidmail travels the same way." I concluded, "Your lead-in trainers will also be your sponsors. They'll show you around."

One of the Soli kids raised a hand. "How's the mess hall?"

I chuckled. *Sounds like a good trainee for Kota, always thinking with his taste buds.* I said, "It's pretty good. There's a flight kitchen, too." I stopped myself from saying something about the food quality being better than the air quality just in time. *That'd raise questions about why weather's on the forbidden topics list.* Instead, I said, "They vortex in float-carts of supplies a couple times a phase. We even get stuff from Tempest and Obolli. There's a good gym, too."

On a whim I said, "I heard about the king retiring the other day." I addressed a young woman who appeared to be Osfelg. "What do you think?"

"It's so sad," she said at once. "He's a good man. He was a good king, but they say his son and top advisors have been conducting the business of reigning for the past year, so I guess it's time."

Several advisors or one in particular? I didn't voice it; I just nodded.

Unexpectedly, the Chalca girl, whose name patch read Chitsa and who'd sat quietly observing me the whole time, said, "In Survival School, they told us about a Chalca pilot who got shot down on Ardonar. His arm was wounded, but he single-handedly captured a high-value target. They said he's still in the 15th, but they didn't give his name. Do you know him?"

I blinked. *I'm a case study for Survival School?* I said only, "Ya, I do."

"What's he like?"

I surreptitiously tugged my right cuff to cover the heel of my hand, to conceal the entry point of the long, livid scar, and said, "He's different than before." *In a lot of ways.* "He's quieter and more serious now." *At least Kota and Rinn say I am.* "And he *really* doesn't like to be pointed out or asked about it."

I felt grateful for Commander Teichert's standing order that people respect my privacy.

The others sat in thoughtful silence for a space, and I regarded them as a group. *I'm a flight commander. Guess I've already started.* I straightened and grinned. "So, what kinds of bugs did they make you eat in Survival School?"

* * *

Our whole group, along with several other personnel who'd been sitting scattered about the waiting area, made the vortex passage to the shipping-crate terminal in the Sathi jungle together. The Sathi pilots peered around hopefully.

Six non-pilot personnel departed within a few minutes for the 11th Aerospace Combat Wing's classified deployment location. An hour or so later, the rest of us, including all sixteen of the new pilots, shoved ourselves through the vortex's invisible icy wall into Lybjevyk Base's austere terminal.

Having been away from it for a phase, Tobe's sulfur-scented air smacked me in the face when I burst through. My nose reflexively wrinkled with distaste.

Mogen and 1st Squadron's two other flight commanders waited at the foot of the shallow ramp, along with Spacer Tech Gennadi, who carried a metal box to collect our personal links. I scanned the warehouse-like space behind Mogen and the others, puzzled by the absence of "veteran" pilots with signs displaying their new trainees' names.

I didn't have time to wonder about it. Spacer Gennadi produced a blocky, gray link from a uniform pocket and held it out to me. "You'll need this as flight commander, sir. It's your duty link. Please initial the issue form here." She thrust a datapad at me, and I drew the glyph for my clan name with my fingertip.

"Welcome back, Ku," Mogen said when he spotted me, and his grave expression lifted somewhat. "Wait here a minute, will you? We have the responsibility of welcoming our new fighter crews. By the way, congratulations."

"Thanks, Mog." My grin split my face again. "You were right. Holding him for the first time…" I shook my head, wordless for a moment. "He has my hair, but I think he looks more like Derry."

Mogen smiled in return. "All the more reason to celebrate. I had something else in mind, but it'll have to wait until we accomplish the task at hand."

* * * * *

Chapter Eight

I nodded, and Mogen announced to the newcomers, "The first thing you'll want to do is unpack your weather mask. We're under Category 2 ashfall conditions at the moment. Your first tip for surviving comfortably on Tobe is to keep your weather mask on your person at all times. I guarantee you'll need it more often than you won't."

I dug my own mask from my travel pack and stuffed it into a pocket, then stood back. Journeyman Officers Sperka and Domokos, the commanders of Arrow and Saber Flights, took turns calling out their new arrivals' names.

Finally, Mogen addressed the seven pilots who remained: Chitsa from Tempest, a man from Obolli, a woman from Solienne, Manoq and a woman from Satha, and two men from Fuago Mono, one of whom was Swa'ako.

I need to connect their names to their faces ASAP, I thought.

"You're assigned to Lance Flight," Mogen said. "May I present your flight commander, Akuleh of Masou clan, callsign Sun Eagle—" he slipped me a sly smirk. "—who happens to be out of uniform at the moment."

I immediately checked my jacket to be sure my rank and unit patches were in place, and caught my new flight mates' surprised expressions and delighted smiles. I gave them a self-conscious *What can I say?* shrug and grin.

"Our promotions became effective yesterday, *Journeyman* Masou," Mogen said. "The orderly room has your new rank pins."

Only then did I notice he now wore master officer rank, appropriate for his recent appointment to squadron commander. My smile broadened. "Congrats to you, too, Mog." I asked him under my breath, "Where are their trainer-sponsors?"

"Otherwise occupied," Mogen replied. "I'll give you the full briefing once we get them checked in and billeted." He peered around my shoulder at the others and said, "Masks on. Let's move out."

On exiting the vortex terminal, we paused in the gravel-covered open area between the base's main buildings and the flightline's hangars and repair facility. As in Osfelga, winter evenings came early to Lybjevyk Base, but even full daylight appeared reddish through the perpetual haze filtering Tobe's sun.

Unlike Osfelga, Lybjevyk regularly got ashfall instead of snow. Even Cat 2 conditions reduced visibility like a thin, dry fog, and the light wind swept grit across my mask's faceplate with an abrasive hiss.

"From this location," Mogen informed the new pilots, all of whom wore scrunched expressions even in their masks, due to the permanent odor of sulfur, *"you can see 80 percent of the base. The flightline is across the stretch of lava rubble behind you.*

"If Lybjevyk Base were an historic fortress, we'd be standing in its main courtyard." He pointed in turn at the encircling buildings. *"Supply is in that two-story nearest the vortex terminal. If any of you are in need of gear you couldn't get at Belsken, you can sign it out there tomorrow.*

"The long, low building between Supply and Headquarters is the base clinic. At least, the front portion of the building is the clinic. The base gym is located in the rear." Evidently recalling Kota's joke about the arrangement,

Mogen added with a wry grin, *"Very convenient for those of you prone to sports injuries."*

The remark garnered a few chuckles.

Mogen started across the "courtyard" toward the central structure. The new personnel fell in after him, their repulsor trunks whirring along at their heels like well-trained dogs.

"Our first stop is Wing HQ," Mogen said. *"In here, you'll find the orderly room, billeting, and the pay office."*

Approaching Headquarters' front doors, he indicated the last two-story building, on HQ's other flank. *"That's Wing Operations, home to Life Support, Intel, the armory, and all three squadrons. Behind Ops, though you can't see it from here, is another long single-story that houses the mess hall, laundry drop-off, a small PX, and the comms center. That last is the most important amenity. Am I correct, Ku?"*

I chuckled. "Got that right, sir."

Through his mask's faceplate, I saw Mogen cock an eyebrow at my use of the honorific for him, but I wasn't about to set a bad example for new fighter crews.

Sperka, Domokos, and I guided our charges through checking in at the various offices. In the orderly room, a cheerful spacer assistant handed me a packet containing four pairs of journeyman rank pins. "Better put these on before the commander sees you, sir," she said. "Congratulations!"

"Now to our quarters," Mogen said when the new arrivals had reconvened in the lobby. "It's about a quarter-range hike. There are railings, but I recommend using your tab lights if you have them readily available." He drew one from a flight jacket pocket and clipped it to his jacket's slide closure before donning his weather mask once more.

I and most of the others did the same. Though small enough to conceal in our hands, the blue-white lights could cut through up to Category 3 ashfall.

With the ruddy twilight succumbing to darkness, we headed out along the boardwalk extending from behind the headquarters.

Each squadron's housing compound stood a quarter to a third of a range away from the main base and from each other in what seemed to be random locations. With the onset of nightfall, the compounds formed blocky silhouettes against the dimming red sky.

"*Why eez our housing so far from ze main base?*" asked the woman from Satha in a pronounced accent. Her name patch read Buchier.

"*Force protection,*" Mogen said. "*If the lumpies or Jax were to find and attack this base, they'd likely strike the runways, hangars, and headquarters first. However, they wouldn't hesitate to kill as many of us as possible if given the opportunity. Spreading out, and concealing our quarters under the ash-colored camouflage netting you saw draped over the main base, makes it a great deal more difficult.*"

Had they arrived during daylight, our pilots would've seen a bone-white plain, punctuated with tufts of blighted grasses, stretching into the hazy distance around and between the six housing blocks. Vapor, from spouting mud pots and hot pools dyed bright blue or green with algae, constantly swirled over the wet surface like ghosts in a hurry.

"*Does it always smell this bad?*" Manoq asked.

"Yes, but you stop noticing it after the first few days," I assured him.

From outside, our housing compound, identical to the others, appeared to be a long rectangle built of twenty-span-high pourstone blast walls, featureless but for the tight seams between the wall sections. The two entrances, one at each end, had been designed with U-turn baffles, and shooting positions perched above for defenders with fire-arms. Blocky Standard characters stenciled above the front entry spelled 1ST SQUADRON.

Inside stood four long rows of boxy cabins constructed of corrugated metal. They'd been set a span or so off the wet ground on pour-stone blocks and painted the same drab gray. One row of cabins stood along each side, against the outer blast wall, while two more rows huddled back-to-back down the center. JO Domokos pointed out the shower and latrine buildings halfway along each lane.

Before directing everyone to their cabins, Mogen said, *"If anyone is hungry, the flight kitchen is always open. Because this base is so small, you'll find it in the regular mess. Take time to do some reconnaissance of the amenities, such as they are."*

On entering our own quarters, peeling our masks off, and finding no one else there, I noticed the chronometer above the door read well past 1900. As if that was its cue, my stomach grumbled.

Mogen grinned. "I suggest we make a low pass over the flight kitchen ourselves. I need to brief you, in any case."

I dropped my travel pack on my bunk. "What was the other reason to celebrate?"

"Our promotions coming through so promptly." Mogen furrowed his brow. "Though the additional responsibilities far outweigh the pay increase."

Thumping along the boardwalk, twenty or thirty arm-lengths behind a handful of the new pilots and hunched in my flight jacket against the chilly wind, I tried to think of a tactful way to mention Mogen's father. I didn't get a chance.

"Rinn and Ga'olani are the new squadron training officers," he said. *"They're already feeling the pressure."*

"From Teichert?" I asked.

"Indirectly. We have a phase-long operational readiness exercise beginning in approximately—" he tapped his mask's temple to check its faceplate chrono *"—eight and a half hours."* Even tinny, coming through the small speaker, Mogen's tone bore irony. *"Welcome to the glories of command, Ku."*

Once we'd cleared the flight kitchen's food line and sank onto chairs at a table in the farthest corner, Mogen asked, "You missed the post-battle briefing, didn't you?"

"Had an early vortex out," I reminded him. I had to squish my sandwich of smoked beef brisket, thinly sliced but thickly stacked, enough to take a bite.

"Right," Mogen said. "We had 68 percent success with the low-level CMP bursts over Jassem. It so happens several of the targets, including the C3 center our group hit, had more sophisticated hardening than Intel had knowledge of. It means the Jax are off our scope for the time being, but most likely not permanently."

"We should eliminate the rest of their war-fighting capability or crush their will to keep fighting before they can stand up again," I said once I'd swallowed my mouthful.

"Agreed," Mogen said. "The twenty-three major cities we struck, because their government *deliberately* placed military facilities in the center of civilian areas, are now embroiled in violence. With any luck, that may be sufficient to destroy their will to fight."

Hope so, I thought. Having taken another bite, I only nodded.

Mogen's grim tone made it clear he needed to vent, so I gave him my attention when he went on. "They should be grateful we didn't simply launch primitive EMP weapons at high altitude over every continent and have done with them. Now I expect we'll be required to send in forces to restore the peace."

I arched a questioning eyebrow.

"Not anytime soon, of course." Mogen gripped his sandwich the same way I had, but let his vision follow the sauce dripping onto the wrapper he'd spread on the table. He hadn't taken his first bite yet.

"Pact leadership is returning its full attention to the Supremacy and its occupation of Nichi," he continued. "I, for one, am not convinced that's wise, but I'm not part of the august circle who makes such decisions. We can't discuss anything here, but I doubt we'll depart Tobe in the foreseeable future."

I stopped chewing. *Conduct ops on Nichi from* here?

Mogen lifted his gaze at last and switched directions. "Have you had opportunity to review the flight commander's SOP?"

I swallowed and said, "Not yet," before I took another bite.

"Do it ASAP." His face and tone grew stern. "Not tonight, however. Until you can make time, here's an overview of your responsibilities: You're in charge of your flight's daily duty schedule. You authorize leave, deal with minor discipline issues, write annual personnel evaluations, and provide feedback to your subordinates.

"You are part friend and part counselor to your people, as much as their commander." Mogen rattled off the points as if he'd memorized them. "You determine who'll fly with whom, notify your flight in case of emergency calls from up the chain—one of the reasons you were issued the duty link—" he gestured at my chest pocket, where I'd stowed it "—and provide mentoring.

"You're also one of my counselors, which means you'll attend squadron staff meetings every phase to make recommendations when we discuss issues concerning individual flights."

I paused from chewing again. *I didn't appreciate Serbinis nearly as much as I should've.*

Mogen offered a half smile. "And if you think *that's* a full munitions load, pray to whatever gods you acknowledge you're never appointed squadron commander."

He finally bit into his now-soggy sandwich and grimaced. "And get used to this." He indicated the sandwich. "It's very much like being a parent, except with adult-sized children who have adult-sized problems."

I nodded. Resumed chewing. When Mogen hadn't spoken again by the time I swallowed, I said, "I heard about your father."

His expression didn't change, didn't reveal any surprise. He gave a slight nod instead and returned his gaze to his sauce-spattered wrapper. He said only, "Yes."

"I'm sorry," I said.

"It wasn't unexpected." He sighed. "We've observed the diminishment of Papa's memory and lucidity for two or three years now." He shook his head with the slow heaviness of a much older man. When he finally lifted it again, he said with all seriousness, "My only consolation is it'll be Sauvar's coronation rather than my own."

I hesitated for several seconds before I asked, "Under the vulture-like scrutiny of Soola ka' Remmet?"

Across the table from me, Mogen froze, and his eyes narrowed. "What do you mean, Ku?"

"I don't trust him," I said. "There's something about him that makes me uncomfortable."

Mogen leaned forward, sternness reclaiming his features, and dropped his voice as well. "Soola ka' Remmet was given to my father as a slave. Highly educated and trained, but a slave nonetheless. My father made him a free man and, seeing his worth, offered him the chief advisor position he still holds.

"Papa didn't require it of him, but Soola swore an oath of fealty, not only to my father, but to all of House Reskag, out of gratitude."

Mogen's intensity straightened me in my chair, but I persisted. "You trust the word of a Jax?"

"More than I trust the word of some Osfelgs," Mogen said.

I held my tongue, but I sincerely hoped his trust wasn't misplaced.

* * * *

Chapter Nine

I stopped at the comms center before making the trek to our compound. *No line for once. Maybe I should come late more often.* When I nodded a greeting to the spacer basic on duty inside the entry, he snapped up from his readpad and returned it with, "G' night, sir."

Given the hour and what time I had to get up, I kept my vid to Derry brief. "Got here safely, along with some new personnel. They look like a good crew. I'll send you a longer vid when I can. *Ti qala bé messa tai messa,* White Bird."

Totally inadequate, I thought, *but messages from Tobe always are.*

Kota, a dark shape curled in his sleeping cocoon on his bunk, rolled over and mumbled something but didn't fully wake when I slipped into our cabin.

I need to talk with him in the morning.

I fell asleep remembering the radiance in Derry's face when I'd arrived home, her serenity on assuring me we'd "sort out" returning to Tempest, and how I'd felt while holding my baby. *My son. The child of my body.*

Six hours later, with the dirty laundry from my travel pack stuffed into a duffle on my shoulder, Kota and I tramped toward the combined mess hall and PX building through what had intensified to Cat 3 ashfall.

Base Maintenance had set up tent-like enclosures over the handwash stations at each entrance. These were equipped with hand brooms on hooks, and signs instructing everyone to brush as much ash off as possible before entering the mess hall.

Lessons learned from earlier ashfalls, I thought.

After we swept ourselves, and I signed my duffle in at the laundry drop-off, I glanced up and down the currently unoccupied hallway, with the mess at one end and the PX at the other, and said, "Wait a minute, Kota."

He stopped, his expression instantly quizzical.

In the most casual tone I could manage, I said, "I happened to be on Tempest for the Coming of Wanikiya Ceremony."

Kota focused his whole attention on me with palpable intensity.

"How familiar are you with the ceremony?" I asked.

"My family goes every year."

"I hadn't participated in it since I lost the man I was apprenticed to," I admitted, "so I'd forgotten a lot of it, but I immediately recognized how they'd changed it."

"They *changed* the ceremony?" Kota, taller than most Chalca because of his Sathi father, questioned from beneath furrowed brows. "Who are 'they,' and what'd they do to it?"

I lowered my tone to grimness. "One guess who 'they' are."

"Should've known." Kota's features tightened into an expression of disgust. He repeated his question. "What'd they do to it?"

I gave him a quick run-through of the first night's ceremony, the discussion at Sunning Lizard House the next morning, and the boarders' decision to hold their own second-night ceremony.

"Do you know who Demothi is?" I asked.

"Isn't he the crazy old hermit with one eye who wanders around the city and yells about times of great danger?"

"Ya. Gram doesn't think he's really crazy, though." I recounted my first exchange with him, about bringing my family home to Tempest.

"How are you going to do that?" Kota asked.

"I'm applying to enter the Qaletaqa," I said. "The idea came to me yesterday. It's been my goal since I was little anyway, but now I've got a real reason to do it."

Kota's eyebrows rose, then bunched together. "How will you convince the Solis to release you from the Aerospace Forces, especially right now? Everybody's been stop-lossed."

"One way to find out. I'll apply and leave it to Shaman Shiye." My words triggered another thought. "There's something else, and this'll mean more to you than it did to Gram or Chanter Wahkan." I told him about Demothi's prophecy in front of the crowd at Old Trade Center, including the part about me ending the war in two years.

Kota's eyes widened. "How are you going to do that?" he asked again.

"No idea," I said, "but maybe that's another reason I need to join the Qaletaqa."

"Maybe," Kota agreed. He jutted his jaw toward the mess hall. We sauntered in its direction, but he said, "Keep talking, Ku. How did the improvised ceremony go?"

"Pretty well," I said, "until the Great Council's private security forces showed up and shut it down. The local people call them enforcers with good reason."

I told him about Bimisi being employed by the Hevos and about our confrontation. I didn't tell Kota about the beating, however, despite the way he questioned me with a pointed stare.

If I told him they cracked a couple ribs, he'd insist I see Doc Moseva, and she'd probably DNIF me. Can't do that with an ORE about to begin, especially when I'm trying to learn how to be a flight commander. My ribs are mostly healed, even if they're still kind of touchy.

Kota appeared aghast even without me mentioning injuries. "You know your stepbrother and Huritt will talk," he said, "if they haven't already. This means an escalation way beyond Huritt's need to win over you at everything. Now you've defied not only his mother the chief, but also the Great Council. You've established yourself as a genuine threat to their agenda, Ku."

"Bimisi called us seditionists," I said. "Everybody on the plaza, from the elders to small children." Anger at the mass accusation overruled everything else I felt right then.

Kota evidently didn't think I was taking the situation seriously enough because he said, "You already know how the Hevovitases deal with people who get in their way."

"Ya, I do." I shouldered the door to the mess hall open and resisted inhaling its aromas too deeply.

I waited until we'd collected our to-go breakfast boxes to continue. We donned our masks and exited through the PX, the shortest route to the side door into Wing Ops and Intel's briefing room. Once on the boardwalk between the two doors, I exhaled to ease a different tension in my midsection and said, "I watched the third night's ceremony on my link, at my grandmother's home. I'd forgotten almost everything in that one."

When I shut up, Kota seemed to sense what I wasn't ready to ask directly. He bowed his head as if speaking to the planks under our boots and said contemplatively, *"There are a lot of opinions about the final battle between Wanikiya and Machitew, Ku. Most chanters say it's symbolic, a warning to our people more than anything. Think about the part where the three eagle-dancer torchbearers come."*

"They raise Wanikiya and two of his warriors from the battlefield," I said, "and take them up to Shaman Shiye."

"What else?" Kota stopped and lifted his head to face me. I could discern his intense expression even behind his faceplate.

I raked through my memories of Wanikiya and the two warriors, renewed in the circle of golden torchlight, as they and their guides crossed the darkened plaza. *I didn't watch that part more than once, just the end of the battle.* I shook my head.

"Only the eagle warriors rise to follow Wanikiya and his companions up the stairs," Kota said. *"The wolf warriors, the people who chose to follow Machitew, they're left lying where they fell."*

"I didn't notice that," I said. "I'll have to watch it again." The tension below my ribs hadn't abated, and I braced myself. "What if it isn't just symbolic?"

Kota gripped my shoulder with his firm hand. His somber expression matched the comprehension stirring in the shadowed future already burdening my soul. *"Whatever happens, you won't be alone."*

I thought of the eagle warrior who'd never left Wanikiya's side throughout the ceremony. I met Kota's eyes. "I know."

* * * * *

Chapter Ten

Kota followed me up the wooden stairs to the briefing room, where we sidled along its last row and plopped onto a couple folding chairs. Except for those preparing for the briefing, we were the first ones there. While we shoveled in hashed *pattat* and smoked herrings, vortexed in from Osfelga, I observed the quiet but bustling activity around the platform in front.

I spotted Rinn Stormun at once, mostly because of his height and solid build. His face, with his military-short dark-blond hair, exuded steady determination as he conversed with a trio of pilots wearing intermediate rank. *Probably the training officers from the other two squadrons,* I thought.

It took me a lot longer to recognize Ga'olani M'oke Keatii, and I started when I did. I elbowed Kota in the ribs. "When did Go shave her head?"

"Right after you left," he said. "It's the mark of a widow or widower among the Bird People. It represents having lost part of oneself."

My heart wrenched for Go. Recalling our conversation before I'd left for my honor-guard duty, I watched her interact with others. Her olive-complexioned face bore serenity and purpose, but her dark eyes appeared larger without her halo of bushy, brown-black hair.

She and Yobo brought me a white flower for peace of heart, she said, when Hanuk was killed. I remembered their visit with a pang. *I should encourage her to continue with* pelu felelei. *I need to keep up with it myself.*

* * *

After the exercise kickoff by Commander Teichert, followed by the ORE scenario's current intelligence briefing, I made my way forward to Go, made the slight bow used for greetings, and asked, "How are you doing?"

She returned the bow. "Keeping busy is good," she said, but I glimpsed a lonely shadow in her eyes.

"Derry sends her love and condolences," I said. "I'm sorry I couldn't bring you a white flower for peace of heart."

A faint smile touched her lips. "You thought of doing it, Ku, and that is, you know, most important."

"I think we should continue to practice *pelu felelei*," I said, "when we have time after the ORE." I motioned loosely to indicate the busy briefing room. "I think it'd be good for you and a way to honor the one you lost."

"Yes," she said at once, "it would be good when we, um, have more time."

We stood silent for a few seconds before I shifted to duty matters. "Did Mog—uh, Master Officer Reskag—already assign lead-in trainers for our new pilots, or do I need to do it? I'm supposed to monitor their progress."

"He did it this time," Go said, "because you were away. It will be your, um, responsibility next time. I have been assigned Chitsa, the woman from Tempest, and Rinn has Manoq from Satha." She named the others and their trainers as well.

"Thanks," I said. "They all seem really motivated."

Kota was clearly relieved he hadn't been assigned another trainee. His eyes still bore the same self-recrimination for losing Ciprianno that I felt about Nawat.

None of the new pilots had attended the briefing, but I hadn't expected them to. The orderly room would keep them running with inprocessing all day. Still, I told Kota as we thumped down the stairs and around the building to its front doors, "They should attend the briefing tomorrow, even if they can't start lead-in until the ORE's over. I want to get them integrated ASAP."

In 1st Squadron's Operations section, I received Lance Flight's sortie orders for the day, including targets, launch times, and call signs.

"Your flight's got nine missions today, sir, each with four ships," said Master Spacer Aitan from the Combat Space Ops Center. "Keatii and Stormun are off the board because they're helping run the exercise. The first sortie launches at 0850 and the second one at 0910."

"What about MO Reskag?" I asked.

Squadron Commander or not, higher rank or not, Mogen still belonged to Lance Flight.

"He said he's available any time after 1400. He's got a load of squadron duties this morning."

"Thanks, Aitan." I scrutinized the flight roster. *My job includes deciding who flies with who.* "Kota," I said, "you lead the second mission, with Maira in the Two position, and…"

It took a while and quite a bit of rearranging to fill nine four-ship sorties on the ops board. Without Rinn, Go, or the new arrivals, who had to regain physical conditioning for flying after a month out of the cockpit for Survival School, I had only eleven of Lance Flight's normal twenty pilots available.

Everybody will fly three sorties. Three of us will have to do four. Lead by example.

"I'll take four sorties," I told Kota. "Can you, too?" When he agreed, I considered. *Can't ask Mog until this afternoon. I'll tag Arturo for my wingman.*

* * *

Our first exercise sortie included penetrating a simulated minefield to reach targets on the surface.

"We took our heaviest losses in the minefield enveloping Jassem," Intermediate Officer Gatika had stated in the intelligence briefing. "The Supremacy took note of their effectiveness and has started using them, too. Until we receive the minesweepers Commander Teichert has requested, it's imperative for you to learn how to avoid mines."

We cruised across Tobe's night-side hemisphere in low-planetary space. For the ORE, the planet's position-finding constellation of satellites had been programmed to broadcast a notional minefield to our threat scopes.

"Call them when you spot them," I ordered.

Within minutes, Arturo, flying the Two position a hundred arm-lengths to my right, shouted, "Visual on a mine!"

"Copy, Two," I said. "Ripper Element, decelerate to .2 now." Slowing to allow more warning and more time to evade had saved people in the Jassem mission.

A heartbeat later, when the first white point appeared in my own scope, the orange-red fireball of Nawat's ship erupted in my memory. My blood iced.

Steady, Ku. You've got to coach the others through this. You got Yobo through the minefield.

I swallowed and called, "Ripper Element, maintain combat spread for maneuvering room. Use your cannon, and stay alert."

Simulated mines appeared in rapid succession from every direction. My hard pitches and rolls soaked my flight suit with sweat under my pressure suit. My team's shouted warnings became a cacophony in my helmet speakers, triggering flashbacks. I forced them away, set my jaw, and fixed my line-of-sight reticle on one target after another.

We accomplished our sortie without "losing" anyone, but I heard fatigue in my team's voices when they reported in. My own breaths raked my earphones. *They'd benefit from a rest before the next sorties. Even one hour would help.*

While heading for the base, a couple minutes before I would've contacted Lybjevyk Approach, a new voice broke in my helmet speakers. *"Ripper Element, this is Ops. Lead and Two have a hot-fuel launch time of 1132. Three and Four for that sortie are standing by. Intel will brief you at shipside."*

I could imagine Arturo suppressing a groan, but I kept my own tone firm and my words crisp. "Ops, Ripper Lead. Wilco." *Set the example... Burn it.*

A late-winter rain we'd been warned about during our pre-mission briefing—little more than a heavy mist—swept in during our sortie. Ash darkened the precipitation and coated the tarmac with a slick slurry. The tower directed us into a holding pattern while ground crews cleared the runway.

Several minutes later, our crew chiefs, armed with red-lighted batons we could see through the drizzly rain, directed Arturo and me to fueling stations. We shut down all our ships' systems and watched our ground crews attach two fuel lines to each fighter. Using dual hoses, they could top off our tanks in fewer than ten minutes.

My stomach growled. *Could use a top-off myself. Long time since breakfast. It'll have to wait, though.* For safety reasons, we couldn't pop our canopies, let alone take off our pressure-suit helmets or even attach relief tubes to our suits during refueling.

Two figures wearing wind-tugged rainshields dashed across from the Operations building, duty links in their hands. Our intel briefers. They positioned themselves to the left of our nosecones, where we could easily see them.

"Sir, Apprentice Porreca," a female voice called through my earphones.

Feels strange to be called 'sir' by Eszter Porreca, I thought. I'd always known her as one of Derry's officemates and close friends. *'Course, it feels strange to have journeyman rank on my collar so soon, too.*

In another second, I realized, *I'm the same rank Russom was as my TO and IP when I went through Basic and Primary Piloting. Hard to believe I was so intimidated by a journeyman.*

Eszter conducted a quick debrief, asking about damage to our targets, the ingress, the egress, and the minefield before she began the next sortie's pre-mission brief with, *"Exercise, exercise, exercise,"* the standard procedure for distinguishing from real-world briefings.

Touching codes into her link's keypad, she said, *"I'm sending the data to your flight computer now."*

"Got it," I said when the flight plan rippled into clarity on my computer's display.

"Good," she said. *"You're escorting a strike package with targets in the northern hemisphere. The lumpies have two known bases, and possibly a third in*

the area—" red encircled three locations surrounding the marked targets *"—so expect them to scramble fighters…"*

I tapped a few notes in while she briefed the mission data. Our flight computers' updated keypads had been redesigned to accommodate our pressure-suit gloves' bulky fingers.

"Questions, sir?" she asked when she finished.

"No, Eszter, thanks."

"Fine. Then I have a question for you." I heard a smile in her tone. *"When do I get to see baby images? You did get some, I hope?"*

I chuckled. "Derry's mother sends loads of vids. I'll forward them next time I'm in the comms center."

* * *

We flew a successful escort mission, eliminating four "hostile" fighters to ensure our notional strike ship made it safely into and out of its target zone.

With an hour before our next flight, Arturo and I sloshed across from the flightline to Life Support, to shed our pressure suits long enough for a relief break and a run to the flight kitchen. Kota, just in from his second sortie as well, along with Mogen, who'd finally escaped an exceptionally long Wing staff meeting, joined us there.

The four of us *thunked* around the Ops building toward the mess hall, our dripping rainshields swishing about the legs of our rumpled flight suits in the dirty drizzle.

Arturo stumbled once. "What's so urgent about this exercise they can't give us more time to rest?"

"Train the way you'll fight," Mogen said before I could. "Like the exercise at the end of Primary Pilot Training, this is intended to simulate real-world high-tempo operations as closely as possible, complete with the same stressors."

"They won't let us exceed a twelve-hour duty day, though," I told him. "Then we have eight hours of mandatory crew rest. Exhausted pilots make stupid mistakes that get them killed."

Arturo nodded acknowledgment.

"Eating helps," Kota said. "I'm constantly starving during these things."

My stomach concurred with a muffled snarl.

A familiar figure, whom I'd only seen twice from a distance since returning to Tobe, narrowly missed plowing into us in the sweep-off shelter covering the mess hall's entry. Huritt eyed me and sneered. "Going to try to smuggle something into your cockpit, Sheggy?"

One step ahead of me, Kota bristled. "That's 'sir' to you, Hevo. You failed to salute two higher-ranking officers."

Huritt gaped at Kota, then Mogen, before shifting his gaze to me. When he spotted the new rank pin at the neck of my rainshield, he froze. His eyes widened, then narrowed, and his square jaw worked with what appeared to be disbelief, closely followed by indignation.

I said only, "The shegruls grew wings, Hevo. C'mon, Kota, we have pre-mission briefs in half an hour."

* * *

I knew better than to hope for an uneventful combat space patrol during an ORE. Predictably, my team got vectored for an intercept within ten minutes of launching. I recalled the lumpy spy ship Kota and I had encountered on a similar sortie during pilot training.

By the time we'd engaged several "hostiles" and returned to base, Arturo and I had spent more than eight hours total in our pressure suits. Our other wingmen sagged in theirs as well. With sweaty hair plastered to our heads, and our eyes glazed with exhaustion, we slogged back to Life Support together.

Newer than me, all of them, I thought, observing them, *but they got it done. I know exactly how bone-tired they are because I am, too, and I've got one more to fly.* I gripped each of their shoulders in turn. "Good job heading their Lead, Arturo. Great shot on the last one, Linnéa. Janos, I'll take you as my wingman any time."

They lifted their heads long enough to slip me grateful but fatigued smiles.

Arturo flew at my wing for the last sortie, too, another ground-attack on multiple targets, but without a minefield that time. We dodged simulated air-defense missiles and high-altitude energy artillery instead.

I spotted Mogen at a table in the middle of the mess hall when I entered its warmth afterward, and I cut straight toward him when I came off the food line. My long day must've shown in my face because he gave me a smirk when I dropped heavily onto the chair facing him. "Learn anything new today, Ku?" he asked.

Seeing the shadows under his eyes, which matched the scruff darkening my own chin, I returned a kidding smile. "I learned a lot about 'the glories of command.' What about you?"

"Much the same," Mogen said and shifted in his chair. "I'm about to add something new to your load. You were recommended in this morning's staff meeting to fly in an aggressor role for the remainder of the exercise."

"Me?" I straightened in surprise and returned my spoonful of venison stew to the bowl. "Don't master officers and prep commanders usually do that?"

"It's experience, not rank, that matters for such an assignment," Mogen said. "The Wing lost several of its most experienced recently. You've flown against lumpies and Jax more than some of the remaining MOs and preps."

I opened my mouth to protest, but Mogen waved me off and pointed out, "It'll benefit your own combat skills as much as the pilots you'll fly against."

He must've seen the lingering self-doubt in my eyes because he added, "You'll start by flying as wingman with Prep Zordisch from Saber Flight."

"What about making Lance Flight's sortie assignments?" I asked.

"You'll still do it. You just won't fly with them." Before I could ask, Mogen said, "I assign 1st Squadron's aggressor missions."

I sagged in my chair and stirred my cooling stew while I considered. I'd occasionally wondered what it'd be like to fly as an aggressor. I'd thought I might even enjoy it. Still, like becoming a flight commander, I hadn't expected the opportunity to arise so soon.

"All right," I said at last and sighed. "Could be worse. I could be the squadron commander."

Mogen arched a copper-colored eyebrow. "Don't say that too loudly, Ku. What is it Rinn always says? 'You say it, you play it.'"

* * * * *

Chapter Eleven

With Go and Rinn off flying duty while they helped run the ORE, their new trainees, rushed through in-processing, weren't going to get any cockpit time.

"I don't want to leave them sitting around," I told Mogen while we pored over the second day's flying roster at the Ops desk, "but they need to get physically reconditioned before they can participate." It usually took a couple phases of lead-in and unit qualification sorties to regain one's flight conditioning after a month or so off.

Mogen gave a curt nod. "Assign them specific simulations at their consoles and set times to review it with them."

"Good idea. Thanks." I blew out a breath. *So much to learn about taking care of my people.*

* * *

I had learning of a different kind to do, too, including getting officially checked out on the old Rohrsprachen Spike I'd fly as an aggressor. Thankfully, the cockpit hadn't changed much, despite other technological advancements to the Spearhead. All the touchpads, switches, and displays lay in their familiar configuration.

Handling it, however, required some mental adjustments. Like the Sevicha-9, it was meant to imitate, the Spike had a greater speed capability than the Spearhead's, but it lacked its tight turn radius.

I'll have to learn to anticipate and compensate.

In my first pre-mission briefing with Preparatory Commander Zordisch, he said, with a heavy, unfamiliar accent, "Consider every sortie actual combat, JO Masou, as you did when you flew against aggressors. Our weapons may be simulated, but our mindset is not. Every time we 'kill' one of them, they learn more than they would if they defeated us."

Learn to think like a lumpy, I thought. *Time to seriously apply the essay in PME about knowing your enemy.*

As I would've done with Lance Flight, Zordisch and I flew at least three sorties a day, at all hours, for the rest of the ORE. Eight other pilots, selected from all three flights in 1st Squadron, and higher in rank than me, also flew as hostiles. We had our own informal flight, with Mogen as our commander.

Though my flight mates knew I'd been chosen to fill an aggressor position, they didn't know which sorties I actually flew until we convened in the briefing room afterward. The Spikes bore only Velika fin flashes. I knew when I engaged members of Lance Flight, however, by their ships' tail numbers.

I didn't need Zordisch's directive to give no quarter. My fighter-pilot competitiveness locked in. I thought only, *I probably have an unfair advantage because I've flown with them enough to know their quirks. But those quirks could be fatal.*

Maira Österdahl, for example, habitually banked off to the right. Knowing my Spike couldn't equal her Spearhead's tight turn radius, I angled across her circle for a lead-pursuit intercept. My sim missile took her out with a clean front-quarter shot.

Kill your signature moves before they kill you, Oyster, I thought.

Arturo, fixed on getting a lock on Zordisch while Zordisch gradually drew him away from his Lead, lost his situational awareness when he failed to keep checking his 180. I dove in after him and, almost at my leisure, launched a sim missile directly into one of his ship's flaring exhaust nozzles.

Ya, I learned that lesson the hard way, too, during pilot training. Never made that mistake again. You learned it today, Art.

Kota attempted the helix braid.

Great tactic, but the lumpies are catching on to it and countering.

I lined my fighter up head-on with his and opened fire with my sim energy cannon. Watching bright red 'hit' markers pepper his canopy in my targeting display, I shook my head.

The Spearhead's longer-reach cannon won't save you, Kota, if you don't start the helix run with your thumb already mashing the firing stud. Whoever shoots first wins.

Now I know what it's like to be an IP, crossed my mind more than once. *I'm wearing Russom's boots.*

Zordisch and I took turns leading debriefings. When I did them, I found myself borrowing a spine from Russom's cactus. Brows lowered in a stern expression, I played each pilot's multi-sensor mission recordings on the small briefing room's tri-D projector. Sometimes I slowed it to second-by-second and froze it. "Watch now, right here," I'd say. "This is where you gave us the opening to kill you."

Most of our students appeared stunned at having made such elementary errors. Unlike HazMat, none of them responded with cockiness.

"What did you do wrong?" I pushed them. "Walk us through the engagement one move at a time. How are you going to handle a situation like this differently next time it happens? Because you better believe it will."

As the ORE progressed, we "hostiles" documented improvement in both single and team strategies and maneuvering. Sometimes we recreated situations in which pilots had failed the first time, and noted with satisfaction when they applied different, more effective tactics on the repeat.

Of course, their success meant we aggressor-instructors got "killed" more often, too.

The "hostiles" held their pre-mission briefings separate from the "friendlies" we'd fly against. We were given the scenario they'd been assigned, and what threats Intel had warned them about, but as with real-world missions, they had to prepare for anything.

Zordisch and I alternated between the lead and wing roles throughout the ORE. With the final day's first two sorties done and two left to fly, I had the wingman position for our third one.

Zordisch keyed the briefing table's tri-D projector to produce a detailed area chart. He pointed out a narrow valley lying amid the ripples and crags of Tobe's buckled surface.

"Tourneau Cleft is approximately 280 ranges north of our base," he said. "Two fighters have been dispatched to fly cover for a lifter inserting a Resistance Pact reconnaissance unit. It is our task to draw away and eliminate the fighters so our comrades can eliminate the lifter and its occupants when it arrives."

A prickling sensation rose at my nape. *The reverse of the mission Mog and I flew in Caerden.* I gave a stiff, "Got it."

"They will be on station by the time we come," Zordisch continued, "and will be expecting enemy actions."

"Are there surface-to-air weapons in the valley?" I asked. "Theirs or ours?" The lumpies had sent Tawfik air defense artillery crews to take down a Qaletaqa exfiltration lifter in Caerden's Stroma Mountains.

"No SA weapons from either side," Zordisch confirmed. His accent gave his speech a certain formality. "It is only us, but they will not know it. They will search for gunners' nests. If they follow Pact SOP, they will establish a combat air patrol track above the valley, to wait for the notional lifter and watch for adversaries." He drew one finger through the projection, shaping an elongated oval that encircled the whole lengthy valley.

"We will make our approach in this ravine," Zordisch said, "and use terrain masking to conceal ourselves as long as we can." He traced a channel between ridges created by the cracking and shifting of the young planet's crust. "When we reach the base of this ridge, we will pitch up and climb swiftly to gain altitude superiority over them, using this slope to maintain our cover." He indicated our designated route, marked in red.

Though smaller than the Rohr-55 Spearhead, the Spike had sufficient thrust-to-weight ratio to accelerate in a vertical climb in atmospheric flight.

"We will carry the standard missile load," Zordisch went on, and keyed up our roster. Ten air-to-air weapons, simulated in this case. "If we must pursue them down into the valley, we will have to close on them enough to use our cannons. This is not a sensible way for us, but it is what lumpies do, and for this training, we must imitate lumpies."

I nodded. *Explains their losses.*

We spent another several minutes considering every possible situation, and courses of action for each, before we headed to Life

Support, then on to our hangar. By that time, I knew, the pilots we'd confront would be well on their way to Tourneau Cleft.

Tobe's lower atmosphere always swirled with volcanic ash, so we cruised at 30,000 spans for most of our flight north. On departing the perpetual reddish-gray gloom of the surface, I never could resist drawing a deep breath. I felt as if I'd burst out of grungy water every time I broke through the cloud cover and saw Tobe's small sun.

With visibility reduced to about 50 percent near the ground, we activated our nav instruments for our descent to enter the ravine. The irregular twists that'd seemed minor in the projection proved sharper and narrower in reality. We banked one way and the other and back with constant twitches of our control sticks.

Like flying down Red Wash in the Darter. Never did it as often as Huk. Now I wish I had.

I started my cockpit chronometer's countdown ten seconds out from the pitch-up point. By then, twenty seconds ahead of me, Zordisch had already begun his accelerated climb, as if using the lava slope for a launch ramp. His dual exhaust nozzles glowed at me out of the gloom like demon eyes.

"Targeting and weapons ready," Zordisch said.

I ordered mine to Ready as well. The targeting reticle's white ring appeared inside my faceplate, and I thought, *Glad they retrofitted the Spikes with this system.* I made a swift check of my line-of-sight target tracker and scanned the row of green lights that confirmed my sim cannon and missiles were set.

Two red darts lit up my threat scope the instant I cleared the ridge. As anticipated, our targets flew a CAP orbit, holding positions on opposites points of their circle.

A few quickened heartbeats later, from a couple thousand spans higher, I watched them form up and swing into their own climb. *They know we're here.*

"Lead, got a visual on both," I said. "They've seen us."

"Roger," Zordisch replied. *"Weapons free."*

"Missile one ready," I snapped and fixed my vision on the leader. My targeting reticle flashed OUT OF REACH.

I maintained my stare. *A few more seconds. They've got the longer reach. Are they going to split or try to take us head-on?* My pulse accelerated.

When a yellow LOCK ATTEMPT symbol blinked on my scope and a warning tone sounded in my earphones, Zordisch ordered, *"Split now!"*

I peeled away from him, arced up and over tightly enough to stress the Spike's capability to break the attempted lock, and dropped in on the Pact wingman's 180. At full throttle, straight and level, I closed on him, staring at his cockpit to line up my reticle. "Locked on," snapped in my earphones.

"Missile one, fire!" I ordered.

He pitched up, a maneuver too swift, too sharp for the Spike to follow. My sim missile simply vanished from my scope.

Typical of lumpy tactics, Zordisch and I reduced the engagement into two one-on-one battles from the Pact-preferred two-on-two, though I never lost track of him. We kept the Pact ships apart, unable to support one another, until I finally dispatched the wingman with a sim-cannon burst in a lumpy-like close-in pass.

His lead immediately spiraled about. I wrenched my ship clear. Began jinking. *If I can open the distance far enough to wheel around on—*

Every instrument in my cockpit flashed red, and my flight computer's cool, female voice stated, "Velika Two is destroyed."

* * *

When aggressor-instructors got "killed," we received the same tough debriefing as our defeated trainees.

A female apprentice, Wexelle from Satha, had flown as Kota's wingman on the sortie. She scrutinized her flight recording from beneath scrunched, blonde brows while it played.

"What happened to you here?" Zordisch asked.

"I became detached from my lead." Wexelle hushed her voice in obvious embarrassment.

"It is a lumpy tactic, one they are very proficient at. And here?" Zordisch paused the vid.

She slipped a sideways glance at me. "I allowed JO Masou to come in too close to me before I fired."

"Yes, yes." Zordisch nodded. "You must never wait. The Rohr-55's cannon has a longer reach than a Sevicha-9's, but lumpies often take the risk. You could have finished him then."

I gave a resigned smile when I dropped onto the folding chair, after Zordisch had finished critiquing Wexelle. Kota, grinning like a well-fed ghost cat, cued up my recording.

He fast-forwarded through most of it, but requested, "Slow to 10 percent," at four specific time stamps near the end. Then he asked, "What do these moves have in common?"

"I started jinking," I said.

"Ya, but more specifically than that."

I crimped my brow in puzzlement. "What?"

"Watch closely," Kota said, and slowed each of the four sequences in turn to one second at a time. "This is how you got yourself killed, Sun Eagle."

I leaned in, still bewildered—until I clearly saw, in the fourth clip, the tracers from Kota's sim cannon *leading* my jink, up and to the left.

"You *always* do it when you start jinking," Kota said. "Up first, then left. What was it you told Oyster the other day?" His grin widened.

"Kill your signature moves before they kill you," I recited and gave Kota a subtle nod of thanks. *Mogen was serious when he said my combat skills would benefit, too.*

* * *

Like the Finals Phase of pilot training, everyone's fatigue accumulated in spite of mandatory crew rest. I had no trouble lapsing into deep sleep no matter the time of day, but waking took a surprising degree of effort. Likewise, I could never get enough to eat.

Huritt noticed when I plodded into Life Support after my fourth mission the last day. He eyed me while his support crew cinched his egress pack over his pressure suit. "What happened to you, Sheggy?" he asked with a sneer. "You look like you've been trampled by a pod of shegruls." He sniffed noisily and made a gagging expression. "You smell like it, too."

As cadets in Basic and Pilot Training, I'd repaid Huritt's frequent provocations with interest. I had a response poised behind my teeth when I glimpsed the stunned stares of the two spacers suiting him up.

HazMat again, I thought initially. A fleeting image of my first lead-in trainee, jeering through his tattooed face, lanced across my mind. I'd only had a few months as an apprentice officer and two major battles behind me then. I'd settled the matter with my fist.

This isn't *a HazMat repeat,* I realized in another instant. *Huritt may not think so, but this has ramifications beyond our private antagonism. His lack of respect toward me in front of enlisted personnel could prompt similar behavior toward other officers if I don't shut it down right now. At least this time I have enough rank to do it.*

I advanced on Huritt, leaned in nose-to-nose, bared my teeth, and locked my warning glare on his. "That is insubordination, *Apprentice.*" I put deliberate emphasis on his lower grade. "I don't care if you hate every bone in *my* body and every hair on *my* head. I don't give a kosa's tail. But if you *ever* disrespect the rank again, you'll answer to a disciplinary board."

I never raised my voice above a growl amid the clamor of lockers and talk in the suiting area, but I felt the thickening silence, like a soggy towel dropped over the room. Stares fixed on me from all sides. Even Huritt appeared shocked.

"You understand me, Apprentice?" I asked.

Huritt said nothing for a long space. I watched his square jaw work. Watched fury smolder in his eyes.

Kota's warning the day Huritt and I had met surfaced from some depth of my memory. "Not smart, Ku," he'd said then. "The Hevovitas clan is notorious for escalating grudges."

Way too late to worry about it now. "Do you?" I demanded again.

"Yessir." Huritt hissed it through clenched teeth. Not for the first time, his glower threatened me with death.

I'd started to move away, keeping him visible in the corner of my eye, when he snarled after me in Chalca, "You'll never hear me call you Wanikiya. That isn't insubordination, Sheggy. It would be sedition."

Ya, he and Bimisi have talked. I spun about, leaned in once more, and said only, in Standard, "You are required by military regulation to call me 'sir' on duty, the same way they—" I jutted my chin in the direction of his suiting crew "—are required to call *you* 'sir.' Now shut up and get out of here."

One spacer broke his brace—though I'd never called them to attention—enough to hand off Huritt's helmet. Huritt seized it, pivoted on his heel, and stormed away, his face darkening under its normal desert brown.

"Sorry you had to see that," I muttered to the suiting crew. "As you were."

I heard a tandem "Yes, sir!" behind me as I strode toward my own locker, but my mind raced ahead. *Huritt belongs to 2nd Squadron. Don't know which flight, but his commander needs to be informed of this.*

* * * * *

Chapter Twelve

Telltale voices issued from our squadron conference room when I entered our duty area after shedding my pressure suit and showering. I quickened my stride. *Am I late for a short-notice staff meeting?* I stopped at the open doorway and peered into a dark room.

Mogen sat alone at the conference table, halfway down one side and silhouetted in the bluish light emanating from the tri-D projection tank on the far wall. He tilted back in the springy chair, his boots propped on the tabletop in a casual manner, but his profile appeared somber.

In the tri-D tank, a newsnet vidcorder positioned on some high roof provided a view down a broad boulevard. People in heavy coats and fur hats pressed nine or ten deep against temporary barriers placed along the street. Many of them waved purple flags bearing the crest of House Reskag, five white stars crowning a regal, broad-antlered elk. A male voice, deep and dignified, provided commentary in quiet Osfelg.

I knew immediately what Mogen was watching.

When I scuffed a boot at the threshold to alert him to my presence, he shifted toward me. "Hello, Ku."

"Still got to submit Lance Flight's final exercise report to Teichert," I said. "I'll copy it to you and the training office."

"It can wait until morning." Mogen motioned at the tri-D tank. "My brother's coronation. It arrived in a mail burst two days ago, but with the ORE ongoing, I haven't had opportunity to watch it until now. Come in."

I picked my way through the darkened room to the chair facing Mogen's across the table.

He noticed my bleary eyes through the dimness and tapped the tabletop control to pause the vid. "Are you all right, Ku?"

"Could use a full day's sleep." I sank into the cushioned seat gratefully. "Just a heads-up. You'll probably be hearing from Prep Commander Ottilie."

Mogen arched his eyebrows in surprise. "2nd Squadron's commander? What about?"

"Huritt." I described the incident in Life Support.

"You were right to put it down," Mogen said. "Letting it go would've cost you the respect of those who witnessed it." He appeared grave. "Please inform me if this continues."

"Yes, sir."

He rolled his eyes and snorted. "And *please* drop the honorific when we're not among our subordinates."

"Fine." I gave him a sly smile and used his callsign. "*Beak.*"

When he chuckled, I redirected my attention to the tri-D tank. "Is that Reskagen? I don't recognize the street."

Mogen resumed the vid. "It's known as the Avenue of the Crown. It runs directly from Parliament to the bench where the temple stands. This view appears to be from the temple's roof, in fact. If they raised the vidcorder's angle slightly, you'd probably be able to see Parliament at the far end."

The vidcorder followed a group of people advancing close together on foot, still some distance down the street. They strode easily up the hill, as if strolling, but with more purpose. I noted how occasional gusts, glittering with powdery snow, slapped black uniform coats against knee-high boots, and rippled the purple standard borne by one of the party.

"Must be pretty cold out there," I observed. "What's going on right now?"

"Sauvar has already sworn the Oath of Fealty before the members of Parliament," Mogen said. "Now the royal party is proceeding to the temple, where the most high priest of Siljan, god of kings and queens, will pronounce the coronation benediction, making it official." He gave a wry smile. "I find the pomp and circum-stuff rather tedious, personally."

My innards tightened. "Sauvar is *walking* the whole way? In the open?"

"It's tradition," Mogen said. "It allows the people to see him, and him to see them, his subjects."

"It allows potential assassins to see him, too," I said. "There could be a sniper on the temple roof as easily as newsnet videographers."

Mogen eyed me. "Security scours the procession route and all accesses to it in the hours leading up to the ceremony, and he's surrounded by bodyguards." He gestured at the tri-D tank. "I can't even see him yet for all the guards."

I straightened in my chair, shaking my head. "They could scour the route every hour for a phase and not find every threat. That's extremely risky."

Mogen didn't answer, but his jaw grew taut. He removed his feet from the table and sat forward in his chair.

Neither of us relaxed until the rooftop view gave way to one from the temple's portico, striped with bands of bright sunlight alternating with gray shadow. The vidcorder followed the prince's party as they entered.

The knot of large men, wearing bronze-colored helmets and cuirasses, parted smartly. In their midst strode a young man with hair as copper-red as Mogen's, but as long as mine. I picked out the fraternal similarities: the high forehead, the ice-blue eyes, the prominent nose.

"How much older is he than you?" I asked.

"Three years," Mogen said. "He's twenty-six now."

Sauvar wore the same bronze-colored breastplate, worked with the Reskag crest, and a broadsword on his back that appeared as long as he was tall. While he advanced toward the dais and the golden-robed figure waiting there, with every step placed at the beat of a majestic anthem, the vidcorder panned the sanctuary.

It paused on the violet-draped royal box overlooking the dais and closed on its occupants, seated in three short rows.

The former king, Sauvar the Third, sat in the center of the front row, flanked on one side by his regal consort, and on the other by a copper-haired girl in her late teens, I guessed, whom I supposed was Mogen's younger sister. Though well-groomed and royally attired, complete with a blue bandolier bearing three large medals, the old man's eyes darted about in evident perplexity, and his mouth hung slack.

Beside me, Mogen swore under his breath. I heard no anger or bitterness in the single word, just sorrow and a deep sense of powerlessness.

While the low-voiced commentator rambled on, I peered into the shadowed corners of the royal box.

I only located Soola ka' Remmet—clad in the same long coat in which I'd seen him before—when he shifted and raised his head slightly. The angle and distance made it difficult, but I scrutinized his wizened face, with its stringy mustache trailing at least a span from each corner of his mouth.

Need to ask Derry if she's found anything on him yet, first chance I get.

The vidcorders switched to and remained focused on Sauvar the Fourth for the rest of the short ceremony. He drew the ancient sword from the scabbard on his back and placed it reverently at the feet of the golden-robed priest.

"The sword, Gällivare, was forged for my eleventh great-grand-parent, Buhrus Ragawyn," Mogen said. "He was the mightiest warrior of the realm, but not a king in the formal sense. His daughter Grynbera became the first queen. Buhrus used the sword in battle, but it serves purely ceremonial purposes now. It symbolizes the monarch's role as the protector and defender of our nation and our gods."

I acknowledged Mogen's explanation with a nod. "Derry and I took a tour of your lodge while we were there, and our guide told us about Buhrus and Grynbera."

We fell silent to watch the most high priest shape symbols in the air over Sauvar's head with both hands. Then he placed his hands on Sauvar's shoulders and recited what I guessed to be a prayer in Osfelg.

"He's requesting the protection and guidance of Lord Siljan upon Sauvar's reign," Mogen said, "bestowing upon him the power to con-quer all enemies who threaten our land and blessing him with com-passion and wise judgment for our people."

I nodded once more. *A lot like the authority Shaman Shiye gave me.*

When the priest pivoted toward the assistant at his elbow and lifted a burnished circlet from the ornate case the youth extended, Sauvar bowed his head. The priest raised the simple crown, recited a ringing pronouncement, and set it firmly upon Sauvar's brow.

Mogen released a long breath as Sauvar rose, and he murmured under his breath, "Siljan's blessings on you, brother."

We didn't stay to watch the processional out of the temple, heralded by triumphant music. I paused long enough to watch the royal family exit, slowed by the former king's halting steps, though he leaned on his daughter's arm. I studied Soola ka' Remmet, too, skulking in their train, and the nape of my neck tingled.

It persisted while we strode to the mess hall, but I held my tongue, remembering Mogen's angry reaction the last time I'd mentioned the old seneschal.

We found the mess hall mostly empty, nearing the end of the regular meal service. I nodded wordless thanks to the servers, who filled our bowls with pungent curry from Marroquin and our plates with black bread and steamed vegetables.

Settled at the first table off the serving line, we ate without speaking. Mogen appeared lost in thought, probably about the coronation, and weariness after flying four sorties robbed me of the desire to do anything but eat.

On leaving the mess hall, I headed for the comms center. "Got a timeslot. I'll come out to our quarters afterward."

Mogen smiled. "My next slot is tomorrow morning. Give Derry my regards."

Recent feeble rains had left a skim of slippery ash mud on the boardwalks, which trembled under my boots at the roars of fighter engines powering up for late launches. I shook my head. *Even with the flightline a quarter range away and beyond the base buildings.*

Once in my vid booth, I hung my flight jacket on a hook inside the door, perched on the hard chair, and logged in.

We weren't allowed to mention missions or training even after the fact, which made the ORE forbidden. If transmissions were intercepted, enemy analysts could piece together enough careless words to study our operations. Likewise, references to our natural surroundings, even the weather, could compromise our location.

"Intelligence work is much like putting together a grea' puzzle," Derry had once told me. "Even tiny pieces can be verra useful."

The restrictions limited our vids to personal stuff. *That's all I really care about, anyway.*

I began my vid with the item burning most urgently at the front of my mind. "Ai, Derry. Remember the matter we discussed soon after Garn was born? Have you learned anything else? It's been on my mind today.

"Eszter asked about you and Garn, so I'm forwarding some of the vids your mother sent. Looks like he's really growing. Can't wait to hold him again."

My smile succumbed to my loneliness. "Wish I could hold you, too. I wish we could fly together under the Awénasa sun, hand in hand, with the wind rippling your hair. I wish I could see it flowing behind you like a river, so I could drown in it, and you could bring me back to life with your kisses."

I imagined the color rising in Derry's face until her freckles faded, and her parted lips anticipated mine. I closed with, "*Ti qala bé messa tai messa,* White Bird."

Opening my first vidmail from her, I wondered if the lumpies had figured Chalca out yet.

* * *

A mail burst a phase or so later brought several vidmails from Derry. I viewed one in particular twice.

"I' was hard, going back on duty today and leaving Garny," she said. She held him in the crook of one arm and angled her link so its lens captured both of them. "Mum dotes on him, of course, bu' I miss him all day. Almos' as much as I miss yew."

My heart gave a small wrench at the longing in her eyes.

"I've no' had opportunity to consul' an exper' abou' our concern," she went on, "and i' may be a while afore I can. I've loads of catching up to do firs'.

"The newsnets were full of coronation pageantry today, and we watched bi's in the office." She described the march up the Avenue of the Crown as she'd seen it from a vidcorder following the prince's party at street level. "The people clearly adore him. He appears to have a grea' deal of suppor'."

She also described the temple alight with amber lamps that night, and festivals in the streets. "With dancing and spor', and loads of food, of course. Yew could hear i' all the way ou' to our area. I'll tell yew more about i' in a proper pos' later."

A "proper post" meant a classified text mail, I knew.

Her affectionate farewell heated me like magma leaping from one of the nearby spouts, but I lay awake afterward for a different reason. *Wonder what she's found and how long it'll take to get here.*

* * * * *

Chapter Thirteen

Rapid pounding on our cabin door, in the middle of a night two phases later, wrenched me out of sleep.

A shout from a male voice followed. "Master Officer Reskag, are you in here?"

I reached the door first, with Mogen and Rinn at my back when I pushed it open.

We recoiled, squinting in a handlight's overly bright beam, before its bearer lowered it, revealing Teichert's enlisted aide. "MO Reskag," he said, "the commander needs to see you right away."

Mogen stiffened. "Coming. Please allow me to dress."

The aide waited outside while Mogen shoved himself into a flight suit and boots. The rest of us, including Kota, Arturo, and Rinn's trainee, Manoq, stood blinking under the room's bare light.

"What's going on, sir?" Kota asked.

"Unknown." Mogen clipped it, his face taut. "Most likely, my father has passed away. If that's the case, I'll be taking emergency leave to attend his funeral." He lifted his gaze from his bootstraps. "Ku, you've got the squadron in my absence."

"Yes, sir." *Think I can handle it for a couple phases.*

Mogen snatched his flight jacket from its hook by the door, gave us a stiff nod, and followed the aide into the night.

"Get dressed," I said when the door clunked shut. "Hopefully it's just some squadron matter, but if he does have to leave, we're not sending him to the terminal alone."

The others nodded and muttered agreement. Once dressed, except for our boots, we returned to our bunks. *Might as well sleep until we find out what's going on.*

More than an hour passed before the door squeaked open. I sat up when a figure halted on the threshold. "Mog?" I asked.

He nodded. Steadied himself with a hand to the doorframe. "It's not my father; it's Sauvar. I've no choice but to return home at once." He crouched to tug his repulsor trunk from under the stackbed. It made a raspy scrape on the bare floor.

Even in the dark, I discerned his waxen face. "What happened?"

Someone flicked the overhead light on. In its glare, Mogen appeared crumpled, diminished.

"They claim it was an accident on the highroad south of Reskagen." His mutter held disbelief. He shook his head. "Barely three phases on the throne."

An icy sensation twisted like an askuk through my guts. *Soola ka' Remmet.*

Mogen flung his trunk open, rose to his locker, and stripped his uniforms off their hangers. Rinn took them, folded them crisply on his bunk, and handed them to Kota to place in the trunk. I gathered his flying gear, his spare helmet, jump boots, and gloves, and packed them in his C-bag.

"I'm next in the line of succession," Mogen explained while he gathered his personal items into his small travel pack. "We've never had a regent, and by law, Sauvar's eldest child is too young to ascend the throne."

"Whatever you do, Mog," I said, "don't trust Remmet." The words came bluntly, but my sense of urgency wouldn't allow me to soften them. "You said he swore an oath of fealty, but the Jax aren't known for keeping their promises."

Mogen wheeled away from his locker to hand another armful of clothes to Rinn before he met my eyes. His own bore a shadow of desperation. "He's the one remaining soul who can prepare me for this."

"He's *Jax*," I said, "by birth and blood, and last month the Pact destroyed huge chunks of his homeworld."

Mogen raised a quelling hand. "He was born into harsh slavery, Ku. He has no loyalty to Jassem." Ducking his head, he said with palpable regret, "He was my tutor. I only wish I'd been a more attentive pupil. I'm completely unprepared to assume such a responsibility."

I stood silent for a handful of seconds, fidgeting with the knowledge I wouldn't sway him from his belief in Remmet. "I'll say the Warding Chant for you," I said at last.

On a thought, I drew the little leather bag out of my flight suit and tipped the oil-paste cup into my palm. "In fact, I can do it for you right now."

Mogen furrowed his brow. "Won't your gods object to doing a chant for a non-Chalca?"

"No, I've done it before," I said. "Will yours?"

Mogen gave a resigned shrug. "I doubt our gods pay much attention anymore, if they ever did."

Certainty lent firmness to my tone. "Mine do. Sit down."

When Mogen sank limply onto his bunk, I dipped a finger in the oil-paste and drew the glyph for shield on his brow with it. The others paused in their packing and pressed close to watch. Curiosity shadowed Arturo's and Manoq's faces.

I recalled doing the pain chant for my Chalca roommate at Basic when he fell on the obstacle course. *No oil, no belief in it myself, but his belief carried it. Opposite situation now.*

"I'll translate it into Standard as well as I can when I finish," I said. Placing my right hand on his head, I began the chant.

Shield him from the spirits of the Dark,
O Sower of the Stars.
Shield his mind against them
that he may know your wisdom.
Shield his heart against them,
that he may have your peace.
Shield his hands against them
that he may work with skill and patience.
Shield his feet against them
that he may walk your Path in safety.
Shield him from the spirits of the Dark,
O Sower of the Stars.

"Thank you, Ku," Mogen said after I translated. "That means a great deal to me." He released a shaky sigh, glanced around our solemn circle, and pushed himself to his feet. "I must get moving."

We sealed the repulsor trunk, strapped his C-bags on its top, and Rinn, Kota, and I maneuvered it from our room.

On exiting our walled enclosure to clatter across the damp board-walk, our tab lights providing the only illumination, I took the lead alongside Mogen. "For your coronation, do *not* walk from Parliament to the temple. It's too much of a risk. If you have a military-grade shielded vehicle, use it. If Remmet balks, keep a close watch on who he's in contact with, and where he goes when he's not on the job."

"Seriously, Ku—" Mogen began.

I waved him off. "Actually, insist that he rides in the vehicle with you, along with your bodyguards. Or do his people have a martyrdom tradition?"

"They don't." Mogen gave me a fleeting smile. "Perhaps I should appoint you my Chief of Security."

"Maybe you should."

He knew by my tone I wasn't kidding, but he shook his head. "The Wing will need you here, but I appreciate your advice."

"Then use it," I said.

A volcano-warmed wind, ripe with sulfur stink, buffeted us all the way through the clustered base buildings to the vortex terminal. The aide who'd awakened us waited there, print copies of orders in hand, along with Spacer Tech Gennadi, who returned Mogen's personal link, and Commander Teichert himself.

As the vortex operators powered up the portal, Mogen exchanged bearhugs and backslaps with all of us in turn. "Follow Rinn's and Ku's examples," he told Arturo and Manoq. "They'll keep you alive."

Kota tugged a jerky bag from his jacket pocket. "In case you have a long wait at some terminal, sir."

Mogen accepted it with a chuckle. "Thank you, Kota. Never stop looking out for your people. And Rinn, never stop being a perfectionist. I'm trusting you to keep these characters in order."

Rinn said, with a resolute tone, "I will, sir."

After a quiet conversation with Teichert, an exchange of salutes, and a solid handshake, Mogen shifted to face me. He flung his arms about my shoulders, and we pounded each other's backs. "It's been an honor to serve with you, Ku."

"And with you, Mog."

He grinned once more. "I warned you not to say it. You *do* know you're going to play it now."

"Yes, sir." I rolled my eyes and smiled.

"You'll do well as a squadron commander."

"So will you, as king. Watch your back."

He nodded, cast a last glance around our circle, popped his well-known satirical salute, and strode with all the dignity befitting his new role into the blue-fire vortex tunnel.

The eastern sky had assumed the smoldering reddish hue of first daylight when we exited the terminal a couple minutes later. We paced, heads lowered and brows creased, everyone wordless in their private thoughts, until a whiff of breakfast aromas penetrated the smell of sulfur.

Kota immediately brightened. "Mess hall's open. We'll be the first in line."

As we had so often during the ORE, our little formation made an immediate course correction toward food.

Kota's prediction proved true. We sidled along the serving line, collecting bacon and sausages, maize porridge with honey or flatcakes with berry syrup, and mugs of strong kasse.

Rinn led off to a table tucked into the farthest corner. We'd barely seated ourselves when he said in a mutter, "I do not believe the death of Mogen's brother the king was an accident."

"I agree," I said at once. Derry's cryptic message of a couple phases earlier echoed in my mind. *I wonder if Intel knew something.*

I'd just scooped up a spoonful of porridge when my duty link chirped. *Didn't take long to begin,* I thought, returning the spoon to my bowl, and retrieved the link from my chest pocket with a sigh.

Commander Teichert's senior aide, a chief master spacer with as much gray at his temples as his boss, appeared in the small display. "Journeyman Masou," he said, "the general wants to see you at 0700."

"Thanks, Chief, I'll be there." *No question what that's about.* My innards clinched. I glanced at the chronometer above the exit. *Got an hour. I haven't even showered yet. Need to clean up before I report.*

"What was that about?" Kota asked, pointing with his chin at the link.

"Flight commander business," I said, pocketing it.

I shoveled breakfast in faster than I wanted to, loped out to our quarters enclosure to shower and put on a fresh flight suit, and loped all the way back. I paused a few seconds to slow my breathing before I entered the wing commander's outer office. *Minute to spare.*

When I stepped inside, the chief gave me an approving glance over his console's monitor and crossed to the commander's open office door. "JO Masou's here, sir."

"Send him in," I heard.

I strode inside, heart hammering, but not from the jog. "Sir—"

He motioned me toward a chair and began to speak before I even sat down.

"I'm sure you understand, Akuleh," Teichert said, without so much as a greeting, "that Master Officer Reskag won't be returning. He'll have to resign his commission to assume the throne of Osfelga. His brother, King Sauvar, was assassinated yesterday."

He believes it, too. "Yes, sir," I said.

Teichert continued, "Since we lost so many people in the strike on Jassem last month, I've spent several hours reviewing the records of personnel in the Wing to determine who's ready to be advanced into leadership roles.

"I know you've only served as flight commander for about a month, but in that time, you've proven yourself capable of greater responsibility. Therefore, I'm appointing you 1st Squadron's commander."

"Yes, sir," I said through a dry mouth. *I really hoped Mogen was pulling my braid.*

"Unfortunately," he said, "you must have a minimum of six months in your current grade before I can recommend you for an additional promotion."

"That's fine, sir." I attempted a smile. "I'm still getting used to being a journeyman."

I couldn't help thinking, *Sure hope I don't get rushed into becoming Wanikiya this way.*

The thought awakened something I'd forgotten about during the high ops-tempo of the ORE, which had occupied every waking moment since my return from Tempest. "Sir," I said, "my plan was to apply for the Qaletaqa once I completed my two-year commitment to the Soliennese Defense Forces. I reached the two-year mark a couple phases ago. I've been meaning to ask you for a recommendation."

General Teichert studied me for a long, silent space. I never stirred under his scrutiny.

"I'm willing to do it for you, Akuleh," he said at last, "though we'd hate to lose you. You certainly may apply, but you need to be aware that MinDef has placed a stop-loss on all separations from active duty for the time being, especially for those in direct combat billets."

"Understood, sir." I paused. "Making me 1st Squadron's commander leaves Lance Flight without a commander. I'd like to recommend Ga'olani Keatii or Rinn Stormun to lead Lance Flight, and Kota of Apenimon clan to become a training officer."

Teichert appeared thoughtful. "Thank you, Akuleh. I'll take your suggestions into consideration. Wing staff meeting is 0800 in my conference room." He gestured at an adjacent doorway.

"Yes, sir," I said and stood.

I trudged down the stairs from Teichert's HQ office and next door into Wing Ops on autopilot, practically unaware of my surroundings due to everything milling in my mind.

Squadron commander. Three flights to watch out for now. I didn't want that any more than Mogen wanted the crown. I haven't even had time to get through the flight commander's SOP yet. I rubbed the itch of fatigue from my eyes with one hand and sighed. *As for the Qaletaqa, that's up to you now, Shaman Shiye. Your call, your timing.*

Minutes later, sinking into the chair in the compact office adjoining 1st Squadron's duty section, I observed Kota peering at me over his own monitor outside the office door, his eyes widening. When they met mine, he asked with a thrust of his jaw, "Does you sitting in there mean what I think it does?"

If I hadn't been so stunned, I probably would've replied with some joking remark like, "No. Just wondering if Mogen's replacement would notice if I swapped my chair for this one." As it was, with my new responsibility not yet a reality in my mind, I mumbled, "Ya. Teichert appointed me squadron commander."

Kota's eyebrows shot up, but only for a second. He grinned. "I knew it. Better you than me."

"Careful, Kota." I returned a warning smile. "I said the same thing to Mogen when he was made squadron commander." Kota's grin evaporated, and I added, "I recommended you for training officer."

He blinked. "I could do that."

I pressed a finger to my console's recognition sensor and my monitor glowed to life. *Let's see what Derry found.*

I didn't have to search. She'd highlighted the subject line of the lead topic in the daily message compilation her office sent—though we received it whenever classified message traffic came through.

CREDIBLE THREAT DETECTED AGAINST KING SAUVAR IV

According to the recipients list, the terse paragraph had been sent to every organization and military unit responsible for the protection of the Osfelg royal family. It included snippets of intercepted communications, with coded phrases that revealed an intimate knowledge of the king's daily itinerary.

Couple phases old by the time it got here, I thought, *but the right people would've seen it in time on Solienne. Wouldn't they? Remmet* had *to be involved in it. Who else would've had access to information like this?* I clenched my teeth. *Burn it, Mog, be wise.*

I skimmed the rest of the message traffic, then downloaded *Standard Operating Procedures for Squadron Commanders, Manual 14-SQ* to my readpad. *Little light reading for tonight.* I rolled my eyes. *Maybe it'll put me to sleep.*

"Later, Kota," I said as I rose. "I've got Wing staff meeting in a few minutes."

Squadron Commander. I shook my head as I pushed through gusts of gritty wind back to Wing Headquarters. *I'm about as ready for this as I am to be Wanikiya.*

* * * * *

Chapter Fourteen

My Qaletaqa application went out in the next mail burst. Teichert's recommendation was so extravagant, I chuckled out loud when I read it. *I'll have to remember some of those lines when I write my people's performance reports.*

Along with the application, I sent a vid to Derry to mark our first wedding anniversary.

"Hard to believe it's been a year already," I told her, "since we've spent so much of it apart. I smile when I remember how beautiful you were in my mother's beaded wedding dress, and those amazing nights at Mogen's lodge. I live on my memories of you until we're together again. *Ti qala bé messa tai messa,* white bird."

About a phase later, the spacer at the comms center entry said, "A box came for you in the latest supply shipment, sir. You can collect it when you leave."

The regular shipments through the vortex usually included people's packages from home. Kota received boxes of food quite often, but I hadn't gotten anything since Gram and Kimama had sent feast foods for Night of Light Ceremony, two months before Coming of Wanikiya. Surprise lifted my forlorn mood. "Thanks!"

I lingered on Derry's vid with her anniversary message. "I treasure ev'ry mem'ry of us, Kew. I miss yer arms 'round me on wintry nigh's, and the sound of yer voice and yer laugh. I see more of yew in Garn

ev'ry day, but i' doesn' make me miss yew any less. I'm sending a gif
to yew. Eszter and Mum made the images."

Among the vidmails, including two from Gram and Kimama, I
found a newsnet feed titled CORONATION OF KING MOGEN
SAUVARSSON RESKAG THE EIGHTH. The title alone brought me some
relief. *Sounds like it went smoothly. Thank you, Shaman Shiye.*

I headed around the corner from the comms center to the Wing
Ops building, my box tucked under one arm. Before Mogen, the small
office at the front of our duty area had been occupied by Commander
Yorgas. I couldn't help thinking about both of them every time I entered.

At my console, I tapped out an immediate message to the squadron. "For all who are interested and not on flying duty at the time,
we're going to watch the feed of Mogen's coronation in the squadron
conference room tomorrow at 1900."

Yorgas' personal items had been carefully gathered and returned
to his family after his death in the Jassem battle, but Mogen had missed
a couple things in his rushed departure. When I found his favorite
kasse mug behind the console monitor, I rinsed it out and set it on a
cabinet in my line of sight.

I admired Derry's precise characters on the plastic shipping box
before using my survival knife to pop its seals. The scent of awanatas,
rich with honey and *piñion* nuts, swept my nose when the cover fell
open. I scooped several of the small, wrapped pastries out, my mouth
already watering, and spied a flat package on the bottom. I removed
it, too. Its paper sheath parted under my knife's blade.

Within lay a six-by-eight-thumb-width image plate. Awanatas
briefly forgotten, I touched the plate on, chose Rotate Images, muted
the sound, and propped it on its built-in tripod.

For several minutes I sat and ate awanatas, savoring the sweetened maize layer enveloping the nutty filling, while I revisited image-prompted memories. *Don't remember Eszter doing these at all. I must've been really focused during our wedding.*

Derry in her wedding dress, and me in Shaman Cheveyo's ivory armor. Derry and me sitting before Chanter Wahkan, the yellow-and-green wedding blanket snug about our shoulders, while he drew white glyphs for unity on our foreheads. Feeding each other maize meal. Standing, with the blanket wrapped tightly around us, laughing and kissing. Cheering friends. Donnol tossing the maize basket.

The last nine or ten images were of Garnan. Sleeping, smiling, waving his arms and kicking. In some, he lay in Derry's arms; in others, he played on a floor blanket with Donnol. I found two of me holding him and grinning. *Derry's mother did those. I sorta remember.*

A reminder chirp from my console snapped me to the present. The message on the monitor read WING STAFF MTG, 10 MINUTES. I re-wrapped the remaining awanatas, stashed the box in my desk, and retrieved my flight jacket and cap with a sigh.

Daily meetings with the Wing leadership, one meeting with my three flight commanders—which now included Go for Lance Flight—training sorties in which Kota and I flew as aggressors against new pilots in four-ship elements, and a couple real-world combat space patrols over Eis Ell with Arturo as my wingman filled the next two days.

I felt gratified when I raced into our conference room to set up shortly before the appointed start time at how many members of 1st Squadron had already arrived. I knew Mogen had a lot of friends in the Wing, but we had to roll in extra chairs and line them up against the walls.

When the tri-D tank rippled to life, it revealed Mogen standing on a platform facing the domed hall of Osfelga's parliament. He wore the same bronze-colored armor his brother had. Though his military-short hair remained uncovered, his normal straight posture appeared unmistakably regal.

The newsnet vidcorder panned the semi-circular chamber. I observed armed guards positioned about the curved rear wall, encircling white Osfelg faces that contrasted with their black-robed mass.

My wariness kicked in. *Those robes of office are so loose and full, they're perfect for concealing weapons. Anybody could have one. I hope everybody was thoroughly searched before they were let in.*

Mogen raised his right hand and recited the Oath of Fealty line by line, as prompted by a stern-faced woman with iron-gray hair. His voice rang, firm and determined in his native Osfelg, while a translation to Standard slid across the bottom of the screen.

He finished, and the dark-clad crowd rose. Applause filled the chamber, the usual dull thunder for a moment or two before it settled into a rhythm. Then the whole parliament clapped in unison. Mogen stood motionless on the platform, his head high, but his expression atypically somber.

A long vehicle, bulky as a ground forces transport with its shielding, the Reskag crest blazoned in gold on its heavy doors, waited a few steps outside when Mogen strode from the government building into winter's clear sunlight. Two armed guards flanked him.

Remmet shuffled in their wake, hunched in his usual long, black coat. To my relief, all four men took what seemed to be pre-assigned places in the passenger compartment, Mogen and one guard sitting opposite Remmet and the other.

If the citizens lining the Avenue of the Crown felt any disappointment at Mogen not marching the route, I saw no sign of it. Purple flags fluttered in waving hands, and children reached over the barriers as they had for Sauvar's procession.

Murmured conversations rose in our conference room during the slow journey up the hill. They hushed when Mogen stepped out of the royal conveyance and entered the temple, where a page presented him with the great sword Sauvar had borne on his back.

Solemnity intensified every face around me. I heard several full breaths released in the conference room when the bronze circlet finally rested on Mogen's head.

Be wise, Mogen, I thought again when Remmet followed the entourage from the granite-gray shadows into the portico.

* * *

On returning to our quarters afterward, I sat on my bunk, my shoulder blades pressed to the chilly wall. I contemplated the empty berth across from mine between jotting notes for my next vidmail to Derry.

Her observations on Mogen's ceremonies had arrived in the same burst as the coronation newsfeed and her anniversary vidmail. "All appeared to go smoothly, though i' was rather more subdued than his brother's coronation. Understandable, really, under the circumstances. The memorials are to be held tomorrow."

She'd also sent more vids of Garnan. "He detes's spending time on his belly. Wails like a banshee, he does, though he can hold his head up longer to look abou' now.

"When Donnol's home from school, he plops down and dangles toys for Garn to see and follow with his eyes." She'd included a clip of them, the tow-headed young boy and the black-haired baby, beaming while they played on the floor, and she finished, "Donnol's almos' as good a nanny as Mum, a righ' helpful big brother."

I felt grateful, but somewhat envious. *Garn's bonding with Donnol. That's good, but how will he react next time he sees me? Will I be a stranger? Will he be afraid of me?* The thought tore at my heart.

A portion of his Birth Chant trailed across my mind.

Follow the flight of the golden eagle.
Follow his Path as far as you can.
Soar in his Path as high as you can,
and learn wisdom in the shadow of his wings.

I considered the words. *What time we'll have together will be up to me. It's crucial. How am I going to make it happen?*

* * * * *

Chapter Fifteen

Mogen's counsel proved correct about a squadron commander being like a father to adult children with adult problems. A few days after his coronation, I stopped at my desk to check messages before my regular *pelu felelei* workout with Go and found an official dispatch. The mother of an Obollan pilot in Saber Flight had recently died after a short illness. Informing him fell to me.

My heart contracted.

I messaged Go first. CAN YOU PUSH *PELU FELELEI* TO 1800? GOT AN UNEXPECTED SQUADRON MATTER.

By the time her AFFIRMATIVE rippled into my Reply file, I'd read through *Notifications of Deaths* in the squadron commander's SOP. It contained one paragraph on notifying next-of-kin about deaths in my unit and one on informing my personnel of deaths at home.

I had to notify the individual's chain of command, which meant both General Teichert and his flight commander, Journeyman Domokos. Then I was to request that his chaplain be present and contact the Casualty Assistance Office to secure emergency leave orders, arrange his vortex journey, and fill any other needs. I found no suggestions on how to actually deliver the news.

Teichert's executive officer took the first call. "I'll inform him, Ku."

When I called Domokos, he told me, "Bahari launched ten minutes ago on combat patrol, ETR four hours. Should I come with him?"

"That'd be good," I said, in a wash of both gratitude and relief for his offer. I knew Bahari, but not as well as his flight commander would. "What about his chaplain?" I asked. We had two Obollans in the chaplains' office.

"Bahari is Ouzounian," Domokos answered. "I think Master Officer Alakka is their spiritual leader."

"Thanks. I'll call him. Let me know when Bahari lands."

I glanced at the wall chrono. *Five hours by the time he debriefs and everything. May have enough time for supper after* pelu felelei. *It's going to be a long evening.*

I contacted the Casualty Assistance Office, then the chaplain. "What do Ouzounians believe?" I asked Alakka after explaining the situation. "What should I say or not say?"

Alakka's voice rolled in the same relaxed manner as one of my favorite instructors during Basic. "We believe our loved ones live on in nature. Mothers are represented by songbirds. Not reincarnation, mind, just as signs of her presence."

"Thank you, Chaplain," I said. *Think I'll leave that part to him.*

I sauntered from my office to the gym, trying out various statements in my mind. *Short illness, the message said, so it may be a shock. I don't want to be like Kekrik was to the families I took the trunks to. Should I lead up to it? How should I do it?*

Still pondering, I changed into my loose *felelei* trousers, removed my sheathed *pelu* from my locker, and withdrew to the small room with padded flooring that served for combatives training and martial arts. Regular practices every phase had accustomed my knees and ankles to sitting with my feet tucked under myself the way Go did. I waited for her without stirring.

She arrived a few minutes later. Although meticulously on time, she glanced anxiously at the wall chrono when she found me already there. She bowed and said, "You are early, Ku."

I'd never gotten used to her shaved head. I experienced a fresh pang every time I saw her. "Needed some time to think."

"You are, um, concerned about something?"

I told her about Bahari.

"Ah. I am sorry," she said. "Just show, um, compassion for him as you did for me."

We spent an hour perfecting a couple new forms. One of them began with a forward lunge, then a pivot to thrust to the rear with the blade inverted. The other consisted of three quick steps forward before raising our *pelus* over our heads for a swift downward cut.

Afterward, showered and changed, I skipped the mess hall and returned to my squadron office, though my stomach protested its emptiness with impatient grumbles. Somehow, it didn't feel right to be comfortably fed in the face of someone's impending sorrow. All I could think was, *Help me do this, Shaman Shiye.*

Chaplain Alakka and Journeyman Renou from Casualty Assistance joined me before Apprentice Bahari, lanky and tall as my friend Ogundo in Basic, arrived with Commander Domokos. Bahari's ebony face displayed apprehension. "Am I in trouble, sir?" he asked the moment they stepped into my small office.

"No, Apprentice." I motioned everyone to the chairs I'd set in a circle front of my desk. Once seated, I leveled my gaze on him, hoping my sympathy showed in my eyes. *No use delaying it.* I drew a breath and said quietly, "I'm really sorry I have to tell you this, Bahari. We received word this morning that your mother has died."

His head drooped, and he clutched his knees. After a short silence, he nodded. "That explains it," he said, barely above a whisper.

"Explains what?" I asked.

"I heard birds singing out on the flightline today, but there are no birds near this base."

I straightened. *He's right. I've never seen one, either. There probably aren't birds anywhere on Tobe.*

Bahari and Alakka spoke together in one of the Obollan languages for a few minutes. Then Journeyman Renou said, "We're making arrangements for two phases of emergency leave. You'll be able to depart early tomorrow morning. Is there anything else we can do for you?"

Bahari thought for a minute, his features stricken, but calmer than I'd expected. "No, sir. Thank you."

Everyone stood, and I briefly gripped his shoulder. "May the birds' songs give you comfort."

Bahari, Alakka, and Domokos left together. I followed a few minutes later, contemplating Bahari's reaction compared to the bereaved families on Tempest.

Night came a little later now, but darkness had fallen when I stepped outside. It brightened the red-orange lava glow of our baby volcano, now visible as a fiery nub on the horizon on clear nights. The wind carried lava heat, too.

I stopped in the flight kitchen for a box of sandwiches and a bottle of fruit-flavored water before *thunking* along the boardwalk to our quarters. Rinn and Manoq had a late sortie, but I found Kota and

Arturo in our cabin, sprawled on their bunks and discussing another PME lesson.

"Rough day?" Kota asked when I dropped heavily onto my bunk.

"Ya." I unwrapped one of the sandwiches. "More of Mogen's 'glories of command.'" I gave the phrase an ironic tone. "I had to give someone bad news from home."

"Consider it experience for the future," Kota said.

Arturo chortled. "Aiming at wing commander already, Ku?"

"Not if I can help it," I said, but I knew what Kota meant.

* * *

I lived for vidmails from Derry, Gram, and Kimama in every mail burst, but my disappointment deepened every time the mail arrived with no response from the Qaletaqa selection board.

They know I'm stop-lossed from the Soli Defense Forces, I tried to console myself. *They're not allowed to accept me until the stop-loss is lifted.*

So I stared when, one afternoon several phases after Mogen's departure, I found a message from Qaletaqa Headquarters in my duty mail queue one afternoon. *Probably informing me I'm not eligible right now.* Bracing for disappointment, I opened the message—and froze at a block of Standard text filling my display.

TO: JOURNEYMAN OFFICER AKULEH, MASOU CLAN.

THIS MESSAGE CONFIRMS THAT YOU HAVE BEEN ACCEPTED INTO QALETAQA TRAINING CLASS 228 WITH A REPORTING DATE OF 03/20/242 ISY AT PAKUNA OUTPOST, AYASHA ISLAND. CONFIRM

Acceptance NLT 01/25/242 ISY. See Attached Documents for Reporting Instructions.

Three-Pinion Chuchip, Eznoh Clan

Amazement paralyzed me for a few seconds. Then I leaped to my feet with a yell in Chalca.

Chairs scraped on the floor outside. In three seconds, six or seven people had crammed my open office doorway, eyes alight with curiosity. I beckoned them inside.

"What is it, Ku?" Kota asked. His eyes glittered. "Did you and Derry start another baby while you were home?"

I chuckled. "She would've told me long before now if we had. This is just as good, though." I indicated my console monitor. "Acceptance into Qaletaqa training."

"What is, um, Qaletaqa?" Go leaned in to read the message, her forehead creasing.

"Officially," I said, "they're the Awénasa Territorial Militia. The name means 'Guardian of the People,' and that's how they got started, because of the criminals deported to Tempest. But in the last few decades, they've earned a reputation as the most in-demand special ops force in the Pact. They used to capture distant-end vortex terminals for the return flights of our combat missions before we had two-way vortex capability."

Go stared. "They did? That was very, um, dangerous."

"Are there pilots in the Qaletaqa?" Rinn asked.

"Remember Five-Talon Noshi?" I asked in return. "The safety officer at pilot training? He's Qaletaqa. He's the one who encouraged me to apply."

Noshi had also piloted the SAR lifter that had picked me up in the mountains of Caerden, but I didn't mention it. Chitsa, who'd once asked if I knew the Chalca pilot who got shot down, had squeezed into my office along with Go.

Manoq squinted at my monitor. "Confirm by the twenty-fifth?" His eyes widened. "Today's the twenty-seventh, Ku!"

I stiffened, my heart stopping in my chest. "Rot! I hope they'll take transmission delays into account." I dropped into my chair and tapped a brief response with jittery fingers. With several others leaning over my shoulders, we read through it a few times before I hit SEND.

By then my pulse had stepped up several notches. I composed a quick message to Derry and wondered aloud, "When does the next mail burst go out?"

No one answered, but Rinn said, "You must tell Commander Teichert, Ku."

"Yes, I must." I punched the comms line to his office. When his senior aide appeared, I said, "Any chance I can get a few minutes of the boss' time today, Chief?"

"How much do you need, sir?"

"About ten minutes."

He glanced away briefly. "He's in a secure vid conference right now," he said, "but it's scheduled to wrap up in fifteen minutes. If you can be here when he gets out—"

"I'm on my way." I rose, swept my flight cap and jacket off their hook, and accepted congratulatory bearhugs and backslaps from everyone on my way to the door.

Kota followed me out. "You know what he's going to tell you," he said in a cautioning tone.

"I left it up to Shaman Shiye when I sent the application," I replied. "If it's supposed to work out, it will."

The overcast had thinned enough—at least for the moment—to let some ruddy sunlight through, and the sulfur smell seemed less pronounced.

I passed Huritt, approaching the Wing Ops building as if from the flightline, though he wasn't wearing a pressure suit. He gave me his typical sneer and a sloppy salute. I smiled and returned the salute crisply. The Qaletaqa acceptance message glowed brightly in the front of my mind.

As I set my boot on the step into Wing Headquarters, a klaxon ripped the afternoon into pieces.

* * * * *

Chapter Sixteen

My heart slammed into full throttle. I spun about and dashed for Wing Ops and Life Support.

A male voice boomed through the klaxon's pulsating wails. "2nd and 3rd Squadrons to your fighters! I say again, 2nd and 3rd Squadrons to your fighters! 1st Squadron, stand by for orders."

1st Squadron stand by? I clenched my teeth. *We're under attack!* Memories of a sweaty night on Ardonar flashed in my mind's eye. *Sure glad Derry's not here this time.*

A sudden realization momentarily checked my stride at Wing Ops' front door. *If Lybjevyk Base has been compromised, Solienne's already fallen. My family's in danger—and what's happened to Mogen?*

Images from intel briefings of slaughtered planetary officials laid out on government plazas flooded my brain. I shook my head to clear it.

Surging adrenaline spurred me forward. *Ironic. Decimating Jassem's warfighting capability cleared the lumpies' way to take Solienne.*

Most of my squadron must've still been in the building when the klaxon sounded. I found Go, Domokos, and Sperka already in the Ops section, receiving information from the wing CAOC—Combat Air Operations Center—officer via a wall-sized holograph projection. Tri-D tracking screens lit the area behind him.

"Good, Masou," he said when I joined them. "1st Squadron has base defense. You'll cover the evacuation by vortex of all non-combatant personnel."

When I nodded acknowledgment, he continued. "We're putting CAPs over the base itself and at the most likely ingress locations, in case lumpy bombers get past our interceptors."

"Or send a separate strike force against the base," I said.

"Affirmative. We'll also have a flight cocked on the runway for ground-alert intercept."

"Good," I said. "When they attacked Ardonar, they vortexed in over the northern pole. We're about halfway between Tobe's equator and south pole here."

"Good point, Masou. Better put one of those CAPs near the southern pole."

Go thrust a hand up. "I will take that one."

I moved off to let my flight commanders decide who'd fly where, but I kept an eye on the holo-projection tracking screens.

When Go, Domokos, and Sperka pivoted away to head into Life Support, Go slipped up alongside me, holding her datapad out for me to see. "Arrow Flight has, um, ground-alert intercept. That leaves five CAPs of, you know, eight ships each, shared between Saber and Lance Flights. Ours is, um, stationed near the southern pole, call sign Catcher."

I scanned the roster on her display. Arturo with me, Chitsa with her, Manoq with Rinn, Maira with Kota. "Looks good," I said.

Having had to wait for 2nd and 3rd Squadrons to leave, 1st Squadron's pilots were still suiting up when we entered Life Support. I glimpsed set jaws and narrowed eyes. Sperka, Domokos, and Go gathered their respective flights for quick mission briefings.

As they had when we'd been attacked on Ardonar, our suiting crews were waiting at their posts. Unlike the night attack, all of them were fully dressed this time.

Spacer Assistant Shokoff motioned me to the bench in front of my locker. "Sit down, sir, and get your jacket off. We'll get your boots."

I sat and shrugged out of my flight jacket. I'd only had shower clogs to kick off last time.

Shokoff and Spacer Tech Galvan each loosened one of my boots with a few practiced tugs, more quickly than I could've unfastened one of them. Galvan hauled my pressure suit from its locker and held it open.

My flight jacket wouldn't fit inside the pressure suit's shell, but I didn't need it. The suit's body-hugging lining provided thermal protection from the absolute cold of space. I shoved stockinged feet into my suit's heavy boots and stood.

"Right arm, sir," Shokoff said, extending the sleeve.

I remembered how Spacer Assistant Zacarious, shirtless and on the verge of hyperventilating, had sealed me into my suit at D'Amarys Main. *He and the rest of the support crews barely got evacuated before the first lumpy troops landed.*

"Now your left, sir."

Galvan's nimble fingers tugged and locked my suit's seals from groin to neck ring. As Zacarious had done in his haste on that sweaty night, Galvan pressed Gram's little bag hard to my breastbone.

Egress pack next. Its straps ran through my pressure suit's shoulder rings, looped under my thighs, and across my chest. I braced against the usual tugs while Shokoff cinched it up and let out my breath when he put my helmet in my hands.

The metallic bangs and clatter had subsided by then. I swept a gaze around Life Support. Only Go and Sperka were still there.

I beckoned to them, then addressed my suiting crew. "Get to the vortex terminal immediately."

They responded, "Yes, sir," almost in unison.

I lumbered to the armory to receive my survival vest and a sidearm in a shoulder holster, the only difference between suiting up for training and for real-world combat missions.

The klaxon wound down as I strode outside, and the voice boomed again from speakers around the base. I shook my head to clear the klaxon's ringing from my ears and swung aboard the waiting bench cart.

"Attention, 2nd and 3rd Squadrons," the deep voice said, "unknown number of enemy ships emerging from vortex, altitude seven hundred ranges over southern pole. Vector to intercept at four hundred ranges."

They knew exactly where to find us, pounded in my head. I glowered. *Seven hundred ranges. They're the decoy. Once they draw our fighters off the base, a new group will pop out of a vortex three ranges away, on the deck, for the real strike.* The thought knotted my stomach under my ribs. *Like they did on Ardonar.*

Those of us who'd fought the space battle hadn't known until afterward. *That's how Derry was injured.*

"1st Squadron," the announcement continued, "stand by for base defense."

The bench cart lurched forward when Go and Sperka heaved themselves aboard. The cart trundled along a sloppy route, its clattering tracks kicking up sulfuric mud that spattered our boots.

As I sprang off the cart, the scream of 2nd Squadron's engines powering up climaxed with the explosive roars of ships launching ten seconds apart. Their afterburner flames lit the murk like so many flying torches.

Branko and Maginn scrambled clear of my ship, disconnecting and hauling away hoses and power cables as they went, when I charged into the hangar.

At least the ordnance crews hadn't had to change our weapon loads. We'd been scheduled to fly escort for a bombing mission against targets on Nichi, so our ships already carried twelve air-to-air missiles in their internal wing racks.

Within minutes, strapped into my cockpit, I watched Branko pull the chocks and step away. She snapped her normal salute as my fighter began to roll. When I returned it, she dropped her hand to let it trail along the wingtip gliding past her.

She did it every time. The affectionate gesture recalled what she'd told me the day I first met her, as a fresh-out-of-training apprentice officer. "She's *my* bird, sir. You better bring her home in the same condition she left."

Three or four urgent voices cut across each other in my helmet speakers. I thumbed the control stick's comms switch to Air Traffic Control's frequency.

"Catcher team." A clipped voice replaced the chatter when my fighter cleared the hangar. *"Proceed to main runway and stand by for launch times. Cloud ceiling is two hundred spans, winds are out of south-southwest at three knots."*

"Tower, Catcher Lead," I replied, "proceeding to main runway and standing by, roger."

I steered my ship onto the taxiway and returned to general comms. "Catcher team, Catcher Lead. Report status."

For planned combat missions, I flew as a member of Lance Flight, as Mogen had. In this situation, I took the lead of the eight-ship element. Go, as Lance Flight's commander, held the Three position.

Seven voices responded in turn. Arturo, Go and Chitsa, Rinn and Manoq, Kota and Maira. I pictured each of them in my mind as they spoke.

We waited, lined up on the taxiway, while 3rd Squadron brought their engines to full power. I felt their multiple shrieks as tremors through my own fighter, and I mulled the situation. *A hundred and twenty flyers in 2nd and 3rd Squadrons. Against who knows how many lumpies.*

2nd Squadron, first into the fight, would eliminate the fighter escorts to give the 3rd a clear field against the enemy attack ships.

As 3rd Squadron's last ship rocketed skyward, Air Traffic Control directed us forward.

My fighter's rumble exuded impatience as I taxied onto the runway. The others rolled after me in single file. Our running lights flashed off puddles of ashy rain on the tarmac, though our helmets blocked the sulfurous odor.

"Catcher Lead, Control." An older voice rang clearly in my earphones. *"From launch, climb to forty thousand spans and take heading eight-niner-five to your CAP track."*

"Roger, Control."

"Supremacy force has descended to six hundred ranges," the man continued. *"Group likely includes Adder surface-attack ships escorted by Sevicha fighters. Tight formation prevents Orbital Early Warning from providing exact numbers."*

"Copy," I acknowledged. *Swarm formation, same as before. We really need extreme-reach missiles with multiple warheads.*

I absorbed every detail as the CAOC continually updated its information. The voice crackled in my earphones as I swung my fighter onto the runway in the lead position.

On the tower's order, I began my engines' run-up. Their idling grumble rose to a roar, then to their characteristic scream, a sun eagle challenging intruders to his territory.

My fighter shook with increasing power, and my heartrate quickened. I kept a tight grip on the throttles and held the brakes hard, as my fighter bucked under the strain like a ghost cat fighting a captor's rope, its muscles straining.

The others took their places behind me. The thunder of their engines awakening joined mine. When everyone confirmed all engines online, I acknowledged and toggled the comms switch. "Tower, Catcher team standing by for launch times."

"Catcher Lead, you are cleared to launch. Catcher Flight, cleared to launch at ten second intervals."

"Catcher Lead rolling." I spread my hand across the throttles and shoved them full forward all at once. Engaging my afterburners felt like a kick in the back.

At two hundred arm-lengths down the runway, I nudged the control stick. My ship rotated, shooting off the tarmac in a vertical combat launch. G-forces flattened me into my seat. I glimpsed Arturo climbing ten seconds off my right wing.

"Enemy strike force descending to five hundred fifty ranges," the CAOC reported.

"Copy, CAOC," I acknowledged.

Tobe's gloomy horizon tilted behind us as we shot through low cloud cover, grunting against the pressure of vertical acceleration. On reaching forty thousand spans, I banked toward the CAP track superimposed on an image of Tobe's surface in my computer's flight profile.

"Combat spread," I ordered. "Threat scopes active, check weapons systems and report status."

My scope revealed my own position in a field of eight blue darts. "Check targeting," I said. "Check energy cannon charge and missile status."

Green lights rippled to life across my weapons panel, and the Ready chime sounded. My targeting reticle appeared, its white circle and crosshairs adrift in my faceplate.

Lybjevyk Base lay about eight hundred ranges north of Tobe's southern polar landmass. We covered the seven hundred-range flight to our patrol track, crossing a band of ocean called the Black Channel, in 35 minutes.

From our altitude of forty thousand spans, craggy peaks layered with perpetual ice gleamed in the distance, rose-colored in Tobe's weak sunlight. The channel frothed below us.

Our oval track paralleled a couple hundred ranges of rocky coastline. We spaced ourselves equal distances apart, beyond visual range of each other, to cover 360 degrees of surrounding sky at all times. Slowing to a fuel-conserving cruise of .8 Mach, we activated all sensors.

I'd barely reported our on-station status to Control when Manoq, seventy ranges across the oval from me, yelled, *"Lead! Lumpy at—"* he rattled off coordinates *"—and thirty thousand spans. No, two lumpies. Now three!"*

Seconds later, my own threat scope bloomed with red enemy-ship darts, visible only through our long-reach sensors. They seemed to materialize out of the clouds below us, flying close together, and heading toward Lybjevyk Base.

"Control, Catcher Lead." I used the general frequency to be sure the other CAPs heard, too. "Lumpies emerging from vortex." I repeated Manoq's coordinates and altitude. "ETA at L-Base 35 minutes. Estimate forty fighters. Intercepting now."

I set my teeth. *Twenty-five minutes until the closest CAP team can get here to reinforce us. The GAI flight will have to cover the base. We're on our own.*

* * * * *

Chapter Seventeen

My heartbeat stiffened when I didn't get an immediate response. *Have they hit the base already?*

"Catcher Lead, Control," I heard at last. *"Redirecting nearest CAPs to you."*

I released a breath of relief. "Copy, Control. Catcher team, combat spread, weapons free."

Adrenaline heightened my pulse as I banked into pursuit. The others locked in their positions.

We've got two advantages: altitude, and heavy overcast to conceal us.

I calculated a lead-pursuit intercept, and we dove on our targets.

At thirty-six thousand spans, sliding along the underside but still veiled within the cloud ceiling, we got our first visual ID. Forty-two Sevicha-9s skimmed the inky channel in close-trail formation, 21 pairs flying in such tight echelon their wingtips appeared to overlap their tail assemblies.

Like carrion hawks on Tempest, I thought.

"That's serious overkill for just L-Base," Kota said.

"Makes me wonder what else they're targeting," I agreed.

"Perhaps they expect heavy losses," Rinn said.

"Coming right up." I didn't miss the grin in Manoq's tone.

I scrutinized the attackers. *That's what swarm formation looks like from above. If we can strike before they break out, each of us can eliminate two ships with one missile.*

"Catcher team," I called, "prox munitions. Lead's taking first lumpy pair. Three, take pair seven. Five, take thirteen. Seven, take the tails. Box them in."

"Three, copy," Go responded.

"Five, copy," Rinn said.

"Seven, copy," came from Kota.

"On my mark," I said. "Missile one, ready."

My missile's amber Standby light blinked green. My narrowed stare locked my targeting reticle on the leader's exhaust nozzle. Spinning digits in my faceplate's periphery tracked the narrowing distance. *Not fast enough, not fast enough.* Sweat dampened the palms of my gloves.

The target-acquired tone sounded in my earphones. I counted down from three. "Mark. Missile one, fire!"

Seven voices echoed my launch order.

I felt the lurch and saw the golden flare as my first missile blasted from beneath my wing. Eight white tracks raced across my threat scope at ten times the enemy ships' speed, almost too swift to see.

Six double explosions and two singles, nearly simultaneous, spawned three more when hurtling wreckage smashed into lumpy wingmen flying too close. For several seconds, expanding fireballs illuminated the dusk before choppy waves swallowed the tumbling debris.

Reduced them to 25, but there are three times more of them than us, and now they know we're here. I locked my teeth.

Red darts swirled in my threat scope like ants from a kicked nest mound. They burst from their tight formation into a spreading climb to meet us. Some paired up, some didn't. Orange tracking icons glowed in my threat scope.

"Catcher team, weapons free," I said. "Two, combat spread. Missile two ready, decoys ready."

Arturo drew abreast, visible at my right wing.

On my scope, five lumpy ships abruptly peeled clear of the mêlée to race north.

They're heading for L-base. I knew it in my gut.

"Control, Catcher Lead!" I called. Urgency laced my voice. "Five bandits inbound, unable to intercept, ETA thirty minutes."

An acknowledgment rattled in my earphones, but the enemy held my full attention. *Eight of us to their twenty. Burn! Still almost three to one.*

I spotted their new lead at once. He and his wingman stayed in echelon to engage, though looser than before. I flicked my datalink, marking them for Arturo. "Two, pincer. Split *now.*"

We rolled apart in a bracketing dive.

Banking into the counterturn, I saw the lumpy lead swing after Arturo. My palms dampened again. When the wingman followed, I had my shot. "Not today, kosa," I hissed through my teeth. I tightened my turn, grunting as nine Gs flattened me in my seat, and fixed my sight on his exhaust nozzle. The reticle locked on, and I snapped, "Missile two, fire!"

Arturo's pincer maneuver took him in a near head-on pass with the lumpy lead. His own shout of *"Missile two, fire!"* rang in my helmet speakers an instant before my missile reduced the wingman's ship to spinning debris.

The lumpy lead pitched up at the flash of Arturo's missile launch. Scarlet bursts from his underside spattered the gloom. Arturo's inbound missile disintegrated in a rupture of phosphorescent white.

What in Yuma's name? I blinked at the afterimage. *Energy guns fast enough to kill missiles?*

My heartrate stepped up when I realized we'd lost visual on the lumpy lead. "Two, combat spread, stay sharp," I called, and swept the murky skies around us. *Too easy to lose him in this.* My nape prickled with the sensation of being watched. I checked my threat scope, which tracked the battle milling beyond us. *Where is he? No way he would've disengaged.*

Arturo locked in at my right, and I said, "Tac left." We swung left together to start a search.

I'd barely repeated the call when a flashing orange icon on my threat scope warned I'd been acquired by a missile sensor. No time to wonder where he'd come from. The orange symbol froze to locked-on red, and the warning honk of a missile launch sounded in my earphones. *Sket!*

My heart leaped to full throttle. "Decoys, fire!" I yelled. Fresh adrenaline quivered in my voice. I pitched up to evade the weapon as my white-hot flares spiraled from their pods.

The missile corkscrewed after the flares, and Arturo's blue dart swung hard left in my threat scope. I recognized his intent to sandwich the Sevicha, but it rolled after him instead. *"Lead, bandit switch!"* he called.

I looped around, straining my neck from looking up and over my shoulder, to keep both of them in sight while the world inverted beneath me.

Somewhere in the mêlée I spotted two Rohrs entangled with five or six Sevichas. Inky smoke billowed aft of one Rohr's cockpit. The other, missing an engine and part of a wing, rocked in a burst it couldn't evade before it nosed over into a spiraling dive. Distance kept me from discerning a tail number, but I knew who it was. "Manoq, eject, eject!" I yelled, though something in my soul told me it wouldn't be possible at that angle and velocity.

Guts knotted, I wrenched my awareness to my own fight.

Arturo reversed, maneuvering to stay out of range while he drew the lumpy across my path. My thumb hovered over the weapons toggles. "Missile three, ready," I ordered. When the light blinked green, and my reticle locked, I snapped, "Missile three, fire!"

Tracking my missile in his threat scope, Arturo pitched right and climbed clear. The fireball as my munition nailed the lumpy illuminated Arturo's ship against ash-heavy clouds. I released a full breath. "Nice one, Two. Combat spread."

Blossoms of combustion ripped apart Tobe's dense sky. Rohrs and Sevichas wove patterns of flashing wingtip beacons and engines' blast-furnace plumes. Myriad voices, panting and clipped, roared in my earphones like tornado winds.

"Catcher Flight," I said, "check in."

"Two," Arturo snapped.

"Three," Go said.

"Four. Damaged but stable." Chitsa panted the words.

"Five," Rinn said, *"I have damage and an injury."*

I stiffened. "Five, an injury? Can you make it to the extraction point?"

"I am stable, Lead," he said.

He's reverting to his native accent. Something's definitely wrong. Innards clenching, I searched my scope for him while I called, "Catcher Six, Seven, and Eight, report."

"Seven," Kota replied. *"Light damage, Lead."*

"Eight," Maira answered.

"Copy," I said. "Report status changes."

It took a couple seconds to pick Rinn out, a lone Rohr with a Sevicha bearing down from behind. "Five!" I shouted to be heard through the cacophony. "Lumpy on your tail! Pitch down! Two, cover me. Missile four, ready."

I watched Rinn pitch down and arc clear as I went inverted and dove after the pursuing hostile. Keeping Rinn in sight, I worked to get a lock on the lumpy while both of them jinked all over the sky.

Red energy from the Sevicha's nose cannon pursued Rinn's ship like ethereal arrows.

Sweat broke across my brow. *They're too close together to use a missile.*

Pulling out of my dive, I jerked my nose up and swung directly in front of the Sevicha. I went nose-to-nose with him, taunting him to draw him off Rinn, and jinking to evade his fire.

My ship bucked, and a red flash appeared on my instrument panel, but the target-acquired tone sang in my earphones. I nailed my energy cannon's firing stud.

The volley tore the lumpy's nearest wing and engine intake apart. Smoke left a trail like a helix as he careened toward the Black Channel.

Lights burned red across on my cockpit display and a persistent beep begged my attention, but I called again, still panting, "Catcher Five, Lead. What's your status? Catcher Six, report."

"Lead, Five." Rinn's words seemed to come with effort in my helmet speakers, but he said, *"I am good... My damage is stable... but I have lost Six."*

"Report status changes, Five," I requested.

"Roger, Lead."

I took a moment to check my own status. The damage lights glowing on my panel marked four directional thrusters—needed for steering in space, but not in atmospheric flight—and a coolant line under my nosecone. *Took those hits in my chicken pass with the lumpy pursuing Rinn. Thrusters aren't urgent, but loss of coolant will be pretty soon.* Still, I shut the beeper off. *Don't need the distraction.*

"Lead!" Arturo shouted. "*Lumpies at three-one-oh degrees high!*"

A glance at my threat scope confirmed two more hostiles closing on blue darts marked Three and Four, who were already mixing it up with two lumpies. Go and Chitsa. "Got them, Two," I said. "Take the wingman."

To my surprise, Rinn locked in at my left wing as we climbed, though his ship seemed to lack full power.

I narrowed my vision on the lead lumpy's nearest engine, my jaw set with impatience while I waited for the white crosshairs to lock on. The tone sounded. "Missile four, fire!" I ordered.

Rinn's call to fire echoed mine.

I felt the usual tug of launch, but no flare zipped into the dark from under my wing. No white track creased my threat scope as it arrowed toward my target. *What's going on?*

A new damage light blinked red, this time on my weapons status display, and three words appeared.

MISSILE FOUR JAMMED

Same side as the damaged thrusters. Sket!

I stared at the missile's panel, Active green, and the digits counting down in it.

28... 27... 26...

Our missiles had a 30-second delay between launch and detonation, the reason we had to be in range to fire. Icy hands seized my insides. "Computer," I ordered, "shut down number four missile."

24... 23... 22...

"Computer, override." Anxiety heightened my voice. "Shut down number four missile."

The green digits continued their countdown.

Got to get clear before it blows. My heart raced; my pulse pounded in my ears. Fresh sweat beaded my face and dampened my glove linings, but I steadied my voice. "Catcher Three, take the lead. L-Base Control, Catcher Lead. Hung missile, punching out, mark my position."

The CAOC would have my ship's track via its datalink.

"Alerting Search and Rescue," I heard.

I glanced right and left to confirm enough space between my ship and my flight mates' before I flicked the control stick. My fighter sank into a steep roll. *Twenty seconds to get far enough away from my team.* Guilt for leaving them harrowed my soul.

19... 18... 17...

My heart felt about to rupture in my chest. It dragged my lungs with it, quickening my breaths to hyperventilation. The sweat that had beaded moments earlier streamed from my forehead and temples to my jaw and about my nose and mouth until I tasted its saltiness.

Time slowed down. I felt fleeting amazement at how much I observed in a split second. I watched Arturo angling toward the lumpies above us while Go and Chitsa rolled and twisted in their deadly dance with their attackers. I *felt* the roar of my engines and the intensifying *beep* of the missile's countdown. Every streak and scratch in the surface of my instrument panel glared at me, and a fleck of dust drifted across my faceplate. The external voices dimmed as I neared my decision point.

Never thought I'd even do this once in my career, definitely not twice.

With ten seconds left on the counter, I aimed my ship at a Sevicha careening toward me over the white-swathed peaks of Tobe's southern polar cap. *Let's play chicken.*

I braced into ejection posture in the seat and tugged the ring with shaking hands.

* * * * *

Chapter Eighteen

As it had over Ardonar, everything happened at once. My torso harness and the straps about my arms, legs, and helmet wrenched me into egress position so sharply I thought they'd dismember me, so tightly they made me gasp.

The ejection's blast swallowed my cockpit in a billow of blinding flame. The sudden acceleration felt like the weight of infinity collapsing on me. It crushed the breath from my lungs, and my vision tunneled.

Somewhere in the eternal, suffocating seconds before the ejection capsule reached its apex, a double fireball ruptured at the corner of my eye. I recognized wings and tail assemblies spinning out of the detonation. My ship and the lumpy's I'd aimed it at cartwheeled toward the icy surface in a fiery tangle.

A moment of regret mingled with odd satisfaction. *I'm sorry to inform you, Chief Branko, but your bird went down with valor.*

Two or three too-fast heartbeats later, hurtling fragments aglow with fire bombarded my escape capsule like a volley from a projectile weapon. I cringed.

The pressure eased as the capsule began its descent. With a *pop* and a jerk, its glider wing unfurled above me. Its vanes extended into the same leaf shape I remembered from before.

"Lead, Three." Go's tense voice rang in my helmet speakers. *"I have visual on your capsule. Do you copy?"*

"Copy, Three," I answered.

My cockpit's instrument panel remained in the ejection capsule, but with only such basic instruments as wind indicator, compass, altimeter, and datalink. It also had stick-and-rudder controls.

Gripping the control stick calmed me. I sucked a full breath into starved lungs and flinched at an ache across my chest, the bruises inflicted by my seat harness. The pain snatched me to full awareness.

The capsule swung in a slow spiral to the left, and I puckered my forehead. *The other one didn't do that. Damage from the falling debris?*

"Lead, Five. Incoming!" Rinn's voice came from behind me in my omnidirectional helmet speakers. Every word seemed strained, as if it took great effort, though it wasn't the grunts of high-G maneuvering. I twisted to look for him and winced at a twinge in my neck.

Another fighter, discernible only by the scarlet flashes from its energy cannon, bore down on me out of the dusk. My heart stopped. My throat closed off my breath. *Here I hang, an easy target, helpless as a fish in a net.*

The Sevicha's wingspan became visible, a faint outline in the murk. Bright tracers like bloody fingers snatched for my capsule, bare seconds before they'd reach me.

I stared, frozen as a tavo in a handlight's beam, my heart racing like a tavo's under my ribs.

The Rohr-55 appeared from nowhere, angling toward the lumpy ship on a lead-pursuit intercept. A Rohr-55 with part of one wing missing, tarry smoke billowing thick as thunderheads from its engines, and lightning from dying electrical systems dancing along its fuselage. Its energy cannon lit up the gloom, brilliant as celebratory fireworks as it stitched the Sevicha's fuselage from nosecone to tail assembly.

The flaming Sevicha tumbled from the sulfur-soured sky in a flat spin, bathing the polar slopes below with ruddy orange. I couldn't tear my shaken sight from its comet of flame and smoke as it plunged toward the mountainside. Its impact hurled burning wreckage across the steep snowfield.

"You are… clear, Lead," Rinn said. His voice sounded calm in my earphones, though his last word ended in a gurgle.

My gaze wrenched up from the crash site in time to see the damaged Rohr wobble slightly, then level out to glide smoothly into the darkness.

"Lift him on the shoulders of air spirits," I whispered. I only got that far before my throat closed. I swallowed but had to mouth the rest of the words without sound. "Let him ride upon them to bear him safely to his destination."

"Lead? Five? Do you copy?" a male voice, I had no idea whose, yelled through my earphones. I started and flinched.

"This is Catcher Lead, I copy." Vision still fixed on the roiling distance into which Rinn's fighter had disappeared, I choked on the next words. "Five is lost."

"Copy, Lead. Calling CSAR." The voice barely penetrated the fog of my grief.

I broke my shocked stare only when my capsule's continued rotation swung the mountainside out of my sight. I swallowed once more and squinted upward.

One corner of the glider wing remained bent, not completely unfolded. *Damaged?* I wondered again. I gave the control stick a sharp nudge.

The stick responded, but I saw no reciprocal movement from the folded steering flap. *Not good.*

Gritting my teeth against a twinge in my neck, I leaned as well as I could in the confines of my pressure suit and harness to study the terrain below.

I hung above the west face of Devil's Comb, the mountains dividing the polar cap. Every slope appeared to be a glacier flowing into the ocean. *Can't see any good places to land even if I could steer the capsule.*

As I had on Ardonar, I murmured the Chalca Pilots' Chant. The whole chant this time, not just the last part I'd sung as a benediction for Rinn. I chanted with a different purpose now. "O, Ancient Ones who formed the winds, who gave the Mother Worlds breath, lift me on the shoulders of air spirits. Let me ride upon them to bear me safely to my destination."

More confident in the chant now than I'd been the first time I had to eject, I repeated the prayer and let go of the control stick. I guided the air spirits with tremulous hands, directing them to send a gust to the glider's bent steering flap. *If it's strong enough, it should straighten the joint and lock it.*

The flap remained useless. The glider resisted my efforts. Its wing slapped at the wind like a child in a tantrum, and it continued its leftward list. My capsule swung above snow-layered slopes pockmarked with the Sevicha's smoldering debris, still issuing coils of black smoke.

My heart clenched once more. *Rinn had my back even when he knew he was dying.*

Contemplating his dogged loyalty prompted concerns about the rest of my flight. *What happened to Kota? And Go and Chitsa and the others? Go sounded all right when she called me…*

I'd ejected from my fighter at an altitude of about twenty thousand spans. A check of the altimeter noted the capsule had descended less than one hundred spans since deploying its glider.

Impatience knotted my fists on the controls. *I could drift up here forever. Need to get to the ground so SAR knows where to pick me up.*

I tapped my helmet's comms switch. "CAOC? Catcher Lead."

No answer. Nothing but white noise crackled in my helmet speakers.

My heartrate had begun to steady by then. Apprehension stepped it up once more. *Hopefully they've evacuated by now. Just hope SAR launched first.*

When I'd ejected above Caerden's Stroma Mountains, I'd detached the glider wing on approaching the peaks' timberline to keep it from getting hung up in the trees. The nironnium capsule had crashed through boughs, bounced off trunks, and trundled halfway down the mountainside before it caught in a cluster of saplings. A wave of queasiness hit me at the memory.

Can't do that here. There's nothing to stop it from rolling a few hundred ranges into the Black Channel. Time for the egress pack.

I doublechecked my pressure suit's backup datalink and telemetry before manually shutting off the capsule's. *Don't need SAR wasting time tracking the capsule.*

I bypassed the overhead clamp that released the glider wing and flipped open the shield cover beside it. Two red handgrips lay behind the cover. *I've only done this in routine training, never for real.* Taking a deep breath, I seized one grip with each hand and tugged.

Another explosion jolted me, though not with the same violence as the first ejection. This one jettisoned the capsule's canopy and glider wing and launched me clear.

With my attention flicking from the altimeter reading, spinning down in one corner of my faceplate, to the sheer peaks rearing like an askuk beneath my boots, I free fell. I couldn't hear the wind wailing past me, though it whistled in the valve where my oxygen hose had been connected. Every loose end of my harness straps fluttered so rapidly they blurred. My heart accelerated as if to keep up, hard as boots pounding inside my ribs, and drove my respirations with it.

At five thousand spans AGL, I yanked the D-ring. The parasail, orange as flame, streamed from the egress pack behind my helmet. Tilting my head back, I watched its full length unfurl above me and watched it blossom as wind caught and filled its rippling folds. I closed my eyes and set my jaw against its abrupt deceleration.

When the parasail settled into a normal descent, my heart began to slow once more and I opened my eyes to survey the surrounding peaks. The wind had begun to carry me south, a few hundred spans above and loosely paralleling the crest of Devil's Comb. Unlike the line of volcanos farther north, this range erupted only with avalanches of snow or fractured mountainside and flowed only with glacial ice.

Still can't see any good places to land.

At the mountains' base, where the glacier spilled onto a tundra, it had hit an obstruction. A surge had compressed it, buckling and cracking the ice floe before it broke through. Later movement had opened the fractures into crevasses I estimated to be an arm-length or more across. Many of them stretched the whole width of the glacier.

Got to try to get past them to the tundra. It's flatter there, better for the SAR lifter.

As the features below my boots gained clarity, I shifted my thoughts to post-landing tasks, as I'd learned to do in Survival School.

With any luck, SAR will find me inside an hour. It'll be dark by then, but I've got signal flares in the survival vest. On landing, I'll improvise a shelter from the parasail and plant a triangle of flares around it to mark my location.

Gliding about a hundred arm-lengths above the glacier, I realized I'd stopped reciting the Pilots' Chant. I resumed at once. "O, Ancient Ones who formed the winds, who gave the Mother Worlds breath, lift me on the shoulders of air spirits. Let me ride upon them to bear me safely to my destination."

The parasail dipped on a downdraft. I worked the suspension lines, fighting to regain enough height to reach the tundra, to bypass the fractured glacier.

The downdraft persisted, strengthened.

"Bear me safely to my destination," I pleaded.

Approaching the surface far short of my intended site, I found the slope steeper than it had appeared from above, maybe 60 degrees, and dusted with recent snow. Even in the deepening twilight, I could make out the glacier's rumpled surface, the cracks across its width. I steered the parasail toward the flattest area I could see.

Two minutes later, my boots struck ice. No chance for the ankle-knee-hip-roll landing we regularly practiced. Deep tread or not, my boots shot out from under me. The left one caught in a crack that wrenched my ankle and twisted my fall onto my side. I struck hard on my hip and elbow. My gasp clouded my faceplate.

The parasail deflated as it settled over me. Half tangled in its suspension lines, I slid sideways. I scrambled, clawing for handholds, but the nubby ice evaded my grasp. I fought to brake myself with my feet, but my boots' tread found no purchase.

Snow swept my faceplate, obscuring my vision, and my helmet struck something hard. It jerked me around so I slid feet first, on my belly. My momentum increased.

If I can't stop, I'll slide into one of those crevasses. The thought slammed my heart to full throttle again.

The icepack grew rougher. That decreased my speed, but it pummeled my chest and abs. Thankfully, the layers of my pressure suit absorbed the worst of it. I reached for chunks of ice to stop myself, but some split off to tumble with me, and others tore from my grip.

Still clawing, still flailing, I skidded into the first fissure.

Its walls, jagged and irregular, bore layers and pockets of stones and gravel. My left foot struck something that twisted my already strained ankle. I closed my teeth on a yell.

Half a heartbeat later, the same protrusion slammed into my left kneecap. I felt something rip and twist. Cold sweat welled on my face, and my vision tunneled. Reflex would've driven a scream from me, except I couldn't draw enough breath.

As the shock through my knee ebbed, and my vision cleared, I fought to expand and fill my lungs.

The effort produced a crushing ache in my ribs, but it drew in very little air. Anxious but not panicky, I sucked what I could in through my mouth.

Several seconds of focusing on breathing calmed me, though my heart still hammered too fast and hard in my chest. I forced myself to focus on my situation.

With my helmet's faceplate pressed to the ice wall, I couldn't move my head to look down. I had no way to estimate the fissure's depth, except that I felt nothing beneath my boots. I had enough space to shift my right leg forward and back a few thumb-widths. Given the pain up and down my left one, I didn't try to move it.

Even that small movement caused me to settle. *Better not do that again.*

The bubble helmet allowed me to peer up, at least. The fissure's rim loomed a couple thumb-widths beyond my fingertips. I stretched to reach it with both arms first, then one.

My egress pack shifted. I settled again. Only about one thumb-width, but enough to increase the pressure on my ribcage. I reflexively gasped.

Rising apprehension sent sweat oozing across my upper lip. *What if I slip all the way to the bottom? Don't even know how deep this is. What if I get jammed in so tight I can't breathe at all?*

The relentless pounding in my left knee sent me from one fear to another. *Feels like the whole joint's torn apart. What if it's so bad it permanently grounds me?*

Oddly, that last thought shocked me into some degree of clarity. *Got to get out. Be careful. Try the suspension lines.*

I twisted the lines around both bulky gloves and tested them with as strong a tug as I could in the narrow space. The parasail must have caught on something. I couldn't hear it sliding on the ice, and the lines stayed taut.

Gripping them like a climbing rope, I dragged myself up a thumb-width or two. Enough to pull in a full breath, though my ribcage felt crushed. Enough to send a new explosion of pain through my left knee. Enough to grasp the rim with both hands.

The lines had sawed into the ice, serrating the rim. I tried to stretch my hands beyond the weakened area.

The rim crumbled and gave way under one glove. Icy fragments rolled down on my shoulder and head, blocking most of my sight. A chunk the size of my helmet fell, pinning my left arm to my side. I tried once to free it and succeeded only in slipping farther into suffocating tightness.

My right hand still reached the lip. I tried to pull myself up one-handed, first gripping the edge, then by the suspension lines. The effort made my lungs ache, sent new shocks through my knee, and left me dizzy.

Relax. Save your strength. You'll slip farther. Be patient, I counseled myself. I closed my eyes to focus on the Warding Chant while I dragged in one scant breath at a time. I tried breathing through my nose to warm the icy air seeping through my helmet's valve, but my mouth kept involuntarily opening as if to capture every molecule of oxygen.

The onset of shivering puzzled me. *Something's wrong. The pressure suit with its thermal lining is rated for the absolute cold of space.*

My mind wandered. I wondered what had caused my missile to hang up. *Did I miss a warning indicator during weapons check? Will the Crash Board blame me? Will my injured knee permanently ground me?*

My knee's throbs matched my heart's increasingly labored rhythm. My right hand, still holding onto the edge above my head, grew numb in its glove. My breath came raggedly through my chattering teeth, and I could no longer remember, for the sake of all the worlds, the last few phrases of the Warding Chant.

* * * * *

Chapter Nineteen

Between pain and deepening cold, I'd lost track of time when the vision came.

I strode for a long time across a nighttime waste, like I'd once seen on Tempest after a tornado had flattened every scrubby tree and shriveled brush. Except this wilderness had gray-black soil and rock, like ash and cinder, not the familiar sunbaked russet, and I shivered in sunless cold.

The sky held no stars. Or maybe the ashy thickness of the air blotted them out. *Is this still Tobe?*

I followed a dim light, wavering on the distant horizon. After what seemed hours of never coming any closer to it, I found myself kneeling in a circular ceremonial lodge. I had no memory of arriving there, but I felt grateful to be out of the desolate chill, in a place of peace after the empty Dark.

I wore only the white, belted tunic of sacred ceremony, and I knelt in the spot reserved for an enclave's chief chanter. I felt no surprise at my clothing, nor any sense of being out of place in the chanter's position. I only felt unprepared.

A series of shadows briefly dimmed the square entry in the lodge's ceiling as my predecessors descended through it one by one. They came on a log ladder with rungs smoothed and polished by millennia of leather-shod feet and formed a half-circle before me.

Huyana shuffled forward first, as she had in my shaman vision. In her gray robe with its long fringes, she might've been Gram's sister, except thinner. Her loose hair, white as winter, fell well below her waist, and the fresh scent of rain wafted about her.

She skirted a fire, burning gently in a circle of stones, to squat before me. "My strength and skill lay in chants to water spirits." She set her ancient hand upon my head. "I have been sent by Star Father to give you, Wanikiya, the powers of water I held in my time, to give life to our people. Learn the chants that call its creatures and its spirits, and when you lack for wisdom, ask."

She smiled reassuringly before she resumed her place.

Wahsapa, younger than Huyana and clad in brown tavo fur, stepped forward next. Her eyes, large and beguiling, reminded me of Derry's mischievous Intel Rogue smile.

She reached to stroke the flames before she knelt to place her warm hand on my head. "Star Father has sent me, Wanikiya, to give you the powers I held, to work with fire and the spirits who wield it. You must teach Anataqa to use them, too. They must be handled with great care to bless our people."

After her came tall Langond, his face painted green and blue. The fragrances of freshly turned soil and growing plants hung about him.

His work-roughened hand lay heavy on my head when he said, in a voice like tumbling gravel, "Under Star Father's direction, Wanikiya, I pass on to you the powers of earth and its spirits, for the strength and fortitude of our people. Do not become discouraged in your labors with them."

Do not become discouraged with earth powers, or with our people? Or both? I puckered my forehead, but he straightened and returned to his place in the circle before I could ask.

Chatima followed, distinguished by his beak-like nose, as prominent as Mogen's, and the cotton whiteness of his long hair. Feathers lined his sleeves, imitating a bird's wings.

The feathers brushed my face when he lay a tremulous hand on my head. "From Star Father," he said, "I give you, Wanikiya, the powers of air, and communion with the spirits of all the creatures that inhabit it, to lift our people's eyes and souls to the Sacred Mountain."

Watching Chatima shuffle to his place, I felt stronger and calmer, but no wiser.

Cheveyo followed them, clad in the ivory armor I'd worn for my wedding. When he put his broad hand upon my head, he said, "By the instruction of Star Father, I give you awareness and insight to protect our people. The time of their greatest danger is coming. Never slacken in your study of tactics and strategies, and of men's minds, that you may keep them safe."

Even in the vision, I stiffened at the phrase I'd heard all my life. I thought of Demothi, always ranting about "the time of greatest danger," and the enigmatic revelations in my encounters with him during my TDY to Tempest several moons ago.

Only two moons ago. Feels more like six or seven.

"What is the time of greatest danger?" I asked Cheveyo before he could step away. "When is it coming?"

"You will know when it comes," Cheveyo said. "Be patient and diligent."

When he returned to the circle, I expected Shaman Shiye to follow. I didn't recognize the sturdy man who worked his way down the ladder instead. He seated himself cross-legged in front of the Ancient Ones, facing me over the low fire, and studied me for a long time. I gazed back, searching his eyes, his mouth, the shape of his face, for any hint of his identity.

At last he smiled, and approval glittered in eyes like flint beads. "Son of my daughter's daughter," he said, and I detected pride in his quiet voice.

"Grandfather," I whispered. My great-grandfather, actually. Gram's father, who'd made the Crossing to Tempest to escape Pahana's War of Extermination more than a century ago.

He affirmed it with a small nod. "I chanted the tales of my people and my life in the link my daughter gave you," he said. He indicated my chest, where the leather bag lay beneath the white tunic. "They can teach you much about the dealings of men with one another."

"Teach me what you learned, Grandfather," I requested.

His smile widened a bit, and he chuckled as he stood. "Listen to the chants, my son. It's very important for you to listen." He touched my head as the Ancients had, with great fondness. "I sang them for you and our people of your time."

He glanced back once, from the ladder, before disappearing through the square entry hole.

Obediently, I removed the link from its bag and scrolled through its contents.

Then Shaman Shiye was there. He didn't use the ladder. He simply stood before me in the shaft of light slanting through the entry. His fiery sun headdress illuminated the lodge, gilding every stone in the curved walls with a golden hue, making the symbols painted on them appear to breathe.

Meeting his gaze, those dark eyes that knew every particle of my soul, but whose depths revealed only understanding and compassion, I swallowed in abrupt realization. *The one other time I met Shaman Shiye face-to-face, I'd also had a fighter destroyed out from under me, had to eject, and been wounded. Is it a coincidence, or is there a reason for it? Is this going to happen every time he has something important to give me?*

I didn't dare ask. I let my head droop. "I'm not prepared for this, Shaman Shiye."

"You will increase in knowledge and understanding," he said, "when you need it enough to *ask* for it. You cannot bear all of it at once."

I opened my mouth, about to protest, but he raised a hand to still my impatience. "Be as a child, my son Wanikiya, humble and teachable in all things." He smiled, an expression of deep, fatherly affection. "And learn patience." He touched my head as each of the others had, and I felt his soul warm mine. "Be at peace. I am always with you."

* * * * *

Chapter Twenty

A voice in my earphones abruptly closed the vision.

"There's his parasail, but where's he? Catcher Lead, do you copy?"

The shifting of heavy fabric rustled in my helmet speakers. I couldn't see their movement in the darkness, but the suspension lines twitched against my right arm when somebody raised the parasail.

Light flooded my icy trap, snow spilled onto my helmet, and a different male voice swore. "His glove!"

"Akuleh?" A female voice pierced my earphones. *"Can you hear me?"*

Doc Moseva. Relief rushed me. I tried to say, "Yes," but the pressure on my chest produced only a sound like a baby kosa's squeak. Unnerved, I gulped.

"Relax," Doc said from somewhere above me. *"We'll get you out, but it's going to take a few minutes. We have to anchor ourselves first."*

"Copy," I tried to say, but managed only another squeak.

"Blast it, Akuleh," Doc said, *"how in all the worlds do you keep getting yourself into situations like this?"*

I didn't attempt to answer.

The SAR team's chatter filled my helmet speakers.

"Kren, we need to put in a bunch of ice screws, to secure us as much as him. Three arm-lengths away from the edge, I think."

"Right," a younger voice answered. *"Looks like the edge's starting to crumble already. More could go about the time we get close."*

For the next few minutes, while I shivered in deepening cold, I heard and felt the vibrations of power drills driving ice screws into the glacier. I counted eight. Each sent a fresh cascade of frosty pebbles onto my helmet.

Then came the *chink* of safety-harness tethers snapping onto the screws, and the parasail scraping across the ice before its suspension lines grew taut.

"Got you, ma'am," the younger voice said.

I detected more movement on the ice, sounds of pushing and grating, before a glove closed on mine. I seized it.

"Good." I heard relief in Doc's voice. *"We've got you, Akuleh. Be patient."* She squeezed my hand and released it.

About all I can be. That's easier now, though.

Two pairs of bulky gloves swept ice chunks and snow off my helmet. I grimaced behind my tinted faceplate at sudden blue-white light glaring from far overhead.

For an instant I thought I'd returned to the interrupted vision. In the next, I realized the silhouetted shapes crouching above me bore no resemblance to Shaman Shiye or the other Ancient Ones. Brief disappointment swept over me. *It's only the lifter's searchlight.*

When one pair of hands uncovered my left shoulder, my arm sagged. I fought for enough breath to utter one syllable, but it sounded like a shaky whimper. Mounting distress covered my face with a new film of sweat.

Doc grasped my hand again. *"Akuleh, are you injured? Squeeze my hand once for yes, twice for no."*

My ankle had gone numb, but my knee throbbed so hard it made me nauseous. I squeezed once.

"Head or neck?" she asked.

I gripped twice.

Use dot code, said Shaman Shiye's familiar, silent voice in my mind.

I squeezed two words on her hand. "Left knee."

The too-bright spotlight behind her made a silhouette of her head, so I couldn't see her face, but her hand tightened on mine. *"Is that dot code?"* I heard her concern through my helmet speakers.

I gave one urgent squeeze.

"Mikel, do you know dot code?"

"Yes'm," said a bulky shape, also starkly black against the light, and a larger glove replaced Doc's around mine.

"Left knee hurt bad," I squeezed out.

"Got it, sir." Mikel let go of my hand and huffed out a breath. I wished I could. *"We'll take care of your knee, but we need to protect your neck first. Kren, stand by with the collar."*

Ice creaked as bodies shifted, and someone leaned into the fissure between me and the spotlight. I watched heavy gloves release my helmet's toggles before they lifted it off.

Frigid air smacked my face, but I couldn't even gasp. I shut my eyes against the spotlight's searing brilliance and gave in to shivering so violent it sent pangs through my injured leg.

A large hand, warm from being in a glove, pressed my neck beneath my jaw. "Pulse is twenty-two, ma'am," Mikel said after a minute.

I knew by the nearness of his voice he'd removed his helmet, too. I opened my eyes and found him hanging over the rim so his broad face hovered less than a span above mine.

Some light-blurred shape handed him a padded collar, and Mikel said, "I'm going to tuck this into your suit's neck ring to immobilize your C-spine." He worked it into place with the same practiced briskness as my suiting crew in Life Support.

172 | D.T. READ

Prompted by that, fear for my crew rushed me. *Sure hope they got out.*

The fear deepened to a sick feeling. *Rinn.* I longed to groan my grief.

The collar cupped my chin, keeping my head up enough to reduce my teeth chattering.

"Now, sir," Mikel asked, "can you swallow? Blink to answer."

I blinked once.

"Good." He twisted briefly toward the rim, then faced me again, holding a thumb-width-long metallic capsule between his medical-gloved thumb and forefinger. "It's a biometric sensor. We need to monitor your vital signs for hypothermia. I'm going to poke it down your throat. Got that?"

He didn't need to explain about biometric sensors. I'd had to swallow one every day during my recovery after I'd been shot down on Ardonar. Nor did he have to ask me to open my mouth; I was still breathing through it.

His thick finger triggered my gag reflex, making me gulp.

"Sorry, sir." Apparently assured I wouldn't puke, Mikel gave me a wicked grin. "Better than poking it somewhere else."

I shuddered at the thought, glared at him, and blinked, "My knee."

"Yes, sir."

The biometric capsule must have started providing readings right away because Doc Moseva said, "Mick, we need to get him on heated O2 ASAP."

"Yes'm," Mikel said. "Kren, make sure the faceplate valve is clear before we put his helmet back on him."

Moments later, Mikel leaned in once more. "I'm going to cover you, sir, to keep the cold off. Then we'll give you some warm air."

It'd help if I could actually inhale it, I thought, but I could only blink acknowledgment.

Mikel reseated my helmet on the neck ring and locked it down. "Now, the O2 canister."

Another figure appeared on the lip, a small oxygen canister tucked in the crook of one arm. Obviously shorter than Mikel, he had to lean into the fissure almost to his waist to reach me.

The edge promptly collapsed under him.

I heard his yelp, but Mikel said, "You're all right, Kren, that's why you're tethered." He swept fresh snow and ice off my helmet. "Where's the O2?"

Kren wrestled to open the oxygen bottle's airflow for a couple seconds before he reached in to connect its short hose to my faceplate's valve. Warm air with a faint metallic scent hissed about my nose and mouth. I strove to drink it in while Kren strapped the canister to the side of my helmet.

When the two medics withdrew from the fissure, Doc took my nearest hand again. *"Getting some air now, Akuleh?"* she asked through my earphones.

I squeezed her hand.

Mikel said, "Let's get him on the backboard."

As tightly as I was wedged into the crevasse, they found no space to slide it in behind me.

"We need to get rid of his egress pack first," Mikel said. "Maybe his survival vest and shoulder holster, too. We need to start with hoist lines."

He and Kren dangled into the fissure once more, trailing sturdy cables that ended in carabiners. I heard the *chink* as they locked into my pressure suit's shoulder rings, and squinted up as well as I could.

Two lines, pale in the searchlight's beam, stretched into the darkness, quivering in a wind. At the edge of my vision, red and green strobes blinked at the blunt tips of abbreviated wings, and a massive rotor churned the overcast. *How high's the lifter?*

Armed with combat utility tools, Mikel and Kren sliced through as much of my survival vest and egress harness as they could reach and tugged them out piece by piece. As the narrow space opened, I sank a couple more thumb-widths, causing a new jolt to my knee before the cables took my weight. I couldn't even gasp.

Something slipped off my shoulder and brushed my right leg as it twisted into the fissure. I didn't hear it hit the bottom.

"What was that?" Kren asked.

"Piece of his holster strap," Mikel said. "I've secured his sidearm. Get the backboard."

With a few more thumb-widths of space, I managed to draw a breath. My exhalation rattled in my voice pickup, and Mikel asked, "Doing all right, sir?"

My ribs felt as if I'd been run down by a double deuce cargo hauler, but I said, "Fine." I didn't squeak that time.

Both medics had to shove repeatedly to push the board into place at my back. That tightened my breathing space and left me wheezing again.

"Sorry, sir," Mikel said. "Arms tight to your sides now." He reached in to tuck them firmly against my body.

When Kren squeezed the trigger grips at the backboard's head, tie-downs snaked out. Steely bands plowed through the ice wall to lash around my helmet, torso, and limbs, like a python tree's tentacles about unwary prey.

I winced at their tightness across my bruised chest. *Like the ejection harness again.*

"Ready, ma'am," Mikel called.

"Copy," Doc said, and addressed somebody aboard the lifter. *"Brandt, ready for extraction. Slowly, he's injured."*

"Roger that," a distant voice carried through my earphones, and something tugged from above.

The moment my chest cleared the crevasse, allowing me to suck in my first full breath since becoming trapped, my left knee met the protrusion again. Pain lanced through my entire leg like forked lightning. It tore a reflexive scream from my throat, and my vision spiraled into darkness.

"Lay him down!" somebody shouted. Doc, I thought. As they tipped the backboard horizontal, the spinning void retreated, and she asked, "Akuleh, can you hear me?"

"Knee," I gasped and swallowed pain-induced nausea. The sweat of shock beaded about my nose and mouth. I gulped once more and fought for air.

Blurry shadows swaddled me in heavy coverings and cinched them tight. Doc's voice swam in my awareness. *"Anchor One, two to bring aboard."*

"Standing by to receive."

A thrumming roar overwhelmed all else in my earphones. Red and green lights strobed across my sight. Snow like storm-driven sand raked my faceplate, and the tugging sensation began again.

Hands seized the head of the backboard, drew me sideways into a steel cubicle with lights overhead, and somebody said, *"I have him, ma'am. Now you."*

Three sluggish heartbeats later, a blond medic hunched above me, his brow creased and mouth set as he unlocked my helmet's toggles. He maneuvered it off and said, "You are safe now, sir," in an accent like Rinn's.

My heart contracted. I squeezed my eyes shut.

* * * * *

Chapter Twenty-One

The medic pressed an oxygen mask to my face. Heated, moist air brushed my nose, and I sucked it in, only remotely aware of him stretching the mask's band around my head.

"Elevate table and activate molecular scanner," Doc ordered from somewhere outside my line of sight. The surface on which I lay rose, the medic at my head scrambled from a squat to his feet, and Doc leaned in to grip my shoulder.

Something heavy *clanged* aft of my boots, and Mikel called, "Team secure, ma'am."

Doc acknowledged with a nod in his direction, snapped her harness onto a ring above the table where I lay, and tapped her headset's voice pickup. "Anchor One, hatch secure, patient secure. Let's go."

The table tilted with the unmistakable swoop of a lifter climbing. When its flight leveled off, Doc reached across to flip a switch on a console beside me and laid her hand on my shoulder once more. "All right, Akuleh, let's check you over."

With my head and neck still immobilized, I couldn't see the molecular scanner's ring make its full pass from my head to my feet. I watched Doc's brow crease instead, as she scrutinized her tri-D display.

"Good, no spinal injury," she said after a short silence and visibly relaxed. She squeezed the backboard's trigger grips, and its tie-downs retracted like a handful of snakes releasing me simultaneously and slithering away. "But your left patella is completely dislocated. It'll require surgery."

"Patella?" I scrunched my forehead.

"Your kneecap." She hesitated, seeming to consider, then said, "We'll discuss it in detail later. Right now..." She shifted to address her medics. "Kren and Brandt, get him out of his pressure suit and collar and into the thermal wraps while I check our other patients. We'll have to splint his left leg, but he'll need a neural block first.

"Mick, I'll need you to help me start an IV and meds." She met my eyes at last. "We'll have you more comfortable in a few minutes, Aku-leh." She patted my shoulder and slipped away before I could ask about her other patients, or even say thanks.

The activity and voices about me seemed more remote and surreal than my recent vision. After Kren tugged the brace out of my neck ring, Brandt took a laser cutter to my pressure suit. I glimpsed ruby flashes against its dark surface, first down my torso, then along my arms and legs. I could only imagine the bitter scent rising on the fine tendrils of smoke because the oxygen mask blocked it.

Kren unzipped my flight suit, Brandt cut away the crewshirt beneath it, and the shivering that had begun to ease resumed. I caught a glimpse of purple bruises crisscrossing my chest, in the pattern of my cockpit harness, before one of them tucked a heated blanket around me.

That brought instant comfort, a sense of safety as much as physical relief. The shivering eased after some seconds, and I finally relaxed.

Doc returned and took my head firmly between her hands, so they blocked my peripheral vision. I felt certain their placement was intentional; she knew how I felt about needles. "Mick, let's get the IV going," she said. "Use the internal jugular. It'll be easier to find than an arm vein while he's so cold."

Internal jugular? I stared up at her.

Mikel peeled the blanket back and unrolled a bundle of bluish cloth across my bare chest with a flick of his wrist. A cold, wet pad swabbed the base of my neck, making me shiver, and a steely shaft glinted in his gloved fingers.

Doc shifted my head away from the corpsman and stroked my forehead with her fingers. "What happened with your fighter, Akuleh?" she asked. "What forced you to eject?"

I flinched at a brief pinching sensation near my collarbone. "Tried to fire a missile," I said through the oxygen mask. "It jammed, didn't leave the rail. It was active, started counting down to detonation. My computer couldn't stop it."

My mind took off and ran with the question. *What made it jam? That's not unheard of, but...*

Doc's brow crimped as she let go of my head. "Are you all right, Akuleh?"

I swallowed. "I'm fine."

She adjusted the IV canister on the hook above me. Warmth began to ease my tension. "That'll help you relax and breathe more easily. I don't want to use a painkiller strong enough to put you out right now. We'll put a neural block in your hip instead."

"Go ahead," I said.

"We'll have to turn you. It'll hurt."

"Jus' do it." The drug, already taking effect, induced a slur.

"Brandt, Kren, support his leg," Doc instructed. "Mick, help me shift him."

Hands closed in and maneuvered me. I locked my teeth against a yell. My breaths hissed between them instead. I glimpsed the glow of Brandt's laser cutting my flight suit and shorts.

"Scanner up." Doc muttered, "Zoom in, zoom in... There's the sciatic. Mick, the clip."

Another chilly pad swabbed my hip. I winced when something sharp pressed into it.

The agony in my knee and ankle stopped as if switched off. I let out my breath in an open-mouthed rush under the oxygen mask—and grimaced at the pang through my ribs.

Multiple hands returned me to my back and tucked thermal wraps about me once more. I relaxed again in the gentle heat enveloping my goose-fleshed skin. *Caterpillar in a cocoon.*

"Mick and Brandt, get a splint on his leg," Doc said. "Kren, put warming mitts on his hands. Then I'll need an assist in berth two."

She returned a few minutes after the others left, put a slim hand on my shoulder, but kept her gaze on what must've been a monitor behind my head. "Feeling better now?"

"Ya," I sighed. "Thanks."

"Good. Your vital signs are starting to stabilize." She patted my shoulder. "You were mildly hypothermic, probably from breathing cold air through your helmet's valve. You'll be all right, but you'll need surgery to repair your knee."

Knew it. I couldn't bring myself to ask about the implications of a dislocated patella for my future prospects in the cockpit. My mouth had dried out. "Thirsty," I said instead.

"Just a sec." She left the cubicle and returned with a drinking bottle. One hand lifted my head slightly, and the other drew the oxygen mask from my face enough to put the tube to my mouth. "Sip it slowly," she said.

Not likely. I slurped the warm water until she gave me a warning frown, withdrew the bottle, and replaced the mask.

"Two minutes to vortex," the pilot's voice crackled from an unseen speaker.

"Team!" Doc called. "Make sure everybody's secure and strap yourselves in."

"Vortex?" My eyes involuntarily widened. "What about my squadron?"

"We've got four, including you," Doc said, cinching straps around me. "There's another SAR ship inbound."

My guts twisted. "How many? Who else?" When she hesitated, I said, "I'm their commander, ma'am. I need to know."

"Not right now, Akuleh. They'll be fine." She tightened the suspension line from the overhead hook to her safety harness and fixed her gaze on the monitor I couldn't see.

"Where are we going?" I asked.

"Carmaux Military Hospital, on the coast of Canutama on Satha. It's near the equator."

I knew the lifter had entered the vortex when a tremor shook it. I closed my eyes.

"Nausea?" Doc asked.

"No, ma'am," I said, my jaw taut. "I just really don't like vortices."

A random image tickled across my mind, of Derry running in darkness, her face pale with evident anxiety.

She hates walking through vortices as much as I dislike flying them. Is that a memory? Please, Ancient Ones, don't let it be prophetic. I choked on dryness.

The lifter pierced "the wall" with a heave much milder than my fighter's usual buck. *Or was that my heart?*

"Ma'am." I had to say it three times to make myself heard, to get her attention.

I must have appeared to be in distress, because she asked with obvious concern, "What's wrong?"

"Derry," I said. "What happened on Solienne? Did you hear anything before you launched?"

Doc Moseva released my shoulder to grip my nearest hand in its mitt, somewhere in the layers of thermal wraps, and her expression grew grave. "I notified her unit when I learned you were among the downed pilots," she said. "I requested immediate orders for emergency leave."

Her slim fingers tightened on my hand. "Right after I sent it, we learned Solienne was under attack, with Supremacy forces landing in major cities around the planet. Her commander acknowledged, but I got nothing else. I'm so sorry, Akuleh."

The thoughts that had struck on my way to the squadron resurfaced. The chill coursing through my body had nothing to do with hypothermia, mild or otherwise.

* * * * *

Chapter Twenty-Two

My dreams returned me to the battle above Tobe. Again and again, I watched Rohr-55s and Sevicha-9s engaged in their deadly aerial dance without any way to intervene. I heard my flight mates' voices in my ears and tried to shout warnings, but no sound issued from my throat. I saw Manoq's fatal spiral to the surface. Heard Rinn report damage and injury, and watched his cannon rip the incoming Sevicha apart before his ship vanished.

I woke in a cold sweat.

When I slept again, I recognized Derry emerging from the depths of a swirling tunnel. She ran toward me, her features more determined and angry than terrified. She clutched a bundle to her chest I knew to be our son, though I couldn't see his face. As she drew nearer, she reached for me with one hand. "Kew!" she called, her voice anxious.

Though she kept running, she remained beyond my outstretched arms. Her voice swelled in intensity and rose in pitch until a baby's wail pierced the nightmare.

My mind flashed to Survival School, and the overloud loop of recordings to which we were subjected during a night locked into pourstone cubicles not much bigger than vertical coffins. There had been wailing songs accompanied by screechy, stringed instruments, a furious tirade by Osaga Safa, a young woman pleading for mercy from her tormentors, and a crying baby. The screaming baby had always roused me from sleeping on my feet.

The baby's weary, persistent howls finally penetrated my groggy sleep. I blinked awake into darkness and an unfamiliar humid heat. Shifting my head toward the source of the sobs, I winced at the ache in my neck.

Two women stood outside my half-open door, blurry shadows in the dim lighting. Fragments of a hushed conversation made it through the baby's ongoing cries.

Finally, the woman holding the baby stepped into the room and pushed the door shut. It doused all light but the amber and green ones flickering on the medical monitor above my head and the wall chronometer's red digits, which read 0154. Just enough light to reveal her silhouette near the bed's foot, but I would've recognized her even without her Caerdish crooning.

"Derry." The relief flooding my soul made me choke on her name. I shoved myself off the bed, grimacing at numerous jabs and twinges through my body, and staggered. It took a second to find my balance on my good but startlingly weak leg and the injured one, numbed and useless in its brace.

"Kew!" She lunged and reached out to steady me. I encircled her and Garnan in both arms.

They smelled of jungle sweat, baby urine, and sour-milk puke. The monitor's blinking lights—which had quickened with my effort to stand—revealed tendrils of limp hair trailing loose about Derry's face, pack straps still snug on her shoulders, and a wet stain down her rumpled uniform front. I held them tightly. "Are you all right, little bird? How did you get here? What happened?"

Garnan's squall swelled, growing more insistent, and his miniature arms and legs flailed and pushed between us.

"He's in despera'e need of feeding and changing," Derry said. She released me with a kiss that promised more later and a hand on my arm to maneuver me back to sit on the bed before she placed Garnan on the mattress where my leg had been propped minutes earlier. Shrugging her backpack off, she said, "Thank the Ancien's we didn' lose his things along with everything else."

"What happened?" I asked again.

She rummaged a few items from the pack and changed Garnan in the dark. "The lumpies captured Solienne." She had to raise her voice to be heard over our infant's wails.

My insides knotted. *All of Solienne. Which means Osfelga. Where's Mogen? What happened to him and the royal family?*

"We had na warning," Derry continued. "They exited vortices on the parliamen' grounds in the hear' of Reskagen. Platoons of foo' soldiers, no' attack ships as they did on Ardonar."

My arm hair rose with sudden gooseflesh. "How did you find out?"

"The newsne's covering Parliamen'. We had the vid on in the office. They were broadcasting live when soldiers stormed into the chamber." She glanced up, her expression and voice grim. "Every newsne' wen' dead within seconds."

Every parliamentarian's probably dead, too, I couldn't help thinking.

"They sounded emergency sirens in the city—"

I interrupted. "Any word about the royal family?"

Derry shook her head and her eyes met mine, barely visible across the darkness. "No' afore the newsne's wen' down. I'm verra sorry, Kew."

Mogen. My heart sank. "How did you get out?"

"Erzie's reques' for emergency leave. I' arrived momen's after the sirens began. Commander Wismond wasted no time. He sen' two officema'es to help us gather our things and said to go direc'ly to the terminal and someone would come confirm my orders."

Finished with changing Garnan, she scanned the dark room for a trashcan, deposited the used diaper in it, and washed her hands in the compact basin in the corner. "Firs' chance to wash all day," she said with a tone of unmistakable relief.

Garnan's howls hadn't diminished with one discomfort eased. Derry scooped him up and sank into the deep chair beside my bed, crooning, "Hush now, hush now."

I hauled my braced leg onto the mattress with both hands and sagged against the pillows to watch her, absorb every long-missed detail of her as well as I could in the dimness. The smooth curve of her cheek and small nose in profile. Disheveled hair quite a bit longer than I remembered it. Slender fingers nimbly unfastening her uniform blouse and bra. The rounded fullness of the breast she uncovered.

When Garnan's hungry wails succumbed to eager suckling noises, she pressed a kiss to his mussed head and asked me, "Where was I? I mus' be rambling. I'm righ' exhausted." She muffled a yawn with her free hand.

"People from your office went to help," I said. "What about your mother and Donny?"

"Aye. Mum was waiting. There wasn' much to do bu' pu' Donny and Garn in their coats and grab our go-bags. I' was verra wise to have them." She smoothed Garnan's hair with gentle fingers while she spoke. "I' took rather longer for the crawler to come 'round."

My jaw tightened. *That long crawler ride. Never did feel good about it. Now I know why.*

"I' was good we lef' sa quickly," she went on. "We saw Security Forces on the move even whils' heading to our house. When we started back, they'd a'ready set up check poin's.

"The crawler stopped a' the main ga'e, and security troops with rifles and helmets wen' through, checking everyone's ID. They held up the crawler for *ten minutes* over Mum and Donnol's refugee status. A middle-aged woman and a child, I ask yew!" Indignation stiffened her tone.

"They stopped us again a' the terminal doors, but Master Spacer Leis was there with my orders. She explained, and they le' us in.

"Tha's when everything wen' dodgy," Derry said. "They'd cu' orders for Garn and me, bu' no' for Mum and Donnol. I showed the portal agen' their refugee forms on my link and told her I was their sponsor sa they *had* to come, but because they weren' on my orders she wouldn' budge. She was abou' to power down the portal.

"Then there was crashing a' the fron' doors, and a lumpy squad broke through." Derry lifted her head to meet my gaze again. "Supremacy soldiers at Belsken Field. I saw their uniforms, Kew. I've no idea of their intentions, bu' they opened fire in the terminal."

An icy fist punched my gut. *My family in the crossfire.*

Her breaths quickened with her next words. "I did the only thing I could. I had Garn in his pack on my fron', inside my parka, sa I caugh' Donny and Mum by their hands and ran headlong into the portal."

What I saw in my dream. More ice trickled down my spine.

She hugged Garnan tightly enough to disrupt his suckling, and he whimpered. "Sa close," she whispered as she relatched him, and for the first time I heard a tremor in her voice. "I' was sa terr'bly close, Kew."

I slid out of bed again, but with my leg braced I couldn't crouch beside the chair. I could only lean in enough to kiss her sweaty hair and stroke her cheek with my fingers.

"I'm a' righ', Kew," she murmured after some moments. "We're a' righ'." Still, when I returned to the bed, she got up onto it beside me and snugged in close.

I wrapped my arm around her. "You lost everything?"

"My valise and Mum's," she said, "when I caugh' their hands to run the portal. Donny was wearing his own knapsack. I' was a good thing he had spare clothes. He and Garn both go' sick in the passage."

"Did the vortex bring you directly here to the hospital?" I asked.

She shook her head against my shoulder. "I' was a terminal in the mountains, like the one yew described, looking like i' was buil' of shipping crates. I though' we'd taken the wrong portal until I spotted other evacuees.

"Only two more people came through after us." Her voice dropped to a shaken whisper. "They said the lumpies had seized the Belsken Field terminal. They didn' know if they'd even make i' through the vortex."

But they entered it anyway. Rather risk an uncertain vortex than the lumpies. My blood chilled, and my vision sank to Garnan when he stirred in Derry's arms. *What if…*

I couldn't bear to think about it.

"We waited five or six hours for them to bring a transpor' up the mountain," Derry said. "Naugh' to ea' or drink bu' wha' Donny had in his knapsack, and he shared mos' of i' with the other children.

"We watched whole units, fifty or sixty soldiers a' a time, come charging ou' of one portal and into the other, faceplates down and rifles a' the ready. I gave up counting after fourteen squads. Carried on for two or three hours, i' did.

"When the transpor' came a' las'," she said, "i' was a bulky thing with grea' tires, made to creep along a switchback track full of boulders and fallen logs. I' bounced and lurched like flying through heavy weather on Tempes'.

"I' took another two hours to travel fifty ranges. All the children were sick and crying by then. Hospital staff were waiting to help when we arrived, bu' Erzie brough' me here to you straightaway."

"I'm thankful she did," I said. "Where are your mother and Donny?"

"In a facili'y the hospital se' up for the refugees," Derry said. "There's food and beds and showers. Mum and Donny are likely sleeping by now."

When Garnan also fell asleep mid-meal, Derry eased him into my arms, rose, and retrieved a pale bundle tucked into the armchair beside her. "I'm in despera'e need of a good wash-up," she said. "Erzie len' me a med-tech's scrub suit to wear sa I can ge' my uniform cleaned, and she showed me the ladies' shower down the corridor. Back in a bi', love."

I settled my child on my lap when Derry left the room, held his tiny hands in my fingers, and studied his sleeping face. He'd filled out in the two months since I'd seen him last, with chubby cheeks and a smoother tan shade to his skin.

Phrases from his Birth Chant whispered across my mind.

My son Hiamovi, called to be the high chief who will raise our people from the dust and lead them in the Light. How do I prepare you for that, little man?

How did my father prepare me to become Wanikiya?

I reflected on my father. How he'd carried me around on his shoulders when I was small. How he'd patiently taught me the first chants and simple rituals. How he'd included me in his chanter duties as much as he could and expressed his confidence and trust in me. *I never doubted for a second that he loved me, even when I needed disciplining.*

I gathered Garnan up in both hands and buried my nose in his abundant black hair. *Oh, Shaman Shiye, give me enough time with him. Help me be for him what my father was for me.*

Garnan stretched full length, almost out of my hold, and yawned. When I returned him to my lap, his eyes opened wide. He stared up at me, unblinking as babies do, and I remembered his searching gaze the night I'd pronounced his Birth Chant.

Then he beamed ear-to-ear and reached for my face with his miniature hands.

I chuckled. "Love you, too, little man." *You have no idea, son, how much I love you.*

Derry returned minutes later, ghost-pale in the gloom. She wore the borrowed gray scrub suit and had twisted her damp hair up in a claw clip. "Horrid humidity," she said. "I showered in cool water and toweled off twice, and I'm still dripping."

"You can wrap up in my robe," I offered, and grinned. "I'll even rub you dry."

She gave a light laugh. "Only if yer robe's still got yew in i'." She settled beside me on the bed once more.

When her head lolled on my shoulder a couple minutes later, I knew she'd fallen asleep.

It took me longer. Her story and my concern for Mogen left me staring for some time into a darkness full of narrowly avoided horrors.

* * *

We both started awake at a rap on the door and blinked groggily when Doc Moseva stepped inside. The wall chronometer read 0642, and daylight oozed between the window blind's slats. Derry gathered Garnan from my lap, rose, and moved away from the bed.

Doc eyed the vital signs monitor. "How do you feel, Akuleh? Did the patch help you sleep?"

"Yes, ma'am," I said, and smiled. "Slept better after Derry got here, though."

"I thought you would." She appeared satisfied. "We'll keep the intracath in place until after your surgery, but we can remove the IV and oxygen lines now." She proceeded to remove them as she spoke. "I don't want you on your feet at all today. Keeping your knee and ankle elevated will help reduce the swelling."

Too late, I thought, but said obediently, "Yes'm." I rubbed my upper lip, where the oxygen line had made it itch. "What about my squadron?"

"I'll fill you in on them later," Doc said. "Right now, we need to talk about what comes next for you."

Something about her tone and the gravity of her features gave my empty stomach a twist. I returned her gaze and waited.

"You've got a strained ankle and a dislocated kneecap," she said, "not to mention massive contusions caused by your harness during ejection. The ankle strain is minor. Last night in Trauma, we injected a regen. Tomorrow you can start putting some weight on it.

"Your knee, as I said aboard the lifter, will need surgical repairs. We'll do that tomorrow morning. By tomorrow evening, we should be able to get you on your feet and let you try it out."

"Good," I said. "Why not do the surgery today?"

"Because," Doc said, "even mild hypothermia, which is what you had, can compromise one's heart. There's an increased risk of complications for a while, even for athletic people like you. Your EKG looks good—" she indicated the silvery discs adhered to my bruised chest "—but I want to give you a standard day to be sure."

I rolled my eyes.

"Back to your knee," she said. "With the appropriate regens and physical therapy, we can expect complete healing in three months."

I gaped at her. "*Three months?* It didn't take that long for my arm injury to heal."

"You had minor tendon damage in your arm," Doc said. "Whatever you hit in that fissure completely tore your patellar ligament. You would've been better off if you'd fractured the patella itself. Soft-tissue injuries require more time to heal."

"Three months," I murmured and ducked my head. The guilt I'd felt at leaving the battle resurged. Half angry, I lifted my head to face her again. "How can I be any kind of squadron commander, ma'am, if I can't fly for *three months?*"

"Akuleh." Doc's voice softened. "You can't. I'm very sorry. This is going to permanently ground you."

My heart seemed to stop. Every muscle in my body stiffened. My breath felt more painfully crushed out of me than it had in the crevasse.

Several endless seconds passed before the shock lifted enough for me to speak. "You said the same thing about my arm, ma'am."

"I told you then it *might*," she reminded me. "The Medical Review Board thought it should've. Detailed examination of your molecular scans, however, made it clear your injuries fell short of the criteria for mandatory grounding. Barely. They finally accepted my request to wait for the results of rehab."

"What's the difference this time?" My words poured out, a plea edged with desperation. "You just said it'd be completely healed in three months. I'll do whatever it takes." *All of it, all of it, all of it.*

"I know you will." Doc's voice remained quiet, an attempt to soothe. "Unfortunately, according to Soliennese military medical regulations, a fully separated, torn, or severed tendon or ligament makes grounding mandatory, regardless of the outcome."

Shock resettled, amid disbelief as smothering as smoke. I sagged on my pillows.

"I'm very sorry," Doc said once more, and I saw in her eyes how deeply she meant it. She gave my hand a firm squeeze before she left the room and closed the door.

On my life.

* * * * *

Chapter Twenty-Three

Derry returned to her place on the bed and placed Garnan, gurgling and kicking, on her lap. She'd grasped my hand before the door even snapped shut.

I didn't draw mine out of hers, but I didn't respond. I couldn't. My lungs felt wrung out within my ribcage.

"Nobody messes with my piloting career!" I'd once shouted in an empty pilot-school briefing room. "*Nobody's* taking this away from me!"

The same helpless fury swelled from the pit of my stomach as it had then. My jaw hardened, my hands fisted—

"Ah! Kew!" Derry jerked her hand free of mine.

Wrenched to the present, I saw pain in her startled eyes. "I'm sorry, Derry. I didn't mean to hurt you." My words came without sound.

Her features softened, her eyes reflecting my distress. "Would you like some time alone, love?"

I hesitated. My humiliated half wanted to withdraw into permanent isolation. The other half ached to grip Derry's hand like a lifeline until the internal storm surge ebbed.

"Ya," I sighed at last.

She rose. Collected Garnan. "I won' be going far," she said, her voice still quiet. "I need to go to Mum and Donny and see how they're doing." She stroked my scruffy cheek with one finger and bent to kiss my mouth. A long kiss, meant to comfort.

I stared unseeing at the door when it closed behind her.

My one-time defiance echoed in my head. *Nobody messes with my piloting career. Nobody's taking this away from me!*

I have taken it from you, Wanikiya, my son.

The silent voice in my mind held the same benevolent firmness my father's had when he'd released a hunting knife from my two-year-old fist before I could cut myself with it. I'd squalled with frustration in my belief he'd stolen the shiny blade from me.

"Shaman Shiye," I whispered from my tight throat. "Why?"

It would have been better for you to give it to me willingly, but you would not.

I stiffened in comprehension. "*You* made the missile hang up, so I had to eject and… get injured again."

I did not cause the missile release to fail, my son. I allowed the action taken by another to be completed.

A fleeting glimpse materialized of Huritt dashing in from the flightline, of his smirk when he saw me, and his sloppy salute. I gaped.

He is also my son, Shaman Shiye said. *His life is also in my hands.*

Resentment simmered in my soul, toward both Huritt and the Ancient One whose voice remained infinitely patient in the face of my indignation. I ducked my head, curled my hands, and wrestled with my bitterness.

Out of it swelled another memory, that long conversation with Gram after Hanuk's death.

"Sometimes," she'd said, "the Ancients require sacrifice. Sometimes, when the outcome is very important, sacrifice is the only way."

"They sacrificed their lives," I'd replied, referring to my parents, and returned my vision to her. "What will I have to sacrifice?"

Recalling it, something fell into place. Understanding replaced my anger. *Piloting has been* my *life.*

Humility followed. "Shaman Shiye," I whispered, "is it my piloting career? Is that the sacrifice you want from me?"

That will be the hardest sacrifice, Wanikiya.

I found reassurance in the soundless words. I nodded and let out a breath. "I'm giving it to you, Shaman Shiye." *And my soul. All of it.*

* * *

I don't know how long I lay there afterward, my sight fixed on the palm-shaped ceiling fan while winged insects butted a random staccato against the window, but a degree of peace gradually settled over me. When the door's latch clicked, I shifted my sight in time to see it open.

Chanter Wahkan stepped inside, his expression tranquil, and crossed to the chair Derry had occupied earlier. "How did you injure your knee, Akuleh?"

He'd asked the same thing after my hands were burned in my damaged cockpit during the battle at Nichi. I'd felt embarrassed to talk about it because it'd been so stupid. I hadn't even thought to use the Chant to Extinguish Fire. *Feels like a decade ago. He's guided me through a lot since then.*

"Had to punch out of my fighter," I said. I described the incident in a few sentences.

"When will they perform the surgery on your knee?"

"Tomorrow morning." I added, more calmly than I would've believed possible a couple hours earlier, "Doc says it'll permanently ground me, though."

Wahkan nodded, appearing thoughtful. "I see. I'm sorry to hear it. You've done very well as a combat pilot. You've proven yourself many times."

I couldn't keep some part of my mind from doubting him. *I've lost two trainees, a handful of my friends, and yesterday I abandoned my flight in the middle of the battle.*

"Derry told me," the chanter said, "after you came home for your son's birth, that you felt you should return to Tempest soon. She said you were planning to apply for the Qaletaqa when you completed your commitment to Solienne."

"I did apply," I said, and paused in surprise. "In fact, I was accepted." *Was it just yesterday the message came?*

I had to backtrack through recent events to confirm it. "Ya, yesterday. But Commander Teichert told me before I submitted the application that I'd been stop-lossed and MinDef would have to approve my separation."

Wahkan gave me a knowing smile. "So someone with greater power had to intervene." The glint in his dark eyes made it clear he meant someone with *far* greater power than Solienne's Ministry of Defense.

I hadn't considered being medically grounded from that perspective, but I motioned at my elevated knee. "This might keep me out of the Qaletaqa, too."

"Perhaps Star Father and Shaman Shiye have reasons other than the Qaletaqa for you to return to Tempest."

I nodded. "I used to think that part of my life was still many years away, but now I think it's a lot closer."

When Wahkan cocked a black eyebrow, I told him about my conversation with Shaman Shiye before his arrival.

"Ya," he said. "It's not too soon to begin preparing." He pushed himself out of the deep armchair with some effort. "We must take care of your injured leg first, however."

Mildly puzzled, I watched him remove his oil-paste cup from the pouch he wore on his belt. He drew the glyph for healing on my brow and immobilized knee before he rested his right hand on my head. Tipping his face toward the textured ceiling, eyes closed, he began the

Chant to Salve Wounded Flesh. The same one he'd performed for my burned hands.

Healings are exorcisms as much as blessings. I mentally steeled myself against the memories I knew the chant would scour from my mind. The fireball of Nawat's fighter in the minefield. The tarry mass of Yobo's fighter on the runway. Rinn's fighter diving in to destroy the Sevicha before it drifted out of sight. I didn't try to suppress my groans.

I'd accompanied my father often enough as a child to know the words and intonations. I mouthed them with Wahkan while he petitioned the Ancient Ones for the cleansing of my soul and the restoration of my body.

"This injury will not keep you from accomplishing what will be required of you in the future," Wahkan said when he finished, and he gave me an enigmatic smile. "Those requirements and your future begin right now."

Without explaining, he hobbled to the door and stepped outside. I heard a couple heavy bumps before the door opened once more, and he guided a floatchair into the room. "There are people who need you."

"Need *me*?" I puckered my brow.

"Get in, you'll see." He maneuvered the chair as close to the bed as he could.

"Have you cleared this with Doc Moseva?" I asked.

Wahkan's smile widened a bit. "She approved on condition that you stay in the chair, and I don't keep you out too long."

I cinched my robe's belt securely about my waist before I levered myself from the bed into the chair. Jabs through my sore muscles and aching ribs prompted a few flinches and gasps. Seated at last, I found a control on the armrest to raise the left footrest to support my leg.

"Do you have the leather bag your grandmother gave you?" Wahkan asked next.

No bag lay on my chest, hanging from its age-yellowed cord. My gut clenched. *They took it off me in Trauma last night. I sort of remember, but where...?* "Check the bedside cabinet," I suggested.

Wahkan rustled through the cabinet's drawer for a few moments before he placed the little pouch in my hand. "We'll need your oil-paste, too," he said. "Is your cup full?"

I opened the miniature container and eyed its contents. "Not full, but there should be enough."

"Good." Wahkan opened the door.

The floatchair had none of my fighter's maneuverability. I had to push and twist the stubby control stick to get it to respond, and then narrowly missed Wahkan's knees in my efforts to clear the doorway. I puffed a frustrated breath. "Handing over controls to you, Chanter. Looks like mine need some maintenance."

He chuckled and gripped the handles on the chair's back.

Unlike the military hospitals in Golmolor and Osfelga, the corridor into which he steered the chair wasn't a sterile passage with wide door-ways at intervals along both sides. Instead, the wall facing my door consisted of transparent panels from floor to ceiling. They provided a view of dew-beaded foliage splashed with flowers in blink-inducing shades of red, purple, and yellow.

"A terrarium?" I asked. "Can you push this thing closer, Chanter?"

Wahkan accommodated me. Studying the contained forest, full of twisting vines and blossoms shaped like flying birds, while he strolled, I heard him say as if to someone else, "There are many chaplains here for personnel from other worlds, but we are the only ones for our people."

"We?" I twisted in the chair to question him with my stare—and cringed at lightning across my strained shoulders.

"You have power to perform the Chant to Relieve Pain of the Body and the Chant to Induce Healing Sleep, don't you?" Wahkan asked.

"Yes, but nothing else."

He immediately stopped the floatchair and placed his warm hand on my head once more. "By the word of Star Father, Akuleh of Masou clan, I bestow on you power to assist me with all the healing chants we may require."

As if oblivious to my open-mouthed surprise, Chanter Wahkan halted the floatchair at a half-open door four down from my own and poked his head into the room. A moment later, he returned to steer me inside.

I recognized the man sitting in the bed as Intermediate Officer Kajika from Arrow Flight. His Obollan buddy, Tabansi, rose from the armchair to greet us.

Kajika's half-open robe revealed the same inky bruises that crossed my chest. He'd also had to eject.

"How are you doing, Kaj?" I asked while Wahkan positioned the floatchair near the bed.

Kajika grinned and indicated my leg with a jut of his jaw. "Better than you, it looks like, sir."

"Bad landing zone." I managed a smile. "Your flight had the hardest job, I think."

"Your element kept the lumpies off long enough for us to do it," Kajika said.

I felt a fresh stab of guilt. *My element. I wasn't even there to lead them for most of it.*

Wahkan rescued me, whether he knew it or not. "We came to offer you a healing chant, Kajika."

"Thank you, Chanter." Kaj shifted against his pillow. "I never knew punching out could bruise you up so much, but Doc says I'll be back in the cockpit in a phase."

Another pang lanced my soul, but I meant it when I said, "Glad to hear it."

"I didn't know you were a chanter, sir," Kajika said when I drew the healing glyph in oil-paste on his forehead. His Obollan friend raised curious eyebrows. Both had arrived on Tobe after my chant to clear the ashfall.

"Chanter's apprentice." I glanced at Wahkan. "This's all I have the power to do right now."

We performed the Chant to Salve Wounded Flesh and moved on shortly afterward to another Chalca pilot from Arrow Flight then one from Saber. Both bore the bruises of ejection. After we performed the healing chants, they and the friends sitting with them described what they'd seen of the battle.

Two doors farther down, Kota shifted his head heavily away from the vidscreen flickering on his wall when my floatchair scooted into his room. Bands and a sling snugged his left arm tightly to his bruise-ribboned chest.

Puzzlement creased my forehead at finding him alone. My innards knotted. *Where's Go?*

* * * * *

Chapter Twenty-Four

I forced away my apprehension and said only, "Kota. What happened to your arm?"

He blinked briefly, as if trying to focus, before his eyes opened wide. "Ku!" Relief swept his face with an attempted grin, and he said, "Broken collarbone. Yuma's beard, I *hate* ejecting!"

His second time, too, I remembered. I said, "Goes for me as well."

Wahkan snugged my chair up next to his bed, and Kota reached out with his good hand to clasp my shoulder. "Doc said they picked you up, but she wouldn't say anything else. What did you do to your leg?"

I returned the shoulder grip, but we mussed each other's loose hair up instead of whacking each other's backs, due to the bruises. "Doc wouldn't tell me anything about any of you, either," I said.

Kota let his hand fall into his lap. His gaze dropped, too. "We lost a lot of people, Ku. A *lot*." He shook his head. "Mogen's trainee, and the new one from Satha, and—" his eyes met mine for a split second "—the big one from Golmolor." The deceased didn't have to be Chalca for us to avoid speaking their names.

We lost Arturo, too? For the second time in a couple hours, I felt as if some massive creature had stomped the air from my lungs.

"The one from Golmolor," I said. "I saw it happen." I bowed my head against a new constriction in my throat. Of all the pilots in Lance

Flight, in 1st Squadron, I'd never thought we'd lose Rinn. I would've pegged him for the next squadron commander.

He died protecting me. He always protected me. He was that way from the minute we became roomies in Basic, teaching me how to snap bedsheets and fold uniforms like an automaton. I thought of how he'd spurred me through physical therapy with his imitations of our training officer, Russom. *He never lost his wry Golmolan sense of humor.*

Kota's face bore the same lines of distress I knew were etched on mine, but he told me, "Doc said they recovered his body. They'll return him to his family."

"Good," I said, and nodded.

Kota seized my nearest hand and wrist with his good one in the ancient Chalca warriors' clasp. We gripped each other hard for several seconds.

Only then did I dare to ask, "What about our classmate from Fuago Mono and her trainee?"

"Chitsa was injured," Kota said. His voice steadied. "She got some bad burns on her legs. Go said she was going to stay with her."

"Glad to know Go's safe," I said, and shot a wordless question at Chanter Wahkan before addressing Kota again. "Why don't you come with us?"

Wahkan nodded approval. "It will be good for you, Kota."

* * *

We rode a lift four levels to the ground floor.

"The more serious injuries are here," Wahkan said. "We'll go to the burn unit first."

Go came to the partly open door when Wahkan peeked inside. Spotting Kota and me in our floatchairs, she gave a slight bow. "Yes, yes, please come in, all of you."

Chitsa lay on her back, her bandage-foamed legs propped on a bolster under the sheet. She stared at me when Wahkan maneuvered my chair close to her bed.

I tried to emulate the chanter's tone when I asked, "How did your legs get burned, Chitsa?"

"My fighter took a hit, sir," she said. "It didn't seem too bad. I finished the battle."

I remembered her reporting she had damage.

"She got, um, two more kills after she was hit," Go said, and I didn't miss the pride for her trainee in her eyes.

Chitsa's expression grew self-conscious. "I made it through the vortex, but something exploded in my nosecone when I landed. The flames came up my footwells."

The same way my arms got burned, I thought. *She's as new as I was then.*

She shifted her head away, fixed her gaze on the whirling fan overhead, and her voice diminished to a whisper. "Doc told me this morning, the burns are so deep they'll permanently ground me."

Something about her deep-brown eyes reminded me of Kimama's the night my stepmother had smacked her across the gathering room. Shock and betrayal overwhelmed the evidence of her physical pain.

"All I ever wanted," she said after a heavy space, "was to be a pilot. My older brothers taught me to fly in our Darter at home, in secret." She gave the ceiling fan a wan smile.

My heart twisted. *I know* exactly *how she feels.*

Her determinedly tearless gaze returned to mine. "I'm sorry, sir." It seemed a plea for forgiveness, as if she'd somehow failed me. "I'm sorry."

I took her hand in the warriors' clasp, as I had Kota's, and something in my soul changed. A little more acceptance of my own loss. A little more peace. An unexpected calm assuaged my own lingering ache. "It's not 'sir' anymore, Chitsa," I said. "This leg injury permanently grounded me, too. It's Chanter Ku now."

Go's eyes widened, and she uttered a tiny gasp.

Kota's good hand seemed to crush the arm of his floatchair. "Aw, no, Ku."

"It's all right," I heard myself say. "It's time for me to move forward." Kota would understand, I knew.

Chitsa didn't close her eyes while I applied the oil-paste glyph to her forehead and legs and reached out to place my right hand on her head. The movement pulled my robe's sleeve up, but I didn't realize it had revealed part of my long scar until I heard her breath catch. When my eyes flicked to hers, I saw *I knew it!* gleaming in them.

"We have others we must see," Wahkan said upon finishing the Wounded Flesh chant and nudged my floatchair out of the room. Kota chose to stay behind.

Wahkan waited until we'd rounded a corner in the corridor to switch the chair off and move in front of it to face me. "I must tell you about Lonato before you see him."

"Lonato from Arrow Flight?" I asked. A few years older than me, he'd pinned on master officer about the same time as Mogen. "What happened?"

"His fighter took many hits and went down near your base in flames," Wahkan said. "The SAR team expected to recover a body.

His fingers and toes, and the structures of his face are gone, his lungs are scorched, and his pressure suit adhered to his flesh." He took a breath. "There is nothing the surgeons can do but ease his pain."

Lonato. I braced myself, dreading the sight of an unrecognizable blackened and blistered form with wounds seeping vital fluids.

We couldn't enter his isolation room even in sterilesuits. A long viewpane, studded with voice pickups set high in the white-painted wall, allowed the only contact. The curtain inside had been drawn, but even if it'd been open, it made no difference from the floatchair. The pane's lower frame lay more than a span above my head.

Wahkan drew close to the viewpane and cleared his throat. "Chaplains for Master Officer Lonato," he said in Standard.

I heard movement inside, and Wahkan reached for my arm. "You'll have to stand, Akuleh."

Do I have to? Really don't want to see this. I clutched the window frame to steady myself on my good leg.

A Sathi woman wearing a sterilesuit parted the curtain a few thumb-widths. "Oh. It is good you have come now," she said. "He is dying. Do your people have last rites?"

I peered past the woman. Glimpsed not a charred, vaguely humanoid shape, but a pale figure like a statue with its face unfinished, a bandage-foamed mummy trapped in a tangled web of tubes and wires. A monitor tracking a spiky green line snagged my eye.

"Not last rites," Wahkan said.

A longing sensation rose in my chest, aching as if my own soul struggled for release. *He wants permission to make his Crossing.* I didn't know how, but the understanding came clearly. *The Chant of Merciful Death. It's all I can do for him.*

Gripping the window frame, I began to chant, "Be calm, wild spirit, be at peace. May your spirit rest in beauty. May your spirit rest in peace. May your spirit find the gentle path to the Sower of the Stars."

I'd used the chant when butchering shegruls as a youth, to calm the creatures and dull the brief pain of pithing them. *Is it wrong to use this for a human? A squadron mate?*

The deep longing compelled me to continue. I sensed Wahkan's stare, but he made no attempt to stop me.

I repeated the chant four or five times before the tension in my ribcage eased. When I drew a breath to start again, the spiky line across the monitor gradually flattened.

"He is gone," the Sathi physician said after a moment.

"He is free," I replied in Standard.

My vision swam, and I swayed.

Wahkan intercepted, caught me at my armpits, and eased me into the floatchair. "Akuleh?" His voice held concern.

"Just really tired." I leaned forward as far as I could to lower my head to my knees. It took several seconds for the dizziness to pass and my shaking to subside.

Wahkan sank to his heels and scrutinized me once I'd carefully straightened. "That was an unusual thing you did. How did you think to sing that particular chant?"

I met his eyes. "I could feel him pleading to be released. It... just came."

Wahkan nodded, thoughtful. "Very kind," he said. "Sometimes chants aren't meant to heal." He paused. "There's one more casualty. Do you have enough strength?"

"Give me a couple minutes," I requested, and concentrated on drawing full breaths to steady myself.

"You know this one," Wahkan said. "Huritt of clan Hevovitas."

I stiffened, and my vision briefly spun again. *Huritt. The one who sabotaged my missile.* My gut wrenched. I stared at the chanter.

"He has a neck injury, severe whiplash." If Wahkan saw my shock, he gave no indication. "The flight surgeon says he'll make a full recovery, but it grounded him, too."

My teeth clenched. The anger of a few hours earlier pushed aside my newfound calm. *Huritt tried to kill me. Again. I'm supposed to offer* him *a healing chant?*

His life is also in my hand, Shaman Shiye had said then. His silent voice added, *You see him only through your own eyes, Wanikiya. I have as much purpose for him as I have for you.*

Bewilderment, then shame, riddled my soul, but I needed several more seconds before, chastened, I agreed. "All right, Chanter."

Wahkan guided my floatchair into a new corridor and through another door.

With his head and neck enclosed in a helmet-like brace, I wouldn't have recognized Huritt if Wahkan hadn't already told me who it was.

He shifted his eyes when Wahkan addressed him—and spotted me. He paled, his square jaw slackened despite the close frame, and horror edged his eyes. Then his mouth curled in its usual sneer. "Come to gloat, Sheggy?"

A few months ago I would've, without hesitation. Now I said, with a composure that surprised me, "No, Huritt. We came to offer you a healing chant."

He glowered. Questioning me. Questioning my motives. I saw it in his knotted face muscles.

"The shegruls have lost their wings," I said. "All of them." I jutted my chin to indicate my knee. "Would you like a chant?"

A long space passed before he tore his gaze away from me. I scarcely heard his whispered, "Ya."

He squeezed his eyes shut when I drew the healing glyph on the small portion of his forehead that wasn't covered and set his mouth in a hard line when I placed my hand on the helmet's smooth crown.

"O Ancient Ones who made us," I began, "who know all our pain, who know our souls…"

Through my own closed eyes, I caught a fleeting glimpse of Huritt standing in a slanting shaft of light at the mouth of a smoke-blackened cavern.

* * * * *

Chapter Twenty-Five

By the time we departed Satha, four days after my knee surgery, my physical therapist had cleared me to use a knee brace and crutches.

"I don't need that," I said when an aide entered my room with a floatchair.

"It is our standard procedure for safety, sir," the man said. Like the female physician in the burn unit, his Standard bore a local accent thick enough to cut with a *pelu*.

Derry, wearing her laundered uniform and her hair up in a regulation twist, helped me secure the knee brace over the leg of my flight suit, which Doc had returned cleaned and sewn back together.

The aide proceeded to buckle me into the floatchair.

"I'm not going to fall out of it," I told him.

"There will be two vortex passages," he said and repeated, "It is our standard procedure for safety."

I rolled my eyes at Derry. She smothered a smile and cinched Garnan snugly to her chest in his baby pack.

Her mother and Donnol joined us in the hallway outside my room. We exchanged greetings and hugs, but the aide tapped his wrist chrono impatiently.

The women followed my floatchair while Donnol stumped alongside. "Guess wha', Kew? We got to play in the ter-*air*-ee-um!" He sounded out the unfamiliar word. "They've a pool with fish this big—" he held his hands a span apart "—and we threw food to them."

I chuckled at his excitement. "I'm glad somebody had some fun here."

In another few strides, he grew anxious. "Where are we going? Will we ge' to stay together?"

"We're going to Tempest, my homeworld," I said.

I didn't know the answer to his second question. The message disseminated by Commander Teichert two days earlier had mentioned only a temporary recovery base some distance from Awénasa City.

Tropical heat, heavy with moisture and redolent of local flora, enveloped us like steamed towels when the hospital doors hissed apart. I blinked in bright sunlight.

Carmaux Military Hospital had its own shuttle pad. An ovoid craft, blurred by shimmers rising from the tarmac, waited several armlengths away, its ramp lowered.

My family and I joined the boarding queue behind Go, who accompanied Chitsa in her floatchair. Chitsa's footrests had been raised to accommodate her bandage-foamed legs, but she appeared in better spirits than when I'd seen her last.

"How are you doing?" I asked her.

"Much better, sir—uh, Chanter Ku." She gave me a shy smile. "I've decided to stay in the Aerospace Force when I'm healed, and cross train into a new specialty. I'm considering logistics or intelligence."

I motioned at Derry. "My wife can answer questions about intel—except for the classified stuff."

Derry smiled. "I'd be happy to."

The shuttle carried us to an orbital military base much like Shemmon Station, where we boarded a personnel transport. Besides 93 wounded military members, the most serious of whom would travel in sickbay, the passenger manifest included 442 non-flying personnel from Tobe, 85 military families who'd been evacuated from Belsken Field, and 14 mortuary transfer cases draped in the national banners of the deceased.

Everyone, military and civilians alike, stood at solemn attention—or sat at attention, for those of us strapped into floatchairs—while the transfer cases were loaded. I noted Lonato's, borne by a Chalca honor guard, with somber interest. A covering of golden tan, representing Awénasa Territory, had been emblazoned in crimson with the glyph of his home enclave.

When the honor guard emerged from the shuttle's cargo bay bearing a casket with the Golmolan flag secured crisply around it, I had to swallow renewed tightness in my throat. *Rinn. Carry him home, spirit birds, to the Sower of the Stars.*

* * *

The transport flight took about four hours. I held Garnan close to my chest and rubbed his back through the first vortex, a smoother passage than I'd ever had in a fighter, but he wailed the whole way.

When the pilot announced our approach to the second one, Madam Graebel reached across to me. "Here now, Kew lad, and le's see what a granny's touch can do." She eased Garnan from my arms.

"Bes' take his towel too, Mum," Derry said, peeling it off my shoulder.

Cradling and rocking and crooning to Garnan proved no more effective than my efforts had. Halfway through, the scent of half-di-
gested milk permeated our seating area. The towel caught it all, but
Donnol said, "Ew-ww!"

I couldn't resist a roguish grin at my mother-in-law. "He didn't do
that to me."

Tempest had only one passenger space station, the hub for its min-
imal spaceliner traffic, but its staff was prepared to berth our military
transport. A handful of ambulance shuttles waited to transfer the
stretcher patients and caskets to the surface before the rest of us filed
to commercial craft in groups of fifty.

Ours made a solid landing with no bounce. I squinted out the oval
window into the glaring light of autumn's early evening and searched
for landmarks. *Wonder where we landed?*

"Welcome to Manaba Outpost, Tempest," the pilot's voice rang
through overhead speakers, "headquarters of the Qaletaqa Militia. Local time is…"

Qaletaqa headquarters! My heart leaped. Then it dropped to my stomach. *What if the knee injury eliminates me when I report for training?*

Under the weight of Tempest's higher gravity, our group shuffled
from the bowl-shaped shuttle bay and bunched together, as if to support each other, in front of two civilian officials bearing readpads.

"Military personnel on medical orders," said the woman in charge,
"will board the transport at my left—" she waved at it "—when I read
your name. You'll spend tonight at Manaba Outpost Hospital, where
your cases will be reviewed by your assigned physicians.

"All civilians and non-patient personnel will take the other transports to on-base Temporary Lodging." She scanned the huddled refugees and said, "The transports will stop at our small Post Exchange

first, for those of you in urgent need. Please board when Alawa—"
she indicated her assistant with a jut of her chin "—calls your name."

When Derry looked toward me, I said, "While you're at the exchange, I need some basic hygiene stuff and a few pairs of shorts."
How do I keep ending up without any underwear?

"Righ'." She grinned and bent to give me a quick kiss. "We'll see
yew tomorrow then, love."

A medic steered my floatchair aboard the hospital transport and
locked it in next to Chitsa's.

A snort from my left drew my attention across to Huritt, who'd
been brought aboard ahead of us.

"What are your plans now, Hevo?" I asked.

The helmet-like brace he'd been wearing when I saw him last had
been replaced with a smaller one, but he still couldn't turn his head
very well. "I'm taking the disability pay and getting out," he muttered.

Jaw set, he shifted to face the seatback in front of him and stared
at it so long and hard I figured he'd shut me out.

Nothing new about that. Better than his usual threats.

I turned to address Chitsa again, but not before I glimpsed uncer-
tainty, even a shadow of dread, in Huritt's narrowed eyes.

*He's concerned about the politics at home. After all I've heard about his
mother, I can't blame him. What's this going to mean for him?*

As if he'd heard my thoughts, Huritt abruptly lifted his head and
glared at me. "What about you, Sheggy? Are you going to stir up your
insurrection now?"

I met his glower. Held it with my own. "I'm not an insurrectionist,
Huritt." *But Shaman Shiye may lead me to become Wanikiya sooner than I
expect if the Qaletaqa reject me.*

* * *

I spent the night in an open-bay ward with fifteen other soon-to-be released patients. Higher gravity or not, I breathed Awénasa's dry air more easily than the humidity-laden stuff at Carmaux. Still, my mind tumbled with *What ifs*, so I didn't sleep well.

Shortly after dawn, a Chalca medic poked his head through the gap in my privacy curtain and said, "Sir, you have a meeting in Consultation Room One in half a sun position."

"A meeting? About what?" I flung the sheet off. "Where're the showers?"

"The meeting is with Qaletaqa Command," the young man said. "The showers are out the door to your right."

Half an hour later, wishing I could ditch the crutches, I rapped on the split-log doorframe of Consultation Room One and said in Chalca, "Three-Talon Masou reporting as ordered." I used the Chalca rank equivalent to Journeyman in the Soli forces.

"Come," said an unfamiliar deep voice, also in Chalca.

Stepping inside, I noticed Chanter Wahkan and Doc Moseva, but my vision locked on the other two men. Taking in the glyphs for their names and rank, I stiffened to attention as well as I could on the crutches. *Feels like another Board of Inquiry.*

Three-Pinion Chuchip of clan Eznoh, chief commander of the Qaletaqa, and equal in rank to a Soliennese general of the third rung, gave me a stiff smile. He said in flawless Standard, doubtless for Doc Moseva's sake, "Carry on, Three-Talon Masou. You may be seated." He pointed with his chin at the remaining empty chair.

I sat, acutely conscious of the brace's dull gleam encasing my gray flight suit's leg, especially when the padded frame made it necessary for me to extend my leg.

Eznoh thrust his jaw toward the man at his right. "One-Pinion Heluska is chief of the Qaletaqa Medical Board."

"Chief." I acknowledged him with a dip of my head.

"It's been brought to our attention," Heluska said, sitting forward on his chair, "that approximately one moon phase ago, you incurred an injury in combat. We understand the injury has permanently grounded you from flying duties in Solienne's Defense Forces, and may prevent you from beginning Qaletaqa training on your report date of the twentieth day of the third month Interstellar Standard Calendar."

Less than two moons away. My heart sank. "*Yah-té.*"

"I've reviewed the medical record provided by your flight surgeon—" his quick glance acknowledged Doc Moseva "—and made particular note of the damage to your left patellar tendon, the surgical repair, and the results of your rehab so far.

"Are you aware that the preliminary conditioning phase of Qaletaqa training consists of climbing, rappelling, combatives skirmishes, and timed distance runs?"

"*Yah-té.*" I said it firmly, but inwardly I braced myself. I set my face in an impassive mask, my gaze locked on his.

"It's your surgeon's opinion," Heluska said, "that with a six-month deferment, the time allocated for medical leave before your discharge from the Soliennese Defense Forces, you can pass the fitness tests mandatory for entering Qaletaqa training." His dark-eyed stare bored into mine. "Do you believe you can be prepared in that time, Three-Talon?"

Hope swelled under my ribs. With every grain of confidence in my soul, I said, "*Yah-té.*"

Four pairs of eyes scrutinized me. I felt the weight of them all, but avoided making contact with any but Heluska.

He shifted on his chair, still studying me. "Then I approve a deferment of six months, reporting date to be adjusted to the twentieth day of the ninth month, Interstellar Calendar."

"*Yah-té*, Chief." I managed to keep most of my excitement out of my voice, but I couldn't wipe the grin off my face.

* * * * *

Chapter Twenty-Six

"Akuleh, I'm releasing you from the hospital," Doc said when we entered the corridor a few minutes later. She sounded stern more than pleased. "We'll talk about rehabbing your knee later. Are you comfortable with a walking stick rather than crutches?"

"Yes, ma'am!" I probably said it a little too eagerly.

"Good. I'll see you and your therapist later. You've got time for breakfast before the Commander's Call."

With one of my major *What ifs* resolved, I ate better than I'd slept, hospital cafeteria or not. At least this one provided familiar fare like shegrul bacon, eggs scrambled with chilies, maize bread, and fresh pimiberries.

Satisfied, I arrived at the hospital viditorium to find Derry already there, saving a seat for me, but she wore a serious expression. "What's wrong, little bird?" I asked.

"We've a few things we need to discuss afterward," she murmured, and pointed to the front.

Commander Teichert already stood at the podium. "Our most important reason for gathering," he said, "is to honor our fallen."

A chaplain conducted a short memorial service before Teichert presented medals. Liberty Bought with Blood medals to most of us, and a handful of Valorous Flying and Valorous Service medals. He concluded by announcing fourteen Legion of Honor medals, the highest recognition given by the Soli Defense Forces, because they were always posthumous.

One was for Lonato, whom Teichert identified as "a Chalca master officer in Arrow Flight," for drawing lumpy attackers away from the base long enough for the last support personnel to escape through the vortex. Others were presented for Arturo and Manoq, then one for Rinn, who was lauded for destroying an enemy fighter closing in on a flight mate who'd been forced to eject from his fighter.

I ducked my head. *The memory of his ship drifting off into the darkness will haunt me for the rest of my life.*

I didn't know most of the other recipients.

Following the medal presentations, Teichert said, "I also need to give you a situation update. The 15th ACW has a new base, the location of which I can't divulge here. Our mission continues with greater urgency. The Resistance Pact's leadership was evacuated from So-lienne in time, to an undisclosed world, and continues to function…"

I hope that includes Mogen and his family. I questioned Derry with my gaze.

"No word ye'," she mouthed back.

If Teichert knew, he didn't say, either.

* * *

Derry slipped her hand into mine as we joined the press of a few hundred people leaving the sandstone-walled viditorium afterward. "We need to talk, Kew."

Something tightened under my ribs. "What about?"

"My duty status. Le's go to the cafeteria. I've no' eaten ye' this morning."

"Good choice. I could use a second breakfast."

We found an unoccupied table against one white-painted adobe wall, away from most of the other occupants, but we'd barely taken our seats when Chanter Wahkan approached and asked, "May I join you?"

"Of course, Chanter," Derry said. "I was abou' to explain my situation to Kew."

Spooning a thick chili sauce over chunks of crumbly maize bread, she told me, "Commander Teicher' requested tha' my bille' be returned to the 15th, to the duty assignmen' I held before yew deployed."

"Good," I said, and Wahkan nodded.

"Bu' we've a problem." She twitched her spoon in a negating motion. "Teicher's learn' tha' my uni' a' Belsken Field, whils' destroying classified materials afore the base was overrun, disintegrated all the personnel records, too. I' was necess'ry to protec' everyone, of course, bu' now there's no proof of my clearances."

"You know there's a backup somewhere," I said.

"Aye, on Ardonar. Bu' under presen' circumstances, i' will likely take months to access them." She sighed. "Which means I'm on indefini'e unpaid leave till then."

"We'll still have my pay while I'm on medical leave." I told her about my meeting with Eznoh and Heluska.

Chanter Wahkan eyed us in turn, his expression hovering between thoughtful and faintly mysterious. "There may be a way to keep your pay as well, Derry." He shifted his attention to me. "It appears the Ancient Ones have cleared this time so both of you can prepare for your future."

A crease appeared across Derry's forehead, puckering her scar. "Both of us?"

"Your calling as Anataqa," Wahkan said, "will be different but no less important than Akuleh's. It's best for you to learn together."

The crease in Derry's forehead deepened to a furrow. "How can doing tha' continue my pay, Chanter?"

"Request education leave," Wahkan said. "Explain the matter of your clearances, and state that while you wait for it to be resolved, you plan to increase your understanding of the Resistance Pact's Chalca allies through several months of cultural immersion."

I gaped at Wahkan and actually came close to chuckling, in fact. *Is he serious?*

"Cultural immersion?" Derry asked. "And wha' of Garnan?"

Wahkan smiled. "He's half Chalca. He needs immersion, too."

The chanter returned his focus to me. "It's time to go to Yellow Rock Enclave and apprentice under Mapiya, the daughter of Chanter Yuma."

Following Wahkan's instructions, and with his endorsement as her chaplain, Derry submitted the request for education leave via her link before we left the cafeteria.

I also called Gram. "We're coming to Awénasa City this evening. Can Derry, Garn, and I stay with you for a few days?"

"I'll be grateful to have you come, Akuleh." Gram's face glowed in my link's display. "I haven't met your son. Kimama will be excited to see you, too."

A few hours later, we and Derry's family joined Kota, Go, and several other members of the 15th aboard a military aircraft to the Awénasa airfield.

Donnol, buckled between Derry and me, beamed the whole way, despite the craft's jouncing flight. He kept yelling questions through the engines' roar. "Is this how soldiers fly? Is this the kind they parachute out of? Have yew ever parachuted out of an airplane, Kew?"

"Only from damaged ones." I suppressed a shudder. *Wonder if we'll have to do it in the Qaletaqa?*

Derry and I accompanied our friends to the vortex terminal.

"I'm supposed to be your backup, Ku," Kota said, unusually solemn.

I knew he meant in my Wanikiya role. "You'll be there when you're supposed to," I said. "Star Father has a way of working things out."

We bear-hugged and pounded each other's backs.

"We will keep in, um, contact," Go said, and bowed.

Movement at the corner of one eye caught my attention as we wished each other well, and I twisted around, still expecting to see Rinn.

Two women and four men in flight suits, helmet bags in their hands, strode briskly toward us. From nine or ten arm-lengths away, I recognized the ebony complexion and piercing eyes of the man in the lead. Habit born from a year under duress stiffened me to attention. Kota and Go fell silent, too.

My one-time instructor pilot, now Master Officer Russom, chuckled. "Carry on, all of you." He studied me for a few moments. Arched an eyebrow on noticing my journeyman rank. "You've done well, Masou." His tone carried commendation. "Not surprising, though. Are you coming with us to the new location?"

"I can't, sir." My words came stiffly. I indicated my knee brace and walking stick. "Medically grounded."

Russom shook his head in evident regret and twisted to address his fellows. "This is the trainee I told you about. Underage runaway from somewhere out in the Territory." He made an all-encompassing gesture. Then he slid me the kind of smile passed between buddies with an inside joke. "I never drove any other cadet as hard as I drove him."

Sudden boldness pushed unexpected words from my mouth. "I hated your guts, sir."

He guffawed. "You were supposed to." To his companions he said, "When I saw what this young man was made of during Basic, I requested him by name to be my pilot trainee. I wasn't disappointed. I never trained a more talented or determined cadet during my whole tour of duty as an IP."

I felt every stare, including Derry's, lock on me like crosshairs on a lumpy ship. My face burned. I dropped my vision to my boots.

When Russom clapped me on the shoulder, I lifted my head.

"Pity you won't be with us, Masou," he said. "It would've been an honor to fly with you." The grip on my shoulder tightened, and his steely eyes narrowed on mine. "Keep that same will and drive, and you'll succeed wherever life takes you."

"Thank you, sir," I said.

I ached to charge into the vortex tunnel with our friends when they disappeared into its depths. I quelled the urge only by wrapping an arm about Derry's shoulders. After a few seconds of watching, we made our way to the terminal's doors.

Russom, I thought, *you have no idea where my life's already taking me.*

* * * * *

Chapter Twenty-Seven

The public transport from the airfield to Old Trade Center spooled billows of russet dust behind it all the way to Awénasa City. Flying grit rasped on the tinted windows like a small creatures' scrabbling claws. Late autumn's chilling rains would dampen the dust soon enough, I knew.

Madam Graebel, seated beside a window, stared across the craggy terrain and murmured, "I never though' to visi' this world again, le' alone come and live here."

When we exited the transport at last, stumbling with fatigue in the higher gravity, I swept the plaza for Demothi. Remembering the incident during Wanikiya Ceremony, I felt an unexpected stab of concern at his absence. *Have the Council's enforcers arrested him as a seditionist? What would they do to a crazy old man?*

"Amber Cliffs Gallery." Madam Graebel sighed on spotting the tall, yolk-yellow structure where she'd once hosted an art exhibition.

Seems like a decade ago. Aloud, I said, "Gram's shop is six doors to the left of it."

Donnol hadn't said anything, but the redness of his face revealed his increasing pain and fatigue.

His prosthetic leg or the gravity. Maybe both.

My knee had begun to twinge, but I handed him my walking stick. "If you'll carry this, I'll carry you."

He replied with a weary nod. Setting my teeth, I hoisted him onto my shoulders.

Kimama flung Gram's shop door open before we reached it and burst outside to greet us. "Ku! Donnol!" she exclaimed. "And the baby!" Beaming, she fell in beside Derry and held out a finger for Garnan to grasp.

Gram welcomed us inside with arms spread wide. She hugged everyone in turn, but couldn't tear her gaze from Garnan. Though he'd begun to fuss with hunger, Derry yielded him into her arms when Gram reached for him.

"I can see both of you in his face," she said and bounced him against her body. "Akuleh's hair, and Derry's complexion."

"My loud mouth," I said with a grin when Garnan's hungry cries grew more insistent.

"Your *eyes*," Gram said, fixing me with a meaningful gaze, and returned him reluctantly to Derry.

"You need to hear his Birth Chant," I told her.

"Dinner first," Gram said. She led us toward the stairs at the shop's rear. "All of you look exhausted."

Kimama sidled up to me as we followed Gram along the main aisle. I didn't need her elbow nudge, the thrust of her chin, or the grim narrowing of her eyes to direct my attention to an empty shelf. I'd already noticed it, stark among the ones laden with colorful tins and jars of imported teas and local honey and preserves. It lay at about shoulder height to a tall man, and it had displayed miniature hand-thrown and painted pots of healing salve.

Before I could ask, Kimama whispered, "I have to tell you about it, Ku. It's important."

Very important, my gut told me.

* * *

Gram had made my favorite maize and chicken stew, and maize bread sweetened with wildflower honey. We adults were too tired to talk much while we ate, though Kimama and Donnol chattered together.

Soon after we finished, Gram said, "Kimama, I'd like you to manage the shop until closing time."

"Yes, Gram," Kimama murmured. She slipped me a pleading expression shadowed with the same anxiety I'd seen earlier when she headed toward the stairs.

"I'll come down later," I told her.

While Gram pointed out their floorbeds to Derry and her family in the adjoining sleeping room, I removed my brace, rolled up one of the sitting rugs to tuck under my knee, and leaned against the warm wall near the dome-shaped oven. When Gram returned, she sank stiffly to the rug beside me, indicated my propped leg, and asked as Chanter Wahkan had, "How did you injure your knee, Akuleh?"

I didn't tell her what Huritt had done to the missile, just said I'd taken serious enough damage to force me to eject again. I told her about the faulty glider wing, about sliding down the glacier, and described in detail the vision I'd had while I shivered in the icy crevasse.

"The Ancients came to me again, Gram," I said. "On Ardonar, they blessed my body with the physical strengths I'll need as Wanikiya. This time, they passed on to me the powers they used during their own lives and gave me the right to use them.

"Then someone else came." I met her eyes. "The one who gave this link to you." I touched my chest, where the small leather bag hung on its cord around my neck.

Her eyes widened when she realized I meant her father, and I nodded confirmation. "He counseled me to listen to his chants and learn about men's dealings with each other, same as you told me. He said he sang the chants for me and the people of this time."

Gram nodded. "They're important for you, Akuleh. The same jealousies and rivalries that existed among our people before the War of Extermination are rising again. There are always a few who believe they should have authority over everyone else, under one claim or another."

I recalled the conversation I'd had with Gram a few months earlier, after the Wanikiya Ceremony. When I'd told her Bimisi had threatened to charge the participants with sedition, Gram had said the great chief felt threatened by what the Wanikiya prophecy meant for her ambitions.

"The ones who want to rule most should never rule at all," Gram said. "People always suffer when they do."

Her statement prompted the image of the stripped shelf downstairs. "They raided your shop, didn't they, Gram?" I asked.

"Only once." She said it in a casual manner, as if trying to make it seem trivial.

It's not *trivial, Gram.* I asked aloud, "What were they looking for? Did they tell you?"

She didn't answer at once. "Ceremonial items," she said after a moment. "That's all. You know I've never sold them, but of course they didn't believe me. They didn't spend much time looking around the shop, but they made me open the storeroom and they took a long time searching it. Then they came up here."

"Into your *dwelling?*" I stared, appalled at such violation. "Do they normally do that, invade the shopkeepers' homes, too?"

"I don't know, Akuleh." Gram shook her head. Her gaze lowered to her hands, clutched together in her lap. "They threw our belongings on the floor and walked all over them, and left them there."

Indignation stiffened me where I sat. "Were they Chalca or off-worlders? Could you see through their faceplates?"

"Both," Gram said. "The one who kept Kimama and me behind the front counter with his rifle was bigger than a Chalca, and he spoke Standard. Their leader and one of the others were Chalca. I recognized—" She cut herself off, and her features grew taut. She paused, then said, "Even with their strange electronic sound, I could tell it by their voices."

My blood iced at the thought of Great Council enforcers holding my grandmother and little sister at gunpoint. *Same thing when they attacked the ceremony. Mostly crims behind the faceplates. What do the Hevos—or crims, for that matter—hope to get out of an alliance?*

"How long ago did it happen?" I asked. Still rigid with horror and fury, I forced the words out between my teeth.

"The evening we came back from Red Wash," Gram said. "We were fortunate they didn't do worse, but Kimama is still very shaken from it."

"I could tell," I said. "I'll go down and help her close the shop. Have you had anyone come help with security since then?"

Gram nodded. "Your uncles are taking turns staying for a few days at a time. Bidzil left this morning because he knew all of you were coming, and we'd need the floorbeds."

"I'm glad they're able to come." I sank back against the wall, but I didn't relax. *Should've expected this.*

We sat in silence for a space. Then Gram managed a wan smile. "I'm sorry, Akuleh. I just wanted to hear your son's Birth Chant."

"You need to." I retrieved the ancient link from its leather bag and powered it up.

She cocked her head to listen intently. "The golden eagle is you," she said.

"I know." I paused the recording. "How can I teach my son wisdom when I need to learn it myself?"

"Wisdom comes from experience," she said. "You'll gain it as you need it."

"Hope so." I touched the PLAY button.

Moments later, Gram remarked, "Derry is the white bird. Is she prepared to become Anataqa?"

"We're preparing together." I told her of Chanter Wahkan's arrangements. "We're leaving for Yellow Rock Enclave in a few days." *Should we leave, though? How long can my uncles keep providing security for Gram and the shop?*

"It'll be good for you two to grow together," Gram said.

Her words returned me to the present. I said, "Listen to this next part."

My voice rose from the miniature speaker. "Learn from little brother creatures on the world you will know. Learn from those that gather and store. Learn from those that build, that you may teach your people."

"Does that mean a different world?" I asked.

"Perhaps," Gram said. "Or it may mean Tempest changed by events to come. It isn't important right now."

She leaned forward, eyes alight, through the parts about Elder Brother Eagle and the white wolves, and straightened at the final lines.

"They have named you Hiamovi, the high chief who will lift our people from the dust, who will lead them in the Light. This is the song of your Path, my loved son Hiamovi."

When the recording fell silent, Gram nodded. "A Path as powerful as yours."

"And as hard." I searched her face. "How do I prepare him for it? How do I teach him?"

She smiled. "By the way you live your own life, Akuleh."

* * *

I assisted Gram to the sleeping room a few minutes later, then descended the stairs to her apothecary. I must've been quieter than I thought, stumping down one step at a time with my stiff leg, because Kimama started violently when I cleared the main aisle and gasped, "Yi, Ku!"

"Sorry, Butterfly." I joined her at the counter and leaned on it while I scanned the shop. My vision immediately settled on the bare shelf. "You said you were going to tell me what happened."

"Ya."

She remained silent for a long time, and I watched her struggle. *Is she figuring out how to tell me,* I wondered, *or does it frighten to her to think about it? Is she having a flashback?*

"It's all right, Kimmie," I said at last, and took her nearest hand. "I'm here now."

"You *shouldn't* be here, Ku!" Her wide eyes beseeched me. "You should leave right now, before they come looking for you again."

"Again? Who's looking for me?" I straightened against the counter and searched her face, but I had a pretty good idea. "Tell me as much as you can."

"They came the day we got home," Kimama said. Once she got started, her words spilled out in a torrent. "They waited until after dark, after the shop was closed. They banged on the door and threatened to kick it in if we didn't open it. Then a crim with a war rifle made Gram and me stand here behind the counter while the others searched the storeroom and upstairs.

"They made a lot of noise, a lot of banging things around and swearing," she said. "They were really angry when they came back downstairs, and one big crim stuck out his arm and swept everything off the shelf as he walked by. All of Gram's little pots of salve smashed on the floor."

Kimama grabbed my hands. They trembled despite their tight grip. "The leader questioned us so long I thought Gram was going to collapse. He kept asking the same question in different ways, and getting meaner and meaner. His voice sounded weird, but I could see his face inside his helmet. It was Bimisi, Ku. They were hunting for you."

* * * * *

Chapter Twenty-Eight

I felt no shock. I only wondered if Bimisi thought I'd never left. If that was so, why had he waited until Gram and Kimama came home to try to capture me? Had he raided the shop purely to terrorize them? *Reeking snake.*

Assisting Kimama with securing the shop, I made note of heavy deadbolts at the door's top and bottom, and three iron bars reinforcing its solid wooden width.

"Our uncles did it," she said, and showed me a button beneath the counter's lip. "They installed this, too. Uncle Paytah said he had to get it from somewhere on Obolli. It was really expensive."

She pressed the button, and a steel curtain unrolled from its tube along the roof's edge like the reed blinds on the upstairs window. It covered the entire front of the building and locked into a rail recently embedded against the foundation. Though energy weapons fire would pierce it like a sheet of paper, it was rugged enough to thwart a common crim's break-in tools.

I shook my head, scrutinizing the steel blind. *Sad we have to take measures like this in Old Trade Center now. Even with all the crims here, we've never had to do this before.*

Limping up the stairs after Kimama when we finished, I almost bumped into her twice when she stopped abruptly and twisted around to give me advice. "Go to one of our uncles' enclaves, Ku... North

Gate opens before it gets light, you can leave that way... Whatever you do, don't go to Red Wash!"

"Does the public transport run all night, Kimmie?" I asked.

"No, but—"

"Too dangerous to travel the city on foot at night," I told her, "and not just because of enforcers. I don't have my military-issue sidearm—"

"The enforcers took Gram's firearms," Kimama interjected.

I gritted my teeth for a moment, then asked, "What time does the first transport come through?"

"0500, I think."

"Then we'll get up at 0400 and be ready to catch it," I said.

In the common sleeping room, lit only by one of Gram's oil-burning lamps, Kimama slid an anxious expression at me and picked her way to the floorbed she shared with Gram.

Extra beds, made up for guests unaccustomed to the Chalca practice of family members sharing them, covered most of the adobe floor. Thankfully, the one where Derry slept lay just inside the door. *Good. I won't kick or step on anybody while I'm trying to cross the room.*

I stood for a time to watch Garnan sleep, swaddled on a bed pad near Derry's head, and Gram's words about him whispered through my mind. *A Path as powerful as yours.*

When I joined Derry on our floorbed minutes later, she roused enough to murmur, "Everything a' righ', Kew?"

"Right now," I replied in a whisper and drew her to myself. *But it might not be come morning.*

* * *

I had no idea how long I lay awake assessing the situation.

I'm not the only one who'll be in danger if some kosa tells the enforcers I'm here. Even if I could leave safely now, they'd probably show up again, accuse Gram and Kimmie of concealing a fugitive, and maybe wreck the shop or torture them. I've got to get them out of here, too. I don't trust Bim any more than the Hevos.

I hadn't slept before I received a surprisingly firm bump to my head. Garnan had kicked in his swaddles. He began to whimper.

Derry whispered and reached to pat him, but his cries became more insistent. With a resigned sigh, she sat up, gathered him, his bag of baby gear, and one of our bed blankets, and tiptoed into the gathering room.

I squinted at my link. Its chronometer read 0336. I pushed to my feet and followed.

She glanced around, appearing mildly startled at me joining her as she settled to her knees on the blanket. "Wha's the matter, love? Yew look like yew've no' slep' a' all."

Because she'd kept her hair pinned in a twist during the day, I hadn't seen how much it'd grown since my three-day pass to Solienne. Rich auburn and wavy, it fell over her shoulders and lay six thumbwidths or so down her back.

"I haven't," I answered, and grimaced at a stab through my knee when I sank to sit on my heels. Speaking just loud enough for her to hear me over our son's impatient fussing while she unwound his swaddling and changed his diaper, I repeated Kimama's account, including her revelation about Bimisi.

Derry's eyes widened.

"We've got to leave in about an hour," I said. "Everyone in the dwelling, as quickly and discreetly as possible. We need to get dressed and go."

"Where?" Derry asked. "And how?"

"Gram's three sons live in enclaves outside the city," I told her. "Kimmie says they've been taking turns staying here a few days at a time since—"

"*Ku!*" If it was possible to whisper a shout, Kimama managed it. I wrenched about to find her standing in the sleeping room's doorway, fists planted on her hips. "Why," she demanded, "are you still here?"

"Because I'm thinking about how to get all of us out," I said. "It's too dangerous for anybody to stay. Can you contact Uncle Bidzil or the others? How fast can they get here?"

"It'd take two or three hours if they launched right now," Kimama said, "either from Willow Valley or Burned Banks." Her crimped brows revealed doubt. "What're—"

"Call them," I said. "Find out if they can come, and where we should meet them. If they can't... we'll figure something out." *Somehow.*

Kimmie disappeared into the sleeping room to retrieve her link, and I told Derry, "You and I will have to go in uniform and keep our travel orders accessible. The last time Bim saw me, I was in civies with my hair loose." *And blood all over my face.* "His thugs won't be looking for me in a flight suit."

I washed, dressed, cinched my knee brace on, and bound my hair in a tight battle braid while Derry fed and dressed Garnan. When I left the washroom, Gram rose on her elbows and asked, "Why are you up so early, Akuleh? Are you ill—or is the baby?"

Madam Graebel and Donnol stirred, roused by Gram's voice, and I said, "Nobody's sick. I was about to wake all of you. We need to leave ASAP. All of us. Kimmie's on her link with Uncle Bidzil to ask about flying us out."

Gram furrowed her brow, preparing to question me, but I waved her off. "Pack your bag like you're going midwifing, and pack Kimmie's for her, too; I'm keeping her busy. She said the first transport comes through at 0500. Is that right?"

"Ya, 0500 Commonwealth time," Gram said, "almost another sun position. What's wrong?"

"A sun position is an hour," I explained to Derry's mother. "You and Donny just bring what you came with."

Both nodded, Donny appearing puzzled, his mother worried.

"What's wrong?" Gram asked again. "I should tell Yamika where we're going and how long we'll be away."

"No!"

I'd *never* raised my voice to her before, so it startled me as much as her. Instantly penitent, I said more quietly, "Sorry, Gram. We can't tell anyone anything. Bimisi's enforcers might find out and come hunting. We have to disappear for a while. I don't know when we can come back. Maybe a few phases, maybe a few moons." I kept *Maybe never* to myself.

Gram, Madam Graebel, and Donnol dressed and packed quickly. Even Donnol spoke very little, whether from anxiety or lingering sleepiness, I couldn't tell.

Downstairs in the shop a little later, Gram handed out small eat-on-the-move food items, which everyone tucked into their bags. I smiled. *Grandmothers are natural supply officers.*

"What've you got?" I asked Kimama.

238 | D.T. READ

"Uncle Bidzil can't leave for another sun position because of a huge storm front," she reported. "Uncles Paytah and Yokolo should've taken off by now, but it'll take longer from Burned Banks Enclave, and they'll have to go around the storm. They'll meet us at our family hangar bays at the airfield. I'll keep up comms with them."

"Thanks, Kimmie." I surveyed our small group. "Here's the plan." *Sounds like a pre-mission briefing,* I couldn't help thinking. *All I need is a tri-D projector.* "We'll have to travel in three groups and pretend we don't know each other—" I gave Donnol a stern gaze "—but always stay within eye contact of each other. Understand? We'll travel from the vortex terminal to the airfield together. It's about half a range."

Everyone nodded.

"Mum and Donny," I said, "if anyone asks, you're trying to get an early vortex to Satha before the storm hits. Do you speak any Sathi language?"

"A bit of Beldesh," Madam Graebel said.

"Good." I told her, "You'll take Garn to maintain Derry's cover. Derry, she'll need his bag."

Derry passed the bulky pouch to her mother, but not Garnan. Not yet.

"Gram and Kimmie, your story is you're vortexing out to Talu-wah—" I named the only other city I knew in the Territory with a vortex facility "—to help deliver a baby. Come up with a cousin or something.

"Derry and I are colleagues returning to our base from TDY. We'll approach the transport stop from Sunning Lizard House so it looks like we've been staying there. Derry, you need to take your earrings off and put them away. They'll shout, 'Married to a Chalca' to any local who sees them."

Derry reluctantly handed Garnan to her mother to fumble at her earlobes and thrust the glittery jewelry into a trouser pocket.

"Let's leave through the storeroom," I said. "It provides better concealment and won't make noise like the steel blind."

We shuffled through the storeroom more by feel than sight. Familiar with it as Gram and I were, we did it easily, but we had to guide the others. Once outside, in a darkness not quite as dense under the dim glow from the nironnium dome, Kimama took a minute to scramble the lock code.

The others headed directly toward the transport stop, but Derry and I kept to the shadows of encircling structures until we drew even with Sunning Lizard House. Then we cut across the plaza. I noted a few off-worlders leaving other public lodges, and a number of residents in workers' clothing. Joining the end of the queue, I deliberately didn't look around. *Don't need any locals recognizing me.*

Still, I felt grateful we wouldn't be the only ones on the lumbering vehicle this early in the morning.

Boarding among the last waiting passengers, I briefly came face-to-face—or rather, face-to-throat—with an armed enforcer who stood behind the folding door at the top of the steps. Derry ignored him; I did my best to do the same, lowering my head like those ahead of us.

Only then did I realize I'd left my walking stick in Gram's shop. *Burn. Would've been good to have an expedient weapon in an emergency.*

To my surprise, no enforcer lurked in the transport's rear.

One was enough for Kimama. I found her, biting her lower lip and her eyes wide, hunched between Gram and a woman in a business jacket. "Warding Chant," I mouthed to her.

When the vehicle lurched into motion, I saw how Gram's gaze lingered on the plaza, on her screened shop, until we entered the arch to the main city. I didn't miss the deep sadness in her eyes, as if grieving a loved one, though she remained stoic.

Commuters came aboard and left all along the city route. By the time the transport exited the main dome for the nine-range route to the vortex terminal and airfield, only a handful of travelers remained besides my group.

The enforcer, rifle cradled in gauntleted hands, pivoted to face us then, as if fearing someone might storm the driver's cab. I ducked my head, folded my arms on my chest, and leaned against the dusty viewpane to feign sleep while I watched him.

He never stirred until the transport halted jerkily at the vortex terminal's entrance. Then he stepped aside enough to let everyone off. I faked a yawn, scooped my small bag off the now-empty next seat, and limped after the others, taking care not to brush him as I passed.

A steel-sheathed hand clamped onto my shoulder from behind.

* * * * *

Chapter Twenty-Nine

"You look familiar, pilot," the enforcer said with his electronically modulated voice, and jerked me around to face him. He released my shoulder to shove his duty link under my nose. "A lot like him. Do you know him?"

An image of me burned in the link's display, with my left eye swollen shut and my nose and mouth bleeding. My heartrate quickened, but I managed not to recoil. *Looks even worse than it felt.*

"Hard to tell," I said, "swollen like that." On a silent prompt, I added, "If it's who I think it is, he used to live in Old Trade Center."

"Where you got on," the enforcer said.

"Yes. Haven't seen him for a while, though. I just came in from Manaba Outpost yesterday." I have no idea how I kept my tone so casual, but I put a hand into my trouser pocket for my link. "I've got my travel orders in here." *Please, Shaman Shiye, don't let him ask to see them. My name is across the top in bold Standard characters.*

"Hand out of your pocket. Now," the thug ordered, leveling his rifle at my chest. "If it's not empty, I shoot."

Heart hammering my ribs, I withdrew my hand slowly and held both out to him, palms up.

He snorted. "Fine. Just tell your friend, next time you see him, he's been charged with sedition."

"Yes, sir." My voice remained relaxed.

I dismounted the transport into a gusty wind bearing the scent of rain and strode to the terminal doors without glancing back, though the prickle at my nape felt like a spider dancing on it. *He knew very well who I am. Why didn't he arrest me right there?*

Did he put a tracker on my shoulder when he grabbed me? Trying to find out where I'm going and who I associate with?

The women and children stood apart near an Arrivals and Departures board, furtively watching the entrance. When Derry noticed me, relief relaxed her features, but she didn't break character. "Wha' was tha' abou', sir?"

"Check my right shoulder closely, front and back," I said. "If you see anything out of place, even a dirty spot, tell me, but *don't* touch it."

Brow scrunched, Derry leaned in to scrutinize the top of my shoulder, then stepped behind me. "Righ' there, sir," she said, "jus' above yer shoulder blade, a sor' of greasy smudge." She came around to face me, any disquiet suppressed, and I admired her ability to maintain her cover. *Maybe it comes with being Intel.* All business, she asked, "Wha' now?"

My heartrate had stiffened again. "Do you have anything for cutting? We learned about stuff like this in Survival School. I'll have to cut it out. It… doesn't react well to being scrubbed off with water."

"One of those ladies migh'." She pointed at her mother and Gram, standing several arm-lengths away and pretending to ignore us. When she approached them and made the request, Gram rummaged in her midwife's bag and removed a single-use, sterile-packaged scalpel.

"A midwife. Wha' luck!" Derry exclaimed on returning to me.

"Thank you, Elder," I called to Gram, as formally as if she were a stranger.

In the nearest men's room, I locked myself in the farthest stall in case the trace contained an explosive. *I'm in your hands, Shaman Shiye.* Teeth set, I undid my flight suit, dropped it to my waist, and twisted the torso part around in front to find the mark.

Keeping the heavy cloth taut with one hand, I cut a generous circle around the thumbprint-shaped smudge. Gram's scalpel sliced through it with ease and nicked my fingertip as well. It stopped bleeding when I sucked on it a little.

At a prompt, I peeled off my crewshirt, too. The dark substance hadn't completely penetrated, but enough lay on the fabric to accomplish whatever was intended. I blew out a breath. *Thank you, Shaman Shiye.*

I didn't cut it out of the shirt. Instead, I wrapped the scalpel and stained piece from my flight suit in the shirt and deposited the whole wad in the trash incinerator.

On emerging from the men's room, I motioned the rest of the group together. Questions shadowed everyone's eyes, but I said, "Later. Kimama, any word from Paytah or Yokolo?"

"They had to reroute because of the storm," she said, "so they landed at Flat River Enclave to refuel the Darters. Uncle Yokolo said 'ETA two sun positions,' whatever 'ETA' means."

"Estimated time of arrival," I answered. "Next time, tell him I can pay for their fuel. How long since you talked to him?"

"About half a sun position."

"We have plenty of time," I said. "Half a range will only take a few minutes. If you've got a coat or wrap, better put it on now."

Derry and her family had escaped Osfelga in their winter coats, Kimama had a jacket, and Gram wore a heavy shawl. My flight jacket, however, had been left in Life Support on Tobe.

While I helped Derry strap Garnan in his baby pack on her chest, so she could close her coat around him, she asked, "Wha' of yew, Kew?"

"If we hurry, we'll beat the rain," I assured her. The wind had strengthened and grown chillier when the terminal's automatic doors opened before us, and the clean scent of rain-washed soil and plants had grown strong enough to taste.

I scrutinized our route ahead as well as I could. Several structures walled the track, a low manmade canyon of warehouses and equipment sheds.

Any building could conceal an enforcer squad. They could have people on the roofs. How long will it take them to realize their tracer's stopped working? Could they have a tail on me already? Hopefully, they think I took a vortex off world. Burn, I wish I hadn't left the walking stick behind!

We leaned into the fitful wind, grimacing and squinting at its grit in our faces. Derry led, with her mother's hand tucked about her arm. Kimama and Gram followed them, Kimama's arm wrapped around Gram's waist. As rearguard, I noticed Donnol struggling and gradually falling behind Kimmie, so I swung him up to ride on my shoulders.

I never stopped scouring our surroundings, including the hazy sky for drones. I moved to face every flutter or slap or clatter of wind-blown objects, prepared to hoist Donnol off my shoulders if we were confronted. He wrapped his arms tightly around my neck. "Wha're yew doing, Kew?"

The first drops fell, tiny bombs of liquid ice, as we entered the gate into the field of private hangar bays. Having flown in and out of Awé-nasa City every time my stepmother needed a supply run, I could've found our hangar bays blind. Still wary, however, I moved up and led our group on an unpredictable route through the grid of lanes first.

Kimama questioned me from beneath puckered brows. "Where are you going, Ku?"

"Shaking off possible tails," I told her.By the time we reached the nearest of two shared family bays, the rain pelted down steadily enough to thoroughly dampen my flight suit, except where Donnol sat. He didn't cover the hole I'd cut, and every drop that struck my exposed shoulder blade prompted a shiver as it trickled down my back.

At the bay's passenger hatch, I lowered Donnol to his feet and punched the lock code. It'd never been changed, but the sand-pitted door grated partway open and stuck. I shook my head. *Never got a lube job, either.* I had to throw my weight against the door a few times to open it far enough for everyone to enter.

The autumn rain heightened the bay's musty dampness until it covered the scents of fuel, lubricants, and the bitter, burned smell of uncounted launches and landings.

"I' feels and smells like a cave," Derry said, wrinkling her nose.

I nodded and said, "Lights."

The pale blue-white ring around the top of the encircling wall flickered wildly for several seconds, like entering a vortex. I shuddered. *No buzzing insects this time, at least.*

A check of my wrist chrono revealed 0749. *Ya, that's about right.* I asked Kimama, "Anything new from Yokolo or Paytah?"

"They haven't answered for a while," she said, and I detected a note of concern.

"Keep trying," I requested. "Tell them we're waiting in bay twenty-nine on Nevus row."

She nodded and strolled across its shallow bowl, keying her link.

Everyone shed their coats and hung them on wall hooks meant for tools and cables and such. I poked through a stack of crates in which we secured supplies in a Darter's hold, hoping to find a rug or two for sitting. I found only the oily mats we'd lain on while doing maintenance under the aircraft.

Three parking stands stood against the curved wall, two of them occupied by dust-coated straddlejets. My own straddlejet, an oversized machine of gleaming black and chrome, had occupied the third stand. I sighed at memories of racing Hanuk across the russet desert and careening through Awénasa City's narrow alleys.

Lost the 'jet and Huk a year apart... I met Derry when I crashed the 'jet into her mother's float-cart.

"Akuleh, come eat," Gram called. I spun around.

She'd spread her shawl on the oil-coated stone floor, and everyone except Kimmie, still talking on her link, had huddled around her. Eager hands opened the packets of shegrul jerky, dried cactus fruit and pimiberries, and hard honey candy Gram had stowed in our travel bags.

Derry hadn't eaten yet. With her coat thrown over one shoulder, and only Garnan's lower half visible beneath it, I knew she was suckling him first. When I sat beside her, she smiled and said quietly, "He's abou' finished, I think. I'll ea' in peace once he's fallen asleep."

Gram noticed the hole in my flight suit's upper back when I reached to accept the jerky bag she handed me. "What happened there, Akuleh?" she asked. "What was it you had to cut out of your uniform?"

I froze for a moment. *How much do I tell her?*

She has the need to know, I decided. *It's the reason we tore her away from her home so suddenly, after all.*

When I described what had happened with the enforcer on the transport, the others pressed closer to listen. I read shock in their eyes and partly open mouths.

"I really don't know what he put on me," I said, "but I suspect it was a trackable substance. Finding out who else I'm supposedly working with to start an insurrection is the only reason I can think of for letting me go."

* * * * *

Chapter Thirty

The snacks weren't enough to fully satisfy any of us, but wearied from our early departure and the morning's exertions and tensions, the others slept as well as they could after eating.

I sat with my back to the hangar bay's curved adobe wall, my bad knee propped over my good leg. From my position, I could monitor activity outside the half-open hatch without being seen. Derry sat curled beside me with her head on my shoulder, and Garnan lay in my lap. Both appeared peaceful in sleep.

My body and blurring eyes and fuzzy mind begged for sleep, too, but I didn't dare snooze. *Enforcers could find us before our rides get here. Whenever they get here...*

"Ku!"

Kimama's urgent voice startled me out of a doze I didn't know I'd sunk into. My head wrenched up so sharply I smacked it on the wall behind me. I winced, fully awake, and blinked at brilliant sunlight outside the hatch. My wrist chrono read 1138.

"Uncle Yokolo's on final approach," Kimmie said. "He's landing in this bay in about five minutes, and Uncle Paytah is in the one over there." She waved in its direction. "Let's get everybody out."

* * *

We had an uneventful flight to Willow Valley Enclave, just less than two sun positions with a tailwind, the trailing end of the storm Paytah and Yokolo had fought all the way to Awénasa City.

Derry, her mother, Garnan, and I rode with Paytah. We'd no sooner reached our assigned cruising altitude than he leaned around his seatback and said with a dim smile, "Bidzil's been trying to persuade Mama to get out of Old Trade Center ever since the raid, but she's refused to stir. How'd you convince her, Akuleh?"

"When Kimmie recognized the raid's leader," I said, "I knew he'd be back if he ever learned I'd even stayed overnight, and he'd do a lot worse than before. I didn't give her a chance to argue, just bundled her out."

"Thank you," Paytah said, and I didn't miss his relief. After some hesitation, he asked, "How did you attract the Great Council's attention in the first place?"

"Wrong place, wrong time," I said. "Participating in a traditional Wanikiya Ceremony is now considered seditious."

* * *

Uncle Bidzil and Aunt Sitala assisted Gram out of Yokolo's Darter when it came to rest on Willow Valley Enclave's plaza. Kimama and Donnol trailed them to their dwelling. Derry, her mother, and I followed, too.

With everyone settled in the gathering room, and Sitala handing out dishes of roasted shegrul and squash, Uncle Bidzil beckoned me outside to the stone landing.

"Thank you for bringing Mama here," he said first. "It was Kimama who called and told me about the raid on the shop. She didn't give a lot of details, and Mama told us even less. She didn't want to concern us unnecessarily, she said. Do you know any more about it?"

I gave him the whole account, from why I'd been staying at Sunning Lizard House, to the attack on the improvised ceremony. I didn't mention the beating.

Bidzil nodded. "The newsnets ran it for days. They showed images of the destroyed merchants' tents and made up stories about how dangerous the people of Old Trade Center are." He rolled his eyes. "A lot of elders with shops that've been there since the Crossing from Solienne.

"They also ran images of you, beaten up." Bidzil eyed me closely. "I thought you were deployed, didn't know you were on Tempest at the time, but they gave your name. They say you're the one who 'stirred up the insurrection' against the Great Council, so now you're wanted for sedition, and if anyone sees you, they're supposed to tell the Council's security forces." Bidzil smiled. "Don't worry, we won't report you."

"Wasn't my idea," I said, "but there would've been too many people to blame, some of whom had come in from the Territory. The security force squad was led by my stepbrother, who's now chief chanter for the great chief. He and I were never really close growing up, so that made me an easy target." I asked, "What about the rest of this enclave?"

"You're safe here," Bidzil assured me. "You can stay as long as you need to."

"Thanks." I sighed, mostly from weariness. "Derry's mother and little brother will have to stay here—they're refugees from Ardonar—so we need to find them permanent lodging. But Derry, Garnan, and

I have to fly to a remote enclave tomorrow. We need to find a pilot. I can pay for the fuel."

"I'll take you," Bidzil said. "I trust the people here, but it's still best nobody knows where you've gone."

* * *

After eating, Yokolo and Paytah departed for Burned Banks Enclave. Derry and I, with Kimama tagging along, made the round of several merchants. Chanter Wahkan had given us a list of the clothing and supplies we'd need, mostly farmers' winter clothing, and plenty of diapers for Garnan.

"No disposables?" Derry asked in dismay, fingering a bundle of diapers made of soft Tempest cotton.

The aged shop owner, who spoke Standard quite well, shook her head. "This is how to fold them for him—" she demonstrated on her countertop "—and knot them at his middle. You'll fold them this way for you, for your female cycles, and tie the ends to a belt at your waist. You'll also need a pot to wash them in, and a stirring rod."

When the woman bustled to the rear of her shop to find a suitable pot, Derry cast me an appalled expression that asked, *Wha' are we getting into?* She hadn't had any cycles while suckling Garnan, and she confided, "I do hope they'll no' star' again till he's weaned, bu' bes' be prepared."

Haggling still made her uncomfortable. "Even for diapers?" she asked. "Is there no shop on this world where I can simply pay a price marked on the goods?"

I chuckled. "Only food venders, little bird. Why don't you and Kimmie go see if you can find some awanatas? That way you won't hear the elder and me yelling at each other." I slid a grin at the woman.

"Actually, Derry, this'd be a good way to start your cultural immersion."

She rolled her eyes at me.

The shop owner had a limited supply of some items, like imported wool socks and women's heavy work shirts. "Shops in Awénasa City would have more," she said.

I replied only, "Thank you."

I got everything we needed at a fair price, including some shirts and socks, and with enough shouting to keep it fun.

"Good to do business with you," the woman said with a smile, and added a backpack big enough Derry could've curled up inside it. "You'll need this to carry everything."

"Thank you, Elder." I stuffed our purchases inside, slung it onto my shoulders, and joined Derry and Kimama across the plaza at a baker's shop.

Aunt Sitala and Madam Graebel had visited Willow Valley's few public lodges while we were gone and found one owned by an elderly widow Derry's mother said was, "Delightful. I' has only one gues' room, on the level above her own dwelling. I's a bi' shabby, so she agreed to le' me pain' murals on the walls and take a share of the household tasks for paymen'."

"Are yew and my sister going to live here, too?" Donnol asked me while we inspected the cozy room. It had a window with a reed blind overlooking the plaza, a few pegs and shelves for belongings, and enough space for three or four floorbeds, but the plaster over the adobe bricks had begun to crack.

"No," I said. "We have to go across the territory to a different enclave to learn some important things." I took care not to name the enclave and wondered if I'd ever mentioned it to Gram or Kimama.

Donnol's eyes widened. "Are yew going to stay there forever? Can I come?"

"Your mother will need you here," I said. "We'll only be gone a few months, not as long as I was deployed."

Donnol relaxed, but asked with his next breath, "Will yew send us vids?"

I chuckled, remembering Kimama's plea when I'd left for Basic. "As often as we can."

* * *

I dressed in farmer's clothing and burned my ruined flight suit in the enclave's midden pit before we left the next morning. Watching the synthetic material dissolve among blue and green flames, I felt the hollowness of loss. *Like a part of myself. That part of my life is finished.*

Derry's mother had the hardest time at our departure. "Surely yew're not taking the baby?"

"He's too young to wean, Mum," Derry said. Snug on her chest in his baby pack, Garnan stared around at everyone and sucked contentedly on his fist. "Besides, he's half Chalca. He needs to learn Chalca ways, too."

"I'll take care of them, Mum," I assured her with solemnity. "They're my wife and child."

Gram stood on her toes to hug us both. "The Ancients will watch over and help you." She took my hand and Derry's and pressed them together, her expression somber. "This will be very difficult. You'll both be challenged in ways you can't imagine. You must learn to be strong together."

* * * * *

Chapter Thirty-One

In the early afternoon sunlight, I spotted Yellow Rock Enclave from a few ranges out, a mound of adobe and stone hunched before the beige foothills of a dwindling mountain range.

"Traditionalists," Uncle Bidzil observed, and jutted his chin toward the structure. "No nironnium dome. We'll have to land outside and taxi in, if their gate's wide enough."

Scrub pines grew in patches, like a dog with a serious case of mange, across the enclave's backdrop of wind-worn mountains. Before the enclave stretched a broad river valley, flat as the Awénasa desert several hundred ranges to the north, but blanketed with grasses dried straw-white under the summer sun.

The river meandering across the plain lay empty this late in the year, but python trees guarded its banks. Gray-beige limbs, thick and sinuous as their namesakes, hung uncoiled in a perverse imitation of willows.

"Starting my final approach," Bidzil said, and swung his Darter into a descending bank.

In the back seat, Garnan began to cry, and Derry murmured to him in Caerdish. "The same thing happened when we landed a' Manaba," she said.

"It's the change in air pressure," I told her. "It affects babies' ears more than ours."

Bidzil set the Darter down with a firm *bump* on a packed-clay track that ran straight to the enclave's east-facing gate. As we taxied toward it, heavy timber doors swung outward, pushed by a pair of rugged men.

The enclosure into which we rolled reminded me for a moment of Greiner Base's vast hangars on Ardonar in a vault excavated from the heart of a mountain.

Only for a moment, though. The Darter's landing lights illuminated the usual tiered, adobe dwellings around a circular plaza of cobbles, but soot-stained log support beams arched far higher than Greiner's granite overhead, with its electrical conduits and gray pipes.

Torches planted about the village and smoke vents in the dome, which admitted dust-laden sunbeams, provided the only light. Still, I recognized it with my next heartbeat. *The third night of the Wanikiya ceremony I watched on my link. This is where it was recorded.*

A teenager, his expression curious, waved us to one side to park. I released my seat harness as the engines whined into silence and suppressed a grimace at my knee's stiffness when I climbed out. I pushed my seat forward and took our wailing baby so Derry could clamber down.

She sighed as she stretched her legs and back. "More than six hours, and i' was the smoothes' fligh' I've had on Tempes'."

"Autumn is *usually* the calm before the winter storms." I rubbed Garnan's back briefly, trying to soothe him, before I returned him to Derry. "I'll get our gear."

Uncle Bidzil had popped the cargo hold by the time I rounded the tail assembly. He hoisted our bags out, and I handed him an extra twenty-rel piece.

"That's more than enough, Akuleh." We exchanged bearhugs. Then he grew serious. "Blessings for your new Path."

He began to prep his Darter for the return flight to Willow Valley, and I shouldered my rucksack.

Scooping up Derry and Garnan's bags, I felt someone watching me. A quick sweep of the torch-lit dimness revealed a female figure, wearing the traditional gathered skirt of native cotton, hobbling toward us across the plaza. She stopped when Derry came around the aircraft to join me.

She's at least as old as Gram. About the same height, but not as plump. Her stoutness reminded me of a thick-trunked desert juniper, survivor of winter blasts and summer furnaces. Her white hair, bound at the nape like Gram's, appeared age-yellowed in the torchlight.

Something about her seemed familiar. Something in her weathered face, with a few scraggly whiskers sprouting from her pointed chin. Was it her protuberant eyes? I couldn't place it. *Have I seen her in a dream?*

"Chanter Mapiya?" I asked.

"Ya." She drew close to me, leaving barely a hand's width of space between us, and tilted her head to peer into my eyes.

I didn't stir, didn't break her gaze for three or four whole minutes. *She's assessing me.*

When she moved back, she swung toward Derry, who slipped me an uneasy question through her eyes and tightened her hold on our squirming baby.

"It's all right," I assured her.

Mapiya grunted when she stepped away from Derry, her features still inscrutable. "I've been waiting for you, Wanikiya," she said in Chalca. She muttered as if to keep the people moving about the plaza's perimeter from hearing. "And you, Anataqa. Now I understand the white bird. I've waited a long time."

All her life, I realized, *not days or sun positions*. I repeated the gist of it to Derry in Standard.

"Come," Mapiya said. "We're staying with Chief Aiyana's family. Tomorrow is Oil-Gathering Ceremony. You must eat and rest and care for Hiamovi." She touched Garnan's head gently with withered fingers before she wheeled about and started away at a surprisingly quick pace.

Following, I inhaled a whiff of childhood memory. *Pine-resin torches. Haven't smelled those since—*

"Willow Valley Enclave wasn' this dark," Derry said.

"Red Wash was when I was little," I said, "before they replaced the logs and soil with the nironnium dome. What you smell is the torches. I used to gather a lot of pinecones and resin to make them." I eyed the intertwined support logs overhead and smiled. "Feels like home."

* * *

Voices in the plaza woke me long before dawn's first shafts slid through the sleeping room's roof vents. Mapiya had left, I noticed on surveying the dim space. I rose at once. *Don't want her thinking I'm lazy.*

When I returned from the washroom, wearing only my shorts and with my damp hair falling loose around my torso, Derry sat up on our floorbed. She watched me tug shegrul-hide trousers and boots on and secure the brace around my knee, and whispered, "Where're yew going, love?"

"Out to see where I'm needed," I answered. "The sooner I can start learning all the stuff I missed out on…"

Skipped out on, I chided myself. *It was my choice to quit my apprenticeship.*

"Wha' of me?" Derry asked.

I saw in her eyes and heard in her voice the same aloneness I'd witnessed when we'd come to Tempest for Hanuk's funeral, and my heart contracted. In this household, only Kaya, the chief's eldest daughter, who'd served four years in Solienne's ground forces, spoke Standard.

I scanned the room. Spotted Kaya sleeping a few floorbeds away. "Come out with Kaya," I said. "Don't be afraid to ask questions. The Chalca phrase for 'How do you say this?' is *Kono di chal.*"

Derry crimped her scarred forehead. "Kono dee shall?"

I grinned. "*Chal,* not shall. It means 'say' or 'speak.'"

"*Kono di chal,*" she murmured.

"Good." I dropped my voice still more. "Don't mention our spirit names to anyone. We're only here to finish my chanter apprenticeship because it was interrupted by military duty, if people ask."

"Righ'."

I peered into her anxious eyes, slipped my hand into her hair near her ear to cup her face, and stroked her freckles with my thumb. "You'll be fine, white bird. *Ti qala bé messa tai messa.*"

She smiled at last. "*Ti qala bé messa tai messa,* too."

"See? You've got that down." I ducked my face to hers and she leaned in, eyes closed, lips parted. Our mouths melded.

Long seconds later, with the warmth of her lips still tingling on mine, I slipped outside and loped down the stone stairs.

Fourteen or fifteen men, shirtless like myself and wielding long staffs, encircled a pod of shegruls. We greeted each other with friendly nods when I joined them.

Shegruls resembled massive caterpillars, eyeless and earless, but equipped with sensory whiskers, and proboscises for smelling and eating. Eight spans long at full development, their leathery, segmented backs reached the middle of my thigh.

While the men kept the shegruls together with gentle bumps and nudges of their staffs, Mapiya shuffled among them. She placed a hand on one here and another there and sang the Chant of Gratitude for Plenty in a croaky voice.

She beckoned when she saw me, her expression indiscernible. "Come help me bless them."

I joined the chant as I pushed through the shegruls to her.

Men shoved the enclave's gate open when the sun's rim surged above the rolling horizon, and we sang the Chant to Welcome Dawn. Women's voices rose with ours, echoing joyfully from the encircling walls, and I peered around.

The families had come out of their third-level dwellings. Young teens, boys and girls, fingered harvesting knives on their belts, and the blades glinted with the in-rushing sunlight. Laughing youngsters swatted each other with broad baskets their mothers had woven from sturdy reeds.

I spotted Derry's fair-complexioned face at once, beside Kaya. Garnan peeked over her shoulder from his pack, riding on her back for a change.

"It's time," Mapiya said, and signaled the shegherds.

As the men steered their charges through the gate, Mapiya asked, "Do you know the Chant of Merciful Death?"

"Yes, Chanter."

"Good. Start singing when the pod approaches the trees and continue until they're all dead."

I'd seen Oil-Gathering Ceremony every year before I'd left home. I'd been a harvester the last two times. It still gave my innards a twist.

Outside the enclave, scents of dried grasses and the wind-borne spiciness of pines replaced the indoor odors of cooking fires and shegrul barns. Autumn's crispness drove the dawn breeze, and gooseflesh rose on my bare chest and arms. *Always chilly for Oil-Gathering Ceremony.*

The riverbank lined with python trees lay a range to the north. We left the hard track and started across the valley. Ten or twelve arm-lengths ahead, the shegherds guided the pod toward one of four clusters of trees.

"It takes four years for bulbs to ripen," Mapiya said, "so we harvest from different trees every year."

The shegruls spread out, galumphing across the plain in the rising light. I counted 56, all fully developed with six segments. Some had even begun to cinch between the third and fourth segments, indicating impending partition into two new creatures.

When my stepmother had ordered me to butcher shegruls for meat and hides, she'd always chosen three-segmented ones, still raw from partitioning. Their former other halves were allowed to mature and reproduce.

Remembering what I'd gotten in trade for three-segment skins before I left home, I did a mental calculation and stared at Mapiya. "That's at least 30,000 rels for the hides alone!"

"Oil has greater value," Mapiya said. "It fuels lamps in the dwellings, lubricates tools, and protects knife blades. It has many medicinal uses and is essential for ceremonies and chants. It's worth the cost of many shegruls."

Maybe the animals smelled the python trees, or maybe their whiskers detected where the grass ended, smothered under acid-riddled bones. Whatever prompted it, they lumbered to a halt.

Mapiya motioned, and we began the chant. "Be calm, wild spirits, be at peace…"

The shegherds' nudges and prods with their staffs became jabs and strikes when individual animals tried to twist away.

"May your spirits rest in beauty," I sang, and urged them forward with hand motions. "May your spirits rest in peace."

The creatures milled, pushing one another into a tight pod, and several brushed sagging boughs. A series of snaps cut the brisk air, like a volley of small arms fire. Too swift to see, tentacles whipped them to the tops of 30-span, pillar-like trunks.

"May your spirits find—"

An eerie whistle, echoed by others, cut through my chant. My vision wrenched from the pod to the nearest tree, to the writhing shegrul it had snared. The icy prickle I remembered from previous Oil-Gathering Ceremonies raced across my scalp. *They don't have voice boxes, but they're screaming.*

"It comes from the respiratory ducts in their backs as air is crushed out of their lungs," Mapiya said.

I remembered the recent pain of bruised ribs, and how the pressure in the ice crevasse had reduced my voice to a squeak. "Makes sense," I said, and quelled a shudder. *Really didn't need to know that.*

"Keep chanting," Mapiya ordered.

It took ten minutes to soothe and chant the last shegruls to their fates, to occupy every serpentine limb. Before the whistling squeals ended and twitching death throes stilled, the rest of the enclave rushed forward.

Besides neutralizing the deadly boughs, binding them about their prey revealed our objectives. Oil bulbs the size of chicken eggs grew in yellow-gray clusters hanging like beards along the limbs' undersides.

Barefoot teens scrambled up scaly trunks, knives gripped in their teeth. They anchored themselves with knees and sheghide belts to shave the clusters free. Younger siblings waited at the bottom to gather the falling prizes into their baskets.

Once filled, the baskets weighed too much for the children to lift. I joined the men and women carrying full ones to the gathering point a few arm-lengths away.

I found Derry with Kaya and some older women, seated in the grass and picking through the baskets for bad bulbs. None of the women appeared shocked at Derry's hair, still much shorter than theirs. A round-faced elder bounced Garnan on her knee and chanted some children's song, and Derry laughed at something Kaya said.

When I faked a stumble, as if to dump my basket in her lap, she rolled her eyes and said, "My spouse," in Chalca accented with a Caerdish lilt.

I chuckled.

Fifteen or twenty minutes later, everyone physically able hefted at least one basket onto his or her head. Hiking back to the enclave, we joined the others in the Chant of Gratitude for Plenty.

Kaya leaned toward Derry. "Now the real work begins, pressing out the oil with our grinding stones. But we'll feast tonight."

Families brought their grinding stones out to the plaza and set them in two long rows facing each other. They fitted the stones with troughs to catch the oil, and everyone sang, partly out of gratitude for the oil, and partly to maintain the grinding rhythm while they worked.

I'd done it before, but Kaya showed Derry how. "Roll the stone like this to press out the oil. Don't scrape it on the grinding surface, or you'll get scraps of bulb skin in it."

Derry recoiled from the scent on her first attempt. "Like rotting mea', bu' no' so strong." She wrinkled her nose. "Why's tha', I wonder?"

"Because the carcasses rot while the python limbs digest them," Kaya said.

Derry grimaced.

"That's why Gram mixes herbs into it," I said.

Derry and I took several turns throughout the day. Baskets gradually emptied, family storage jars gradually filled, and songs and friendly laughter rang within the enclave. Smoke coiling from pits near the wellhouse revealed a few more shegruls had been sacrificed for the anticipated feast.

"Help me bless this oil," Mapiya said, indicating a large jar painted with sun eagle figures. "Chanters will use it to make oil-paste for healings and sacred ceremonies."

I'd seen my father bless fresh oil, but it'd been years ago. "I don't remember the chant, Elder."

Mapiya pursed her mouth briefly. "Watch and listen to me, and follow." She knelt to place her bony hands about the jar's neck.

My knee twinged when it met the cobbles. I ignored it. Facing Mapiya over the jar, I rested my hands on it as well, and the cheerful songs around us ebbed to silence.

"O, Ancient Ones, who shaped the worlds," she sang, "who give us gifts from all the trees and beasts, purify this oil for healing. Purify this oil for use by holy hands and lead us to walk in beauty."

I followed as she sang it three times, until in my memory my father's voice mingled with the melody. An unexpected warmth flickered at the center of my chest and flowed through my frame.

Somewhere on the Sacred Mountain, my parents are rejoicing with me.

* * *

When I dreamed that night, I stood again on the river valley's plain facing a single python tree. Its fleshy limbs hung loose, rippling like a wrestler shaking out his muscles before a match. A chill coursed through my spine.

I jumped at a *crack* like a whip and blinked. The tentacles hadn't coiled about a shegrul, but a world. I recognized the dark-blue oceans and ochre landmasses with sick dread. Tempest.

I also recognized the face that gloated from the top of the trunk. Osaga Safa, mastermind of the Supremacy.

My *pelu* lay in its sheath on my back. I snatched it free and swung. The long blade felled the tree with a single blow. The snaky boughs thrashed, and my homeworld rose free in the night sky.

The python tree vanished, but a new one grew in its place. Its limbs swayed like a dancer's, seductive in their movement, soothing and hypnotic.

Another *snap*, like a tripped trap, rang across the plain. Once more, serpentine limbs entangled Tempest.

This time, Machitew leered at me from the tree's top. The semi-familiar eyes that laughed at me through an ash-blackened mask gleamed with triumph.

I raised my *pelu* again and swung as I had before, a decapitating stroke.

This time my blade lodged halfway through the trunk. I tugged at it, twisted. I tried sawing the trunk.

My blade stuck fast.

When I glanced up, the strangling tentacles had tightened about my homeworld. I watched them crush it to dust.

I lunged upright on the floorbed beside Derry, panting as if I'd run five ranges, and streaming with cold sweat.

* * * * *

Chapter Thirty-Two

Asense of helplessness weighed on me long after the dream dissipated. The same helplessness I'd felt at seeing Nawat hit the mine and Yobo crash on the runway. I sat with elbows on knees, gripping my head in my hands. *Just a dream. Probably triggered by the python trees.*

I knew better. My dreams had held specific meanings too many times for me to ignore this one. When I lay down again, I stared at the log ceiling beams, mulling possible meanings, until Mapiya stepped close to our floorbed.

"We'll set out at dawn," she said. "We have sixteen ranges to walk."

I sat up. "To where?"

She scrutinized me for a couple seconds, eyes narrowed and lips gathered, before she said, "To my home."

Surprised, I asked, "You don't live in the enclave?"

"No. Too many people and distractions."

That explains why we stayed with the chief, I thought.

Gaining my feet sent pain like a leather awl's jab through my knee. I winced. *Should've elevated it last night after all the activity yesterday.*

I didn't wake Derry until I'd returned from the washroom and dressed. While she bathed, I changed Garnan and carried him out to the gathering room when he began to wail for his breakfast.

"Can't help you there, little man," I said, pacing with him. "You'll have to wait for your mama for that."

Mapiya inspected our packs while Derry suckled Garnan. She indicated the energy rifle strapped across my rucksack. "That stays here." Her no-nonsense firmness reminded me of Doc Moseva. "And your handlights and talking things." She shaped rectangles like our links with her fingers.

"Won't I need the rifle for hunting?" I asked.

She favored me with the same long stare of mild annoyance she'd given me earlier. "No. You won't have these things in the time that's coming. I must teach you—" she included Derry with a nod "—to hunt as the grandfathers did."

The time that's coming? She sounds like Demothi.

Mapiya spoke only Chalca, and Derry slid a querying glance at me. I interpreted.

"Wha' abou' Mum?" Derry asked. "She'll be expecting vids of Garn and us."

That time Derry received the unblinking stare.

"Call her now," I said. "Tell her we're going to be out of range for a couple months, and we'll call her when we get back."

Derry conversed with her mother in Caerdish for four or five minutes, then handed her link to Mapiya with a somber but resolved expression.

Kaya loaded pouches of food into Mapiya's backpack, tucking them around a large jar of python oil, and we filled gut waterskins at the enclave's well. When the sentries opened the timber gate far enough for us to sidle through in our backpacks, we stepped from smoky near darkness into the frosty blue of predawn.

"This way." Mapiya's words hung on motionless air in a small vapor cloud.

She started south, along a well-worn path toward a valley between grassy foothills. I motioned Derry to follow her, and I brought up the rear.

We climbed a small rise to sing the Chant to Welcome Dawn when the sun pushed above a brush-strewn hill. Too dry for dew here, dawn's first breeze rustled the grasses, stirring fragrances of wildflowers and sage.

Derry sang the chant without hesitation, and I queried her with my eyes.

"Chanter Wahkan taugh' me while yew were deployed," she said. "Tha' and other chan's we use the mos'."

On the trail once more, I asked Mapiya, "Chanter, what did you mean about the time that's coming? Why won't we have any technology?"

She peered at me around her shoulder, the same hard gaze, before she said, "I had a dream. I saw a falling star, except it rose like an arrow and didn't come down.

"At the peak of its flight, it flashed and went out. All the city lights went out, too, and the city noise went quiet. I heard faraway cries because everything had stopped."

My gut knotted like a cold fist in my midsection. Ice slithered up my spine, straightening my frame. "An electromagnetic pulse." I knew it as surely as I knew my name. "When, Chanter?"

"Maybe moons," Mapiya said, "maybe years. I don't know." She shrugged. "You must be ready."

My eyes only partially took in the surrounding terrain and our route. I couldn't dispel thoughts of a future EMP attack. *How much time have we got? How much do Derry and I have to learn? Will we be well enough prepared to make sure our people survive it?*

We hiked at an easy pace. Our gradual climb followed a broad stream winding from tree-covered mountains through a valley between folds of hills. The stream sparkled in the early sunlight, and its splashing and gurgling over round stones sounded like light laughter.

After Mapiya's apparent resentment of my previous queries, I hesitated to ask again. Then stubbornness set in. *How does she expect us to learn if we don't ask questions?*

I stiffened my tone along with my resolve. "Where does water come from this late in the year? In Awénasa, we don't have anything but rocks and gravel in riverbeds by now." *Probably why there aren't trees like this, either.*

"Springs," Mapiya said. "They flow all year."

The high-altitude breeze warmed as the sun climbed. We shed our light jackets and stuffed them into our packs.

"You must protect Hiamovi from the sun," Mapiya told Derry. When I translated, the elder lifted the dozing Garnan from his baby pack—which woke him, of course—and handed him to me to bounce him while he whimpered. Mapiya removed the baby pack and replaced it under Derry's loose shirt. "This way."

Derry watched the process, her eyes appearing startled at Mapiya's brisk handling. "Now I know wha' a pony feels like, being saddled."

Thankfully, Garnan returned to his interrupted nap when we resumed our hike. The breeze bore the mustiness of fallen leaves moldering in mountain loam, the perfume of flame-shaped flowers, and whispers through the remaining leaves.

"Never knew Tempest had a place with so many trees," I said.

Mapiya identified their varieties as we went along. "Many willows in this area. Those are downywoods—" she nodded toward a timber grove on the streambank "—with flowers like down from white doves."

Sunlight ribboned between narrow, dark-green leaves, and I peered through swaying shadows.

Mapiya paused often to point out new plants, various small animals' burrows and runs, or a nest of tangled branches in a crag far above.

"Sun eagles," she said. "That pair has lived there for twenty years and raised many chicks."

Eyes shielded with my hand, I squinted after one soaring bird for some time. Blinked at a flash of sunlight off its golden wings. *My spirit guide.*

Mapiya studied us every time we stopped. "Drink more water," she ordered. "Stand still and breathe deeply."

She hobbled slowly but steadily. Another time, I might have grown impatient, but my knee ached despite the brace, and my ankle twinged if I trod carelessly. *Sure wish I'd brought the walking stick.*

Two strides ahead of me, Derry sagged under the double load of her backpack, smaller than mine, and Garnan cradled on her chest beneath her shirt. It'd take her longer than me to acclimate to the gravity difference, I knew.

I drew up alongside her and noted her head bowed to lean into the shallow incline. Her breaths sighed through her open mouth. "Doing all right, white bird?"

"Keeping up," she said with determination. In her eyes I read, *Barely.*

"Want me to take Garn for a while?"

She eyed me, bearing my rucksack that rose as high as a cockpit's seatback behind my head and protruded several thumb-widths beyond my shoulders. "I'm a' righ'," she said. "He's no' verra heavy. How's yer knee faring?"

I attempted a shrug. "It's been worse."

At mid-morning we found a large log, stripped of bark and gray with age, for a place to sit and eat. We shed our packs, revealing sweat-dark patches on our sides and backs. Derry dug a small blanket from hers and spread it on thick grass in the log's waning shadow.

By then, Garn needed a change, another meal, and some tummy time to kick and stretch and lift his head. Derry unlaced her shirt's front to lift him out and placed him on the blanket while Mapiya opened my rucksack to find the bundle of new diapers stuffed in on top.

"You rest, Anataqa," Mapiya said. "I'll tend to food while Wani-kiya tends to his son." She pushed a new diaper into my hand and gave me her steady gaze. "Those who would be great leaders must care for their weakest people in the humblest way."

"I used to do this for your Aunt Kimama when she was your size," I told Garnan while I cleaned him up and swapped his soiled diaper for the fresh one.

Garnan waved his arms and crowed and favored me with his toothless smile. Unexpected joy swelled under my ribs, and I chuckled.

I returned him to Derry before I scrubbed his used diaper in a swift current far downstream and spread it on sunlit grass to dry. When I returned, Derry had settled against the log and cradled him under her shirt to suckle. Her nose and cheeks glowed pink, and her freckles had multiplied.

"You're sunburned, little bird." I teased, "Put some python oil on your face. It'll help."

"Ugh!" Derry shuddered. "I canna abide the smell of i'."

We munched on smoked shegrul rolled with tangy chilies in flat circles of maize bread. After the morning's hike, I couldn't get enough.

"Why, Chanter," I asked Mapiya between mouthfuls, "do you live so far away from the enclave?"

For once she didn't glower at me. "I live where I was born and grew up," she said. "I was the last child. When my sisters and brothers went away to have their own families, my father gave responsibility for the sacred things to me."

"Your father was Chanter Yuma?"

She gave a scant nod.

"The sacred things?" I asked.

Another nod. "The things you must learn, Wanikiya." Her gaze grew stern once more, so I dammed up the flood of new questions welling in my mind.

"Finish what's in your waterskins," Mapiya said. "There's plenty of water at my dwelling."

She pointed out purple-black berries from bushes along the streambank. "They're good for winter. We'll come soon to harvest them. They're easy to store."

We gathered some into an emptied food pouch, as well as our stomachs, before we set out again. Their tartness freshened our mouths, and their seeds crunched between our teeth.

* * *

Shortly after the sun passed its zenith, we veered left into a narrow side canyon. Massive columns of wind-battered beige stood guard at each side of its mouth, grim and towering.

I stopped short. *Like the columns that tore loose in Red Wash and crushed my brother. Like Yuma's Knife that cracked in the lightning strike and threw down my father.* My eyes narrowed, and my hands tightened.

"Wanikiya?" Mapiya demanded.

I shook myself out of the flashback. "Nothing," I said, but my jaw remained set.

The chanter regarded me for a long space before she beckoned sharply and said, "This way."

I drew several steadying breaths and followed.

Our trail paralleled a tinkling creek that fed into the large stream we'd followed. The trail led down a gradual bank to a shallow ford, and I studied the damp soil bordering the water.

Tracks of all shapes and sizes lay imprinted on each other in firm mud, most of them less than a day old. Twiggy, four-toed tracks of running birds. Heart-shaped hoofprints three thumb-widths long. The alternate round and long prints of hopping tavos, with their alert ears, twitchy noses, and meaty haunches.

I picked out clawed canine prints, slightly wider than my palm and as long as my palm and fingers together. Desert wolves, I knew, grew fangs like ivory daggers, had keen night vision, and feared only fire.

By the size of these prints, their shoulders are probably level with my hip.

"Large pack," I said, indicating the massed spoor.

"I've counted sixteen hunting together," Mapiya said.

I spotted a single set of feline tracks, paw prints broader than my spread hand. I smiled and pointed them out to Derry. "That's a ghost cat." *Her spirit guide.*

Her weary features lit up. "I'd dearly love to see one."

"We probably won't," I said. "They're shy, stay away from humans, and their coat markings make them hard to see from a distance unless they're moving. That's how they got their name."

"A female," Mapiya said. "She has kits sometimes, but not this year."

Half hidden in the leafy mold at the trail's edge, a string of tracks—familiar, but with odd differences—caught my eye. Large as the ghost cat's, they appeared somewhat reptilian, with a knobby center pad and three clawed toes. Toe prints overlapped heel prints, and I visualized their maker's rippling movement. *At least three pairs of legs, maybe four.*

The tracks twisted away under the trees on our side of the creek. For an arm-length or more on either side of the prints, the soil had been randomly scooped and clods broken as if by a careless farmer with a shovel. Off-white tufts like dirty wool had caught on raw ends of chewed and broken branches as high as my chest.

Looks like a city transport with a plow rammed through here. Tracks could be a shegrul's, except they're three or four times too big, and shegruls don't have claws. And where did the clumps of hair come from?

I stared a question at Mapiya.

She picked her way to me and eyed the tracks I crouched beside. "Mountain shegrul," she said. "Different from the tame desert ones. They have keen senses of smell and touch, and they grow heavy wool." She indicated the tufts stuck in the brush.

"They don't eat insects, carrion, and droppings like desert ones. They have tusks, like boars in coastal jungles, to root in the earth." She motioned at the torn soil. "They eat burrowing mammals, snakes, ground birds and their nests, and roots and cones. Their teeth can grind bones."

Mapiya eyed me. "Early in spring, before the last snow fell, I found a place in the large canyon where wolves attacked the shegrul. They tore off a back foot."

She squatted to stroke dank, blackened leaves from the tracks with careful fingers. "See?"

No toes. Like somebody had pounded the mud with a badly chopped post. I said, "Yes, Chanter."

"It killed two wolves and wounded more," Mapiya said. "I found two carcasses. One was partly eaten."

"It's lived in this canyon since then, farther up than my dwelling. It's very destructive. It tears out grasses and saplings, so soil is washed down the creek when it rains. It destroys other animals and their habitats. There have been no whistling grouse since early summer."

She pushed herself to her feet by leaning on my shoulder and studied me where I crouched. "It's very aggressive, but it will provide much meat for the winter, and its hide will keep your family warm. You must kill the mountain shegrul, Wanikiya."

* * * * *

Chapter Thirty-Three

"Come, now," Mapiya said. "My home is half a range away. We have much to do today."

She led us across the creek, only ankle deep, but cold enough we didn't linger in it. From there the trail ascended the side canyon's east wall, steeply enough that climbing replaced casual hiking. Fragments of stone rolled and slipped under our feet. My knee panged with every step.

The canyon curved gradually southwest. We left behind willows and downywoods for scattered junipers and piñions, scrubby and bare. Their distinct scents flavored dust-laden air, and we spat grit. Several arm-lengths farther, we left the trees for a hillside of gray rock, washed with sun and wind.

Where the trail widened, Mapiya stopped and waved across the canyon. "My home."

Between the tops of several trees, I made out a rounded cave, like an open mouth halfway between the canyon's floor and the cliff's top.

In the next moment she shifted our attention to a prickly cactus with slim branches growing near the trail. "The yellow fruits at the ends are called honey barrels. You must wear heavy gloves to harvest them. They're sweet and dry well for winter.

"Those are paddle cactus, plainer than red cactus fruits. The baked, flat leaves taste like bread.

"More piñion trees. The nuts are ready. We should gather some cones while we're here.

"That—" she pointed at a plant with elongated, spike-tipped leaves about its base and slender stalks rising from its center "—is Many Uses. Young, tender stems are good food. When they're old and dry, the stems have strong fibers to make twine and nets. I make soap from its roots, and its spikes are my needles."

Beside me, Derry nodded acknowledgment while I translated. Her breaths came in weary puffs.

In another hundred arm-lengths we rounded a blunt outcrop. The trail descended to a log-and-stone dam with a timber bridge along its top to cross the narrow canyon. The pool behind the dam extended ten arm-lengths at most. Below its rippling surface, I guessed the water to be no more than twelve spans deep.

"The creek flows all winter," Mapiya said. "The pool only freezes at the edges." She pointed toward the dam's base. "The mountain shegrul did that, too."

With the rucksack on my shoulders, I didn't lean too far. Not that I needed to. At the foot of the dam, under a log-framed opening for overflow, I discerned the tumbled remains of a six-by-six-span stone enclosure.

"For cold storing," Mapiya said. "The shegrul knocked it in to eat the meat and pelts I had there."

"I can rebuild it," I said, "during winter when there's not much water in it."

Mapiya eyed me again before she said, "Look up past those trees."

Three firs towered near the bridge's end, shaggy spires sighing in the canyon's breeze. Derry and I shifted to peer around them.

They shaded a gravelly clearing at the base of a beige, striated cliff. Its layers resembled an athlete's well-defined abs, carved by millennia of winds and water. A rugged ladder, built from stripped logs about four thumb-widths in diameter, leaned against the natural wall.

I sized up the ladder. *Forty-five or fifty spans high.*

Its top rested on a stone shelf protruding like a lower lip below a cave's mouth. The first of a handful of caves, in fact, lying in a fairly even line across the cliff's face.

Early afternoon sunlight slanted into the nearest cave, which arched at least twenty spans high. Even from a distance, I could see a partial wall within its shadowed interior. I turned toward Mapiya.

"My enclave," she said and brushed past us on the bridge. "Come. The ladder is strong enough for all of us."

She climbed more easily than she'd hobbled along the trail. The ladder didn't bounce or rock. Its feet rested in stone-braced holes about a span deep.

Beside me, Derry hadn't stirred, hadn't uttered a sound. When I glanced around, her wide eyes locked on me, and she swallowed. "I don' care for heigh's, Kew," she whispered, "any more than for tigh', dark spaces."

I hadn't known about her claustrophobia until after she'd led her officemates from their bombed building, crawling on her belly through a narrow, tar-black tunnel.

"Come," Mapiya ordered from the shelf, and beckoned with evident impatience.

"You made it out of the burning vault, white bird," I said. "That was a lot more dangerous than this. Keep your eyes on Mapiya and take it one rung at a time. I'll stay right behind you. I won't let you fall."

Derry sucked her lower lip between her teeth and set her hand on an eye-level rung. Hesitant boots followed on the lower ones.

She started up shakily, and I swung onto the ladder behind her. My injured knee protested with a jab. I gritted my teeth, but stayed close enough to place a hand on Derry's back when she faltered. "I'm right here, little bird. You're doing fine."

Mapiya stretched out a wizened hand to Derry when she reached the top. "Hmph," she said. "You'll climb faster next time." It sounded like an order, and I winced for Derry.

When I dismounted moments later, I gave the ladder an experimental push. *Solid and heavy. Don't think I could haul it up by myself. How does Mapiya do it?*

I studied the cavern's interior. About twelve spans wide and maybe fifteen deep with a slightly sloping floor, it seemed to have been scooped out of the cliff's face. Though cool and shady after our hike in the sun, it smelled of canyon breezes, not guano or lichens.

The partial wall I'd glimpsed from the bridge was composed of stone chunks, flatter than typical adobe bricks, though just as long and wide, and mortared together. It stood two or three spans inside the cave's mouth, as high as the middle of my chest, and extended halfway across the opening. *Like a livestock pen. But how would animals get up here? Maybe this is a storage area?*

A few seconds' scrutiny overhead, through shadows and water stains, revealed a modern pulley system anchored on the ceiling. Its heavy rope, ending in an iron hook large enough for the ladder's top rung, hung coiled on a bracket at one side. *Good. We can bring the ladder up quickly if we have to.*

Satisfied, I let out a breath and shed the rucksack while I surveyed the canyon.

The side on which we stood faced south, which meant the caves would receive all the low-angle sunlight available until winter darkness arrived. From the lip I could see most of the way down the side canyon, to the point where it bent to enter the broad valley from which we'd come.

Sharp scents of junipers and piñions, mingled with those of dying leaves, wafted across my face and ruffled the front of my hair. *Once the leaves drop, we'll be able to see the canyon floor. Looks like 150, maybe 175 spans from here.*

From this position I had an unobstructed view across the bridge to the trail we'd followed, and of the elevated clearing at the ladder's foot, which sloped directly to the reservoir's bank behind the three firs.

I nodded in satisfaction. *Also good. Clear visibility of the approach. Unless there's another path farther up the canyon, bringing up the ladder makes these caves close to inaccessible. Wolves can't leap this high. Don't think even a ghost cat could, but I need to do some reconnaissance.*

Mapiya, watching me, seemed to guess my thoughts. "The only other trail from the caves goes up." She jutted her chin toward the cliff overlooking the canyon's mouth. "My garden is on the mesa. We'll start harvesting this afternoon, but we must eat and rest first."

The stone lip on which we stood fronted most of the cave complex. The lip varied from four to six spans wide, and it dipped here and rose there. Around its mild curve we entered a second cave three times the width and depth of the first.

Little daylight slanted into it. Faint, infrequent dripping reached my ears, and its chilly dankness produced gooseflesh on my arms. I grimaced at its musty odor.

When my eyes adjusted, I made out three compact dwellings, all two stories, snugged against the rear wall in a semicircle around a gathering area with a fire pit. As with dwellings in manmade enclaves, the builders had created high windows, timber-framed doorways, and left enough space between the roofs and cave ceiling for adults to stand upright.

Though a quarter the size of Red Wash's and Willow Valley's dwellings, I appreciated the other similarities, using the cave instead of a man-built outer wall and dome.

The walkway shelf ended a few arm-lengths farther on, where the cliff's face bulged across it. Shielded by the natural buttress, a third cave's mouth stretched wider but lower than the others.

Mapiya led us into its sunlit front chamber, where a clay jar about an arm-length tall stood beside broad stairs built of rubble and mortar. The jar held several pine-resin torches. Mapiya hefted one, fished briefly in her belt pouch for a flint-and-steel, and lit it with a few strikes.

"Come," she said, and Derry and I followed her up the steps into a broad chamber.

The air felt drier in the upper cavern, not so chilly, and it smelled more of burned wood than bat guano. Its silence prompted me to stand still, as if sound would violate something holy.

The shallow mouth below blocked the sun from the higher level, but wavering torchlight revealed a cavern large enough to hangar a couple Rohr-55s. Heavy soot coated the ceiling. A covering of fine gravel and sand leveled the floor around a large fire pit.

Another natural stone ledge, about four spans high and somewhat slanted, crossed the rear wall, and I noticed several barrels and large jars lined up on it.

"My father's ceremonial lodge," Mapiya said, "when three generations of his family lived here. The jars and barrels hold things for ceremonies. You'll learn to use them. Now follow me."

She led us to the right, where light angled in around a stone corner. "This is the passage to the next cave, the only way in. Be careful; the floor is uneven and the ceiling is low."

Derry and I picked our way and ducked a low ridge where the passage turned. The smoky light revealed Derry's determined expression.

The fourth and fifth caves, one an extension of the other, contained dwellings, too. Each cave appeared as broad as the ceremonial chamber, though only half as deep, and much more open to the outside. That allowed air to move freely through them, but I smelled lichens and noticed dark streaks of moisture on some walls.

Most dwellings hugged the caves' rear walls. Their doorways faced an open front area with a bumpy floor that sloped toward the arched mouths. None of them bore any resemblance to another. A few had two stories, and most were more or less square, but some proved to be walled-off natural alcoves.

Mapiya used one of those, constructed in a nook between two ridges where the fourth cavern opened into the fifth. Her door faced a relatively level and spacious area with a group of five fire pits. There she planted her torch.

"Choose your place to sleep," Mapiya said. "We'll eat and work out here."

Derry and I peered into several empty residences before we found a rectangular space about ten spans deep and twelve wide. Just inside the fifth cave's mouth, the room's doorway, covered by a faded blanket, faced inward. Immediately outside its door to the left lay the clustered fire pits, and beyond them, maybe ten spans away, stood Mapiya's sleeping space.

The cave wall blocked winds, but our room's east-facing constructed wall, with its two small, high windows, had been set far enough forward to catch early-morning sunlight. *Explains why it's not as dank as interior living spaces,* I thought. Dust motes swirled in the light angling through its windows, heightening the dry smell.

I made a quick inventory of its contents. In a far corner, a broad paddle with a long handle for sliding food in and out leaned against the dome-shaped oven. Two wooden water barrels, three spans high and two across, stood upside down inside the doorway, along with a twig broom. Several rolled mats or blankets lay in a near corner, and every wall bore stout pegs, and niches for oil-burning lamps.

"It's better equipped than our townhouse at Belsken Field was," I joked.

"'I' will need a good sweeping." I heard Derry's attempt to sound hopeful in her reply, but weariness overwhelmed it.

Scuttling movement at the base of the natural wall caught my eye. *Shouldn't rodents be dormant by now?*

I snatched the broom and swept the creature into a patch of sunlight slanting through one window to the rough floor.

It might have been a baby kosa, with its coat of black spines and beady eyes. Except it had *four* pairs of eyes, and it scrambled on four pairs of jointed legs as I corralled it with the broom. It would've filled my cupped hand.

"Whatever is tha'?" Derry asked with undisguised revulsion.

"Crack crawler," I said. "They come into enclaves during the winter and raid food stores, like kosas. Their spines are venomous. Not deadly, but they raise welts that burn for days."

I stomped on the thing, swept its flattened carcass out the door, and began fiercely sweeping the seamed walls. A tickle at the back of my neck warned me not to put off torching every crevice in the room.

* * * * *

Chapter Thirty-Four

"You can make your home after dark," Mapiya said from behind me. "There's work to do while there's still daylight."

I was about to ask her to wait, but she planted fists on hips and ordered, "Come *now*. Daylight is short."

Another Russom. I suppressed a scowl and returned the broom to the corner with great reluctance. *Don't forget to torch the room, Ku. It's important.*

We ate the piñon nuts and purple berries we'd gathered, jerky from Mapiya's stores, and water from her barrel. Not enough to assuage my hunger, but she said, "We'll roast sweet tubers and maize tonight."

When Derry had changed and fed Garnan, and returned him, wailing in protest, to his baby pack, Mapiya pointed us to a cobwebby storage space beside her sleeping room. We collected several deep reed baskets with double handles, three pairs from a pile of leather gloves, and two axes. The little oval room also held jars and bowls, skin buckets, and several folded tarps.

Mapiya handed an axe to me. "We must chop firewood this afternoon."

The trail to the mesa led from the fifth cave and climbed past the mouth of a sixth, which had partly collapsed. While not steep, the trail narrowed to two spans wide, and Derry gripped the rough wall until we reached the mesa's gently rounded top.

A chilly wind bearing the scent of sun-dried grasses tugged at our shirts. I found it refreshing, but I noticed Derry's brief shiver.

Mapiya had planted a couple acres of garden. Faded maize stalks, wilting chili plants, and various herbs rustled like ghosts in the breeze. Long rows of poles and stick frames, sagging under laden beanstalks, swayed in the gusts.

Orange tubers poked from the soil beneath their squatty plants like huge eggs in a gravelly nest, and squashes and melons stretched out prickly vines. I shook my head, amazed. *This'd feed a whole family for a winter. Does she plant this much every year, or does she trade some of it?*

Aloud I asked, "How do you keep tavos and summer birds from eating your crops?"

She fixed me with her appraising stare once more before she said, "Hawks and sun eagles eat many of the birds and tavos, but there are plenty for us to snare."

Why does she stare at me like that? I wondered. *Russom only did it when I messed up somehow.*

We dug plump tubers, gathered several ears of maize, and one bush's load of red chilies into one basket, then started along rows of beans. Early frosts had shriveled their leaves to black, and the pods hung in dappled clusters. We stripped them into baskets slung on our shoulders and sang the Chant of Gratitude for Plenty while we worked.

When we'd picked two rows of beans, Mapiya said, "We'll harvest the rest of them and the maize tomorrow. After supper we'll shell beans and spread them on tarps to dry. Now we must chop firewood and fill your water barrels."

Derry stared when I translated. Fatigue lined her sunburned face, now smeared with python oil and dirt. I read dismay along with exhaustion in her eyes and wondered, *What have I dragged her into?* I gave her hand a discreet squeeze.

"We must take the baskets to the cave," Mapiya said, watching us both.

I counted the baskets. *Eight full of beans, another with tubers and maize, and we haven't even chopped the firewood. We'll have to make several trips to carry it all.*

Maybe I appeared disconcerted, too, because Mapiya said, "There's a hoist."

A solid tree stood on the brink, its bottom limb protruding over the edge. The heavy rope secured about its bole, like the one for the ladder in the first cave, ended with a hook large enough for two baskets' handles.

"It lowers in front of your cave, Anataqa," Mapiya said. "The staff is in my sleeping room, with a crook for pulling the baskets inside when they come down."

Derry eyed me for an interpretation, then said, "Yes, Chanter," in Chalca. She started for the path at once, cradling our unhappy baby inside her shirt.

While we waited, Mapiya and I carried the baskets to the hoist. She pointed out sun-bleached fallen trees outside the cultivated ground, ideal for firewood.

"There's enough to last," she said, "but we need to bring in wood before winter comes. When we're done with other tasks every day, we'll chop firewood until it gets dark."

"When I was little," I said, "we went into the hills above Red Wash for wood, before the snow came. Can't do anything once it's a couple hundred spans deep and always dark." I surveyed the canyon below us, imagining it filled to the rim. "How deep does it get here?"

She preceded her answer with that stare. "Only one or two spans. The cold is worse than the snow."

"I'm here!" Derry's voice rang from below. It carried more energy than I'd thought she had left.

I lowered the baskets two at a time, feeding out enough rope for Derry to swing them inside and unhook them. When I hauled the rope up the last time and looped it around a branch, I shouted, "We'll come after we chop wood."

Mapiya chose a wind-warped fallen juniper near the garden. Its weathered trunk split with a few well-placed axe strokes. The sharp *pok, pok, pok* of our tools rang across the narrow canyon and echoed from its facing wall.

While I bound oven-length chunks into bundles to carry on our shoulders, Mapiya stuffed splinters and dry weeds into her belt pouch for kindling and tinder. On a thought, as we crossed to the path's head, I chose several poles from the rows of beans we'd picked.

Mapiya eyed me. "Those won't burn well."

"Good," I said. "We need a rack for drying diapers after we wash them. Do you have twine?"

"Ya." For the first time, Mapiya appeared approving.

We reached the cave to find Derry seated on a woven mat in the gloomy gathering area, her back to a stone-and-mortar wall, and her grimy shirt and bra pushed up to suckle Garnan. She'd hauled the baskets of beans inside and found a pottery basin into which she'd piled the tubers and chilies.

She started when we briefly blocked the last light through the entrance and broke off her Caerdish crooning. "I'll scrub the tubers and husk the maize when I've done here," she said in a rush, as if to preempt additional requests.

In the next breath she added, "One baske' a'mos' burs' when I hauled i' in. I' needs mending. And I've no idea wha' to do with his diapers. I've four in there now—" she pointed with a Chalca-like jut of her chin at the pot we'd bought "—all needing washed."

Still got to haul water. I lowered my shoulder-load of wood to the floor with a clatter and a resigned exhalation. My knee ached, but I asked, "Chanter, how many buckets do you have?"

"Thirteen." Mapiya deposited her firewood near mine, relit her pine resin torch, and shuffled in the direction of the first cave and the ladder. I followed.

The skin buckets stood, neatly stacked, behind the partial wall. Each held about three gallons, I guessed. "I'll go down and fill them if you can bring them up on the rope."

Mapiya said, "Hmph," but removed the coiled rope from its hook.

At the reservoir's edge, dipping one bucket after another into the glassy water, I watched the receding sunlight ignite high-altitude clouds into flaming streaks of red and gold. *Don't think I've ever seen a sunset that brilliant before.*

I would've liked to watch the colors change and fade, but darkness had already enveloped the caverns by the time I climbed the ladder and hauled it up, too. Mapiya went ahead to light a few torches, and I seized two sloshing buckets.

While Mapiya started a supper fire in one of the gathering area's fire pits, I washed our water barrels. Storing them upside down had kept small creatures from falling into them, but fat spiders had filled them with dense webs.

Derry watched me in the flickering torchlight as I set down one bucket of water. "Yer limping's worse, Kew. Yew need to ge' off yer leg. I've rested a bi' now; I can carry the water."

I'd ignored the pain during the afternoon's labors, until the pangs and twinges and jabs had melded into a throbbing ache. Still, I balked. "No, that's my job."

Derry and I had spoken in Standard, so I started when Mapiya said in Chalca, "Tasks are tasks, Wanikiya. It doesn't matter who does them." She beckoned me. "Come, sit."

When Derry stood, I eased myself to the rug beside Garnan. Fed, changed, and content at last, he beamed at me, gurgled, and waved and stretched with evident pleasure. I scooped him up, grinning, but felt mildly useless watching Derry collect the water buckets.

"Your knee, Wanikiya," Mapiya said and took Garnan from my arms. She cradled him, fingered his hair, kissed his forehead.

I had no idea how much my knee had swollen until I removed the brace and rolled my trouser leg up. The brace had left deep marks in my skin through my trousers. My ankle didn't appear much better.

"Your knee needs something cold." Mapiya returned Garnan to me, climbed to her feet to enter her sleeping room, and returned with a handful of rags. Efficient as a military medic, she soaked them in one of the buckets I'd brought and wrapped my knee and ankle.

Finished with me, she used a small paddle to scoop a hole beneath her fire's coals and buried some tubers and maize ears. Within minutes, aromas of roasting vegetables drifted through the gathering area.

Derry made several laborious trips back and forth through the cave complex, hauling two buckets each time. After setting the last pair down, she shook out her arms and sank to the rug beside me. "Isn' there a chan' to call water spiri's to fill the barrels?" she asked, catching her breath.

Mapiya's head snapped up. In the embers' ruddy glow, her face appeared craggy as old juniper bark, and her voice rattled like gravel. "The spirits of Star Father's creations are not slaves to summon for our common tasks, Anataqa. We call on them only for sacred purposes, or when there's an urgent need, with approval from Star Father to use his power."

Mapiya's tone bore unmistakable rebuke. I bristled for Derry's sake when she turned to me, clearly stricken, though she didn't understand the words.

I explained, and Derry asked, "How do you say 'I'm sorry, I didn't know?'"

"*Tai epesso* means 'my sorrow' or 'I'm sorry,'" I said. "'I didn't know' or 'I don't know' is *ti telá-ma*."

Derry bowed her head toward Mapiya in a manner reminiscent of Go and said with genuine contrition, "*Tai epesso*, Chanter. *Ti telá-ma*."

Mapiya eyed her for a moment before she said, "Hmph," and returned her attention to the fire pit.

I glowered. *Worse than Russom, especially when Derry's trying so hard.*

The aches in my leg and foot ebbed under fresh cold wraps while we ate roasted maize and sweet tubers, bright orange in their crackly skins. Food in my belly eased the day's fatigue as well. After we ate, I lashed the sturdiest bean poles into a drying rack.

Mapiya dumped a basket of beans in a mound on the floor and began to shell them into the clay basin Derry had found.

"*Kono?*" Derry asked, watching her. "How?"

Mapiya demonstrated the shelling technique without speaking, and Derry dug in, diligent but silent.

A starfield as dense as summer dust filled the sky outside the high cavern. *I've only seen this many stars from orbit.*

My thoughts immediately went to Kota, Go, Allandra, and my other friends in the 15th ACW. *Wonder how they're doing, wherever they are? How many missions have they flown since I left? Are they all right?*

"First frost tonight," Mapiya said. Her voice, chilly as the impending temperature, snapped me from my reverie. "Build a fire in your oven."

I nodded in response. *Legs ache, arms ache, back aches. How long will it take, learning to live the way my grandfathers did? Or will Mapiya decide we're unworthy?*

* * * * *

Chapter Thirty-Five

Mapiya taught us how to swaddle Garnan correctly to keep him warm before we withdrew to our room. By the light of a python-oil lamp, I built a fire that'd burn slowly through the night. Derry improvised a cradle from a large basket she padded with maize husks, and she shook out and arranged an old rug and faded blankets into a floorbed.

We washed with water heated in a bucket beside the oven and shared a towel from Derry's pack. She spoke very little until we'd settled into the blankets. Then, lying with her head on my shoulder and a hand on my bare chest, she sighed. "I don' think Mapiya approves of me."

I'd contemplated Mapiya's brusqueness while building the fire, but Derry's words revived my memories of pilot training. "Maybe she's like Russom. I thought he was trying to wash me out of pilot training the whole time, when he was really pushing me to excel."

"I've a feeling I'll be saying *tai epesso* a lot."

I chuckled. "So will I, probably. Keep asking how to say things in Chalca. Ask *everything* you have a question about, so she'll know you're taking it seriously."

"Righ'."

"But not tonight." I eased her onto her back and grinned. "I want to count all your new freckles." I started by kissing the tip of her nose.

Eventually we sank into sleep, snug in each other's arms. On the familiarity of a floorbed, I slept deeply, though I fell asleep to the tiny scratchings of night creatures in the cave. *Got to burn them out of all the crevices tomorrow...*

* * *

G arnan woke us with his usual hungry cries when the first faint pallor touched the sky outside our high windows. Derry stirred beside me and groaned.

"What's wrong, white bird?" My breath clouded on the crisp air.

"I'm sa sore I can scarce move a muscle." She set her teeth as she lifted Garnan from his basket cradle. Autumn's high-desert chill raised gooseflesh on her arms, and she quickly gathered him to her breast under a cloak of our blankets. He squealed and tried to squirm in his snug swaddling.

The previous day's exertions seared my muscles, too. Teeth gritted, I shoved off the floorbed and crossed to the oven on bare feet. The floor's uneven stones felt like river ice under my soles.

I poked through the ashes with the oven paddle until I uncovered live embers from the night's fire. With new kindling, gentle blowing, and fuel, I coaxed new flames to life, then dipped a bucketful of water from one full barrel. I'd just set it by the oven to heat when a step fell at the doorway behind me. I started.

Mapiya peeked around the door blanket. "Good, you're awake. There's maize porridge. We must eat before Dawn Chant. We have much to do today."

With our stomachs full of hot porridge sweetened with lumps of crystalized honey, we started up the trail to the garden. Our voices echoed from the canyon's facing wall in the words of the Dawn Chant.

Fingers of sunlight sketched our shadows, lean and long as bean poles, and eased Derry's shivering beneath her jacket.

We spent the morning picking beans, chilies, and maize, gathering squashes and melons, digging more tubers, and lowering filled baskets to the caves. I barely noticed my knee's soreness for the ache through my shoulders and back, and I saw Derry's cringes when she bent and lifted, too.

Mapiya called to us when the sun reached its zenith. "Now we eat and rest," she said. "Then I'll teach you to use hunting tools."

She made a stew of beans, squash, and maize, with herbs and chunks of jerky for flavor, and we divided a juicy moon melon between us. Its silver-colored flesh gave it the name. I ate like a partitioned shegrul after the morning's labors.

"Chanter," I said, ladling seconds from the pot into my bowl, "Wahkan sent us to you to learn the sacred ceremonies and chants. I need to finish my apprenticeship. When will we start? We haven't even talked about it."

Mapiya leveled her piercing stare on me. I returned it.

At last she asked, "What does your name mean, Wanikiya?"

"Preserver of the People," I said.

She gave a curt nod. "How can you preserve our people in the time to come if you don't know how to preserve yourself?"

The time to come. The EMP. I stiffened. *How much time do we have?*

"I can teach any apprentice chants and ceremonies," she said. "I've taught many. You're not *any* apprentice. There are *many* things you must learn as Wanikiya. You're here to learn *all* you need, farming and hunting and healing, and growing in your soul." She pressed a palm to my chest.

"Others are coming to help hunt the mountain shegrul," she said. "We must prepare for them. You'll start learning the ceremonies when they return to Yellow Rock Enclave."

"Good." Placated, I dug into my second bowl of stew.

* * *

With the cooking gear washed and shelved, Mapiya retreated to her sleeping space and came back with two long bundles, wrapped with care in supple leather. One sheathed a rugged spear with a hardened steel head. The other contained a wooden bow, about two-thirds my height in length, and a quiver of arrows.

Mapiya handled them with the same reverence Go had taught me for the *pelu*. "They were my father's, brought here on the Crossing. He taught his children to use them, and I've taught many others. Now I will teach you."

We returned to the garden for her training. In the dry heat of afternoon, I peeled off my shirt while I built targets from maize stalks. Their dusty scent drifted around us on particles that stuck and itched on my sweat-damp skin. They prompted a couple sneezes while I gathered them into rattling bundles and bound them with smooth twine.

"The twine comes from Many Uses plant." Mapiya rolled it between her wizened fingers with evident satisfaction. "I'll teach you to make that, too, but not today."

Having only one set of weapons, she worked with us one at a time. "Come." She beckoned to Derry and placed the bow across her hands.

From where I sat under a shaggy piñon, with my stiff knee elevated on a lichen-encrusted rock, and Garnan propped in my lap to look around, I couldn't hear Mapiya's coaching. I saw her demonstrate the shooting stance and watched Derry imitate her.

Though I couldn't see the targets, I knew Derry missed her first shot by the way her shoulders slumped.

Mapiya positioned her wrists and elbow with firm hands, gave her another arrow, and stepped away.

When Derry missed again, something occurred to me, a memory of sparring together with wooden practice knives. *Is she trying to do it righthanded?* I tucked Garnan into the crook of my arm and crossed to them. "Derry, do you shoot your military pistol right- or lefthanded?" I asked. I already knew the answer.

"Lef', of course," Derry said.

I gave Mapiya a firm glance. "No different with archery. Try it lefthanded."

Mapiya scrunched her scraggly brows, but Derry's next effort at least struck the bundled stalks, if not the moldy squash I'd set on top.

"Better," Derry said.

"You'll get it." I slid a reassuring hand across her back and returned to my spot under the tree.

When Garnan whimpered for his afternoon meal, Derry picked her way through the harrowed soil with confidence in her step and smugness on her sunburned face. "I'm no' ready for moving targe's jus' ye'," she said, "but I hi' the spoil' squash from a distance of thirty arm-lengths."

I bounced Garnan and chuckled. "Hear that, little man? Never torque off your mama."

Derry relieved me of our wriggling son and grinned. "Now le's see wha' yer da can do with a spear."

The weapon Mapiya held out to me consisted of a seven-span, two-thumb-width diameter shaft topped with a steel head ten thumb-widths long. Its blade widened to three thumb-widths from the point, with a span-wide crosspiece forward of the tang, where three heavy bolts secured the head to the shaft.

This isn't a primitive weapon. I hefted the spear in my hands, finding its balance. *Six or seven lugs, I think, weighted toward the head.*

"It isn't a throwing weapon," Mapiya said, watching me. "A mountain shegrul's fleece will deflect a thrown spear, and you must never be disarmed. They're very aggressive. This is for thrusting."

She squatted to trace the outline of a four-segmented shegrul in the dirt with a finger. "You saw the tracks. They have a narrow base. They can be tipped over.

"Here's the best place to strike." She tapped the drawing between its first and second segments, where any other animal's heart would be. Shegruls had a two-chambered heart in each segment. "It'll thrash, and you'll have to hold it down, but if you hit it here, it can't twist enough to rend you with its tusks."

Rend me? I masked shock and said, "Good to know," in the most matter-of-fact tone I could muster.

"You'll have to put your whole weight into your thrust to knock it down," Mapiya said. "Most hunters run at it, but if it picks up your scent or the vibrations from your steps, it'll charge you." She repeated, "They're very aggressive."

I remembered the askuk tracking me by my footfalls in Red Wash Enclave's burial ground. *No grave pillars here. Do mountain shegruls ram trees?*

"What if it charges?" I asked.

"Drop to one knee, anchor your spear, and level it like a pike. The shegrul will impale itself."

I arched a questioning brow.

"It weighs fifteen hundred lugs and has four pairs of legs," Mapiya said. "Once it has momentum, it can't stop quickly. And once it has your scent, it won't swerve away. It's very—"

"Aggressive, ya." I concealed my tension under a dry tone.

"That's why the spear has lugs." She slid wrinkled fingers along the broad crosspiece. "They keep the shegrul from running up the shaft at you. If you must take it head on, angle the spear up through its mouth, into its skull, and keep your grip until it stops thrashing."

Fifteen hundred lugs of shegrul thrashing at the end of my seven-span stick. I'll have to dig out those work gloves Wahkan recommended. Hope the palms have a good gripping surface.

"Ya, Chanter," I said.

I spent the next hour or so under Mapiya's critical gaze, charging at split melons and bug-eaten squashes placed in the crotch of a dead piñon.

"More thrust," she said. "Lunge as if you're throwing it at the last second."

The spearhead pierced the discarded fruits and dry wood up to the lugs with a satisfying *thunk* I felt more than heard. It roused something in my warrior soul I hadn't experienced even in a six-G vertical combat launch. *The primal part. The part my ancestors knew.*

I roared as I drove the blade into the piñon's trunk. My bellow echoed at me from across the canyon like the acceptance of a challenge. I continued the lunges and thrusts until the old tree split under my repeated strikes, and my palms tingled with increasing friction.

"Chopping firewood is half done for today," Mapiya said when we finished, and for an instant I glimpsed teasing in her eyes, "but we will have to inspect and sharpen the spearhead."

* * *

Mapiya set the routine for our days. Mornings, we harvested crops or hiked down the canyon to gather the last piñion nuts, berries, and cactus honey barrels. Afternoons, we exercised with the spear and bow.

Once Derry switched to shooting lefthanded, she proved to have a keen eye with the bow, even better than mine, but she found the spear too long and heavy to handle well.

When the spearhead sank into soil for the fourth time on another attempt to charge with it, I teased, "At least you'll be able to pole-vault over the shegrul if it charges you."

She laughed and pitched a pinecone at me that would've hit my chest dead center if I hadn't snatched it out of its flight.

Mapiya rolled her eyes and muttered, "Lovebugs."

After chopping wood and hauling water, Derry and I sat knee-to-knee to shell beans, sort berries and chilies, cut up melons and squashes, and shuck ears of maize onto tarps to be spread on the cave's lip to dry in the next day's sun. During those quiet evenings, a sense of fulfillment settled on my soul. Derry and I exchanged glances and small smiles, and I knew she felt it, too.

Mapiya sprinkled the laden tarps with bitterleaf seeds to repel squirrels and kosas. Once they dried, we'd store the fruits and vegetables in covered clay jars, and strip maize off the ears into cloth bags.

Later, while Derry fed, changed, and swaddled Garnan for sleep, I boiled his diapers and our underwear clean in the laundry pot, and hung everything to dry on the bean-pole rack beside the oven.

"Thank yew for doing i', Kew," she said more than once.

"A task is a task." I said it in Chalca and shrugged. Then I teased, "I'd be happy to trade off, but I'm not equipped to feed Garn."

One morning I set snares across a few well-used runs that entered the garden. That night we had spit-roasted tavos for supper. Mapiya stuffed them with herbs and wild onions, and we relished the fire-seared meat and sweetness of cooked onions.

Once lengthening shadows drew darkness like a blanket over the canyon, we worked by firelight. Mapiya taught us the right way to flesh tavo skins and stretch them on drying frames, and to store the brains in a jar for tanning the skins later. She showed us how to grind dried maize kernels into meal and braid fibers from Many Uses plants into twine.

The soreness in our muscles faded. The swelling and ache in my knee and ankle decreased, and Derry grew stronger in the higher gravity.

Garnan adapted, too. Swaddled at night, he woke less frequently than before. He giggled and cooed for Mapiya when she held or bounced him, and when we laid him on a blanket near us during the day, he wiggled and burbled and beamed at us until we laughed.

Between chores, I roamed the narrow canyon in search of suitable poles and lashed together drying racks for the meat from our upcoming shegrul hunt.

I explored for another reason as well. *What if we have to bring our people here after the EMP? How would I bring them here? How could I defend this canyon from marauders?* And always, *How much time do we have?*

By our tenth evening at the cliff dwelling, rising impatience made me fidget while I inspected and sharpened the razor-edged spearhead. "When are we hunting the shegrul?" I asked. "It'll take a couple phases to make its hide usable."

Mapiya quirked a thinning eyebrow. "Killing and butchering it is a task for many hands. We must wait for the hunting party to come."

"*When* are they coming?" I insisted. "We lose a few more minutes of sunlight every day, and it's getting a lot colder at night."

Mapiya stopped weaving new reeds into the broken basket and fixed me with her long stare in the wavering light. Evaluating me again. "Soon," she said.

* * * * *

Chapter Thirty-Six

Eerie stillness blanketed the canyon two days later. The soft splash of water spilling from the bucket I hefted out of the reservoir sounded like a torrent.

The trio of firs by the bridge stood as motionless as if holding their breaths. My vision slid up their slim trunks to where their tops vanished in low, heavy clouds as dense as gray smoke. *First snow by morning.*

I snatched the last empty pail and stooped to the water, but straightened when movement across the canyon caught my eye.

A dark-clad man appeared around the outcrop where the trail led down to the bridge. A second man followed, then a third and fourth.

I kept my eyes on them while I filled the last bucket. I seized the previous one and hauled both to the foot of the cliff. The rope and hook rotated slowly at waist level. Hanging the buckets on the hook, I said, "We've got visitors."

Mapiya, waiting on the cave's lip to draw up the buckets, squinted across the canyon. When she called to the approaching figures, I relaxed.

By then the first two men, spears on their shoulders, had started across the bridge. When the leader shouted a greeting to Mapiya, I strode forward to meet them. All wore backpacks, and hunting knives at their belts. Those without spears carried bows and quivers.

The party consisted of nine people, all of whom I'd met during the Oil-Gathering Ceremony. Kaya had come, along with two other women.

Now I know why Mapiya asked me to set tavo snares again this morning. We'll have more than ten sharing supper tonight.

While most of the newcomers explored the cave complex to choose sleeping spaces, their leader, Adahy, and I hiked to the mesa's top to chop and bundle firewood.

Adahy reminded me of Chanter Wahkan in some ways, with his ready smile, though lankier of build and a few years younger. "Do you like living here?" he asked.

"It's different from the enclave I grew up in," I said. "Quieter here. I like that."

"This is a sacred place for apprenticing." Adahy scanned the blue-shadowed mesa around us. "Our well-known chanter lived here. Chanter Mapiya is his youngest daughter."

I knew that. I simply nodded.

When we checked the snares, we found tavos dangling, one still warm and twitching, in eight of the ten I'd set.

While Adahy split their skulls and scooped out the brains for tanning the skins, I dug a hole in the middle of Mapiya's garden. Burying the blood and offal there would benefit next year's crops.

Adahy stopped me. "Save as much of that as you can carry in one of the skins to use for bait tomorrow."

Scrunching my nose at the stench, I piled steaming entrails onto one raw pelt and knotted the legs together.

We strung the gutted tavos by their tied hind legs, along with the grisly bait bundle, on a weathered branch and carried it down the trail between us. We reached the caves as twilight deepened into night. I left the smelly bait bundle outside the first cave, near the ladder.

The others had built fires in the gathering area's five pits. The flames had reduced enough for cooking by the time Adahy and I arrived. Everyone cheered at our catch.

Kaya examined the tavos' pelts and gave Derry a smile. "Warm clothes for your baby. We'll flesh and stretch them on drying frames before we sleep tonight."

The first snowflakes drifted lazily past the cave's mouth while we devoured roasted tavos and halved squashes filled with berries and wild honey, baked on the glowing coals. The snow increased in density during the next hour.

"Snow will make tracking easier," someone remarked.

Derry and I found snow swirling through our windows when we entered our room. A fine dusting already lay on the craggy floor beneath them.

"Oh, my hear'!" Derry cried. "I was only thinking of sunligh' when I saw the windows."

While she revived the fire in our oven, I dug through the storage space Mapiya had shown us. Only one tarp remained. Holes chewed by rodents had rendered it unsuitable for drying beans or berries. By the light of oil lamps, I tied one ragged edge to a row of wooden pegs above the windows and weighted the bottom to the floor with head-size rocks. "Have to do for tonight."

Derry drew Garnan's basket cradle close enough to canopy it as well as cover us with the musty blankets. "I will be sa good to have the fleece to sleep in," she murmured.

I gathered her close, her back to my chest. "I'll keep you warm until then."

* * *

Mapiya woke us before the stars began to fade above the canyon's eastern rim. "Much to do, and a short day to do it."

Everyone stood around the fire pits, bleary-eyed and quiet, shoveling in maize porridge, shegrul jerky, and baked paddle-cactus leaves, and guzzled strong blackmint tea from pottery bowls.

Only Adahy spoke, mostly to me, offering advice between mouthfuls of food. "Snow will make the shegrul's white coat harder to see, so watch for movement between the trees. Throw the bait bag as close to it as you can. The smell will attract it. It's best to catch a mountain shegrul in the trees so it can't maneuver and charge as well.

"Whoever spots it first will give a birdcall, and the rest of us will surround it. We'll start stomping then, to confuse it with vibrations from all directions. You'll have to spear it as quickly as you can, because sooner or later, it *will* charge."

I nodded. My mouth felt dry despite the tea.

"Its mouth and the base of its skull are the best spots for the kill," Adahy continued. "If you hit it broadside, it'll turn on you. You can knock it over, but then you'll have to hold it down with your spear until one of us finishes it."

"Got it," I said. *A seven-span spear against a fifteen hundred-lug animal.*

Derry watched, gently rocking Garnan, while we clipped sheathed knives to our belts, donned our parkas, and shouldered our packs of hunting gear. Then Mapiya swooped in and lifted our baby from her arms. "Get your bow. You must go, too. I'll care for him."

Mapiya had always been tender and affectionate with Garnan when she'd looked after him during the past couple phases, so he didn't protest. When he reached for her nose and giggled, she nuzzled his hair and murmured some baby song.

Mild apprehension shadowed Derry's features. She slid a nervous glance at me.

I understood her maternal qualms, but I chuckled. "He'll be fine. I think she likes him better than she likes us."

Derry gave an uneasy laugh, but she bundled into her parka and slung the bow and quiver onto her shoulder.

The bait-bag had frozen where I'd left it. *Just as well. Cuts the stench.* I hung it on my spear for our hike.

We descended the ladder as the sun's diffused light eased above the canyon rim, so we stood in the clearing at the cliff's base to sing the Dawn Chant.

The canyon had received about two thumb-widths of powdery snow, but clouds brooded on the mountains above us, as if contemplating releasing more. Their shroud had reduced the cold to little more than chilly. *May want to take off our parkas before long.*

We skirted the small reservoir and followed the tiny stream that fed it farther up the canyon. We crept along in single file, picking our way with care where the snow made grassy spots and steep slopes slippery.

Half a range above Mapiya's cliff dwellings, the canyon forked. We saw where the shegrul had torn out vegetation and rooted along the streambank. Undercut by years of spring runoff and eroded after the loss of its undergrowth, the bank had collapsed.

Adahy jutted his jaw at a trail cut through the woods. "They make runs like tavos between their feeding and bedding grounds."

Snow didn't conceal the pattern of spade-like scoops along the way. It only emphasized the loss of underbrush.

A hundred arm-lengths on, we entered a small valley still draped in predawn shadow and populated by wind-blasted fir trees. We'd climbed high enough for the clouds' underbellies to fill the valley, so we strode in their gray haze. Sound seemed as muffled as the light, and the temperature dropped.

With the trail wider there, Derry drew up alongside me and slipped her gloved hand into mine. I slid a smile to her and saw contentment in hers.

The trees' rough boles, like uneven black stripes painted on the backdrop of snow, distorted my depth perception. I had to see the trees' roots to be sure how near they stood.

"Spread out, five or six arm-lengths apart, with your spears and arrows ready," Adahy said. "Walk lightly to reduce vibrations in the ground. Whistle if you spot it."

Like line-abreast formation, searching for the enemy on combat space patrol, I couldn't help thinking.

Derry, jaw taut as she drew an arrow from her quiver, eased off to my left. Two youths moved out beyond her. I dangled the bait-bag from my throwing hand and leveled my spear with the other.

Layers of needles, damp with snow filtered by scraggly branches, cushioned our careful steps and raised the scent of moldering pine. Only an occasional creak of boughs shifting overhead disturbed a nearly tangible silence.

Our line had advanced about thirty arm-lengths when crunching caught my ear, and a shape like an off-white mountain eclipsed half the black trunks ahead. Broadside to me, maybe another thirty arm-lengths away, it headed to my right.

Where did it come from so suddenly? Was it standing there all along?

I gave a trilling bird whistle and changed course to head it off. *A lead-pursuit intercept.* When the others glanced to me, I pointed with my spear. They began to converge.

The massive creature, pale as a bank of old snow on the move, rippled among the distant trees like a caterpillar in spring grasses. I watched it pause now and then to unearth and devour leafless underbrush.

Then, with a dexterity that triggered memories of the askuk in the enclave burial ground, it doubled around and froze. I couldn't see its head from that distance, but I could imagine it snuffling the air. *It discovered us. How?*

The icy draft sweeping off the mountains, pinching my nose and tickling my face with crystalline snow, assured me we were downwind of the beast. I peered over my shoulder.

Helki, the boy at the far end of the line beyond Derry and the other youth, had broken into a run to close his side of the circle. *So much for stealth.*

The mountain shegrul lurched into motion like an Awénasa City transport. Increasing in speed and momentum, and slamming between trees, it curved directly toward Helki.

He froze, but sudden adrenaline shoved my heart to full throttle. I didn't need a tracking scope to calculate where the shegrul would intersect with him. *No-o-o!*

Arrow nocked, Derry sprang between boy and beast. My racing heart stopped at the sight, but my legs charged toward her.

Her first shot grazed the creature's face. It broke stride, shook its head as if shedding flies, and Derry let fly again.

The second arrow lodged in a woolly shoulder. The shegrul twitched but lumbered on.

Fear for her spurred my pounding run. "Derry!" I screamed. "Stand still! Let it pick up my bootfalls." As in space combat, my voice pitched up a couple notches.

Desperation strengthened my arm when I hurled the bait bag. The bundle burst when it struck the ground, an arm-length or two ahead of and on my side of the charging shegrul. With a boar-like bellow, the creature careened after its prize, sideswiping a tree with enough force to shake it. Its bulky wool coat didn't muffle the *thunk*.

It overran the splattered bait bag and struck two more trees as it twisted to a halt. Grunting, it scooped the slimy contents off the snowy loam with its tusks. It lacked only the small eyes and upright ears of a boar.

Ten arm-lengths away, straight through the trees. Better to close the distance myself than give it time to build momentum again. My hands, sweat-damp inside my heavy gloves, tightened on the spear. I roared as I had on the mesa, another challenge, and charged.

The shegrul stood still, grayish tavo guts trailing from its jaws while its shovel-like snout tested the wind. It snorted through red-flared nostrils and lowered its head.

With the ripple of its galumphing leap, I felt the turf beneath my boots tremble under its multiple clawed feet.

Big as a city transport. I broke into a sweat.

Lunge into it as if throwing the spear at the last second, Mapiya said.

Teeth clenched, I leaned into my thrust and rammed my weapon into the shegrul's wide-open maw. I glimpsed molars as ragged as a saw's blade. The raw stench of its breath struck my face, churning my stomach.

The spear sank to the lugs, which protruded from the sides of its mouth like a horse's bit. I staggered at the violence of the collision and scrambled to brace my feet.

It lurched, razor tusks straining to reach me around the lugs. My boots skidded backward on snow-slick groundcover. I stayed on my feet only because of my grip on the spear. *How long can the thing keep moving, skewered this way?*

When it tried to swing its broad head from side to side, I realized my mistake. I swallowed. *Wrong angle with the spear. I missed the brain, just made it mad. Need to get astride it...*

Indistinct shouts rose at the edge of my awareness.

I leaned into the spear once more. Strained until fire seared my shoulders and chest, while I scoured the frosty sod for a root or rock sufficient to plant the shaft.

The shegrul lumbered forward, its grunts spattering my face, arms, and chest with hot blood. Its mass forced me backward one step, then another. Fresh sweat broke along my ribs under my parka. *If I lose my footing, it'll trample me.*

A *thok* cut across the creature's snorts. Derry's arrow shivered in the side of its head where a boar's eye would've been. It swung to confront the new threat.

That's it. I let go of the spear and leaped forward. Gripping handfuls of fleece on a shoulder higher than my own, I swung up behind its head. *More than one way to get to its brain.*

Without my pressure on the spear, the shegrul leaped into a rippling run that dragged the weapon alongside it. I gripped with my knees and reached for the hunting knife on my belt.

When I'd butchered tame shegruls for my stepmother, I'd dispatched them with a swift blade through the neural cluster that served as a brainstem.

"Be calm, wild spirit, be at peace," I said through gritted teeth. In that moment the universe went silent. Nothing existed but the mountain shegrul and me. "May your spirit rest in beauty. May your spirit rest in peace." I plunged my knife into the precise spot at the base of its head. "May your spirit find the gentle path to the Sower of the Stars."

Its galumphing stride faltered. Its front pair of legs buckled, pitching it forward into a ground-shaking fall.

* * * * *

Chapter Thirty-Seven

I dove headlong off the shegrul and tucked to roll clear as it collapsed. I gained my feet, my healing knee throbbing, and stood panting while I examined my kill. Relief overwhelmed satisfaction. *More dangerous than an askuk in some ways.*

Shouts from behind prodded me to wheel clumsily about. The rest of the party jogged toward me through the trees, grinning and hooting and waving their weapons.

Except for Derry, in the lead. Her face bore scarcely more color than the trampled snow as she rushed me. I opened my arms, and she flung hers around me and held on. "I feared i' would trample yew, Kew." Her words came through panting, too. "Are yew a' righ'? Yew're covered in blood."

I wrapped her tightly in my arms. "I was afraid it was going to trample you, too. You're a deadeye shot, white bird."

"Ai, you two lovebugs!" somebody hollered behind us. "That shegrul's not going to butcher itself."

Everybody laughed. I chuckled, and Derry's cheeks grew rosy.

She detached herself from me and slipped away among the trees, hands pressed to her nose and mouth, when I slit the main artery in the shegrul's neck. Hot crimson melted what remained of the snow and rolled across the deep loam. An older, heavy-set man called Doho-san opened its belly, and the stench rose on spiraling vapor in the still air.

Three men removed the large, twisty gut. Once washed out and dried, we'd create storage pouches, buckets, and strong cord from it. Others dug for the primitive hearts, one in each body segment, which lay against the loose-jointed spinal column.

My mouth watered in anticipation. *Nothing like a fresh shegrul heart, salted and roasted on the coals, and these are huge.*

We found only a small brain when Adahy axed the skull open. Not enough to tan the whole hide. We had to harvest the neural cluster from the spinal bulge in each body segment as well.

The hide itself, twice the size of a Soliennese horse's and covered with dense fleece, proved the most difficult to handle.

"Where are we going to stretch this to dry?" I asked.

"We have to get it back to the caves first," said Helki.

Kaya and Dohosan, with his gray-streaked hair knotted at his nape, dragged the hide upwind of the carcass, and Derry, still somewhat pale, joined them.

Kaya drew a couple fleshing knives from her pack and handed one to Derry. "Same as the tavo skins, just bigger. Be sure to remove every scrap of flesh and fat so the hide won't start to decompose."

The next time I glanced their way, they and another woman were kneeling on the skin, intent on their task.

Though I'd had plenty of experience butchering shegruls, the massive size of this one would've overwhelmed me without the others' help. We took turns sawing the skeleton apart and carved most of the pale meat off it in ten-lug slabs.

"Leave some meat on the ribs," someone suggested. "We can smoke them for supper tomorrow."

By mid-morning the cloud cover had dispersed under a strong sun. The day warmed, and we shed our parkas. Our loose work shirts got soaked with snowmelt and smeared with blood and slime.

Looks like we've been in hand-to-hand combat, I thought. *Smells like it, too. Good thing it's too cold for goreflies, or they'd eat us alive.*

Shortly after midday we piled the meat, skeleton, and every edible or useful organ on the fleshed hide. Three people tugged it closed, and another man and I bound it.

"Everything fit inside the skin when it was alive," Helki's buddy Guyapi said with some puzzlement.

Dohosan and Adahy lashed two slim fallen trees together to form a simple sledge and used our last rope to secure the hide bundle to it. Helki and Guyapi dragged it down the canyon, along a trail now slippery with mud instead of snow.

My knee ached during the trek. I resisted limping and locked my teeth to keep from wincing at each step, but Derry spotted it. "What'd yew do to yer knee, Kew?"

"Twisted it, I think." I tried to remember exactly when it might've happened. "It's not bad. It'll be fine once I get off my feet."

Still, I couldn't stop wondering how badly I'd reinjured it. *Will it keep me out of the Qaletaqa?*

Garnan's hungry wails reached us as we circled the small reservoir. Through the trees I spotted Mapiya at the first cave's mouth, watching for us and rocking our unhappy child.

"Ah, Garny!" Derry cried. She pushed past the sledge to dash ahead, and sprinted up the ladder without hesitation. When Mapiya settled Garnan in her arms, Derry pressed a kiss to his head and disappeared in the direction of our sleeping space.

Mapiya eyed our gore-smeared party from the cave's lip when we gathered in the clearing. "Good. I'll send down baskets for the meat, but you must take the hide and gut downstream and wash them before you bring them up." She pointed members of the group to various tasks with the briskness of a flight commander.

With its burden emptied, Adahy, Dohosan, and I rolled the hide and hoisted it to our shoulders. We had to pick our way downstream a quarter range to find a natural pool large enough to thoroughly scrub blood, mud, and pine loam out of the span-long fleece.

Our parkas and boots got soaked through, and the icy water quickly induced shivering. My fingers and toes felt pinched with cold before they grew numb. Our gloved hands shook so violently we fumbled at our task, and our teeth chattered too much to speak.

We rolled the hide tightly, flesh side out, three times to wring water from it, but we staggered under its increased weight. In our shivering, we stumbled often, and my knee came close to buckling once while we hauled the hide to the hoist.

Mapiya had tasked people to haul water for washing. While several buckets heated by the cooking fires, one man had taken his axe to a couple water barrels in one unused dwelling. Split lengthwise, they became four compact bathtubs.

My crew and I came in last. By then, gritty, tepid water ran freely across the first cave's sloped floor and spilled from its lip. The improvised bathtubs had clearly been emptied and refilled several times.

People had scoured their clothes after washing themselves. Work shirts and hide trousers had been draped over the partial wall or dripped from pegs. The clothes smelled like wet dog.

Shortly after our morning departure, Mapiya had set large pots of speckled beans to simmer in the fire pits. Aromas of seasonings reached me before the smoky warmth enveloped me on entering the first cave. The scents overwhelmed the dog smell and triggered eager snarls from my midsection.

I dismissed the growls. *Got to stretch the hide, but not until we've washed up and thawed out.*

Once I'd sunk into a tub of heated water and my shivering had begun to ease, I examined my knee. It hadn't swollen much. *Not as bad as I thought. Got to expect some swelling after activity like this. It'll be fine.*

Dohosan returned to the improvised bathhouse as I pushed a foot into my spare pair of trousers. "There's enough space to stretch the hide in the second cave," he said. "We'll drive pegs between stones in the facing walls of the two front dwellings. It'll get enough light and air there. The boys are cutting cords from the gut to tie it with."

"Good," I said. "Be there in a minute."

We drove pegs into the walls, and Dohosan showed me the best way to punch holes around the hide's edge with an awl. I appreciated his knowledge. "Thank you, Elder."

We needed the whole group, some squatting on the roofs of the facing dwellings, to heft the dripping hide on end. We worked from the top down, everyone tugging and straining to expand the skin as much as possible before we anchored it.

Derry watched from one side, Garnan asleep in his baby pack on her chest. Her washed hair hung in auburn strands that fell well below her shoulders. She kept tucking damp tendrils behind her ears with fingers bloodstained from slicing slabs of meat into narrow strips for drying. When our eyes met, I mouthed *"Tai messa"* to her. She smiled and mouthed it in return.

With the sun sinking in a blaze of red and orange beyond the canyon rim, everyone converged on Mapiya's fire pits, most of us shaking

318 | D.T. READ

out our arms and hands from stretching the hide. Mapiya and Kaya scooped beans into pottery bowls and carved sizzling meat off slabs suspended on skewers above the coals.

"May I have one of the hearts?" I asked, extending my bowl.

"Your privilege, Ku, as the one who slew the shegrul," Kaya said, and everyone concurred with cheers or clapping my back. She worked the organ off its skewer into my dish. Even roasted, its size matched both my fists pressed together.

"Want a taste?" I asked Derry. "Organ meat is richer in nutrients than regular muscle. Good for suckling mothers."

She ate the piece I sliced off for her but pulled a face. "Too strong. I prefer whi'e mea'."

Helki grinned at me. "I've never seen anybody ride a mountain shegrul before."

Easier than riding an askuk, I thought.

Mapiya arched questioning brows, and the others joined in telling the tale. Guyapi acted out my wrestle with the creature at the end of my spear. It was a good thing I didn't have my mouth full, because I probably would've choked from laughing.

We celebrated with candy made from honey and dried melon strips, hot mugs of honey-sweetened tea, and a lot of mirth.

I drifted to sleep that night warmed by an acceptance I'd never known before among my own people, a warmth deeper than the comfort of fresh meat in my belly or even of Derry curled close beside me.

* * *

The group from the enclave stayed for a few days, long enough to help slice all the meat for the drying racks. The cave complex rang with voices and laughter, people coming and going and squatting around the fire pits together, and I thought, *It must've been like this when Chanter Yuma's family lived here.*

Kaya and the other women helped Derry with tanning, softening, and smoking the tavo pelts. I noted Derry's increasing Chalca vocabulary, though she struggled with sentence structure.

Watching the women place the small skins on frames to keep them open like bags inverted over smoky fires, I considered my options for doing the same thing with the shegrul hide.

May have to build a huge frame. I'd need a hoist to get the skin onto it. Wonder how long it'll take to smoke something that big? My stepmother used to smoke tame shegruls' hides for a couple days, I think.

Adahy smiled at my scrunched face. "Wondering how you're going to handle the hide by yourself?"

"Got a couple ideas," I said.

"Good. We may need them," he said. "Dohosan and I will stay until it's done."

"Thanks." I glanced from one to the other. "I'm learning a lot from both of you."

It took more than a phase for the hide to dry properly, mostly because of the dense wool. The rest of the party had returned to the enclave by then, bearing pouches of shegrul meat as gratitude gifts. The cave complex felt empty without them, but nocturnal rodents and insects became active again.

Still haven't burned all the cracks in our sleeping space. Need to do that soon.

* * *

While the hide slowly dried, we spent diminishing daylight hours on the mesa. Dohosan, Adahy, and I scoured the scrubby woods surrounding Mapiya's garden for every dead log and limb and chopped them for the ovens in our sleeping spaces.

Occasionally, we spotted canine tracks along the fringes of the wooded area beyond Mapiya's garden. They never left the trees but seemed to pace at the edge of the cleared area before returning to the shadows.

"Not normal wolves," Dohosan said the first time we found their spoor. His forehead creased, and the lines about his mouth deepened into grimness. He didn't crouch for a close examination, but actually stepped away to point out the details. "Too long and narrow, too shallow of an impression for an animal so large, and they do not come into the light."

I noted the differences from the wolf tracks we'd seen the day we arrived in the canyon—and something else struck me. "I've never heard any howling."

"They don't howl." Dohosan leveled his serious gaze on me. "They are chucapas. They fear only fire and the Warding Chant. If you must leave the dwellings during darkness, always take a torch, and chant aloud. Better to go with others. Truly, best to stay inside."

"Never heard of chucapas," I said.

"Demon wolves." Dohosan kept his voice low. "Some call them Machitew's dogs of war."

An icy finger traced its way down my spine.

* * *

Derry came with us when Mapiya was willing to tend Garnan. I taught her the correct way to use an axe. "This is safer. If you missed, doing it that way, you'd split your shin open."

As with archery, once she mastered the technique, she became very efficient. We didn't talk much while we worked, but I often saw the competitive glint in her eye when I glanced her way. She routinely chopped as much as me and the other men.

If she felt me watching and looked up, I mouthed "*Tai messa*" to her. She always beamed and returned the endearment.

Once I offered to haul her wood to the cave along with mine, but she said, "I can carry i' myself, Kew."

When I blinked in surprise, she explained, "Gram told me, whils' working on the wedding dress, tha' I'm no' as sturdy as Chalca women, and I need to be, so I'm working a' i'."

I chuckled. "You're doing fine, white bird."

When the time came to tan the shegrul hide, Derry overcame her squeamishness to simmer the brain matter with water and mash it into a smooth slurry with a wooden pestle. Lips pressed in a tight line at the smell, she dipped her fingers in the slimy stuff along with the rest of us and helped us rub it firmly into the skin side.

"Smells goaty," she said, "but i' will be verra good for keeping us warm a' nigh'."

She and I crouched head-to-head as we worked. "Speaking of goa's…" She put on her Intel Rogue smile and gave my beard a playful tug.

"Yi!" I hadn't realized how long it'd grown. *Three or four phases since I last used beard foam. I probably look as wild as Demothi.*

That prompted a grimmer thought. *Sure hope he's all right.*

* * *

S moking the shegrul hide completed the process. Adahy, Dohosan, and I strung a rope between the two dwellings we'd used for stretching and drying and draped the hide over it. Using holes we'd already punched, Derry and Mapiya stitched the sides closed. We used wooden pegs to anchor the opening of the hide bag around a large fire pit.

All of us took turns on smoker duty during the next three days. When not tending the low fire, by feeding water-soaked woodchips onto glowing coals to maintain steady billows of smoke under the hide, we hauled water or chopped firewood. Chopping included reducing some oven-length branches to smoking chips.

Derry arrived during my smoker watch late on the third day, carrying Garnan and a rug from our sleeping space in her arms and a tavo-skin bag on her shoulder. With longer nights had come colder temperatures. Derry wore her jacket most of the time when not sleeping and kept Garnan loosely swaddled in a blanket.

"No more goat smell," I said, poking a few fresh chips under the hide pouch. Blue-gray tendrils wafted out the top, pungent with the scent of juniper.

"Will we have i' tonigh'?" she asked.

"Probably."

"Lovely!" She handed Garnan to me, shook out the old rug, and settled on it cross-legged. The posture had become natural to her by now. She dug into her bag for bone needles, shegrul-gut thread, and a half-sewn baby coat with a hood, fur side in.

"Way too big," I said.

"He'll outgrow i' soon enough," she replied.

Perched on my knees between my hands, Garnan crowed and reached for my face with drool-damp little fingers. Though not thin, he'd lost some pudginess as he'd grown these past few phases. His miniature frame had an unexpected solidity.

"He's doing baby push-ups now," Derry said. "He'll be sitting on his own soon."

"Push-ups?" I placed Garnan on the rug on his belly and dropped to my own, facing him. "All right, little man," I said, smiling, "let's see what you've got. See if you can keep up with your pa."

Garnan gave a delighted squeal and flailed his limbs, then stopped kicking long enough to push his chest off the rug with both arms. I couldn't keep from laughing.

He imitated me for seven of them, then scooted forward to grab at my horsetail while I pumped out the rest of fifty. "Got to start somewhere," I panted to him. "Tomorrow, we'll get you up to ten."

Adahy and Dohosan's chuckles at our little competition announced their arrival.

"Let's put the fire out and get your rug down," Adahy said.

Two or three buckets of water, sloshed on hot spots and stirred with an oven paddle, reduced the smoking fire to soggy ashes. Derry and Mapiya unlaced the sewn sides and lifted the ends clear, while Adahy and Dohosan untied the rope from which it had been suspended. Even dry, it took the three of us to roll it and haul it through the cave complex to our dwelling.

Folded in two, fleecy side in, the hide covered half our room's floor. The scent of juniper smoke lingered about it, and Derry inhaled deeply.

"No more trying to sleep around bumps in the floor," I said. "No more kosa-chewed rugs." After the other two left, I added with a seductive smile, "No more socks in bed, little bird. You won't need to wear *anything* to stay warm in that."

324 | D.T. READ

She blushed in the lamplight. "Yew're thinking the same thing I am."

With fleece a span long, we sank into the hide as if it were a pillowy mattress. The weight of the half covering us surprised me. *It's going to be too warm for me.*

Derry lay with her head on my shoulder and released a deep sigh. "Puts me in mind of our nuptial journey."

"Better than our nuptial journey." I smiled. "We've got six months of nighttime coming."

She replied with her Intel Rogue chuckle.

* * *

Persistent sharp rapping at our doorpost wrenched me upright, from deep sleep to fully alert. A gust through our high windows, icy on my bare chest, warned me not to lunge out of the sleeping hide.

My gaze shifted from the gyrating flame of a hand-held oil lamp to the weathered face it dimly illuminated. I blinked and asked, "What's wrong, Chanter?"

"It's late," Mapiya said. She sounded annoyed. "There's much to do today, Wanikiya. It's time to begin your apprenticeship."

* * * * *

Chapter Thirty-Eight

I found Adahy and Dohosan sitting by a glowing fire pit in the gathering area, finishing their breakfasts.

"Good sleeping, Ku?" Dohosan greeted me. His mischievous smile deepened the creases at the corners of his mouth.

My face warmed, but I said, "Very good sleeping," yawned, and dropped to my heels alongside them. "Thank you for staying to help."

Both shrugged, and Adahy scanned the gathering area. We'd stacked firewood shoulder high in every corner, after filling three unused sleeping spaces.

"Now you're prepared for winter," Adahy said, "so you can concentrate on apprenticing. Chanter Mapiya says you have much to learn before Night of Light Ceremony."

I started. *Night of Light. That's in early spring, about six months from now. I have to make up eight years of missed apprenticeship in six months?*

Ya, I have a reporting date for the Qaletaqa in six months… unless the EMP happens first.

I felt overwhelmed as I watched them head down the canyon before the lowest stars had begun to fade above its eastern rim.

* * *

The odor I'd barely noticed while simply passing through intensified when we stood at the center of the ceremonial cavern. "Bats," I said. I glanced at Derry, carrying

325

Garnan in his baby pack, and hitched the fire-building bag higher on my shoulder.

"They're gone right now," Mapiya said. "They migrate for winter and won't come back until spring. I scrubbed when I knew you were coming."

"How did you know?" I asked.

If Mapiya heard me, she ignored my question. She moved ahead of us and lifted her lamp. "There's—"

Derry and I locked gazes. "—much to do today," we mouthed to each other, and Derry stifled a snicker.

Darkness absorbed Mapiya's feeble lamplight before it reached the ceiling. Having seen it by bright torchlight the day we arrived, I knew the cavern's size. The lamp's wavering light guided us across the deep mix of sand and fine chips of stone, soft underfoot.

Understanding replaced my original puzzlement. *They held dance ceremonies here. They leveled the floor for dancing.*

Mapiya stopped at the rim of a sunken fire pit two spans deep, five spans in diameter, and walled with fitted stones. "We'll begin here." She squatted at the fire pit's edge. "Fire is the beginning and ending of all ceremonies. Do you know the Chant to Ignite Fire, Wanikiya?"

"Ya, Chanter." *The first chant every apprentice learns, as much to build confidence as to serve a purpose.* I hopped into the fire pit.

It had been carefully cleared after its last use. No partly consumed wood chunks remained, just several stones larger than my fists, stained with soot and dry bat droppings.

By the flickering lamplight I selected four large stones and placed them at the points of the compass, then opened the fire-building bag on the pit's rim. It contained two pouches, for tinder and kindling, and a parcel of forearm-length sticks for fuel. *I performed this for my purification before Garn's Birth Chant, but I had a hearth there.*

With tinder and kindling arranged in the space between the four stones, I began to chant. "O, Ancients, who light the skies with stars and warm the Mother Worlds with sun, send me fire spirits from the stars to light this lodge. Send me fire spirits from the sun to warm this lodge, and teach me to live in beauty."

I continued the chant while I touched the tinder, three balls of dried grass, with my finger. A tiny flame rose from each in turn. Holding my loose hair out of the way with one hand, I hunched to blow gently until the kindling ignited. When it caught, I added the first small sticks of fuel.

Dancing flames like liquid gold cast a flurry of sparks, an inverted meteor shower striking the ceiling, which arched ten or eleven spans high. I estimated the cave at fifty spans across.

The sloped natural shelf I'd noticed before stretched the width of the rear wall. The jar of python-tree oil Mapiya had brought from the gathering ceremony now stood among the barrels, jars, and pouches on its uneven surface.

Mapiya's voice reclaimed my attention. I shifted to face her and spotted Derry. She sat at Mapiya's shoulder, Garnan sitting in her lap, her eyes wide with awe in the swaying firelight. I'd once told her how chanters worked with spirits of nature, but she must've never seen it before. I knew she'd never seen it from me. I smiled at her.

"Today," Mapiya said, "I'll try your knowledge, Wanikiya, to see what you've already mastered."

"I finished most of the first cycle with my first teacher," I said. "We'd just started earth chants when he died." The thought stirred latent resentment.

Mapiya shook her head. "There's more to do than I thought."

Apprentices began at the age of eight and completed one-on-one instruction at about twenty. During the first cycle they learned common chants to request assistance from spirits of the four elements and began to memorize songs and ritual dances for annual ceremonies.

The second cycle expanded on the first. Youths increased their understanding of nature's spirits and how to work with them, and they received power to summon them for specific purposes. We learned drum rhythms and flute melodies for ceremonies and the basics of healing, using prayer chants and herb lore for simple illnesses and injuries.

Gram had taught me a lot about herb lore. I expected to do well there.

In the third cycle, apprentices received instruction and power to perform rites like marriages and funerals, and to work more complex healings. By that time, most had discovered the element with which they had the greatest affinity and focused their training with its spirits.

I remembered how Chanter Elsu at Red Wash Enclave had become so adept with water spirits he could instruct them to combine hydrogen and oxygen molecules to create it. As a child I'd seen him bring rain during a drought.

I'd heard of chanters who called on air spirits to change the course of tornados or reduce them to dust swirls, chanters who guided fire spirits to extinguish or redirect massive desert wildfires, and chanters who'd ordered spirits of earth to cause ground quakes or call earth creatures from their dens.

Students' apprenticeships ended when their teachers felt they were fully prepared. In the presence of the enclave, the chanter placed his or her right hand on the apprentice's head and called upon Star Father to grant them the power to serve their people.

Who will do that for me? I wondered. *Chanter Mapiya, or Chanter Wahkan if I don't finish here?*

Mapiya eyed me. "We'll start with chants to air spirits." She fished a dry leaf from the kindling pouch. "I want you to fly this leaf around the cave."

"Ya, Chanter." I instantly recalled a yellow leaf drifting from a tree on the piloting school campus and the amber glider wing of my ejection capsule above the Stroma Mountains. I slid another smile to Derry, who leaned forward to watch when I lay the leaf before me.

I sang with certainty. With a one-handed motion, I directed air spirits to lift the leaf from the gravel. It hovered for a moment, level with my face, before I steered it toward the wall. I let the spirits tumble and bounce the leaf in a playful circle before they brought it back to Mapiya's lap on a soft gust.

"I think you enjoyed that, Wanikiya," she said with typical sternness.

Something tightened in my soul. "Is it wrong to enjoy performing chants?"

"Do you think Star Father enjoys it?"

"Ya!" I said at once. "Especially creation chants."

Mapiya said, "Hmph. They may be used *with* joy, but not for mere enjoyment. Do you understand the difference?"

"Ya, I do, Chanter." The haunting by Machitew in which he'd tried to possess me had happened after I used this same air chant to show off for Go.

Mapiya turned to catch Derry's eye and placed the leaf in front of her. "Now you do it, Anataqa."

Derry appeared perplexed. "Teach me the words, Chanter."

I took Garnan to let Derry have the use of her hands and seated him snuggly in the crook of my arm while Mapiya coached her through the prayer chant. When Derry closed her eyes, I chuckled. "You have to see where to guide the spirits, white bird."

After several attempts, she finally whirled the leaf around our heads, and laughed in delighted surprise.

"Now blow it across the cave and back," Mapiya requested.

Derry caught the leaf as it spiraled toward the floor. "Won' i' ge' in the fire?"

Mapiya arched a scraggly eyebrow. "You fear fire, Anataqa. Fear holds one back. As you overcome fear, you discover new strengths." She rummaged in the tinder pouch, withdrew another grass wad, and pressed it into Derry's palm. "Say the Chant to Ignite Fire and touch it with your finger as Wanikiya did."

Apprehension pinched a crease between Derry's eyebrows and rippled her scar. She cast me an anxious glance but repeated each line of the chant as Mapiya recited it. When she touched the wad with her finger and a nascent flame spouted, she gasped and immediately dropped it.

"Do it again," Mapiya ordered, and put another grass ball in Derry's hand.

"It won't burn you," I assured her. "Hold it on your palm until it goes out."

Derry did, but with her teeth gritted the whole time.

* * *

Throughout the morning I performed every first-cycle air chant I knew as Mapiya requested them. The spirits responded as freely to me as the element they inhabited. *Definitely the most natural element for me.*

Between testing me, Mapiya talked Derry through first-cycle chants to fire spirits. Derry never relaxed. With each new chant, she grew more tense. She winced and repeatedly jerked her hands away from flames.

At last Mapiya said, "Wanikiya, show me the Chant to Guide Many Winds." She rose and shuffled about the cave to place seven dry leaves in various cracks and niches, then hefted Garnan from my arms.

I moved a few arm-lengths from the fire pit's warmth and closed my eyes to detect the natural drafts. The strongest blew fitfully through the large entrance, but others sifted in from smaller openings. *I'll need to call several air spirits.*

"You must draw the leaves from their hiding places and gather them to you, using two or three winds at the same time," Mapiya said, cradling Garnan in her lap.

Arms uplifted, I began the chant. "O Ancient Ones who formed the winds, send spirits of air to work your will. Send spirits of air to serve your purpose and teach me to guide them in harmony."

I felt I'd returned to aerospace combat, directing several pilots at once. This time the leaf "fighters" depended on my guidance of air spirit "pilots" to fly them. My attention flitted from one leaf to another to keep all seven aloft.

A flash at the edge of my sight sent me into a headlong dive. Yellow-orange flames arched over the pit and struck the spot where I'd just been standing with a burst of sparks.

"Kew!" Derry stared at me, her expression panicked. "*Tai epesso, tai epesso!* Are yew a' right?"

I chuckled and regained my feet. "You did *that*? Yi! Throwing fire is a second-cycle chant!"

"I didn' mean to." She inspected one palm. "I misspoke the words and i' burn' me, and I tried to fling i' away."

Mapiya eyed Derry for a long minute and shook her head. "That's enough for today. You can perform the extinguishing chant, Anataqa."

Derry exhaled in obvious relief and smothered the fire pit's gentle blaze on her first attempt.

I'd forgotten how draining it could be to practice chants all day. I saw the sag in Derry's shoulders, too, so I persuaded Mapiya not to take time to cook. We ate a supper of dried sweet tuber slices, berries, shegrul jerky, and blackmint tea, and gratefully retreated to our sleeping space.

Once we'd done the washing, fed and swaddled Garnan, and crept into the sleeping hide, I said, "You seem really uncomfortable about fire chants. What's wrong?"

Lying with her gaze fixed toward the unseen ceiling, she murmured, "When I was ten, a townhouse in my da's stree' took fire. They made everyone leave, ou' of fear i' migh' ligh' the neighboring ones.

"The woman's two little dogs were trapped inside, and we could hear their cries across the park. When the fire brigade go' to them, i' was too late. I still hear them sometimes when I see leaping flames." Her voice trembled.

"I'm sorry, Derry." I drew her to me. *Like my flashbacks of Shirik.*

A few months before fleeing Red Wash, I'd watched, helpless in my circling Darter, as my fifteen-year-old half-brother and half my stepmother's shegrul pod vanished under a sheet of sliding snow and a crash of stone columns when a section of the wash's bank collapsed.

Again and again, I'd shouted the only chant to earth spirits I knew. They'd mocked me with cracking roars of boulders breaking and tumbling into the wash.

Same as my father. A lightning strike had caused the avalanche on a stone pinnacle called Yuma's Knife, but earth spirits had done nothing to protect the chanter performing a storm-stilling chant on the sacred peak.

Anger more than grief tightened my jaw. *I have no affinity with earth spirits, that's for sure.*

I didn't have any nightmares that night, but I slept as I had on deployments, with half my mind on alert.

* * *

Settling near the fire pit in the ceremony cave the next morning, I tensed when Mapiya said, "Today we'll work with earth spirits. What earth chants do you know, Wanikiya?"

"I was learning the first one," I said, "when the man who taught me was killed."

Mapiya leaned forward to scrutinize me across the dimness. "There's anger in your voice."

Without giving specifics, I told her about my father and brother. I clipped the words, my jaw taut.

Mapiya never blinked. "You won't master earth chants as long as you're angry, Wanikiya. Bitterness and resentment are greater barriers than Anataqa's fear. The spirits do not respond to those who don't respect them."

I gave a curt nod. Glowered at my lap.

Mapiya's next words impaled my soul. "You cannot perform as shaman if you're not in harmony with all the spirits of Star Father's creations."

* * * * *

Chapter Thirty-Nine

By afternoon of our second day in the ceremonial cavern, Derry had learned the Chant of Rolling Pebbles, the practice chant my father had taught me two days before his death. The rhythmic *thrum* of the words stuck in my throat every time I tried it. Watching pebbles tumble over each other brought images of boulders crashing down the face of Yuma's Knife, and I had to walk away.

We began the third day with the Chant to Scatter Water. I knew it and the other water-spirit teaching chants very well. I'd learned them as a child as easily as air-spirit chants.

Huk and I learned them together. He got the water ones a little quicker than me. Just a little, but I got him back.

Remembering with a smile how Hanuk had demonstrated his new skill, I glanced sideways at Derry. She sat with her eyes closed and palms cupped above a half full pottery basin while she chanted. Joining in the song, I guided water spirits as I did air spirits, with precise hand movements.

Derry gasped and jerked up straight when several chilly drops splashed on her head and shoulders. "Kew, dra' yew!"

I chuckled. "The day I learned this, the one who made us laugh did that, except he rained his whole bowlful on me."

Mapiya scowled. "Remember what I told you, Wanikiya, about using the chants *with* joy but not for *enjoyment?*"

I sobered at once. *"Tai epesso,* Chanter." *I don't want any new Machitew hauntings.*

"Do you know the Chant to Move Sand?" she asked.

"No, Chanter."

"Press your palms to the earth and sing the words low in your throat. I want you to ask the spirits to shift the soil back and forth without moving your hands."

My midsection tightened. I placed my palms on the coarse sand before me, half expecting a shock or something.

Nothing happened, but I sang the chant three times, with increasing urgency, before the sand spirits heeded my request. Then they acted with deliberate stubbornness.

Mapiya said, "Hmph," at the feeble sand ripples. "Why should they help someone who doesn't like them? These aren't the earth spirits who caused you harm. Don't blame them."

I hadn't considered that. I drew a breath, closed my eyes, and tried to pour reconciliation into the prayer song.

"Better," Mapiya said, her tone grudging.

A miniature dune stood between my planted hands.

"I'll know you're making progress," she said, "when you can persuade them to form a bank of sand two spans high against the shelf."

"Ya, Chanter."

I moved farther into the cavern, sat facing the uneven rear wall, and lay my hands on the soil once more. I whispered the chant and listened for responding whispers of shifting sand.

I labored at the Chant to Move Sand through most of the afternoon. Though I scarcely stirred, the efforts of my mind and soul left me sweaty and spent.

During those hours, Derry grew comfortable enough with water-spirit chants that by the time we finished for the day, she could direct them to bear the contents of one bowl into another basin ten spans away in a graceful arc.

By then I'd succeeded at mounding Mapiya's requested two-span-high revetment against the storage shelf, too. When she inspected it, she said only, "Keep practicing, Wanikiya," with an expression reminiscent of Russom.

* * *

We settled quickly into the apprentice routine.

As daylight hours continued to diminish, and when snow-laden clouds didn't obscure the sky, I tracked the time of day by the positions of stars and moon. Within a phase, I'd trained myself to wake a sun position before Mapiya, to establish a routine of my own.

On the first morning, I revived the ashy embers in our oven and fed them a stick or two to start warming the room before I bundled into my boots and parka and hefted my rucksack to my shoulders.

The rucksack no longer contained gear. I'd put a pile of fist-size rocks in it to simulate the loads under which I'd have to do timed runs during Qaletaqa training.

Remembering Elder Dohosan's counsel about the chucapas, I left our cave armed with the hunting spear and a slow-burning, hardwood torch. The snow clouds had blown off, and I could see clearly by a partial moon as it glowed off new snow.

As it always did, the stunning starfield took my attention first. *Miss being out there in the middle of it. Wonder how Kota and the others are doing? Are they seeing a lot of combat? Where is the war going now? Will it be the lumpies or Jax who drop the EMP on Tempest?* I even found myself wondering what Huritt was doing these days. *Probably cowering before his mother.*

Ghost-cat prints marked the trail to the mesa, prints that only led up, as if the cat had come out of our cave. My heart lurched. *Did she enter our cave?*

My search revealed no sign of her coming down, but falling snow might've covered earlier tracks. Oddly, the prints didn't sink into the snow, but barely marred its surface, as if she trod lightly on top of it. *Like the chucapas spoor.* Still, their clarity proved they were fresh. I raised the torch, lowered the spear, and crept to the mesa in silence.

The ghost cat tracks wound off to my left, following the canyon's rim.

In a moment, and with another clutch of my heart, I spotted her. The ethereal lioness lay directly above the first cave, where we lowered the ladder to the reservoir. Motionless, but with ears alert, she surveyed the canyon.

Though I stood frozen, she sensed my presence. She shifted her face toward me. Gave me Mapiya's stare, long and appraising with silvery eyes, before she briefly lowered her regal head as if in recognition and resumed her vigil. *Mosi, Derry's spirit guide.*

I lifted my gaze to scan the inverted bowl of wintry sky.

Movement caught my eye, cast against high altitude wisps of clouds. A large eagle, as ghostly as the cat, rode the night wind, tilting on the gusts as it circled the plateau. As it drew near, it dipped in its flight to spread its wings over me, then climbed again. *Migisi, my spirit guide.*

Another realization swept me. *They're guardians as much as guides. They're watching over us.*

Peace enveloped me. I planted the torch and spear at the edge of Mapiya's garden and jogged a couple laps around the fallow soil to warm up. Then I slid the spear shaft through my rucksack's straps and hoisted the load above my head.

Pressure on my locked elbows and tension across my pecs made it far more strenuous than a regular run, but the Qaletaqa fitness guide said we'd do a lot of running while carrying loads over our heads.

I set out along one of the six or seven trails rambling about the gently rounded tableland, trails Adahy, Dohosan, and I had discovered in our hunts for firewood. Most meandered for three or four ranges.

That first time I chose a winding path among scrubby trees. It circled a low rise, then dropped into a shallow hollow.

Close to twenty hewn pillars, ten spans high and a span in diameter, stood in the cleared space. Grave markers, like the ones in enclave burial grounds.

I eased my load to the path and approached with reverence, close enough to discern the totems carved in them. Unlike the stone pillars at Red Wash, these were logs. I scrutinized each in turn, but never found Chanter Yuma's.

Maybe the tales of him disappearing into the desert are true.

* * *

Mapiya and Derry had risen by the time I returned to the caves. I hauled water and set a full bucket near our oven to heat, then finished my workout with push-ups, sit-ups, and pull-ups. I used pegs in an outer wall for the pull-ups, still wearing my rock-filled rucksack.

I found Derry wrapped in the fleece and suckling Garnan when I returned to our room to wash up minutes later. "How was yer run, Kew?" she asked as I peeled off my shirt.

"Pretty good." I scrubbed my face and met her gaze, with water dripping off my nose and running into my beard. "You should come with me sometime. I saw our spirit guides on the mesa. They really are *spirits*."

Her eyes widened. "Mosi was there?"

"I think they're our guardians, too," I said, and sloshed tepid water over my head.

Derry appeared awestruck.

I didn't mention it while we ate a generous breakfast of shegrul bacon and maize porridge with dried berries and honey barrels. *Too sacred. Only to be known by Derry and me.* Instead, I said, "I found a burial ground while I was running, Chanter. Your family?"

Mapiya nodded. "My older siblings only came home to be buried."

"I couldn't find a marker for the chanter everyone remembers," I said.

"He's not buried there," Mapiya said. "He isn't dead."

"How do you know?" I asked.

She leveled her trademark stare on me, which I returned without blinking, before she said, "Bring my grinding bowl, Wanikiya. We'll rest from practicing chants today. You and Anataqa must learn to use healing plants."

* * *

I started the fire in the ceremony cave first, to provide warmth as well as light to see by, then retrieved the containers Mapiya requested from the rock shelf.

Garnan, snug in his oversized tavo-fur coat and leggings, rolled and scooted around on his belly on a blanket beside Derry. He babbled and shook a tiny striped gourd to make its seeds rattle, while Mapiya showed us how to distinguish bundles of dried vegetation.

"This plant is five-footed tavo," she said, offering a stem with five fuzzy, grayish buds on the stalk. "You can chew the leaves to relieve fever or use them for tea or poultices when they're dry like this.

"These bulbs are from spring sunshine flower, the first to bloom even before the snow melts. Mash them very smooth and mix it with python-tree oil until it looks like cream. It heals skin that's dry and cracked by winter cold. We'll need a lot of it.

"This is bitterleaf root. We used its seeds to protect our drying food from rodents. When you crush the root, it produces strong-smelling juice. You mix it with python oil, and it draws the venom out of insect bites and stings. It also heals small burns. We'll make more today. I don't have much left."

She demonstrated how to crush the roots properly to release the juice and had us take turns mashing it. The potent scent stung our noses and watered our eyes.

"One part juice to three parts python oil," Mapiya said, watching Derry mix it in a pot. "It's very strong."

While we worked at crushing roots and grinding various seeds and leaves to powders, some of which Mapiya showed us how to mix for particular remedies, she taught us the healing chants to accompany them.

"Sing the Chant for Curing Headaches with this one," she said. "Draw the glyph for pain in oil-paste on the person's brow while you sing. See?" She touched a dab to our faces. "It's made from fresh speckled wort stems. Do you feel the tingle? It's used to revive the unconscious, too."

Through the day she taught us about teas for upset stomachs and to soothe coughs and sore throats, how to wrap long strips of cloth tightly about sprained wrists and ankles, and how to make poultices to drain infection from wounds.

I remembered teaching Derry's mother to make poultices when I was wounded in Caerden's mountains, and a verse she'd recited came to my mind. "'Pucker root's good for both inside and out, but for fever and chills, best use corliswill.' Do you know about pucker root or corliswill, Chanter? They grow on Ardonar."

Derry appeared surprised and mildly amused, but Mapiya drew her brows down grumpily. "Never heard of them." Still, she nodded approval when I explained how to make an herb poultice.

She taught us remedies for colicky babies, how to use vapor from herb-infused water to clear nasal and chest congestion, and which leaves stopped bleeding when pressed to a wound.

"That's as good as the hemostatic wraps in our military first-aid kits," I said, recalling how swiftly the bandaging had halted the bleeding from my torn arm.

By suppertime I didn't think my head could hold any more medical knowledge. I sat quietly while I shoveled in a savory stew of tavo, maize, and wild onions, and mentally sorted treatments and which plants to use for them.

Derry apparently felt the same way. "I's all verra interesting," she said through a yawn when we'd settled in the sleeping hide, "bu' I do hope I never need i'. Wha' if yew or Garn ge' sick or hur', and I forge' or do the wrong thing and make i' worse?"

* * * * *

Chapter Forty

Winter's perpetual darkness closed in during the next few phases. The lack of light didn't concern me as much as the cold. With no sunlight to counter it, the chill continued to deepen. Wind often roared through the small canyon, sometimes carrying stinging crystals of snow, and always a deeper cold.

Even in our dwelling, our breaths constantly clouded on the air, and ice crusted our water barrels every day. Derry lived in her parka, except when sleeping in the fleecy hide, and dressed Garnan in layers. Constantly growing and becoming more active, he squalled when she tried to bundle him into the baby pack to carry him inside her coat.

"Before our grandfathers made the Crossing to this world," Mapiya said as we shivered through breakfast one morning, "they had a way to keep heat inside their bodies. They coated their skins with the fat of a certain large mammal.

"Those mammals don't live on Tempest, but python oil works just as well." She produced a small pot from within the blanket she wore about her shoulders and set it before us. "Spread it everywhere but in your hair. Rub it on Hiamovi, too."

Derry stared at her, clearly horrified. I could imagine her thinking, *We'll smell like rotting carcasses, the lo' of us.*

Mapiya must've read her thoughts because she said, "Python oil loses much of its odor with time. This pot is three years old." She

344 | D.T. READ

actually smiled, and her eyes glittered in the golden firelight. "You'll want to help each other apply it."

"Good idea." I slipped a sly grin at Derry. She returned it a bit dubiously. Finished with eating, I scooped the pot up.

"Wait until it's time to sleep," Mapiya said. "There's much to do today."

* * *

To my surprise as much as Derry's, coating our bodies with python oil really did seal in our heat, and by the next morning we no longer noticed the residual smell. Derry didn't shed her parka, but she didn't shiver as much, either.

Except during blizzards—a rarity compared to the days-long whiteouts of Awénasa Territory—I continued my "morning" runs and workouts. Three months after the injury, my knee had regained its full strength and range of motion and no longer twinged or swelled.

I carried a torch on the days I didn't run with my loaded rucksack over my head. Always I recited the Warding Chant aloud, though it came out broken on my panting breaths.

Twice I thought I glimpsed yellow eyes peering from wooded tangles, but when I leveled my gaze on them and chanted more loudly, they vanished. I couldn't shed the creeping sensation of their surveillance, however.

How did they get up to Mapiya's mesa? I wondered. *Did they come down from the mountains? Is there a way to fortify the mesa and canyon from that direction?*

Of course, if they're chucapas as Dohosan said, not real wolves, no physical barrier will block them.

Battle braid or not, my hair rose on the back of my neck.

Occasionally I spotted Mosi or Migisi, spectral presences barely visible against the snow or star-dense sky. I smiled. *Derry would call them guardian angels.*

I used some morning ventures to do reconnaissance. If real wolves could get up here, so could human attackers. *If I had to defend the mesa and canyon, how would I do it?*

* * *

Mapiya changed the lessons, if not the routine, every few days. Sometimes the cavern echoed with drum-beats as deep and steady as a giant's heart, and flute melodies as fluid as birdcalls on spring breezes.

Garnan, sitting propped in a bundle of blankets, stopped gnawing on a leather teething toy to pat his fur-clad knees while Derry and I practiced drumming rhythms for different ceremonies. He squealed and clapped mittened hands in evident excitement at the echoing thunder.

"You'll have the responsibility of leading ceremonies, Wanikiya," Mapiya said. "You and Anataqa must learn drumming and flute melodies for all the dances."

One day, Mapiya opened the largest bundles stacked on the natural shelf. Each contained dancers' ceremonial regalia. Murmuring a reverent song under her breath, Mapiya untied one bundle as if the action itself were sacred.

"Time of Planting Ceremony," she said. To Derry she added, though she spoke only Chalca, "When we plant our crops every spring, we remember two Ancient Ones of long ago."

From the hide wrapping she lifted a gray robe with two-span-long fringes falling from its sleeves, and cloud patterns embroidered in silvery beads about the neck. "This is worn by the dancer for Shaman Huyana, whose chants to Star Father brought rain to parched lands."

She shook the robe to ripple the fringe, and bitterroot seeds scattered from them. "The fringe symbolizes falling rain."

Derry nodded. Her understanding of Chalca had improved with immersion in the three months since we'd come, but she still switched between Chalca and Standard when speaking. I sometimes teased her about using Chaldard.

Mapiya laid down the robe and took up a farmer's shirt and trousers of soil-brown leather. Leafy plants, created in green beadwork, twined up the trousers' legs and across the shirt. I inhaled the scent of ancient leather emanating from them.

"Shaman Langond," Mapiya said, "the one to whom Star Father gave understanding of plants and soil, and wisdom to use it for growing crops. He saved the people from famine in his time. Our people still use his knowledge. The dancer always carries fans made of leafy plants."

We spent the day learning the rituals of the Planting Ceremony. While Mapiya worked with one of us, teaching us our roles, the other cared for and played with Garnan. I expected him to start crawling any day. He already knew how to roll off the blanket to play with the gravel chips, which he usually tried to stuff into his mouth.

The second day she opened a bundle whose contents I knew at once. *Saw this regalia when I watched the ceremony on my link months ago.*

I didn't comment, and Mapiya leveled a stern eye on me as she laid out the bird dancers' regalia with great care on the uneven stone shelf. "My family made these when I was small. They aren't sun eagle feathers. They haven't been worn in many years. I hope you know this ceremony."

"Ya, Chanter, I do."

I examined wings painstakingly built on willow frames, and hoods with beaks carved from wood and painted eyes. The brown and white birds. I held the white one up for Derry. "This represents you."

"I know." Awe softened her voice.

For the golden bird, brown feathers had been coated with yellow maize pollen. A lot of it had brushed off. "This will have to be redone," I said.

Mapiya concurred with a nod.

The wolf regalia I'd seen on my link consisted of whole pelts, with the upper half of the wolf's head worn atop the dancer's. All had been rolled with bitterroot seeds, but some appeared patchy anyway.

I recognized Shiye's sun headdress and examined it with reverence. Intricate details made clear it had been carved and painted by a skilled craftsman. I asked, "Who dances Shaman Shiye?"

"The enclave's chief chanter," Mapiya said.

As he should. I nodded.

At the shelf's end lay a bucket-like mask made of wood. Its hinged jaws opened and closed, and several horns protruded in asymmetrical directions through a mane of grease-black rags. I steeled myself to pick it up, and in sudden defiance poked two fingers through its eye holes.

"You will never wear that one," Mapiya said.

Already have, I thought, *in his hauntings.*

In another heartbeat, unexpected words spilled from my mouth. "Is the end of the third-night battle prophetic or symbolic, Chanter?"

Mapiya appeared mildly surprised by my question. "What do you think, Wanikiya?"

"I think it's prophetic."

"Why?" she asked.

"Because," I said, "the events in the first and second nights' ceremonies happened a year ago."

When she raised questioning eyebrows, I described how the enactment paralleled my life. I concluded, "The battle in the third night I saw seemed pretty real."

"If it is, what does it mean to you?" Mapiya persisted.

I avoided a glance at Derry. "I'll have to lose my life to save our people."

"You believe the Path of a prophecy can't be altered?"

Puzzlement puckered my brow. "It wouldn't be a prophecy if I chose not to fulfill it, would it?"

Mapiya shook her head. "A prophecy does not take away your right to choose, Wanikiya."

As we discussed the ceremony in depth, her statement kept shifting my mind in search of alternate endings to the battle.

"Wanikiya," she said at last, "you can't make the right choice without the right knowledge, and you won't receive the right knowledge until the right time. For now, you must stay in the present."

Though that didn't answer my question, I felt relief. *Maybe there'll be more options when the time comes.*

* * *

Mapiya never went more than a few days without teaching us new chants, but it seemed forever before she said, as we entered the ceremony cave one morning, "We'll start second-cycle chants today, with water."

She poured water from a bowl into the gravel chips on which we sat. "This is the Chant to Recover Spilled Water. You must return all the water to the bowl."

I considered. *Have to guide the water spirits, like the air spirits carrying leaves.* I placed the bowl in the fire pit, its lip against a crack between stones in the wall.

As I repeated the chant after her, I visualized water seeping through gravel. I directed the water spirits with scooping and drawing motions of my hands to gather water into a channel and carry it toward the basin.

They didn't cooperate at first. The water remained lost in the coarse sand and didn't move to the bowl.

Eyes closed and hands cupped together, I murmured the words again and again. "O Ancients, who give the thirsty worlds rain, send water spirits to join drops to the river, to gather drops to the stream, so they will flow together and become one in beauty."

After three hours of practice, the basin in the fire pit remained empty. My soul felt empty, too. Drained.

Mapiya peered at the bowl and clucked in disappointment. "Water spirits are like tame shegruls, Wanikiya. If you guide them properly, they will come."

I furrowed my forehead. *How do I guide them properly? Tame shegruls turn away from nudges.*

I imagined nudging water spirits in the right direction and used my hands along with the chant to urge them on.

The water only spread farther through the sand. I groaned.

Several different attempts later, and growing increasingly impatient, I stopped chanting. *Got to rest a minute.*

I sagged where I sat. While I kneaded my temples to ease the tension in my head, I pictured the water simply trickling where I wanted it to go, through the crack in the fire pit wall.

350 | D.T. READ

A splash on pottery straightened me with a start. I stared into the fire pit, at the bowl. A drizzle slid from between the stones, darkening the one over which the water spilled.

"What changed for you, Wanikiya?" Mapiya asked.

It took me a minute to make the connection. "I imagined the water going where I wanted it to. I guess I *showed* the spirits what to do."

"Ah." Mapiya's head bobbed. "Do it for me again tomorrow, so I know you've learned it, before I teach you another."

* * *

She didn't return to water chants the next day. She set Derry a second-cycle fire chant, and me an earth one.

Seated far enough away with Garnan to avoid distracting her, I watched Derry.

"Today," Mapiya said, "I'll teach you to do with purpose what you did from fear before." She placed a tinder wad of dry grass several arm-lengths from where Derry sat. "With this teaching chant, you'll direct fire spirits from your hand to go light the tinder ball."

Derry pursed her lips briefly, then echoed Mapiya's words as she sang the prayer. Derry started when a small flame rose in her palm, but this time she didn't drop or fling it. With her expression one of concentration, she gazed at the tinder ball, straightened where she sat, and repeated the chant with firmness.

Her first attempt fell short because she broke off in mid-chant when the flickering tongue *leaped* off her hand, but she succeeded at her second and third tries.

Only when Mapiya appeared satisfied with Derry's efforts, having encouraged her to launch a small fireball the width of the cavern, did she shift her attention to me.

"You must build a windbreak in front of the fire pit using the loose stones," she said. "You must call on earth spirits to place them correctly for you."

My innards tensed. I drew a long breath. *I succeeded with sand chants. This shouldn't be any different.* "Ya, Chanter," I said.

I started with an under-my-breath repetition of the Warding Chant, and my tension lifted. With another deep breath, I began the Chant to Build with Rocks.

The oddly shaped stones had to seat firmly, not wobble, so I had to rotate them in the air to examine their sizes, shapes, and uneven surfaces. My visualizing lesson from the previous day served me well, until I didn't give it close enough attention. Then one misplaced rock toppled a hole in the windbreak.

Though no larger than both my fists, the tumbling stones touched off a flashback of Red Wash. I stiffened where I sat, fists clenching and sweat breaking on my face.

"Wanikiya," Mapiya said from behind me, and I started.

"I know." I said it through my teeth. Loosened my fists with great effort. "These aren't the earth spirits who killed my people. Don't blame them."

"Walk around," Mapiya said. "Drink some water. Then come back and do it again."

I nodded and noticed Derry watching me, concern in her eyes, when I shoved to my feet.

A few minutes of pacing the cavern calmed my heartrate and pushed the images away, but it took me the rest of our practice time to finish constructing the windbreak.

* * * * *

Chapter Forty-One

As more phases passed, Mapiya's lessons in healing skills, interspersed with everything else, advanced to setting broken bones, stitching wounds, and diagnosing illnesses. Derry never flinched, but the thought of sewing wounds, let alone practicing on freshly snared tavos, made me queasy. *Never liked needles.*

"Think I'll stick to chants and herbal medicines," I said during supper after a couple days of it.

Mapiya shook her head and suppressed a smile. "You have enough knowledge now, Anataqa," she said, "to learn about midwifing. You, Wanikiya, will do the daily tasks and care for Hiamovi tomorrow."

"Good." I probably sounded more relieved than I should've. "Hear that, Garn? Father-son day tomorrow!"

He jabbered and grinned at me through the mashed orange tuber smeared around his mouth. At a few days from eight months old, I guessed he weighed about twenty lugs. He had four teeth now, two on top, two on the bottom, so we were gradually expanding his diet.

He'd begun crawling about three phases earlier and could take off like a tavo. Except for the fire pit and the drop-off at the cave's front, the ceremony cavern held few hazards and provided plenty of room for him to play, but Mapiya had started working with Derry and me separately so one of us could keep an eye on him.

With that in mind, on returning from my run the next day, I took a lamp and searched the storage space for the balls of twine we'd wound a couple months earlier. *Probably should tether him so he doesn't get away while I do chores.*

When Derry and Mapiya left for the cavern, I set Garnan in the middle of the sleeping hide with the three toys we'd made for him and plopped beside him to cut a length off the twine ball. "Don't know if your mama would approve," I said, tying one end loosely around his ankle with a quick-release knot, "but this way I won't have to stop working every few seconds to get you out of trouble."

I made a loop at the twine's other end and hung it on a peg in the wall, then positioned myself where he could reach me, but not the stone oven and its tantalizing flames.

He seemed content to watch while I ground maize. I sang the traditional grinding songs while I progressed from cracking dry kernels to milling them into meal. He tried to sing along, drooling down his front, clapping wet hands, and bouncing on his diaper-padded bottom.

Washing his diapers and our undies became another adventure for him. Hearing the water sloshing in the laundry pot while I stirred it with the rod, he tried to thrust a hand in.

"Yi, Garn, no! That's hot!" I moved the pot beyond his reach. "Let me find one for you."

He pouted and whimpered in frustration while I sized up the cooking vessels stacked near the oven. One appeared suitable, with a broad base to prevent tipping easily, and a neck too narrow for him to fall into. I dipped a little cold water from one of our barrels and set it before him. "There you go, little man. All yours."

Pudgy hands promptly reached into the pot and started splashing. He laughed and babbled.

I grinned. "Enjoy it while you can. When you're big enough, you'll have to wash stuff, too."

Garnan had begun trying to imitate our speech, so we paused to listen when he responded to us and tried to mimic his sounds back to him. He'd recently mastered syllables like "da-da" and "ma-ma."

His *Where are you going?* wail followed me to the cave's lip when I left to dump the wash water. I returned to find him poking his head past our room's door-blanket, his leg with the tether stretched out behind him. I let the pot drop with a *clunk* and scooped him up. "I'm right here, Garn. How about some food?"

Once he'd calmed, I set him on the sleeping fleece again and put bits of dried melon and honey barrel from a storage pouch into a bowl for him. One by one, he grabbed the pieces with a clumsy fist and shoved them into his mouth.

How I felt eating lefthanded, I thought, and said, "It gets easier, little man, I promise."

Derry arrived after I'd made maize porridge and corralled Garnan in my lap to feed him. She settled beside me and smiled when I repeatedly scooped it off our son's chin to spoon it into his mouth again.

"I swear he gets his food by osmosis," I said.

She laughed. "Here now, let's try a bit of suckling." She pushed up her shirt and bra without removing her parka and hefted Garnan from my lap to hers.

He wasted no time latching on, so I divided the remaining porridge into two bowls, offered one to Derry, and asked, "How's midwifing going?"

She sighed. "Sa much to learn. I'd no idea sa many things could go wrong with birthing."

"I don't know how you do it even when everything's normal," I said.

"With the help of yer pain-easing chan'," she said, and leaned to kiss me. On glancing down to find Garnan asleep, she returned him to my arms. "Time to nap, but he's in wan' of a changing firs'." She smiled and tucked her shirt in. "Maybe yew can nap with him."

Garnan woke while I was changing him and didn't want to sleep again. I stretched out on my back and placed him on my chest, inside my jacket to keep him warm, but my shirt's leather lacings caught his eye. *Better those than my beard.*

I watched, chuckling, when he tried to stuff one lacing into his mouth.

He lost his hold, reached for the ties again, and his hand went inside my shirt. I braced for a tug at my chest hair, but he'd found Gram's little leather bag.

"Not that, little man." I extracted the bag from his grip with care, drew its cord off over my head, and stashed it in the hide behind me. "Time to sleep now."

I closed my jacket around him once more, and eventually he snoozed, thumb in mouth. *Napping's a good idea.*

I never fell asleep. After a while I eased Garnan to the hide beside me, patted him to sleep once more, and located the little bag. *Never have listened to any of Grandfather's chants.*

As I had in the mountains of Caerden, I lowered the ancient link's volume, but not so quietly I had to press it to my ear this time.

The journal didn't start with my great-grandfather. Upon scrolling to the beginning, I discovered recordings by a General Cheveyo.

Shaman Cheveyo? I wondered. *The Ancient One? Gram said he was my ancestor.*

The general spoke with the ancient formality of the chants and an oddly familiar accent, but neither masked the gravity of his voice. *Hard to believe this was recorded centuries ago.*

"A man named Malack has come before the Great Council," Cheveyo said, "a man who claims direct descent from Huyana, she who sat as high chief and shaman of the people a thousand years after the coming of Shaman Shiye to our world.

"This Malack has put forth his claim as rightful great chief by virtue of his lineage, and has called for the Great Council to be dissolved. He has declared the Council an innovation to appease rivals following Shaman Huyana's Crossing.

"The people of small and scattered clans," Cheveyo went on, "to whom the Great Council gives equal voice with people of large clans, are rising up and crying out against the Council's removal. This Malack, being a cunning man, is calling upon clan chiefs himself. If they will establish him as great chief, he promises to grant them authority in their own territories."

I quirked an eyebrow.

In his next entry days later, the grimness in Cheveyo's voice had deepened. "The Great Council has become a place of noise and contention. Malack fears his claim for great chief will not be supported when put to the voice of the people. I have received a report that he seeks an alliance with the Pahana if the vote fails, to take the chieftainship by force."

I stiffened. *An alliance with the Pahana?*

"If that occurs," General Cheveyo concluded, "we will have no recourse but to take up arms against our brother Chalca. We cannot allow Malack to impose his tyranny upon the people."

Garnan's noisy yawn and a kick at my leg when he stretched his leg wrenched me from listening. When I peered at him, he smiled broadly and reached for my face. I fumbled the old link into its pouch, quelled the questions in my mind for the moment, and scooped him up. *Wet again. Where does all the water come from?*

* * *

"Today, Anataqa," Mapiya said, "we'll practice third-cycle fire-spirit chants. There is still much to learn, and there are less than three moons until Night of Light Ceremony."

Less than three moons? I started at Mapiya's announcement.

Derry had mastered most of the fire chants, including basic casting from her hand, but she'd never quite lost her apprehension. I read it in her eyes when she whispered to me, "I'd rather practice stitching wounds."

Still, she took her place beside the ceremonial cavern's fire pit while I retreated to a far corner with Garnan.

Mapiya's croaky voice carried across the chamber while she shuffled about, planting oven-length logs at various locations. "Today you must learn the Chant to Use Fire in Battle. Wanikiya will not be the only one who must fight for our people."

I furrowed my brows at that and saw Derry's raise in surprise.

"Directing the fire spirits accurately and with great power is important," Mapiya continued, "because casting fire uses a great deal of energy. You must not waste it in a battle.

"Once you can consistently strike still targets," she added, "you must learn to hit moving ones."

Derry slid a wide-eyed stare at me. I mouthed, "You can do it, white bird."

As with archery, she had better accuracy when she used her left hand to point the fire spirits to the logs. Most of her first attempts struck, but they only scorched or fractured the wood.

"More power!" Mapiya ordered. "You must summon enough fire spirits to burn the logs to cinders."

Derry took a deep breath, narrowed her eyes, and repeated the chant. Her voice, her clipped words, held determination. The gouts of flame she launched from her palm seared crimson across the dimness, briefly illuminating the whole chamber.

By the time Mapiya called a halt for our midday meal, Derry had reduced six logs to blackened ash.

"You're better at fire chants than I am," I told her as we made our way to the gathering area.

"I's a lo' like archery for me," she said, "bu' with a differen' kind of arrow. And I'm famished!"

She ate as much as I did and fell asleep while suckling Garnan after.

On returning to the ceremony chamber later, Mapiya set a small pile of fist-size wood chunks near one side wall and motioned to me. "You must throw the targets for her, Wanikiya. You can throw faster than I can."

I questioned her with my eyes.

"Not at first, of course," Mapiya said, "but as her confidence grows, you must increase the speed and force. Don't hold back. Your lives may depend on her ability one day."

Also like archery, Derry learned quickly to gauge angle and velocity to anticipate exactly where the fire spirits had to meet my hurled chunks of log.

Mapiya ended our training day early when Derry swayed on her feet in obvious exhaustion. The chanter motioned at twenty or so crumbling lumps scattered across the cavern. "I'll go make our supper. You must gather those and put them in the fire pit." She said it gruffly but favored Derry with a satisfied nod.

Entering the uneven passage toward the gathering area, once we'd cleaned up her charred blocks, I grinned at Derry. "You would've been killer with a Rohr's energy cannon!"

"Fire's a ghastly weapon to use on a living creature." She shivered, and I saw the shadow of her childhood nightmares in her eyes. "I hope I never have to use i'."

"Careful, little bird," I warned. "That's what I said after I completed my ejection qualification."

* * *

*F*our moons already. I sighed, staring at the ragged ceiling that night. *Little more than two moons left until Night of Light Ceremony. This is going too fast. There's so much I still have to learn. I don't feel any more prepared now than when we first got here.*

A mild tremor silenced the normal skittering of nocturnal creatures about the cave and startled me from my ruminations. I raised myself on my elbows, straining to hear through the wind's muted roar in the canyon. A crack and rumble reached me, like thunder on the desert. I listened for some time after it faded.

Nothing else. I sank into the fleece, but not to sleep. Not for some time, anyway.

Rapping at our doorframe startled me awake who knew how much later. I sat up at once. "Chanter?"

"We're starting fourth-cycle earth chants today," Mapiya said through the door blanket. "A rockslide sealed the canyon's mouth last night. You must clear the avalanche so we can leave when it's time."

Rockslide. So that's what I heard. Clear an avalanche? My innards instantly knotted at memories of the one at Yuma's Knife.

"I'll start breakfast," she said. "You'll need to eat well, Wanikiya. There's much hard work to do."

* * * * *

Chapter Forty-Two

The trail curved northward along our side canyon's eastern wall. Heart already pounding with anticipated horror, I squinted toward its mouth. By scant starlight I perceived, above the skeletal branches of barren trees, the new gap in the facing cliff's profile.

The wind-lashed column at the mesa's point, whose top had loomed above the side canyon's mouth like an anvil's heel, no longer existed. Darkness and distance left me wondering if it'd taken the trail-head to Mapiya's garden along with it.

We saw the complete blockage before we reached the canyon's floor. A section of the collapsed column, longer and broader than a public transport in Awénasa City, had obliterated the ford where we'd examined animal tracks when we arrived.

The creek's icy trickle already begun to back up, forming a pool behind the fallen stone. More fractured slabs, some large, many smaller, lay at haphazard angles upon and against the broken column.

The flashback struck in an instant, with such clarity I might have been transported to the winter-dry bed of Red Wash. In my mind I faced a different rubble heap of stones, russet instead of gray-beige.

Along with the images came sensations. My heart thudded under my ribs, and my hands grew damp in my gloves.

Shaking, I maneuvered around some boulders and scrambled over others. I barked my shins, lost one of my mitts.

The stone column, parted from the seventy-span bank with a rending crack and an avalanche of old snow, lay crumpled in front of me.

"Shirik!" I screamed. I tore through icy rocks and gravel. My back and shoulders strained to heave large chunks aside. "Shirk, can you hear me?"

I went rigid, gorge rising in my throat, when I uncovered his boot, protruding from under a boulder, and I clamped my teeth closed so I wouldn't shout his name again.

"Wanikiya."

Mapiya's voice wrenched me from the flashback. Nausea coiled in my gut, and sweat broke beneath my parka. I staggered off a few steps, bent to clamp my hands on my knees, and swallowed the urge to retch.

She remained silent, though I felt her gaze on me, keen as a hawk tracking a tavo. When I straightened at last, still facing away from the rockslide, but with my heartrate and ragged breathing returning to normal, she said, "You still bear your anger toward earth spirits."

"I told you what happened to the people I knew." I couldn't keep the venom out of my voice.

Mapiya regarded me for a long while, her wavering torch casting her face into witchy crags. "Come with me." She swung toward the left branch of the side canyon, where the mountain shegrul had been heading when we'd first seen its tracks at the shallow ford. I followed.

A third of a range in, we entered a clearing where the snow lay untouched even by animals and birds. Mapiya's torch shed a faintly golden light upon it. I hesitated under encircling trees, unwilling to disturb its serenity, but Mapiya shuffled forward. The snow reached her knees. At the clearing's center, she shifted about and beckoned.

She peered at me through the swaying light when I joined her. Flinty eyes deepened by creases probed mine. "You've carried the weight too long, Wanikiya, like carrying a boulder ever since your loved ones died. It's time to put it down. It's time to forgive."

I managed not to snort at the absurdity of it. "Forgive earth spirits? How do I do that?"

"With the same heart where you're carrying your anger."

I studied her face by the torchlight for any indication she might be mocking me. Though always stern, she'd *never* mocked me. I detected no hint of it now.

"It's very important for you, Wanikiya," she emphasized. "*Most* important for you. Earth spirits will be essential in accomplishing your greatest purpose as shaman. Earth is your most natural element."

I shook my head. "No, it's not, it's—"

She shrugged. "I saw how naturally you worked in my garden. I watched you calm the shegruls during Oil-Gathering Ceremony. Tavos come to your snares as if to a feast, and I heard how you conquered the marauding askuk at your enclave."

I gaped. "How did you hear about that?"

"Word comes to me in many ways." She waved a dismissive hand. "That's not important. It *is* important for you to learn to work with earth spirits. Talk to Shaman Shiye. I'll wait at the rockslide. Come when you're ready."

She took the torch with her. I watched it bob away, an orange flare among bare branches.

Alone, I blew out a tremulous breath. Watched its vapor wisp away on a gust. I swayed where I stood.

"Shaman Shiye," I whispered at last. My voice seemed a shout in the total stillness. "I need your help. I don't know how to forgive the earth spirits."

My knees felt weak. I let them buckle, sank onto them. The healing one struck a stone under the snow, and I flinched.

"Shaman Shiye," I pleaded, "how do I do this? What do I need to do?"

It seemed a long time before I heard the quiet voice, calm and clear in my mind. *You must give your anger to me, my son Wanikiya, along with the sorrow from which it came.*

Cold penetrated my trousers and pinched my knees until they ached. Shivering swallowed me. "Give my anger to you? As if I can just decide not to feel it anymore?"

You can *decide so, my son.* The soundless words came with certainty.

Reservations riddled my mind. "How?" I whispered my plea. Again it sounded like a ringing shout in the clearing's silence. "How do I stop feeling it?"

Do you want to stop feeling your anger?

"Ya." I said it through chattering teeth.

Do you believe I can take it from you?

Years of anger and ache. Years *of it.* Lingering doubt made me hesitate before I ventured another, "Ya."

Then choose to, my son, and offer your anger to me with your whole heart.

I drew a shuddering breath and filled my lungs with icy air. "I *choose* to, Shaman Shiye." My whispered words shook, as much with determination as from cold.

A particular moment from my shaman vision seared my mind. I extended my trembling arms as if offering a gift. "Take it out of me, Shaman Shiye. Take all of it."

Calm came first, followed by comfort, as if unseen arms had wrapped around my shoulders. When the heaviness in my soul lifted, I drew another deep breath. Peace flowed in with it.

Now, my son Wanikiya, I heard, *I can help you make strengths from your weak things.*

I gained my feet with a lightness I hadn't expected after kneeling for so long in the snow. A high wind had swept the clouds away, revealing a waxing moon and myriad stars so clear, I might have been soaring among them. They gave the snow a brilliance I'd only seen before at dawn.

It is *dawn, my son,* the quiet little voice said in my mind. *It's dawn in your heart.*

Every detail of the woods and the canyon walls above them stood out as I retraced our footprints to join Mapiya. I didn't rush. To do so would have violated the peace, the sanctity of the moment. I wanted to absorb it, to hold it inside as long as I could.

Something behind my abs tightened when I drew up alongside Mapiya to study the transport-size stone column. *Shield me from the spirits of the Dark, O Sower of the Stars...*

I quelled the tension and addressed her. "I'm ready to learn now, Chanter."

* * *

We started with the Chant to Reveal Hidden Things. I stiffened when Mapiya sang the first words. *They used that chant to see how to lift the boulders off Shirik in Red Wash.*

Again, I overwhelmed the memories with the Warding Chant. *Shield my mind against them that I may know your wisdom. Shield my heart against them that I may have your peace.*

Standing before the rockslide with my eyes closed, images of chunks and rubble within the debris mound invisible to my physical eyes coalesced in my mind. I saw points where pressure alone maintained a precarious balance, and what would happen if this cracking slab or that boulder shifted. The great size of most of the fragments made the avalanche unstable.

Seeing the blockage in such a way left me lightheaded. I plopped onto a long-ago fallen log to catch my breath and hoped my head would stop reeling.

Mapiya drew a drinking gourd from within her blankets and thrust it to me. "You must open the way for your people to pass, Wanikiya. It may be narrow, but it must be straight and sure."

I nodded and glugged half the gourd's contents. *Blackmint tea, very strong. It's still warm.*

"You won't accomplish it in one day," she said. "Not without help. You'll have to work at it every day."

"I'll have to take down the debris pile first," I said. "It's shaky, jammed together this way. Then I'll have to rotate the huge block on the bottom so it lies against one wall instead of across the canyon."

Mapiya taught me the Chant for Lifting and Moving Heavy Things. "You'll feel the weight," she warned me. "The chant doesn't make the stone lighter, but earth spirits make it easier to bear."

I started with the uppermost slab, one the size of a Rohr-55 teetering atop the mound. *Got to move it and put it up on the opposite rim before it slides into the canyon.*

After raising it off the scree, the spirits of the stones seemed to balk. The slab, hovering several arm-lengths below the rim, wobbled like a wagging tongue when I motioned them to hoist it higher. My arms and back burned with the effort, and I gritted my teeth.

"Remember what you learned about recovering spilled water," Mapiya said behind me.

I spared an acknowledging nod. I didn't dare stop chanting, not with the slab hanging so precariously. Eyes closed and arms outstretched as if hefting it, I visualized it drifting to the intended location and settling with a spray of snow and pebbles.

My eyes sprang open when the sensation of weight on my arms lifted and a muffled *thump* reached me. I shook out my arms.

The slab lay exactly where I'd pictured it, well away from the facing cliff's edge. I released a breath of both relief and amazement and glanced at Mapiya.

"Hmph." She nodded. "Now you know how to do it."

* * *

When the Winter Dancer constellation wheeled to the clear western horizon, marking late afternoon, Mapiya said, "Good, Wanikiya. Now it's time to eat and rest."

With my shoulders and lower back aching as if I'd bodily hoisted every massive stone, I paused halfway up the trail to peer back at the rockslide. *Can't even see what we've done.*

An unexpected peace permeated my soul despite the apparent lack of progress. *I'll get it done.*

The aroma of roasting meat wafting through the caves roused a hopeful snarl from my stomach. I found Derry crouching beside one fire pit in the gathering area, roasting three winter-lean tavos on spits.

"We climbed to the mesa after yew lef'," she said, and nodded toward Garnan, sleeping in a sort of pen she'd constructed in a cozy niche. "I wanted to see where the cliff gave way, and I se' some snares. They'd caugh' only these three when we wen' back."

"You skinned and gutted them yourself?" I asked in amazement.

"Aye." She shuddered with obvious revulsion. "And I scraped and stretched the skins. Garn's outgrowing his clothes." She waved at three drying frames hanging on the rear wall. "I knew yew'd be verra hungry, so I pu' swee' tubers in the coals, too."

I drew her to her feet and into a tight hug. "You have no idea how much I appreciate you, white bird."

* * *

On the third morning, I sloshed across the expanding pool, where the blocked creek lapped at the massive column, and scrambled to the boulder's top. I didn't need Mapiya's torch, which we carried to ward away chucapas. The moon, not quite full, illuminated the small canyon's slightly widened mouth and highlighted the remaining rubble's blocky shapes.

"Not much left to clear," I called to Mapiya. "I'll finish by this afternoon, and tomorrow I'll pivot this thing and lay it against the canyon wall."

In mid-morning, by the constellations' passage, while I stood atop the fallen column to clear another tumbled slab, a bird's shrill cry snatched my attention. A spectral eagle dove at me, flapped above my head, called out, and wheeled toward the caves.

When I didn't move at once, puzzled by the display, it circled and stooped again, so low its phantom wingtips would've brushed my face if they'd been physical. Its cry grew more insistent, more urgent.

"Migisi," I said under my breath.

The eagle banked away once more, clearly wanting me to follow, and a ghost cat's scream echoed from the canyon.

"Mosi." A chill, icy as the creek's water, shot through my soul. I leaped off the stone block, heart already racing.

Something's happened in the caves.

* * * * *

Chapter Forty-Three

"My family's in trouble!" I yelled to Mapiya. As I sprinted up the trail, a terrifying scenario tore through my mind. *Garn crawled to the oven, his clothes caught on fire, he's seriously burned.*

My boots slipped on icy patches. I landed on my knees more than once. I grasped at jutting rocks and brittle plants to haul myself forward, never breaking stride, and charged across the icy dam.

Silence from the caves as I raced up the ladder multiplied my fears. "Derry!" I shouted on reaching the top.

"Kew!" Desperation colored Derry's distant reply. "In here!"

I found her in the ceremony cavern, sagging over the stone shelf at the back. A single lamp at her side revealed our baby sprawled there. She glanced up as she began a series of quick chest compressions with two fingers. "Hear' stopped, no' breathing," she gasped before covering his mouth and nose with her lips to give him several puffs of breath.

By the time she returned to chest compressions, I'd yanked the little bag from around my neck so sharply I snapped its ancient cord. I dumped the oil-paste cup into my palm and fumbled it open with shaking hands while she repeated the breaths.

When she straightened to do chest compressions once more, I drew the glyph for life on Garnan's forehead in two swift strokes. Even in the lamp's light, he appeared ash-gray, his miniature mouth too dark.

"Keep going," I told Derry and cupped our son's head with my right hand. I felt a surge through my soul, strong enough to make my voice tremble when I said, "Garnan Kerk, having received power from Star Father, I command you to live and to heal, for you have much work to do for him in your life."

My hand didn't leave his head while Derry breathed for him again. He never stirred.

Everything inside me felt torn apart, a blaze of agony like the evisceration in my shaman vision. Eyes closed, teeth locked, I tipped my face skyward. *Hear me, Star Father. You called him to be Hiamovi, to lead our people. Please spare his life.*

It seemed an hour before Garnan stiffened under my hand. I opened my eyes in time to see his little chest expand. Pink flooded his pale features, and he released his full breath in a scream.

Derry clutched him to her heart, rocked him, buried her nose in his disheveled hair, and kissed his head. Only with the crisis past did she let tears come. "Ah, my poor babe, my poor babe!"

Her voice's quaver penetrated our baby's squalls. I wrapped both of them tightly in my arms. Derry's frame shook against me.

Mapiya stumped across the cave to us, puffing. "What happened, Anataqa?"

"Crevice crawler." Derry swallowed and lapsed into rambling in Standard, still rocking the crying baby. "He chased i' across our room and grabbed i'. I couldn' catch him in time." She lifted her questioning, wet eyes to me. "Yew said they weren' fatal, Kew." Accusation touched her tone. "Yew said only painful wel's."

I shook my head, sharing her shock. "I've never seen this happen before. Allergic reaction?"

"Anataqa," Mapiya said across Garnan's continuing screams, "there's blood on your hand. Wanikiya, take your son."

Derry surrendered him to me with great reluctance to let Mapiya see her hand. "Stung me, too, when I took i' from him. I threw i' in the fire."

While Mapiya examined Derry's hand, I caught Garnan's wrist in my fingers to see his injury. His whole tiny hand burned a furious red under Mapiya's torchlight. Swelling had doubled its size already, and it felt fevered in mine.

Mapiya opened her jar of bitterleaf salve and applied it to Derry's hand. I spread it thick as honey on several welts bulging from Garnan's palm as well. He stiffened again, arched his back, and cut loose another lung-straining shriek.

It shredded my heart, too. I pressed him to my chest and rocked him as Derry had, stroking his mussed hair with clumsy fingers. "I'm sorry, son, I'm so sorry." With my throat so tight, I could only whisper.

Mapiya scorched one of Garnan's clean diapers over the fire pit to sterilize it, something she'd taught us phases earlier, then tore it into strips for bandages. While I held Garnan's arm still and attempted to comfort him, she wrapped the strips into a mitt that reminded me of the bandage foam on my burned hands.

"I'll keep his fingers uncovered," she said, "so we can be sure they don't go cold."

Garnan's howls eventually subsided, but from exhaustion more than relief, I thought. I bounced him gently and murmured the Chant to Relieve Pain of the Body. "O Ancient Ones who made us, blood and flesh and bone, drive away the spirits of suffering. Drive away the spirits of pain and bring peace to your child." I sang it over and over.

By the time I finished, Mapiya had bandaged Derry's stung hand. Her left one, of course.

"Two of her fingers and her palm," Mapiya said. "They're too swollen to bend. We'll need to change their bandages and apply new salve every day."

I performed the pain chant for Derry as well. Then, while Mapiya steadied her and carried Garnan to the gathering area, I entered our room. I shook out the sleeping hide and swept and torched every corner and crack in the walls, rebuking myself the whole time.

Should've done this when you saw the first crawler, Ku. It's your fault this happened. Your fault for not doing it when you first got here. Garn could've died.

I found two more crawlers, one gorging on half-ground maize on the stone Derry had been using. I dumped the contaminated grain into the smoldering oven along with the stomped-on vermin.

Assured of my family's safety, Mapiya said, "We must return to the rockslide, Wanikiya. There's still much to do."

I read Derry's lingering pain in her feverish face and tight-lipped expression. She sat curled on the sleeping fleece, cradling our miserable baby.

"Did the chant help?" I asked.

"Aye, verra much." She sighed it. "Thank yew."

"Will you be all right if we go back to work?"

"I think sa." She nodded, but I didn't miss the distressed shadow in her eyes.

* * *

With Garnan's screams and the sight of his swollen hand still vivid in my mind, I couldn't concentrate on earth-spirit chants. Once I let a boulder drop rather than mentally showing the spirits how to set it down. It split into four torso-size chunks and sprayed us with jagged splinters.

On returning to the caves at last, troubled and restless, I found Derry grinding more maize, using the heel of her right hand to work the stone. She'd tried to wash the diapers, too.

"I couldn' wring them onehanded," she said, motioning at them dripping soggily from the drying rack.

"I would've done it when I got back," I said.

Mapiya stewed jerky with beans, chilies, and wild onions for supper. Derry managed clumsily, eating with her right hand, and refused my offer to feed her. "Yew did i' after yer injury. I can, too."

I held Garnan after supper. He fussed a lot and wouldn't take anything to eat but Derry suckling him. I performed the pain chant and the Chant to Induce Healing Sleep for both of them before we settled in.

They slept well at first, but Derry woke with a gasp every time she bumped her hand in her sleep. Garnan woke a few times, too, and we took turns cradling and chanting him back to sleep, huddled together in the heavy fleece.

The bitterleaf salve had reduced much of the swelling and soaked their bandages with amber fluid when Mapiya and I changed them the next morning. The redness and heat persisted, and so did the pain. Derry winced, but Garnan started wailing again.

I skipped my morning run on the mesa to change and dress him, things Derry couldn't do onehanded, though she tried. I brought her breakfast and extra firewood to our room, filled the oil lamps, and performed pain chants for them again.

With Derry more relaxed, and Garnan calm in her arms for the moment, I asked, "Better now, little bird?"

"Much," Derry said.

I dug into my trouser pocket, where I'd stuffed Gram's little bag after reviving Garnan, and tipped the cup of oil-paste out of it. "You've been given the power to do the pain and sleeping chants for him yourself, you know."

"Aye. The firs' ones Mapiya taugh' me when we started the lessons on healing."

I crouched to set the little container beside her and bent to kiss her, then knotted the bag's broken cord and returned it to its place under my shirt before I joined Mapiya in the gathering area.

* * *

For the next two days, I concentrated on removing the rubble from against the canyon wall where I'd have to place the massive column to reopen the pass. Some boulders appeared to be portions of a second column. They required all my patience and visual guidance of the earth spirits to roll them out of the canyon below the pass or lift them onto the mesa with the first slab.

Mapiya and I returned to the caves after our labors to find Derry pacing with our crying baby. Weariness etched itself in fine lines about her eyes. "Can yew take him for a bi', Kew?"

"Soon as I've hauled the water," I said.

"I'll do it, Anataqa," Mapiya offered with outstretched arms. She cradled Garnan to her chest and set to crooning a Chalca lullaby.

By the third day we were ready to shift the toppled column. I felt the heavy presence of the earth spirits when I imagined for them the column pivoting to its new position.

It refused to budge, and I sensed disappointment from the spirits, low voices like stones grating together. Sweating from exertion under my parka, I sank onto a fallen log, planted my elbows on my knees, and concentrated on breathing until my labored heartrate slowed. Then I closed my eyes and began the Chant to Reveal Hidden Things.

With its clarity, my vision locked on a detail I hadn't noticed in my concern about the instability of the original rubble pile. A sense of deepening frustration, the increasing pressure as each day passed to clear the canyon, and endless exhaustion draped despair on my soul like a rain-soaked blanket.

"It's too long to pivot," I told Mapiya. I couldn't keep my discouragement out of my voice. "It's jammed too tightly between the canyon walls."

* * * * *

Chapter Forty-Four

I stared at her, numb in mind as well as body.

She watched me. Waited.

"I'll have to tip it on end to move it, if we can get it loose at all." My mouth felt thick. My words slurred. "Might knock down more columns, bring down more rocks."

The thought of moving more broken stone instead of starting the process of rebuilding the pass pressed me into a slump. I stared at my stained and battered boots and shook my head. "Don't think I can do this by myself, Chanter."

"You don't have to, Wanikiya," she said.

I lifted my head. Questioned her with my gaze. "You said, when it happened, *I* had to clear the avalanche."

"Not alone," Mapiya said. "Some things you can't do alone. None of the Ancients, even Shaman Shiye, accomplished everything they did by themselves. You won't be able to serve as shaman by yourself, either." She held out the drinking gourd.

I accepted it, but I stared at her for several heartbeats with mounting annoyance. "You mean I could've asked you and Anataqa to help me the first day, and you would've?"

She nodded.

Annoyance swelled to anger. I didn't speak until I'd taken control of my voice. "We've wasted so much time." I jutted my jaw toward the side canyon. "Now Anataqa's hurt, and my child almost died because they were left alone in the cave. Why didn't you tell me?"

Mapiya held my stare with hers, the unblinking assessment I hadn't seen for a while. "You had to learn to ask. Answers only come when you ask."

"Your 'lesson' endangered my family." I snarled it.

"I'm sorry," Mapiya said. "I never expected such a thing to happen." She indicated the drinking gourd in my hand. "Drink, Wanikiya, and take time to calm yourself. Only evil spirits respond to anger."

I removed the gourd's stopper. *More blackmint tea.* I downed the whole thing, but I needed several minutes of pacing to shed my seething frustration.

"I'm ready," I said at last.

Standing beside me, Mapiya raised her arms as if lifting. We raised our voices as well, hers sing-songy, mine deeper and firmer, in the Chant for Lifting and Moving Heavy Things. "O Ancient Ones who built the worlds, who gave them hearts and ribs of stone, send earth spirits to our aid. Send earth spirits to lift with us, to work in harmony and beauty."

I fixed an image in my mind of exactly how we needed to tilt the column enough to swing it to its new place. Impatience edged my straining effort, and I sensed wariness from the earth spirits.

As I'd feared, one of the column's sundered ends struck a nearby ridge protruding like a buttress. Boulders split from the cliff's face and rolled into the pass. I roared my aggravation, the earth spirits fled, and the massive column struck the canyon floor with a ground-shaking crash.

"We'll clear it tomorrow," Mapiya said. For the first time since our arrival, she sounded out of breath.

We trudged the trail to the caves without speaking.

Garnan's cries and the odor of a messy diaper greeted me when I stumbled into our gloomy dwelling. He lay loosely swaddled in his basket cradle.

Derry, her face drawn, peered up from onehandedly grinding maize again. She leaned into the stone with her right arm, keeping her bandaged hand tucked against her body. Lamplight accentuated her pallor and contrasted with the lank strands of dark hair hanging across her face. "Kew?" she beseeched me.

"In a minute," I groaned. "Give me a couple minutes." I sprawled headlong on the sleeping hide.

A hand shaking my shoulder wrenched me out of deep sleep, and I wondered how I could've slept at all with Garnan's yowls echoing between the close walls. I eased onto my back, grimacing at the fire in my muscles, and met Derry's weary eyes.

"Kew," she said, "will yew *please* see to Garn?" I didn't miss the impatience in her expression and voice.

"Sorry." I shook off sleepy fog and staggered to my feet. *Need to do the washing after I change him.*

My bucket struck the bottom of one barrel when I dipped it, and I found the other barrel low as well. *Hauling water. One more thing for the list.*

Garnan's crying abated slightly once I'd changed him and placed him in Derry's arms so she could feed him. For a while we heard only sniffles between his suckling sounds.

Mapiya set out a pot of maize porridge with dried berries when we gathered around the fire pit for supper. I recognized fatigue in her face, too, but she asked, "How is your hand, Anataqa?"

"Slowly healing," Derry said in Chalca, and left it there. With Garnan settled in her lap, she persuaded him to take a few small spoonfuls of her porridge.

After supper, when Mapiya and I changed Derry's and Garnan's bandages, she nodded in evident satisfaction. "Ya, they're healing well."

I performed the pain-relief and sleep-inducing chants for Garnan and Derry when we finished the bandaging. Garnan fell asleep in my lap, and I blew out a hopeful breath. *Maybe he'll sleep through the night this time.*

He didn't.

His sleep remained broken for the next two nights as well, though his hand continued to heal.

Because of it, Derry and I didn't sleep well, either. A couple times I shrugged into my parka and paced with Garnan in the frost-rimed gathering area.

When I tried the pain-relief and sleep-inducing chants for him in the middle of the third night, neither worked. *I'm drained. I don't have anything left to draw from my soul.*

The promise I'd made Derry's mother pounded in my skull during those hours of walking around the faintly glowing fire pits. "I'll take care of them, Mum. They're my wife and child."

Guilt cinched my innards. *I'm not taking good care of them. I'm failing as a husband and father.*

On the fourth morning, Garnan *finally* sank into a restive sleep an hour or so before Mapiya rapped at our doorframe. At her quick taps, his thin wail picked up as if he'd never left off. I groaned between gritted teeth.

He cried while I changed his bandage and diaper and dressed him in tavo-skin clothes already becoming too tight. He cried while Derry tried to feed him. He cried when I took him to rock him so Derry could eat her breakfast.

How does he keep it up nonstop? I wondered. *Wears me out just listening to him. Worse than clearing the rockslide.*

Secretly, I couldn't wait to escape to the rubble in the canyon's mouth, but I asked Derry, "Is there anything else you need before I go?"

"Aye, there is, in fac'."

Her clipped words and sharp tone, in Standard rather than her pidgin Chalca, fell like a hard slap. I blinked.

"Yew can take us back to civilization, Garn and me," she said. "I've had qui'e enough. I's all wrong, having to wear my winter things in my... 'house.' I've no' had a proper bathe since we lef' Yellow Rock. Everything's about knives and gutting and eating wild stuff. I's a miracle we didn' die long ago, especially Garn."

Her tirade touched off a conflagration in my own soul, as if all my weariness and stress were a tinder-dry forest and her words a lightning strike. My hands reflexively fisted, and I switched to Standard, too. "We came here to learn how *not* to die. Did you think it'd be easy? Chanter Wahkan and Gram both told you you'll have to be strong to be Anataqa. What were you expecting?"

She ducked her head. "I don' know, I don' know, but no' *this*," she said to her lap. "Garn barely eats, he scarcely sleeps, he jus' cries. All day. I'm weary of i', Kew. Bone weary. Bu' yew keep going off every day, leaving us sitting in a *cave* whils' yew play with yer rocks."

"*Play? My* rocks?" Indignation fanned the flames licking at my temper. "Those rocks have sealed this canyon. You want out of here,

Derry? You want to go back to civilization? The sooner I clear out *my* rocks, the sooner you can go."

I glowered all the way down the trail. Scowled as I strode among the new boulders and slabs, and calculated how to reinforce the crumbled canyon wall. *Won't be so much straining today. These are smaller than most I've handled.*

With only a glance at Mapiya, I lifted a beckoning hand and began to chant.

Nothing happened.

It felt different from my lack of energy to perform the pain chants. Different from my struggles while I'd learned to guide the spirits. I'd never doubted my power to use the chants. This time I seemed to speak into a vacuum. The words evaporated as they left my mouth. *What's wrong? I've been using these same chants for at least a phase.*

When my second effort rang as empty as the first, I cast a furious stare at Mapiya.

She leveled her purposeful gaze on me. "Something's broken, Wanikiya. You must repair it before you can repair this."

It took me several seconds in my exasperation to realize what she meant. The embers in my soul flared again. "I didn't start it, Chanter."

"I'm not accusing you," she said. "She must learn to repair broken things, too, but this time it's most important for you." She pointed with her chin toward the smaller canyon.

I still didn't know why Mapiya considered the place so special, except for its solitude, its quiet. *Maybe Chanter Yuma used to come here when he needed peace from his children in the cave.*

I followed our boot prints from days before into the clearing. While I trudged, Gram's parting words to us stirred in my mind. "This will be very difficult. You'll both be challenged in ways you can't imagine." *Never thought she meant our marriage.*

On reaching the trampled spot where I'd knelt before, I returned to my knees, more carefully than the first time. The bruise hadn't completed healed.

"How do I mend this, Shaman Shiye?" I asked in a whisper. "This's a *lot* more important to me than forgiving earth spirits. Teach me what to do."

While I huddled there, with my knees growing numb in the crusted snow, I thought about Derry. I recalled everything she'd done for me, all the time and effort she'd dedicated to me.

She was there every evening during my recovery from the shootdown. Sat there with me when I wasn't good for anything else. She sent all those packages and vids while I was deployed. She gave birth to Garn alone and risked her life to get him off Solienne.

She snared and roasted those tavos the other day. She hates gutting things, but she did it because she knew I'd be hungry.

Shame bowed my head.

Go and do the same for her, came a clear impression.

"I will, Shaman Shiye," I whispered, and rose. To Mapiya I said only, "My family needs me," before I headed up the trail.

* * *

Derry lifted her head when I pushed aside the door blanket to our room. Her arms tightened around our crying baby. Lamplight etched a glare in her eyes, emphasized her tight jaw, and the furious pucker of the scar across her forehead.

I froze in the doorway. *This girl can cast fire from her hand with deadly accuracy.*

My heart wrenched, seeing her huddled in the flickering dimness. I swallowed to clear my throat. "I'm sorry, white bird." I had to raise my voice to make myself heard through Garnan's weary wailing. "I'm sorry about what I said earlier… May I come in?"

She nodded. Watched me cross the small space to join her on the sleeping hide. I didn't sit too close.

Close enough, however, to truly study her as I hadn't for… I don't know how long.

Her face had grown thinner since we'd left Willow Valley, but not gaunt. Her freckles had disappeared along with the sun, and her cheek or nose or forehead always seemed to be smudged with soil or ash or maize meal. Arid cold had cracked her lips until she'd resorted to python oil to ease their smarting, and her eyes bore the shadows of overwork.

Winter's dryness, along with the daily chores, had worn at her hands long before the crawler stings. I knew they must smart, because I'd seen blood on her cracked knuckles from time to time. Chapping had roughened her skin despite daily applications of python-oil-and-sunshine-bulb cream, and small scars marked nicks on her fingertips. She used one of my knives to trim her nails and kept them as short as mine.

The additional gravity hadn't weighed on her for some time. These days, she moved as easily as I did, and though she hadn't bulked up, I felt steeliness in her body when I held her at night.

"This's been a lot harder on you than I thought," I realized aloud. "*Really* hard. You've learned to do things *I* didn't know before we came here. I've seen you wear yourself out day after day without complaining. I love you for that, white bird. I respect you more than I know how to say. I'm very thankful for you."

She eyed me for some time before she said, "*Ti qala bé messa tai messa*, Kew." Her voice trembled, but she reached out to touch my whiskered cheek with her uninjured hand. "I'm sorry, too. I' was wrong to say wha' I did, even if I'm worried and exhausted."

"We'll work through it." I caught her hand, leaned in, and kissed her long and deeply. "I'll take Garn for the rest of the day so you can sleep."

First, however, I revived our oven's fire and retrieved several buckets and one of the half-barrel bathtubs from the first cave. Mapiya had returned by then. She squatted by one of the fire pits in our gathering area and watched me come and go with evident interest.

Having placed several filled buckets around the oven to heat, I set up the bathtub. "Not much of a spa," I said with a sheepish smile, "but it's the best I can do. You'll sleep better after a bath."

Derry smiled for the first time since the crevice crawler bites. "Yew're sa sweet, Kew." She teased, "When yew think to be."

I emptied the heated water into the tub for her since she couldn't pour the buckets onehanded. Then I relieved her of Garnan and swung the fire-building bag to my shoulder. As I passed Mapiya on my way to the ceremony cave, she favored me with an approving smile.

By the wavering light of a small blaze, with Garnan snug against my chest inside my jacket, I paced the cavern. The fine gravel crunched under my boots as if to accompany my chanting.

When his wails reduced to whimpers, finally spent, I sank cross-legged to the rug Mapiya had left there, cradled him in my lap, and drew Gram's little bag out from under my shirt. Unhurried this time,

I traced oil-paste glyphs for sleep and pain on Garnan's forehead, placed my right hand on it as before, and repeated the chants.

Energy drained from me. What I had left. Relieved to find I had any at all, I sagged where I sat, held my son, and chanted to him. I didn't stop until his whimpers subsided to the even breaths of sleep. I murmured a chant of gratitude then. Still cradling him, I struggled to my feet.

The oven's glowing coals provided the only light in our room when I came in. Derry roused enough to smile sleepily when, after swaddling Garnan, I placed him in his basket cradle near her head.

The bathtub's water had grown cold. I bailed most of it with a bucket and poured out what remained from our cave's lip. While I stood there, leaning heavily on the draining barrel and watching powdery snow fall, the faint howls of wolves reached me from the main canyon.

Real wolves, I thought. *The ones whose tracks we saw the day we came. Dohosan said chucapas don't howl.*

A ghost cat's scream slashed the night. *She's on the mesa above our caves again,* I knew. I glanced skyward and made out a ghostly eagle riding the thermals high above our canyon. It screeched as if in warning, and the distant canine calls fell silent.

I relaxed and smiled. *Thank you, Migisi and Mosi. Thank you, Shaman Shiye.*

Still, the urgency I'd felt the night of the rockslide returned full strength. *So much I still have to learn. I'm running out of time.*

* * * * *

Chapter Forty-Five

Even with Mapiya's help, I needed three more days to clear and reinforce the canyon pass. By the time we finished, Derry's and Garnan's crawler stings had diminished to small scars, and the pain had faded. Garnan's usually cheerful personality resurfaced, and our vigilance heightened when he began pulling himself up to things.

Mapiya altered her curriculum, if not her routine. "I have no new chants to teach you," she said the first day we returned to the ceremony cavern after completing our labor in the canyon, "but you must keep practicing what I've taught you."

We continued to spend most of our waking hours in the ceremony cavern, where Mapiya set tasks to test or stretch our growing abilities. Derry and I worked at the chants together, often spelling each other off, or combining our efforts on one chant, or using similar chants for different elements' spirits to request their cooperation on the objective. Mapiya coached us while strolling after our curious and fast-crawling baby.

She advised us in other areas during our meals.

"Being the shaman of our people requires more than knowing chants and ceremonies," she said once. "I couldn't teach you some of the most important things you had to learn here. Only experience can show you things you need to know about yourselves. How do you act when you face difficulty or failure or danger? How do you treat others when you're discouraged or exhausted or in pain?"

I hung my head. *Not very well. I get angry too easy.*

"Watch for unworthy traits in yourselves," Mapiya said, "and work to fix them so you can earn the loyalty and trust of our people. You'll have to be examples to them in the times to come, when you'll face much greater challenges than these."

My innards tightened. *I already know it.* I resisted touching the spot where an enforcer's baton had connected with my left cheekbone.

"Wanikiya," Mapiya said, leveling her flinty gaze on me, "you've been chosen to be the voice and hand of Star Father by the words of Shaman Shiye."

I nodded. I couldn't speak. Trying to comprehend it filled me with a humility so deep my soul seemed about to burst with its magnitude. *To speak for Star Father...*

"You, Anataqa," Mapiya addressed Derry, "have been chosen to be Wanikiya's strength when he's weary, his hope when he's discouraged, his completer. He can't accomplish his part without you. You must do this side-by-side."

Derry, her features somber, also nodded.

"Both of you were chosen," Mapiya went on, "to lead our people in the time of their greatest danger."

Her words, the echo of Demothi's, returned me abruptly to the present. "What does that mean, Chanter? I've heard it my whole life. How is the time to come different from the Pahana's War of Extermination, or the dangers my grandfathers chanted about as long ago as Shaman Cheveyo?" I tapped the old link in its little bag under my shirt.

"Those times," Mapiya said, "were battles for our people's lives and freedom. The time to come will be, too, but the real battle will be for their souls."

* * *

"The moon is waning," Mapiya said during supper several phases later. "Night of Light Ceremony always comes at the new moon. It's time to return to Yellow Rock Enclave. We'll leave in three days."

Derry and I both stared.

The solemnity, the lack of preparedness I'd felt before, intensified during the next two days while we meticulously repacked the ceremonial regalia we'd used. Derry helped Mapiya store the food supplies she'd need when she returned.

On our last night, Derry and I packed our well-worn gear into our backpacks, then sat together on the fleecy hide in the stony space we'd called home for the past six moons.

"I'll miss this," Derry said, fingering woolly strands, "bu' no' the dir' everywhere, or washing our things in a po' on a fire, and I *certainly* won' miss always being cold!"

"I'll miss the solitude," I said. "Even Willow Valley is noisy compared to this. You can *think* here."

In the morning, when Derry wished aloud that we could take the fleece with us, Mapiya said, "Sprinkle it full of bitterleaf seeds, roll it up, and bind it tightly. It'll be safe here until it's time for you to return."

Somehow, I knew she didn't mean to finish our apprenticeships. *We've had all the training we're going to get. The rest is up to us, and asking the*

Ancients who came before us when we have questions. Wonder what will bring us back here?

* * *

Though well past mid-winter, the interminable darkness hadn't yet begun to fade into spring, even for a few minutes at midday.

"I'll bring a torch," Mapiya said. "You bring the weapons."

We set out after a filling breakfast of maize porridge, smoked shegrul bacon, dried melon and berries, and plenty of blackmint tea.

"Enough to keep us until we get there," Mapiya said while we thoroughly doused the fire pit.

Garnan, ten moons old and making his first attempts to walk, hadn't fit in the baby pack for a couple moons. Bundled into larger tavo-fur clothing, he rode on my shoulders, astride my neck with my rucksack for a seatback. I kept one hand on his leg to steady him while my other gripped the spear shaft like a walking stick.

When we emerged from the narrow side canyon, we found unbroken snow as deep as Derry's and Mapiya's knees filling the main canyon. Derry plowed through it in the lead, the bow and an arrow in her hands and the quiver on her shoulder. Mapiya, carrying the torch, walked between Derry and me. I would've preferred to break the path for them, but an undefined uneasiness warned me to keep the rearguard position.

As we had coming in, we paralleled the stream at the broad valley's center. The dark water, bordered with translucent ice, still tinkled and gurgled around the bases of rocks we'd seen submerged before, the only sounds in a windless calm. The trees we'd last seen carpeting the low hills in autumn ambers and oranges now wore layers of frozen snow like shawls of shaggy pelts.

Unlike our stroll into the mountains, we moved as steadily as possible on our journey out.

Garnan jabbered nonstop, and his free foot kicked an excited rhythm on my collarbone. One mitt or the other constantly pointed at things around us. Just as well; he tended to cover my eyes when he held onto my head, and I had to keep detaching him.

With a start, I realized this whole world was new to him. We'd never taken him outside the caves.

The call of a wolf from the main canyon behind us, where the valley grew narrower and deeper, stopped me short.

Another wolf answered.

Real ones. Hand tight on Garnan's leg, I spun around in the snow to peer in the direction from which we'd come. The moon in its new phase provided no light.

Two or three ranges away, I estimated. *There'll be others. How many? Are they pursuing us, or hunting elsewhere?*

I assessed our surroundings through narrowed eyes. *No high ground within half a range. No climbable trees any closer. Nothing to put our backs to.*

My heartrate quickened, but months of learning and practicing chants had developed one new reflex at least. Like muscle memory in my soul.

"O Ancient One," I whispered, soundless. Only my breath curdling on the still air bore my words. "O Ancient One who formed the winds, who gave the Mother Worlds breath…"

I trailed off. *What now? What do I say next?*

Ask for what you need, my son, came Shaman Shiye's patient counsel, followed by the memory of Mapiya's. *Answers only come when you ask.*

I need to see the wolves, see where they're going. How do I do it?

With several chants I'd learned, especially for water and air, I'd shown the spirits what I needed them to do through my eyes. *Can I turn that around? Is it possible to see with a spirit's eyes? Guess I won't know unless I try.*

Remembering the banshee hawks the Supremacy had used for surveillance platforms on Ardonar, I drew an ice-crisp breath. "O Ancient One," I said, "send Migisi, spirit of the wind, to guide me. Let me see the danger with his eyes so I can protect my family." I repeated the request once, then twice.

"Kew?"

I jumped at Derry's voice so close. She'd drawn up at my left. "Wolves," I told her. "Call for Mosi to come protect Garn and Mapiya."

She wrinkled her brow but didn't hesitate. "O Ancien' One…"

A sun eagle's cry cut the silence. I searched the star-sparkled sky. Migisi seemed to materialize from the midst of it.

Migisi, wind spirit, I called in my mind, *let me see with your eyes. Show me the wolves and where they are.*

I thought the spectral raptor would head northwest, up the main canyon. He didn't. From an altitude of maybe four thousand spans, he tucked his wings and dove like a fighter on a surface target, somewhere to my left. I wheeled on my spot to follow him. Watched as he leveled out to skim the treetops shrouding the valley's south hillsides.

My sight *changed.* Even in darkness, every detail held an eagle's razor clarity. I locked onto a movement as if with my Rohr's targeting reticle. Ten—no, eleven—canine shapes angled down the slope in our direction beneath the concealing trees.

Not IR. At least I'm not seeing thermal signatures. In fact, they appear colder than—

Because these aren't the same wolves I heard a couple minutes ago. I swallowed at the revelation, and my vision returned to normal. *These are chucapas, and they're heading straight for us!*

"Where are they?" Derry asked, following my gaze with hers. She clipped the words. She had an arrow on the string, but held the bow loosely. Behind her, I glimpsed Mosi already twining to and fro, frost-colored tail switching, ears flattened to her skull, dagger fangs bared.

"Coming from the trees," I said. Keeping one eye on the forest's edge, I planted the spear in front of Mapiya and hefted Garnan off my shoulders to hand him to her over the ghost cat. "Hunker down, give me your torch, and don't move."

She nodded, and I caught a glint in her eyes that told me she knew exactly what was about to happen.

With no time to question her, I told Derry, "Eleven of them. Chucapas, not wolves."

Her eyes widened. She shed the bow, sheathed the arrow, and raised her hands as if for combatives, her left one extended.

Without Migisi's vision, though he circled overhead, it took a few heartbeats to realize the tarry beasts had already cleared the forest's murk. They leaped over the snow at a speed impossible for true wolves, never breaking the surface, though they matched Solienne's bears for size.

Habit from combatives and *pelu* practice set me in a ready stance, slightly ahead of Derry and with Mapiya's torch angled to shield her.

"They fear only fire and the Warding Chant," Dohosan had told me.

Derry has the fire, I have the chant. Come and take us, Machitew dogs.

"O Ancien' One who made the suns…" I heard from my left. Derry didn't have to speak the Fire for Battle Chant aloud, but she'd always said doing so kept her focus. "… send fire spiri's to protec' us. Send fire spiri's to destroy the evil threa'ning us…"

The chucapas *did* need to hear the Warding Chant. I sang it as if to the beat of a war drum, over the rising thunder of incoming unnatural paws and guttural snarls.

When they closed to a few arm-lengths, I braced the torch to impale the charging alpha. Its momentum plowed it into my flame, and it ruptured in a fireball. *Like a missile striking an enemy fighter, minus the wreckage. Minus any remains but a dark hole in the snow.*

The others screeched, unearthly, soul chilling, and spread out to circle us. They lunged, snapped, withdrew, lunged again. I swung the torch across bone-white eyes and shouted the Warding Chant.

"O Ancien' One who made the suns, who gave their flares such deadly power…" I heard from my 180.

Derry had shifted back-to-back with me, with Mapiya shielded between us. Through the corner of one eye I spotted the chanter huddled in the snow, covering our whimpering baby with her shawl. I saw her lips moving but couldn't hear her words.

A chucapa saw her, too, and charged her. Plowing into my chant's ward hurled it to its back. Mapiya ducked when Mosi and Migisi dove in, claws and talons flailing. The chucapa disintegrated.

Red-orange flares ribboned the dark around us like single precise bursts from an energy cannon. A glance over my shoulder revealed Derry awash with the golden-red light balled on her palms. They highlighted the fierce set of her jaw and the lightning in her stormy eyes. I didn't try to count her kills. I just perceived the beasts' numbers dwindling.

I didn't notice how far my torch had burned down, either, until it sputtered when I swung it at a chucapa's face. My throat had given out, too. My voice had gone hoarse.

The demon dog pawed and snapped—and pierced my faltering ward. I shoved my smoking torch into its maw, still rasping the chant.

In an instant I knew they weren't enough. The chucapa drove itself onto the torch and kept coming, like the mountain shegrul on the spear. Teeth like an askuk's parted, expelling frigid breath scented with death.

"Shield me…" No sound came out.

I recoiled from billowing heat on my face, blinked at vivid after-images, and staggered.

Through a rain of flickering ash, I discerned Derry swaying on her feet. Tangled tendrils of hair stuck to sweat rolling down her flushed face, and her breaths came as raggedly as if she'd just finished a twenty-range race. "Kew," she mouthed my name.

I wrapped her in my arms. For two or three minutes, we simply stood there holding each other up on our feet, catching our breaths, and kissing the small burns on each other's faces.

When we finally looked around, Mapiya smiled. "You passed this test," she said. "There will be others."

* * * * *

Chapter Forty-Six

Still clutching Garnan with one arm, Mapiya worked a drinking gourd from her belt under her shawl with her other hand and passed it to Derry. "Share it between you," she said, glancing from Derry to me. "Drink all of it."

Restored by her strong blackmint tea, I relieved her of Garnan. Still too dazed for much talk, I hugged him tightly and kissed his forehead before I boosted him to my shoulders once more. He squealed, and I grimaced when he grasped my hair.

Mapiya returned the spear to my free hand and chanted a small flame to life in her palm to replace her smoldering torch. "It's acceptable to use a chant when you've lost the normal means for doing things."

* * *

The snow decreased to ankle depth once we left the canyon for the foothills. Beyond the hills stood the enclave. Its log-and-soil dome could have been a gray boulder set in the vast plain of snow. Thin curls of smoke rose lazily from roof vents, the fingers of a beckoning hand.

Its residents clearly been expecting and watching for us. The gate swung open, sending a path of yellow light across the night-blue snow. When the sentries hailed us, Mapiya waved an arm above her head and called their names.

"Blessings to you, Chanter," one of the young men said. "Chief Aiyana welcomes all of you to her home."

The chief greeted us herself, arms outstretched, when we slogged into the torchlit plaza. "There's tea and rest and heated water for washing," she said. When I lifted Garnan off my neck to my chest, she beamed. "Ah, see how much he's grown!"

"You and he can wash up first," I told Derry when Garnan reached out for her, his hands opening and closing in a request for a meal.

I avoided interacting with people any more than necessary until I'd had my own turn to clean up, after Derry and Mapiya. No one in the enclave had any beard foam, so one of the chief's sons showed me how to use his razor. I only nicked myself twice.

Derry did a doubletake when I returned from the washroom before she brightened into a smile. "Took me a bi' to recognize yew withou' yer beard."

Garnan stared at me, clearly bewildered and wary. I didn't push it. *He doesn't remember me without a beard. He'll get used to it in a few days.*

Chief Aiyana returned our links once we'd settled in the gathering room's warmth, and Derry, with Garnan sitting in her lap, immediately made a vid call to her mother.

I checked my link as well. *Hope there's something from Kota or Go. It'd be good to know how they're doing. And Gram and Kimmie!*

Kimama had sent a handful of vids a few months ago, but Go's and Kota's had come recently. Kota's latest one had arrived two days earlier. *I'll watch Kimmie's later,* I decided. *Start with the newest ones and work my way back.*

Tension about Kota's eyes and mouth in his vid, in place of his typical grin, shot an alerting tingle up my neck.

"Ai, Ku," he said. "I hope you get back from wherever you are and find this really soon. They say the lumpies are targeting Tempest now, so we're preparing for action. I hope we'll see you in a few phases." He gave a fleeting half-grin and popped a salute.

See me in a few phases? I wrinkled my forehead. *The Solis medically discharged me. Are they considering reversing it?* Hope glimmered in my soul.

Watching his vid again increased my heartrate. *The lumpies are targeting Tempest. The Wing is preparing for action. Will this be the EMP attack? He never said anything about Mogen.* My heart sank at that.

I tried to relax and converse with Chief Aiyana's family while Derry, speaking Caerdish, must've described our entire sojourn to her mother in intricate detail. I had no idea what she might've said about Garnan's close call, but he giggled and attempted to grab the link when Madam Graebel spoke to him from its display.

When Derry finally pocketed her link, appearing content, I handed her mine, keyed for Kota's vid. "Was there anything about this in your messages?"

"Wha'?" She handed Garnan to me to check her link once more. He continued to stare at me, but didn't cry. When Derry brought up a newsnet, we watched a couple reports together. Intel-officer intensity narrowed her eyes and pursed her lips, and I knew she itched for a detailed classified message.

* * *

According to tradition, supper on the evening before the ceremony's first day, which concluded with the Night of Light, consisted of clear broth or the bitterleaf tea we drank during mourning fasts. Not what I really needed after our battle with the chucapas, but I understood the meaning.

Mental replays of Kota's message caused more sleeplessness than my snarling stomach.

Savory smoke and aromas of cooking already drifted about the enclave when Derry and I rose, though the celebratory feast wouldn't take place until late evening. Only the very young and very ill didn't fast all day.

Everyone gathered in the plaza early in the morning, as they would have to welcome the dawn. I remembered how people had thronged for the Wanikiya Ceremony, except everyone wore their shabbiest clothing and solemn expressions this time. Even normal household decorations like wooden carvings or painted pots had been put away, giving the enclave a forlorn mood.

Derry and I spread a sitting rug on the cobbles among the chief's family. We hadn't been seated long before several people spotted us. Helki and Guyapi came first, eager as always, and followed by Kaya's two friends. Like Chief Aiyana, the women exclaimed at Garnan's new tavo-fur clothing and how much he'd grown. Adahy, Dohosan, and the others from the hunting party arrived, and we exchanged greetings and kidding.

The pageantry played out through the day in distinct parts divided by two- or three-hour breaks, like most annual ceremonies.

This one began with a man poised on the wide lintel stone above the enclave's gate, to represent the top of an enclave's wall. Elussit the Stranger, as the sacred tales named him, wore crude clothing made of hairy pelts and painted his face with dark teardrops trailing from his ice-pale eyes. No one ever saw him come or go. Some people called him a phantom.

A torch illuminated the dancer's eerie face. Accompanied by a gentle drumbeat, he stretched out his arms and called, "In two years,

Shaman Shiye will come to walk on our world, the Healer of All Wounds, the One Who Fills Darkness with Light. He will show you the Path to Star Father and the Sacred Mountain. It's time to prepare for his coming."

A crowd of dancers at the gate's base portrayed the people of the enclave, proud and violent. They danced to a faster, louder drumbeat, wearing regalia heavy with stone jewelry and tinkling with tiny bells. They shook weapons red with the blood of greed and vengeance, and shouted curses and threw stones.

Recalling the ceremony I'd attended in Awénasa City months earlier, I wondered, *How have the Hevos changed this one? Or have they banned it altogether? Don't think I want to know.*

Elussit never flinched. None of their stones hit him. "I tell you what to watch for!" he shouted. "When Shaman Shiye appears on our world, there will be a night with no darkness. You will see the sun set and rise again, but the sky will be bright as midday all night. He will come to us in two years."

More curses, more stones, but the Ancient Ones protected Elussit. Untouched, he jumped from the wall and vanished, ending the first part of the pageant.

When the second part began, a few dancers representing those who believed what Elussit had said left the riotous group and shed their costly regalia. Clad in simple farmers' clothing, they danced in unity.

The richly garbed dancers shoved and struck the ones in plain clothing and mocked them with contorted faces and wagging fingers.

Then their leader took his place on the lintel stone. "The time spoken of by Elussit of a night without darkness has passed!" he shouted. "You were foolish to believe his cunning lies. You are foolish to

believe in a mysterious being called Shaman Shiye. You are too foolish
to live.

"A day has been set. If that night does not stay light, all who believe will be destroyed. We will burn you, and our great fire will be the
light of the night." He threw back his head in a roar of laughter.

The jeweled and bangled dancers stacked a massive bonfire in the
center of the plaza, between the shallow, rounded roofs of the underground ceremonial lodges. The drumbeat mounted, threatening and
deep as thunderheads on the desert, and the second part of the pageantry ended.

Uneasy and restless, I used the lull to pace the enclave's shadowed
perimeter. *Only early afternoon. Feels like it should be evening by now.*

Derry joined me. "Kaya has Garn," she said, and studied my face.
She slipped a hand into mine. "Is i' Kota's message?"

"Ya." I blew out a breath to relieve the tension under my ribs. "I
feel like it's imminent, and I need to do something."

"Wha' can you do here?" she asked.

"I don't know, I don't know." I shook my head.

We returned to our places before the next part began, and Derry
reclaimed Garnan.

Young men extinguished every torch in the plaza, except a single
tall one at the center. The lone light flickered in smoky darkness above
the cluster of believer dancers, seated around the great drum as if in a
ceremonial lodge. The single torch emphasized the threatening stack
of their enemies' bonfire.

Beside me, Derry threw a blanket over one shoulder to suckle Garnan. "Does the darkness have a meaning?" she asked.

"It represents the people's sadness," I said, "and their fear the
promise be fulfilled in time to save them."

In their midst, one of the enclave's chanters portrayed Napashi, the believers' leader, wise and faithful. The melody of a lone flute drifted from their circle, haunting and melancholy above the muted heartbeat of the drum, and the chanter began to sing.

Everyone seated around the plaza clasped hands. I caught Derry's free hand at one side, Mapiya's on the other. Some people bowed their heads, others tipped their faces skyward, but all closed their eyes to join in the Chant of Mournful Waiting.

Come, O come, Shaman Shiye.
Your people wait for you.
Your people plead for you
to save us from
the forces of the Dark.
Come, O come, Shaman Shiye
and bring the promised Light
that we might walk in beauty
and rejoice with you.

As we came to the phrase "to save us from the forces of the Dark" a second time, an icy prickle crossed my nape. I startled and stared about myself.

The darkness surrounding me was no longer the enclave. The torches' smoky flares seemed to have been snuffed out to be replaced with stars, the familiar constellations of Tempest's northern hemisphere. I studied them, forehead furrowing. *What's going on? What am I supposed to see?*

Then the first cobalt-blue beacon appeared, too close to be merely a brilliant star. It glittered, and my breath caught. *A vortex portal?*

A second scintillating light, immediately followed by a third and fourth, confirmed my suspicion. Their blue fire scored the depths of space. Four vortices twisted across it like illuminated snakes.

Discerning them deepened my urgency. *Is this the attack Kota meant? Are they lumpy vortices?*

When six lumpy attack ships in trail formation entered the first vortex, I saw each one more clearly than I would've in my fighter's threat scope. I stiffened where I sat, and my hands reflexively clenched Derry's and Mapiya's.

Both tugged their hands free. Mapiya shot a questioning glare at me, but Derry gasped, "Ow, Kew!"

"Tempest is about to be attacked," I hissed. "I just saw six lumpy ships entering a vortex."

In the time it took to say it, three more attack groups vanished one by one into their portals.

"Four groups of six ships," I whispered. The weight of the knowledge hunched my shoulders, dried my mouth. I tipped my head back and closed my eyes. *Shaman Shiye, what must I do? How do I stop them?*

The calm, quiet voice I'd learned to seek spoke clearly to my mind. *Use the chants you've learned, my son.*

There are no chants to space spirits. I groaned aloud.

Use what you've learned from the chants.

I saw where each would expel its strike group, above the four largest cities scattered about Tempest's globe. The first was Awénasa.

How do I stop them from coming through the vortex?

The memory of three flight mates lost at the end of a battle brought an idea, though no comfort. *How do I collapse the vortex? What about the other three? I don't think there's enough time to take them out one by one.*

I sat there sweating, straining for an answer, hands fisted in my lap. The chants I'd learned in the last months milled in my mind. The ways I'd struggled with them blurred and confused my thoughts. *The Chant to Reveal Hidden Things. The Chant for Lifting and Moving Heavy Things. The Chant to Recover Spilled Water. The Chant to Guide Many Winds.*

The solution presented itself in a tentative glimmer. *Take control of all four vortices, like the many winds. Turn them somehow... That's it! I've got to lock all four exits on the same coordinates in space.*

I pulled in a deep breath and began, "O Ancient Ones who formed the winds, send spirits of—"

I stopped. *Are there spirits of space?*

Out of roiling images, a memory of one night during pilot training opened as clearly as if I'd searched for it on my link. Machitew's bodiless mask hovered in my chilly sleeping space, urging me to sabotage Huritt's ship. "Space belongs to the spirits of the air," he'd said.

There's an irony. Thanks for the tip, Machitew. But can I trust it? I swallowed. My heartrate quickened with driving exigency. *Only option I've got right now.*

I straightened and started again, dry mouthed. "O Ancient Ones who formed the winds, send spirits of air into space to work your will. Send spirits of air through space to serve your purpose and teach me to guide them in harmony."

With my eyes closed, I didn't see Mapiya's stare, but I felt her stiffen next to me.

The visuals of space combat, of tracking multiple fighters in my threat scope, returned as if I'd done it yesterday. As with guiding the air spirits to carry the leaves in the ceremony cavern, my attention shifted constantly from one vortex to another. I used my hands to direct the ice-blue lightning coils.

No substance to guide. No air in space. Those attack ships have, at most, a three-minute transit through the vortices.

My concentration swelled to throbbing in my skull. My pulse matched the urgent beating of the distant ceremonial drum. I chanted through gritted teeth. "O Ancient Ones who formed the winds, send spirits of air into space…"

Around me, hundreds of voices intoned, "… save us from the forces of the Dark…"

My spirit vision flicked from one vortex to the next. All remained locked on their surface targets.

"Send spirits of air through space to serve your purpose," I chanted, "and teach me to guide them in harmony."

Focusing on four vortices at once heightened the pounding in my head. I winced, sucked in a breath, fixed my spirit vision on each blue lightning track piercing space. I willed them, each in turn, to shift. "O Ancient Ones who formed the winds, send spirits of air into space…"

Sweat oozed under my arms. My hands outlined a bend here, a curve there. I beckoned one to arc halfway across a hemisphere. "… to work your will. Send spirits of air through space to serve your purpose…"

My breathing grew ragged. It came with increasing effort. "Chanter," I panted to Mapiya, "I can't stop the attackers by myself. I need your help."

She patted my arm. I heard her raspy whisper, though I had no idea what she said, or to whom.

Before my spirit eyes, the sparking azure tracks refused to bend. I glimpsed fiery plumes from the ships accelerating within them.

"… teach me to guide them in harmony."

The Chant to Recover Spilled Water. I had to show the water spirits what I wanted them to do. I let my hands drop to my lap.

The drumbeats inside my skull sharpened, like axe blows splitting wood. I dragged in a deep breath. Released it slowly to push out the swelling pain.

Four blue-flashing, spinning tunnels filled my spirit sight, still open above four scattered cities.

I focused briefly on each one. Clenched my teeth against the agony inside my cranium. *Got to show them what I want them to do. Got to* show *them…*

With some detached sense, I recognized people stirring and pressing around me. Hands, some light, some firm, sometimes single outstretched fingers, touched my shoulders, my back, my head. Strength flowed from their touches, refilled my flagging energy. Their voices chanted as if from dense fog, lending power to mine.

Come, O come, Shaman Shiye.
Your people wait for you.
Your people plead for you,
to save us from
the forces of the Dark.

Sweat beaded from my temples, cold as if I were in shock. I sagged where I sat. I had to strain to lift my head. *One more time. That's all the strength I've got left.*

Stress heightened the voices singing around me.

Come, O come, Shaman Shiye

and bring the promised Light
that we might walk in beauty
and rejoice with you.

"O Ancient Ones who formed the winds," I chanted. The words slurred on my tongue. "Send spirits of air into space to work your will. Send spirits of air through space to serve your purpose and teach me to guide them in harmony."

Vortices, this is what I need you to do. I visualized them converging on each other, their strobing, cobalt portals yawning wide as vipers' mouths, all facing the same pin-point coordinate in space.

A brilliant flash filled the blackness, as if every star within my sight had simultaneously gone nova. It blinded even my spirit eyes and burst like a cleaving blow at the crown of my head.

This is how I die.

* * * * *

Chapter Forty-Seven

I woke lying on my back with gentle fingers smoothing something cool and tingly across my forehead, and several voices chanting quietly a couple arm-lengths away. A dull headache remained, but the tingling gradually eased it. I opened my eyes.

Derry bent over me, clutching a jar of speckled wort oil. Despite the dimness, I saw relief in her face. "Oh, Kew, praise the Ancien's," she murmured in Chalca, and glanced around as if to signal the others.

The chanting ceased, and several figures drew closer. *Nine of them,* I counted when my eyes cleared. I discerned Chief Aiyana, two of the enclave's chanters, Kaya and one of her sisters, Adahy, Dohosan, Helki, and Mapiya. Concern puckered their brows, but wonder filled their eyes.

The blast that had robbed me of consciousness seared across my memory like an afterimage. "The attack," I said. It came out in Chalca. I struggled to sit up. "What happened?"

Derry pressed my shoulder to the floorbed. I felt weak enough that I didn't resist. She peered around at the others, evidently uncertain what I'd asked.

Chief Aiyana crouched beside me first. "Your chant worked, Aku-leh. The attacks were averted."

"Good," I sighed.

411

Mapiya joined her, and I saw the others pressing in close around them. In the lamplight, their features seemed to sag with relief, but curiosity burned in their eyes.

"How," Mapiya asked, her tone and expression stern enough to suggest I'd cheated somehow, "did you think to send air spirits into space?"

I wasn't about to reveal the actual source, especially before this many people. "Memory of something from pilot training," I said.

"It was a very strong chant," Adahy said. "*Very* strong." He shook his head in apparent amazement. Dohosan nodded agreement.

Helki nudged in beside Derry. "You passed out just when they lit the Night of Light bonfire, but some of us went outside the enclave to look." He still appeared wide-eyed with astonishment. "There were streaks in the sky in the northeast. Lots of them, like a meteor shower, but a *lot* brighter! They went on forever!"

Four lumpy attack groups reduced to meteorites. I tried to picture the multi-ship conflagration at the edge of Tempest's atmosphere but found I didn't want to. *My own people are safe.*

"We thought it'd killed you at first," Kaya said. Relief shaded her tone.

"Nearly did." I touched the top of my head, where I'd felt the splitting blow. *No bump, no soreness.* "How long was I out?"

"Through the whole Day of Rejoicing," Chief Aiyana said. "It's evening again."

"Explains why I'm so hungry." I pushed myself up fully that time. "Any food left?"

"Maybe a few crumbs," Helki said with a grin. "I'll see what I can find."

Celebratory music pounded outside the dwelling. Rapid, complex drum rhythms and trilling flutes accompanied voices raised in joyful singing for the coming of Shaman Shiye.

Helki returned a few minutes later, bearing two bowls heaped with roasted shegrul and chicken, honeyed squash and cactus fruits, and a thick maize pudding filled with piñion nuts and dried fruits. I inhaled, and my stomach growled. I smiled at the youth. "You're a good hunter, Helki."

A solid meal restored my depleted energy, and Derry, Garnan, and I went out to watch the dancing in the plaza. Feast dancing, celebratory dancing now, no longer ceremonial.

Torches had been planted on the roof of every structure, and the central bonfire still blazed, bringing near daylight to the enclosure. Ragged clothes had been changed for feast-day best, with bright beadwork and stone jewelry to rival the evil people in the tale of Elussit.

While Derry gripped his hands to keep him from plopping on his bottom, Garnan bounced on moccasined feet and squealed with excitement at the colorful activity around us.

People approach us, all exuding a shyness that puzzled me, when they noticed us on the sidelines. I hadn't met any of them, but they clearly recognized me. Reverence lit their faces when they searched mine. Women clasped my hands, men bear-hugged me and slapped my back, youths and children simply stared through wide eyes. Self-consciousness engulfed me.

They all murmured variations of the same thing.

"You saved our enclave last night."

"You're the one who killed the lumpy ships."

"You're as powerful as the Ancient Ones."

I shook my head at the last statement. "No, I'm not. You chanted with me. You touched me to share your strength. You helped me do it. I couldn't have done it alone."

Somehow, I knew it would also take others' touches to save them in the time to come.

* * *

Mapiya shook me awake the next morning. "My father has come to talk to you and Anataqa," she said. "They're gathering in the great lodge." She pointed with her chin toward the plaza.

I stared into her weathered face. "Chanter Yuma?"

She nodded. "Take time to wash, but don't eat. It's best to come fasting."

Derry and I exchanged incredulous gazes. When she glanced at our still-sleeping son, Kaya sat up on the next floorbed and offered, "I'll look after him."

A short time later, washed but hungry, we climbed down the log ladder into the ceremonial lodge. We found it well lighted with torches and a fire on its hearth. The circular chamber appeared capable of seating at least twenty.

Yellow Rock Enclave's eight chanters had arrived ahead of us and occupied part of the stone bench lining the wall. Their steady stares at me prompted a nervous swallow. Then I moved away from the ladder to face the chief chanter's seat and swallowed again, this time in shock.

The fire's ruddy light clarified the figure seated there. *Demothi?*

He must have seen the surprise in my face because he chuckled, a sound as cracked and ragged as his features. As if he'd heard my thought, he said simply, "Ya."

Mapiya's father. Chanter Yuma. I shifted my gaze from Demothi to Mapiya. *Same nose, same jawline. Even the eyes, though she has both of hers. Now I know why she reminded me of somebody the first time saw her.*

"Chanter Yuma?" I whispered. I stood frozen. Years of Demothi's shouts and pointing finger flashed across my mind. A flood of questions followed.

He had doubtless expected it because he said, "I'll answer all your questions, Wanikiya." He peered past me at Derry, who'd followed me down the ladder, then around at the chanters seated behind us. "There's much that needs to be told." He gestured at a rug spread before him and the glowing hearth fire. "Come and sit down. Warm yourselves."

We sat. Derry appeared wary.

Demothi studied us first, then addressed the circle of chanters on the bench. "I was no older than Wanikiya," he said, indicating me, "when our people made the Crossing to this world. I was the only chanter left alive. The Pahana had killed the elders, all the wise ones.

"We settled in the Awénasa and built our first enclave. The early years were hard. We weren't used to the high gravity at first, and the extreme seasons. We had to fight strange, hungry animals and criminals who raided our crops. Many people died."

No one in the lodge had a hand drum, but Demothi-Yuma spoke as if to the rhythm of one, with more clarity and lucidity than I'd ever heard from him. No one in the lodge stirred.

"People cried, 'We need a shaman to guide us. We need someone who can plead to the Ancient Ones for us. Yuma, you are our only chanter. Go and ask if the Ancients will make you our shaman.'

"I told them, 'I won't do that. I wasn't chosen to be shaman.'" He shook his shaggy head.

"Our people stayed in the Awénasa Enclave for many years," he went on, "and it grew very large. Too many people; too much noise." He waved a gnarled hand as if shooing a fly. "It came time to settle in new places and build new enclaves.

"My clan and a few others came here to the Yellow Rock. We lived in the caves while we built the enclave. My family chose to stay in the caves even after it was built. We had much sickness and danger that year. My wife died. Two of my children died."

Yuma fell silent. His head drooped to his chest, and he sat motionless for so long I wondered if he'd fallen asleep. I heard anxious whispers and shifting behind me.

At last, giving a sigh, he lifted his head and continued. "Again people said, 'We need a shaman to lead us, a shaman to plead for us. Yuma, you are our chanter. Go and plead with the Ancient Ones to make you a shaman.'"

Silence settled once more. When he'd remained still for a long space, Derry slipped me an anxious gaze. I leaned forward to peer at him, saw the fixated stare of his remaining eye, but something cautioned me not to disturb him. *He's in a spiritual communion.* I mouthed "Wait" to her.

After several minutes, he started. He glanced first at Derry and me, then around the lodge, and drew a shaky breath. He didn't ask where he'd left off, he simply went on.

"I gave heed to my people that time," he said. "Because of my wife and my children, I thought, 'Maybe if I'd been a shaman, I would've known what to do. Maybe my family and so many other people wouldn't have died.'

"It was summer, with no darkness. I took no food or water because I wanted to fast. I traveled north of these mountains—" he motioned "—to the desert, where I made a shelter under a leaning rock. I chanted to ask for a vision."

Yuma's subdued voice resumed its chant-like rhythm, so steady I wanted to tap its beat on my knee.

"The heat and the dryness became too much," he said. "In my sickness, I stared at the sun. I believed it to be the light of a vision, and I pleaded to the Ancient Ones.

"In their mercy, they sent a traveler to me. I didn't see his face, for he covered his head with a cloth. He cared for me until I was well, then gave me a message from the Ancients."

Yuma never glanced at Derry or me, or any of the chanters while he spoke. "The Ancients took the sight from my right eye, the traveler told me, because I had sought for things I wasn't meant to see. But they healed my left eye of the burns.

"With my left eye, I would see many things," he said, "of the spirit as much as the world. I was to spend the rest of my life seeking Wanikiya, whose role I had coveted."

Yuma finally raised his leathery face and leveled his one-eyed gaze on me with such intensity I recoiled. As I always had. "You were a small child the first time you came to the city with your father. Not even as high as my belt. But when I saw your eyes, I saw your soul, and I knew you were Wanikiya. I've watched you ever since.

"And you, Anataqa." He shifted his attention to Derry. "Not until I saw you in the market with Wanikiya did I understand the chants and ceremonies that described you as a white bird, the one meant to fly side-by-side with the sun eagle."

I remembered the confrontation at Old Trade Center in which Demothi had advanced on Derry with his wild-eyed stare. His constant wails of "I know who you are! I know what you will become!" echoed in my ears.

"You scared me when I was little," I said. I struggled to suppress years of resentment. "Scared me in a different way when I got old enough to believe my stepmother saying I'd be Death Bringer. Your rants made people believe her, made them fear me."

I knew it was forbidden to discuss someone's Birth Chant until they heard it in their Coming-of-Age Ceremony, but I said, "You could've encouraged or reassured me, even if you couldn't tell me."

Yuma bowed his head. "That was my hope, my only intention, Wanikiya, but every time I spoke to you, the Ancients bound my tongue out of fear I'd tell you too much. It wasn't time yet."

I studied him for some seconds: the withered frame, the loose hair, the downcast face. *My chanter called Yuma speaks the truth,* Shaman Shiye whispered in my mind. Nothing else. No explanation. Still, I relaxed. My anger subsided. "I understand," I said.

The other chanters had held their silence, though I'd heard subtle movements on the curved bench. I felt them watching me, the pressure of their gazes greater than the physical touches of the night before.

Yuma saw it, too. He slid a firm stare past my head, around their circle. "The coming of Shamans Wanikiya and Anataqa is not to be spoken of outside this sacred lodge. Shaman Shiye will name the time and place of their declaration, but it's important for you, the chanters of the Yellow Rock, to hear my witness and to see them, to know who they are. They will need your help in the time to come more than they did last night."

Solemn murmurs of assent rose behind Derry and me.

Apparently satisfied, Yuma smiled. "Now I can make my Crossing to the Sacred Mountain and be at peace, but for you, Wanikiya and Anataqa, there is much to do before the time of greatest danger."

# # # # #

About the Author

According to her mother, Diann "DT" Read began writing as soon as she could pick up a pencil, though her first "stories" were mostly drawings of horses. By age 10 she'd appropriated her father's old college typewriter and learned to type, with two fingers, because it was faster than pushing a pencil. At age 14, with the encouragement of a schoolteacher aunt, she entered the Utah League of Writers Contest for Young Writers and won 1st place in the Junior High Division. She started her first novel, a fantasy based on the Arthurian legends, in high school, but got sidetracked into science fiction in college and never finished that book.

Her first military science fiction trilogy, The Sergey Chronicles, was published by Tor in the late 1990s. Now available for Kindle, Nook, and Kobo, the Sergey trilogy continues to earn royalties after all these years. She also has a handful of published short stories.

Diann took a hiatus from fiction writing when she was mobilized to active duty in the wake of 9/11. She served for 23 years in the U.S. Air Force, and retired as a lieutenant colonel in 2009 to return to writing. Diann learned her craft from such mentors as Orson Scott Card, Elizabeth Moon, and David Farland, and worked for David as an editorial assistant for several years. She is married to Jon Read and they live in Texas.

Connect with Diann at www.facebook.com/d.t.read.author, www.patreon.com/DTRead, and her website https://d-t-read-author.com.

* * * * *

Get the **free** Four Horsemen prelude story "**Shattered Crucible**"

and discover other titles by Theogony Books at:

http://chriskennedypublishing.com/

* * * * *

Meet the author and other CKP authors on the Factory Floor:

https://www.facebook.com/groups/461794864654198

* * * * *

Did you like this book?
Please write a review!

* * * * *

The following is an
Excerpt from Book One of the Lunar Free State:

The Moon and Beyond

John E. Siers

Available from Theogony Books

eBook, Audio, and Paperback

Excerpt from "The Moon and Beyond:"

"So, what have we got?" The chief had no patience for inter-agency squabbles.

The FBI man turned to him with a scowl. "We've got some abandoned buildings, a lot of abandoned stuff—none of which has anything to do with spaceships—and about a hundred and sixty scientists, maintenance people, and dependents left behind, all of whom claim they knew nothing at all about what was really going on until today. Oh, yeah, and we have some stripped computer hardware with all memory and processor sections removed. I mean physically taken out, not a chip left, nothing for the techies to work with. And not a scrap of paper around that will give us any more information…at least, not that we've found so far. My people are still looking."

"What about that underground complex on the other side of the hill?"

"That place is wiped out. It looks like somebody set off a *nuke* in there. The concrete walls are partly fused! The floor is still too hot to walk on. Our people say they aren't sure how you could even *do* something like that. They're working on it, but I doubt they're going to find anything."

"What about our man inside, the guy who set up the computer tap?"

"Not a trace, chief," one of the NSA men said. "Either he managed to keep his cover and stayed with them, or they're holding him prisoner, or else…" The agent shrugged.

"You think they terminated him?" The chief lifted an eyebrow. "A bunch of rocket scientists?"

"Wouldn't put it past them. Look at what Homeland Security ran into. Those motion-sensing chain guns are *nasty*, and the area between the inner and outer perimeter fence is mined! Of course, they posted warning signs, even marked the fire zones for the guns. Nobody would have gotten hurt if the troops had taken the signs seriously."

427

The Homeland Security colonel favored the NSA man with an icy look. "That's bullshit. How did we know they weren't bluffing? You'd feel pretty stupid if we'd played it safe and then found out there were no defenses, just a bunch of signs!"

"Forget it!" snarled the chief. "Their whole purpose was to delay us, and it worked. What about the Air Force?"

"It might as well have been a UFO sighting as far as they're concerned. Two of their F-25s went after that spaceship, or whatever it was we saw leaving. The damned thing went straight up, over eighty thousand meters per minute, they say. That's nearly Mach Two, in a *vertical climb*. No aircraft in *anybody's* arsenal can sustain a climb like that. Thirty seconds after they picked it up, it was well above their service ceiling and still accelerating. Ordinary ground radar couldn't find it, but NORAD *thinks* they might have caught a short glimpse with one of their satellite-watch systems, a hundred miles up and still going."

"So where did they go?"

"Well, chief, if we believe what those leftover scientists are telling us, I guess they went to the Moon."

* * * * *

Get "The Moon and Beyond" here: https://www.amazon.com/dp/B097QMN7PJ.

Find out more about John E. Siers at: https://chriskennedypublishing.com.

* * * * *

The following is an

Excerpt from Book One of This Fine Crew:

The Signal Out of Space

Mike Jack Stoumbos

Now Available from Theogony Books

eBook and Paperback

Excerpt from "The Signal Out of Space:"

Day 4 of Training, Olympus Mons Academy

I want to make something clear from square one: we were winning.

More importantly, *I* was winning. Sure, the whole thing was meant to be a "team effort," and I'd never say this to an academy instructor, but the fact of the matter is this: it was a race and I was in the driver's seat. Like hell I was going to let any other team beat us, experimental squad or not.

At our velocity, even the low planetary grav didn't temper the impact of each ice mogul on the glistening red terrain. We rocketed up, plummeted down, and cut new trails in the geo-formations, spraying orange ice and surface rust in our wake. So much of the red planet was still like a fresh sheet of snow, and I was eager to carve every inch of it.

Checking on the rest of the crew, I thought our tactical cadet was going to lose her lunch. I had no idea how the rest of the group was managing, different species being what they are.

Of our complement of five souls, sans AI-assist or anything else that cadets should learn to live without, Shin and I were the only Humans. The communications cadet was a Teek—all exoskeleton and antennae, but the closest to familiar. He sat in the copilot seat, ready to take the controls if I had to tap out. His two primary arms were busy with the scanning equipment, but one of his secondary hands hovered over the E-brake, which made me more anxious than assured.

I could hear the reptile humming in the seat behind me, in what I registered as "thrill," each time I overcame a terrain obstacle with even greater speed, rather than erring on the side of caution.

Rushing along the ice hills of Mars on six beautifully balanced wheels was a giant step up from the simulator. The design of the Red Terrain Vehicle was pristine, but academy-contrived obstacles mixed with natural formations bumped up the challenge factor. The dummy fire sounds from our sensors and our mounted cannon only added to the sense of adventure. The whole thing was like fulfilling a fantasy, greater than my first jet around good ol' Luna. If the camera evidence had survived, I bet I would have been grinning like an idiot right up until the Teek got the bogey signal.

"Cadet Lidstrom," the Teek said, fast but formal through his clicking mandibles, "unidentified signal fifteen degrees right of heading." His large eyes pulsed with green luminescence, bright enough for me to see in the corner of my vision. It was an eerie way to express emotion, which I imagined would make them terrible at poker.

I hardly had a chance to look at the data while maintaining breakneck KPH, but in the distance, it appeared to be one of our surface vehicles, all six wheels turned up to the stars.

The lizard hummed a different note and spoke in strongly accented English, "Do we have time to check?"

The big furry one at the rear gruffed in reply, but not in any language I could understand.

"Maybe it's part of the test," I suggested. "Like a bonus. Paul, was it hard to find?"

The Teek, who went by Paul, clicked to himself and considered the question. His exoskeletal fingers worked furiously for maybe a second before he informed us, "It is obscured by interference."

"Sounds like a bonus to me," Shin said. Then she asked me just the right question: "Lidstrom, can you get us close without losing our lead?"

The Arteevee would have answered for me if it could, casting an arc of red debris as I swerved. I admit, I did not run any mental calculations, but a quick glance at my rear sensors assured me. "Hell yeah! I got this."

In the mirror, I saw our large, hairy squadmate, the P'rukktah, transitioning to the grappler interface, in case we needed to pick something up when we got there. Shin, on tactical, laid down some cannon fire behind us—tiny, non-lethal silicon scattershot—to kick up enough dust that even the closest pursuer would lose our visual heading for a few seconds at least. I did not get a chance to find out what the reptile was doing as we neared the overturned vehicle.

APPRENTICE TO THE GODS | 433

I had maybe another half-k to go when Paul's eyes suddenly shifted to shallow blue and his jaw clicked wildly. He only managed one English word: "Peculiar!"

Before I could ask, I was overcome with a sound, a voice, a shrill screech. I shut my eyes for an instant, then opened them to see where I was driving and the rest of my squad, but everything was awash in some kind of blue light. If I thought it would do any good, I might have tried to plug my ears.

Paul didn't have the luxury of closing his compound eyes, but his primary arms tried to block them. His hands instinctively guarded his antennae.

Shin half fell from the pivoting cannon rig, both palms cupping her ears, which told me the sound wasn't just in my head.

The reptile bared teeth in a manner too predatory to be a smile and a rattling hum escaped her throat, dissonant to the sound.

Only the P'rukktah weathered this unexpected cacophony with grace. She stretched out clearly muscled arms and grabbed anchor points on either side of the vehicle. In blocky computer-generated words, her translator pulsed out, "What—Is—That?"

Facing forward again, I was able to see the signs of wreckage ahead and of distressed ground. I think I was about to ask if I should turn away when the choice was taken from me.

An explosion beneath our vehicle heaved us upward, nose first. Though nearly bucked out of my seat, I was prepared to recover our heading or even to stop and assess what had felt like a bomb.

A second blast, larger than the first, pushed us from behind, probably just off my right rear wheel, spraying more particulates and lifting us again.

One screech was replaced with another. Where the first had been almost organic, this new one was clearly the sound of tearing metal.

The safety belt caught my collarbone hard as my body tried to torque out of the seat. Keeping my eyes open, I saw one of our tires—maybe two thirds of a tire—whip off into the distance on a strange

trajectory, made even stranger by the fact that the horizon was spinning.

The red planet came at the windshield and the vehicle was
wrenched enough to break a seal. I barely noticed the sudden escape
of air; I was too busy trying, futilely, to drive the now upside-down
craft...

* * * * *

Get "The Signal Out of Space" now at: https://www.ama-
zon.com/dp/B09N8VHGFP.

Find out more about Mike Jack Stoumbos and "The Signal Out of
Space" at: https://chriskennedypublishing.com.

* * * * *

Made in the USA
Coppell, TX
10 February 2023

12608107R00243